JOHANN C.M. LAESECKE

The Roaring Road

The Roaring Road Series Book 1

ROAD TRIP DOG
PUBLISHING

To Lori,
The love of my life, who told me to stop talking about writing a book and start writing it.

The Roaring Road is a work of historical fiction. Names, characters, organizations, places, events, dialogue and incidents portrayed in this novel are products of the author's imagination or used fictitiously.

Road Trip Dog Publishing
An imprint of The LaureDan Company

The Roaring Road website: www.theroaringroad.com

Cover design and illustration by Don Henderson
Henderson Graphic Design & Illustration www.hendersongdi.com

Print ISBN   978-0-9964861-0-1
Kindle ISBN 978-0-9964861-2-5
Epub ISBN   978-0-9964861-4-9

RAILROAD CROSSING, LOOK OUT FOR THE CARS

The engine roared when the Elgin Six Victory Scout automobile jumped sideways after hitting a rock in the road, carelessly pushing the rear wheels adrift toward the outside of the curve. Tires struggled for traction in the hard-packed rough gravel. Calmly looking over the side from my seat at the right rear of the open automobile, the tires appeared to be losing the battle for traction as we slid ever closer to the edge. When the wheels dropped into the narrow roadside ditch at this speed, the car would flip over. I wondered how many times it would roll and if I would be thrown clear or trapped under the car.

Would the engineer in the thundering locomotive on the tracks two hundred feet from our left rear laugh when he saw our car roll? He was not a very pleasant fellow when we met before the race. Even so, I was confident that my father's driving skill would keep us in the race.

As if he knew what I was thinking, Dad downshifted and flicked the steering wheel, correcting the slide. The tires spun and spit gravel, slowly scrabbling away from the road's edge. With the sideways slide corrected, we regained forward momentum and the engineer acknowledged our continued presence on the road with long angry blasts from the locomotive's whistle.

My notes from our three practice runs indicated the road ahead was a long rough left handed curve of about a mile before the next railroad crossing. I tapped Jake, our mechanician in the front seat ahead of me on his shoulder to make our predetermined road condition hand signs, since voice communication was impossible over the roaring road, wind and locomotive sounds. Jake nodded and repeated the signs for Marvin.

The young man sitting to my left in the rear seat was an official competition observer from the *Chicago American* newspaper's Automobile Department. Chester Foust was looking pale as he hung on for dear life when Dad began swerving to avoid the worst of the potholes and ruts. My father was one of the top rated drivers in the Elgin National Road Races but even he couldn't avoid every rock and rut. Our racecar bounced, jolted, slid and became airborne a couple times as we covered one of the most dangerous sections of the road at high speed. Good thing Jake replaced the standard wood spoke wheels with steel disc wheels, or they would have been smashed to smithereens by now.

I looked over at Chester and grinned, and a few seconds later we began laughing our fool heads off to relieve the tension. My Dad yelled "Shut up you two weirdos or I'll stop this car and throw you both off" which of course made us laugh harder. Even Jake chuckled at his friend's toothless threat. Dad couldn't dump Foust off because without an official observer our race win could not be certified, and I knew my father wanted to win the race more than he wanted to drop me off in the middle of nowhere. However, I decided not to push things too far.

The track ran straight while the road curved toward the crossing, so the constant side-to-side movements to avoid road hazards caused us to lose some of our lead. Looking back I saw the white hot steam from the locomotive's stack showing that the fireman knew his onions about managing the fire in the locomotive's firebox. I wondered if he was pushing the steam pressure limit. Never had I seen a train going so fast or heard a steam engine so loud. White flags at the front of the locomotive indicating its special status were pulled straight back in the over seventy-mile-per-hour wind. There was only about four hundred yards of road ahead before we hit the crossing.

My route notes showed that at the end of this long curve there was a rough track crossing. Chester warily looked back at the monster locomotive, the smokestack spewing huge clouds and the big wheels turning so fast the side rods were just a blur. The engineer leaned out his side window watching us as he raced to deny our crossing the tracks ahead of his locomotive.

Poor Chester Foust was trying to decide if he should jump now or hope for the best. But he had confidence, knowing my father's reputation as a smooth, fast driver and our Elgin automobile was running perfectly.

Wednesday, August 27, 1919 was a hot, humid summer day in Indiana. I was 16 years old and this was my first automobile competition. The motor club competition rules stated that the automobile had to carry four people and luggage to approximate what a family of four would have loaded into the automobile. I begged and pleaded with Dad to let me ride in the fourth seat while my mother begged and pleaded with him to leave me at home. I laid out every point I could make to convince Dad. I reminded him a hundred times that race car driver Charlie Merz drove a National automobile in a 100 mile race at the Indianapolis State Fairground when he was 17, and at 23 he drove to a 7th place finish in the first Indianapolis 500 race in 1911. I finally overwhelmed his defenses, or at least he let me think I did.

The week before our race with the Chicago to Indianapolis express train, my mother, with tears in her eyes, agreed that I could ride as observer. She knew I was determined to follow in Dad's footsteps and she had to let me grow up.

On the day of the race Dad, Jake, Chester and I, wearing white racing coveralls with the name "Elgin" printed in an arc across the front were as ready as we could be. Before the race my mother gave me a box and told me to open it. Inside there was a brand new pair of racing goggles to replace my old scratched and pitted hand-me-downs, thus showing her reluctant acceptance of my participation in the race. She hugged me and said "Hang on and to do exactly as your father tells you, without question."

"Thank you for the goggles Mother" I replied, even though her instructions were unnecessary. My father had sternly laid down the rules and the penalties for disobedience would be severe. One of them was that I could be thrown from the car when it hit a bump if I was not holding on properly. The worst was that my father would never let me ride in another competition event with him, should I fail to follow his instructions.

During his pre-race talk, Dad told us that he had confidence in us, Jake's thorough preparation of the automobile, and our pre-race test run notes. He looked us each in the eye to see if any of us had doubts, but we all said we were jake and everyone laughed when I noted that even Jake was jake. In the test runs made before the race I served as the map man and scribe, sitting in the front seat writing road notes that Dad dictated while he drove. I also made sure the route map was kept folded correctly to our exact location. During the test runs Jake rode in the back seat with his big railroad pocket watch, giving me elapsed times through each route section to add to the notes.

Jake's toolkit and spare parts were clipped within easy reach so he could jump out and fix any problem with the motorcar should the need arise. On the seat next to me was a large box with more parts and tools. My job was to open it if we had a mechanical breakdown. I knew each part and tool by name and use so I could hand them to Jake as he called out what he needed. We practiced this until I could anticipate what he needed.

Jake listened to the motor and the chassis and suspension working over the rough road. Jake could tell a lot about a car by listening. If something was not right he would know it before anyone else. He said automobiles talked to him and Dad believed him. Chester Foust might never want to ride with us again but I gave the young newspaperman credit as he resolutely hung on, writing in his reporter's notebook whenever we were on a smooth piece of road.

Foust's eyes got big when he looked back at the locomotive and ahead at the decreasing distance to the crossing. This was his first time as an official observer for a motorcar race. It had been considered a dangerous event by *Chicago American* management and the senior reporters declined the assignment. Chester Foust was not married and the new guy, so he took it. At the start he was excited but that excitement was now tinged with a healthy amount of fear. I tapped Jake on the shoulder and pointed back to the train. He turned and looked, then gave my father the hand sign to pick up speed and go for it!

Almost as if we had rehearsed it, each of us braced ourselves, expecting a rough track crossing. The engineer gave us two long warning blasts on the whistle. Jake looked back and repeated the go for it sign. Dad later said the engineer was trying to intimidate us, to make us worry and slow down so the train could take the crossing first while we waited for the railroad cars to clear. The danger was that at the speeds we were traveling, there would be nothing left of us but memories if the worst happened and the locomotive smashed into our Elgin racecar.

As we got closer to the grade crossing the car lurched and jumped wildly but Dad remembered this part of the road and the line he wanted. Without lifting on the gas Dad drifted through the curve of the road toward the grade crossing. Jake took a last look back to the locomotive and gave Dad the 'go' sign for the final time. *Was the train picking up speed too?* But now we were committed, we would not be able to stop in time. It was mere seconds to the crossing but for me time seemed to slow down. Each of us, except for my father who concentrated on the road, looked back and forth at the distance to the crossing and the rapidly closing locomotive. The engineer gave us another long mourning wail from the whistle, but my father remained calm, trusting Jake's call to go for it. Jake sat there like a rock, holding on to the grab bar he had welded in after the first practice run. I was holding on to my grab bar and Chester gripped his so hard his knuckles turned white. He looked like he was going to pee his pants.

We were only about fifty feet in front of the thundering locomotive when the Elgin Six Victory Scout hit the crossing and became airborne. It flew two or three feet above and fifteen or twenty feet along the road until the automobile landed with a solid thump.

The car held together and there were no sounds or vibrations of broken suspension parts or burst tires. I looked back at the locomotive and the stoker, Sven the Swede, smiled and waved. He was a cheerful fellow and not upset like the engineer was about the race. Dad smoothly turned the steering wheel as the road curved to the right and then straightened out parallel to the tracks. We had made it. For a few seconds the only sound was from the roaring road and the train engineer's series of short angry whistle blasts. Then we started laughing and waved to Sven, who probably expected to see human body and automobile parts strewn all over the landscape. I imagined the engineer cussing Sven, having lost the race to the crossing. But we still had a lot of road race ahead of us. We had only gone about a quarter of the 163 road miles from Chicago to Indianapolis.

For the next hundred miles it was a battle with the train gaining when we slowed down for road intersections and rough or muddy spots, then we would pull ahead when the road got better. The track crossings became smoother as we neared Indianapolis and we were steadily moving ahead of the express train.

Arriving at the train station in Indianapolis, Chester Foust and I ran to the telegraph office to get a time stamp for proof of our arrival time. People stopped and stared at us in our dirty coveralls with our faces looking like raccoons with all the coal dust, dirt, sand and mud making an outline around where our goggles had been. A railroad gumshoe gave us the evil eye and followed to see what we were up to. We got the time stamp and figured the elapsed time to be four hours and six minutes, then raced back to give it to my dad. I still have the Indianapolis Star newspaper clipping:

"A New Elgin Six, standard stock Victory Scout model, Series II, No. 826 carrying four passengers and luggage, covered the 163 miles between Chicago and Indianapolis today in four hours and six minutes running time, an average of forty-seven and seven-tenths miles per hour. This breaks all records for a standard stock car with full passenger load over this route and beat the Monon 'Hoosier Limited' express train by fifty-six minutes. The official observers were Chester Foust of the Chicago American newspaper's automobile department. The driver was Marvin Lindner of the Elgin Competition Department, the mechanician, Jake Winiarzski of the Elgin Engineering Department. The fourth crew member was Daniel Lindner."

"Gasoline average, sixteen and one-third miles per gallon. The Elgin Six finished the run in fine condition and was driven back to the Elgin factory the next day. Motor worked perfect, no additional water required."

"Meeting the victorious automobile and crew was B. M. Wylie, Indianapolis distributor for Elgin Motor Car Company and C. F. Jamieson, Elgin Engineering Department. Elgin Motor Car Corporation president C. S.

Rieman sent a telegram of congratulations. Also present was Arthur P. Lane of the Monon Railroad and Patricia Beebe, 1919 Miss Indiana State Fair."

When we got back to the car, Elgin and Monon representatives and Indianapolis newspaper reporters were interviewing Dad and Jake. Also waiting for us was a photographer and a very pretty girl.

The dignitaries held no interest for me after I cast my peepers on Miss Indiana State Fair of 1919. Jeepers creepers what a kitten! I already wanted to drive racing cars, but I figured if the race winner got one of these for winning I would be well motivated to win. Miss Indiana State Fair looked to be 18 or 19 and had dark brown hair and a curvy body. She looked me over and decided I was 16, which was true, and proceeded to ignore me. Well, that was tough luck for her. I made sure to introduce myself and tell her my name because I thought some day she would ruefully remember the time when she could have had me all to herself. The photographer took a lot of photos and agreed to send copies to us at Dad's shop. Somehow I finagled the photographer to take a picture of Miss Indiana State Fair with me. She kept a smile on her face, but then, that's what she was supposed to do.

One thing for sure, our Elgin Six was a tough motorcar. Jake inspected the chassis and suspension, listened to the motor, changed two of the wheels and test drove the car and pronounced it roadworthy for our return trip to Chicago the next morning. Dad allowed me to drive part of the way back. I pretended that I was Charlie Merz driving a real racecar in the Indianapolis 500 on my way to winning the race and Miss Indiana State Fair, until I got a little carried away and my father growled at me to slow down so we could get home in one piece.

The impressive win was printed in newspapers nationwide. My father and Jake each received a bonus of a new Elgin Touring Six Victory Scout. A few years later it would become my first car.

THE STORY OF THE COLT M1911 PISTOLS

Marvin Lindner modified and raced motorcars, building a reputation as one of the best drivers in the Elgin National Road Races. In 1915, my father won a National Trophy race driving a Stutz, and the competition director for the Elgin Motor Car Company met Marvin after the impressive win and signed him to drive for the company.

Jakob Winiarzski emigrated from Poland to the United States and lived with his family in Argo, a small town south of Chicago. Jake had no formal mechanical training but his natural ability became evident soon after he landed a job at the Elgin Motor Car Company. He was able to fix anything and came to management's notice because he often helped the engineers re-design components when there were patterns of failures. When Marvin was signed as a factory driver, management promoted Jake to mechanician in the Competition Department and assigned him to work with Marvin, and they became best friends.

The Elgin Motor Car factory was located in Argo, and like many automobile manufacturers Elgin entered races and endurance events to enhance their reputation. Elgin found a winning combination with Marvin and Jake as they chalked up a long list of victories and awards, and they paid Dad and Jake handsomely for showcasing the speed, strength and endurance of Elgin motorcars.

In May 1917 my father drove an Elgin up a ramp at over fifty miles an hour and the automobile landed 60 feet 5 inches from the ramp. Mom and I were there and saw the car come down with a solid bang on the macadam road at Fort Sheridan in Illinois, where one of the Army officers watching the event was a captain by the name of George S. Patton. After Dad, Jake, and the Chicago Motor Club official observers inspected the motorcar, it was declared safe and Dad repeated the jump to the delight of the cheering spectators. After replacing a burst tire it was inspected once again and found roadworthy, so Dad drove Mom, my little sister Claire and me fifteen miles home to Long Grove.

The U.S. government turned to conscription to raise troops for the war in Europe and the Army decided it needed Marvin and Jake. Their draft notices ordered them to report to Ft. Sheridan, where they were sent to different training camps and lost track of each other. Jake was given a rifle and assigned to sniper training, but in a lucky twist of fate an officer took notice when Jake fixed a troublesome Army truck and he was re-assigned to a truck motor pool unit. Upon completion of basic training, the boys were separately shipped out to join General Pershing's Allied Expeditionary Force in France.

"Dad, tell us The Story of the Colts." My Mom and my sister Claire groaned, but they stayed to listen. I never got tired of hearing it and sometimes he told parts of it differently. Jake told me that Dad exaggerated a few details, but the substance of the story was true.

In June 1918, Marvin was in France tasked as a supply clerk and test driver in a tank maintenance unit of the 304th Tank Brigade, commanded by Lt. Col. George S. Patton. My father came to Patton's attention because of his ability to acquire things that were not available by normal requisition through military channels.

One day Jake was at a supply depot to finagle some hard-to-get parts for his truck maintenance unit, and found Marvin doing the same for the 304th Tank. The two friends were glad to be reunited, and Marvin helped Jake get the parts he needed. Later that day, Marvin told Col. Patton that his best friend was a mechanical genius in a truck unit. Col. Patton asked for his name but didn't say anything else. The next day Jake received orders to report for duty to Patton's 304th Tank Brigade.

It wasn't long before Marvin and Jake were called to Patton's HQ together. After praising their work, he told them "You two have done a great job in your shop and my other tank maintenance units need help. Sometimes more than half our tanks are out of service. I can't have my tankers sitting in a battle getting killed because a motor won't start. I heard it was both of you who prepared and drove that automobile up the ramp and made those jumps at Ft. Sheridan. You two got moxie and I want you to get my maintenance units jumping. I won't tell you how to do your jobs, and I won't ask questions. Do whatever it takes, but do it quick" Patton told them. "And I'm promoting both of you to sergeant. Now get out of here and get my tanks running!" Patton laid down the challenge. Marvin and Jake stood up, said "Yes, sir" and saluted. Challenge accepted. Patton stood up and returned their salute.

"You get the list of things I need? Jake asked when they were on the way back to maintenance HQ.

"Yes, already got over half. There's a truckload heading for you first thing in the morning" Marvin answered. "And I'm sending a couple guys who were truck mechanics in Chicago for you to check out. If you like 'em, I'll get Patton to have their transfer orders issued before lunch."

Marvin scrounged hard-to-get parts and supplies and scheduled the jobs. Jake motivated, trained and supervised mechanics, often helping on the tough jobs. Almost overnight the 304th Tank Brigade readiness went from lousy to great, and Patton protected them from being snatched away by other motorized units. The boys liked working for Patton. He was a tough taskmaster but his soldiers were loyal and did not want to serve anyone else.

Patton commanded his tank brigade from the front, and in September of 1918 the 304th Tank was in the Meuse-Argonne offensive near a French village called Cheppy. It was foggy and as usual, Col. Patton was leading the attack when his tank was hit and Patton was seriously wounded in his left thigh. Patton's orderly, PFC Joe Angelo, got him out of the tank and into a deep shell hole for protection as the battle raged around them. For a while they were pinned down by a German machine gun nest and because of his wounds Patton couldn't move fast enough for evacuation. PFC Angelo performed basic first aid and helped Patton get orders to his tank units during the battle while they waited for an ambulance.

Sgt. Marvin Lindner was helping load and move the headquarters company when word came that Col. Patton was wounded and needed evacuation. Marvin ran to find Jake, appropriated a 1917 Dodge staff car, and they were on the way, Jake having grabbed a 1903 Springfield and ammunition clips. The boys got about a half mile from where Patton was and had to hoof it the rest of the way. With the assistance of PFC Joe Angelo, Col Patton's aide, they moved Patton to the road, Joe and Marvin helping the colonel and Jake watching for snipers.

When they got to the Dodge they found the enraged captain to whom the car was assigned with his driver trying to start the car. PFC Angelo had put a coat over Patton's shoulders so snipers could not see his rank insignia and the captain didn't recognize Patton. The pissed-off captain began ripping Marvin and Jake new assholes, telling them they were under arrest and they would be court-martialed for stealing the Dodge. Patton silenced the officious captain when he spoke in his distinctive voice, telling him "Captain, I am reassigning this staff car to the sergeants as of yesterday, and you WILL NOT court-martial them. You WILL report to me when this action is over. IS THAT CLEAR?"

That's when Jake pulled the coil wire out of his pocket to the goggling eyes of the captain and installed it while PFC Angelo got Patton into the back seat of the Dodge. The captain, afraid of Patton's temper, decided to walk back to headquarters. Patton said "OK boys, I saw you at Fort Sheridan, how fast can you jump us out of here?"

Marvin drove the rough roads as if his pants were on fire, but Patton ordered him to stop at his HQ to file his action report before being taken to a field hospital. Patton laughed as he recounted the look on the captain's face when Jake took the cable from his pocket. Jake claimed he did that so the Germans couldn't steal the Dodge.

In the hospital recovering from his wounds, Patton wrote letters to their families about what the boys had done and how proud he was to have such fine soldiers in the 304th Tank. He also sent each of them new U.S. Army Colt M1911 pistols in presentation wood boxes. PFC Joe Angelo received the Distinguished Service Cross for getting Col. Patton safely out of the line of fire and communicating Patton's commands to his tanks. Dad and Jake were promoted to First Sergeant and received letters of commendation, but they treasured Patton's personal letters and Colt M1911s most of all.

Jake and Dad returned from the war and Elgin management put them back to work in the competition department. Jake also worked in my Dad's repair shop in Long Grove Illinois.

I never tired of hearing The Story and I have my father's Colt M1911. The framed letter to my mother from Lt. Col. George S. Patton is proudly hanging on my office wall.

Max Flack

A YELLOW MARMON ROADSTER

On a hot Midwestern July day in 1921 I was working in Dad's shop doing odd jobs, running errands, pushing a broom and learning everything I could from my Dad and Jake. Dad paid me sometimes, enough to go to Cubs Park in Chicago now and then. I had been there last weekend and met Max Flack, the Cubs right fielder. Max was not a popular player, having made the famous throwing error in the third inning of the sixth and last game of the 1918 World Series between the Boston Red Sox and the Cubs. His error allowed the Red Sox to score two runs and the final score was Boston 2, Chicago 1. Many people blamed Max for the Cubs losing the series and accused him of throwing the game. I arrived at Cubs Park early because younger fans were often allowed on the field to meet players before the game. Max was a nice guy and I got his autograph. He didn't seem to me to be the kind of guy who would throw a game.

Long Grove Illinois is a small village northwest of Chicago, a farm community with a general store and a few other shops, a church, a tavern, a blacksmith, a one room schoolhouse, a few dozen houses and a covered bridge. Our shop was just out of the village, a half mile from our house. The shop was busy, with Dad working full time and I helped after school and in the summer. Jake worked at the Elgin Motor Car Company in Argo where he and his family lived. Recently, Elgin announced that they were cutting back because sales were dropping. When the competition department was cut back and Jake did not have enough work at Elgin, he came up to Long Grove to work for us. Dad asked Jake to join us as a partner, but Jake's wife and family wanted to stay in Argo. Sometimes Jake would go to Gauthier's Field near Wheeling, where the local pilots flew aeroplanes. Jake was building a reputation as a talented airframe and engine mechanician.

Dad had a truck driving job which took him away from the shop for several days at a time. Jake was often there when Dad was driving the truck. I was learning the automobile repair trade and Jake told me I had a natural ability. It was a good thing, because I had been somewhat casual about school until the train race a couple years ago, when I decided I wanted to race cars. I started working hard, amazing my dad who thought I had been turning into a sheba chaser. I asked Dad to take me with on his truck job, but he said no, it was boring work and my mother needed me at home while he was away.

My mother had gone to visit her brother in Arlington Heights and Dad was away on his truck job. At noon Jake sent me to the Long Grove Village Tavern to pick up sandwiches and beer for lunch. In 1921 Prohibition was the law but many small town taverns remained open. It was only a half mile so I walked to the tavern because the road took me past Nancy Linford's house and if she was outside I would stop and visit. We were going steady and Nancy would ride with me to the lake in Dad's Elgin for a petting party and sometimes more. She was a great kisser, but what was important was that Mom and Dad liked her and thought someday we would get married. She was an attractive brunette, fun to be with and a willing companion at the submarine races.

Hutfilz bought the Village Tavern two years before Prohibition and was doing as good a business now as before. Town Constable Sherman was often seen there having a beer with his friends. Arriving at the tavern, I noticed a new-looking bright yellow Marmon Touring Convertible parked in the lot. No one in town had a car like that, so I deduced that we must have a well-heeled visitor in town. The car pulled me to it like a magnet and I circled it to look at every detail. It was the bee's knees, the berries, the cat's meow all rolled up in one. I was dreaming how I would look driving it with Nancy sitting next to me. The Marmon was a two-seat roadster so only one girl at a time could ride and the others would be envious and line up for rides. *Maybe they would even fight over who got to ride next!*

Hutfilz stuck his head out the door to call me inside. I reluctantly turned, not knowing why on earth Hutfilz would be calling me. "Danny, I just called the shop and Jake told me you were on the way over and for you to try to fix that Marmon or hitch a horse and pull the car down to the shop. I'll get your sandwiches ready while you take a look at the car. Here's the driver. Wally, this is Danny, son of our local auto repair shop owner." I turned and first noticed a beautiful woman a couple years older than me with a chassis that easily was the equal to the sexy Marmon roadster waiting outside. I inspected her carefully. She wore a pale yellow summer dress that set off her beautiful blonde hair. If I could have taken her picture I would tear down that old photo of me with Miss Indiana State Fair and put the photo of this girl in the frame on my bedroom wall. I must have just stood there for a few seconds and the man named Wally next to her laughed.

"Dawn has that effect on young men. But if I can pry your peepers off her for just a minute, I'd like you to take a look at my Marmon. The engine began running rough and we were lucky to be coming into this charming little village and better yet, this fine tavern." I was still staring at Dawn. I was sure to have dreams about Dawn for the rest of the summer. Dawn smiled sweetly back at me.

"Danny, would you do us a favor and look at the car?" she asked, trying to break the eye lock I had on her body. That woke me up and I looked at the man, his face in a shadow for a moment and I started mumbling an apology for being rude. Then I stopped, as if I were suddenly paralyzed. It couldn't be. Here in Long Grove? We were a long way from Hollywood but I was sure it was him. I had seen his movie *The Roaring Road* and just a few weeks ago Nancy and I had gone to see *Excuse My Dust*. I had seen some of his other movies too, but Wallace Reid made the best auto racing movies.

Tall and handsome, he had a reputation as a musician and a fast automobile driver who did his own stunts. Wally was at the top of the Hollywood popularity list with both men and women, young and old, right up there with Valentino and this new guy Chaplin. The magazines called him "the screen's most perfect lover." Men liked him for his daring racing and girls swooned at the thought of being his lover.

My knees were getting wobbly and I might have collapsed to the floor but Wally grabbed my hand to shake it and put his other hand on my shoulder to steady me. He must have had a lot of experience like this with young women and men meeting him for the first time. "Pleased to meet you Danny, can I get you a soda or a beer or something?" Wallace Reid had a reputation of being a great guy, and here was the proof. I had just finished mentally undressing his girlfriend yet he treated me as if nothing unusual had happened. Moreover, he was even better looking in person than he was in the movies. Even my mom and dad liked his movies.

"Yes sir, Mr. Reid, I'm sorry sir. I don't know where my mind went off to." *I knew damn well where my mind was and will probably burn in hell for telling a lie,* I thought. "I'll be glad to look at your car and if I can't get it running right, our mechanician Jake is a genius with both aeroplane and automobile motors. Thank you sir, for the soda." Hutfilz was trying to keep from laughing as he brought me an orange soda. He knew I liked orange soda or Coca-Cola. Hutfilz said no beer until I looked at the Marmon.

"Please call me Wally. Relax, drink your soda pop and then let's take a look at the Marmon." Dawn motioned me over to a chair next to her and my knees were buckling again, but I grabbed hold of myself, trying to remember every detail of Dawn, even her scent. Dawn was a lovely kitten and I recognized her from the flickers.

I was starting to calm down and the hyperventilating went away. Finishing the soda I stood up, mindlessly taking Dawn's hand to help her up. She gave me a smile brighter than the sun and Wally laughed again. *He must really think I'm some kind of feeble idiot*, I thought to myself. *Here I am making an ass of myself in front of Hollywood royalty, even taking his girl's hand like she was my date, and Wally was amused at my antics. OK Danny, it's time to get yourself under control.* Hutfilz called out that the sandwiches were ready but to come in and get them when we were leaving so the beer would stay cold.

Wally and Dawn walked out with me following so I could watch Dawn's backside as she moved. Wally started the Marmon and it ran smooth for a few seconds but then began to run real rough, but it would run.

"Mr. Reid – I mean Wally, I think it would be best if Jake took a look at your car. The engine isn't making any dangerous sounds, just running rough. Let's try driving it to the shop, it's only about a half mile that way and if it starts sounding bad I'll run ahead and get Jake" I said, pointing down the road. "I'll get the sandwiches and beer and meet you there."

"Why don't I wait so you can stand on the running board and we can arrive together? Dawn can hold your sandwiches and beer." Wally was a gentleman. I had been a big fan of his but now I would charge up the hill for him if he asked. Dawn treated me real nice too. I thought someday I would have a wife like her. Wife? I mean girlfriend! I ran in and got the sandwiches and beer,

Hutfilz grinning at me. He would have stories to tell his customers for days afterward. I ran back to the Marmon, handed in the sandwich bag and bottles of beer to Dawn, hopped on the running board and grabbed hold of the windshield post.

The trip to the shop was exciting. First, I was standing on the right side looking down Dawn's dress and could see her magnificent breasts. As we went by Nancy's house, she was outside cutting flowers and saw me riding on the yellow roadster's running board. I waved to Nancy. Then she saw Wallace Reid and her eyes got real big. She dropped the cut flowers and scissors and put her hands to her face in total surprise.

Wally noticed. "Friend of yours, Danny?" he asked.

"Um, yes sir, and a fan of yours too, she went with me to see *Excuse My Dust*." Wally pulled the car over, got out and asked me to introduce Nancy. I was glad to see Nancy was just as star struck as I was.

After a couple of minutes visiting with Nancy and giving her an autographed photo and a kiss on her cheek, Wally got us back on the road to the shop. Nancy told me later that she had to go inside the house and lay down to recover from meeting and getting a photograph and kiss from Wallace Reid.

By the time we got to the shop, Hutfilz called Jake to tell him we were on the way and probably tipped Jake off to the Wally situation. Jake did not go to the movies, so Hutfilz had to tell him that Wally was a big movie star. Jake came outside when he heard the sound of the Marmon's rough engine approaching. He waved Wally to pull the yellow convertible inside the shop. I got off the running board, opened the door for Dawn, and took her lovely hand. She seemed amused by my chivalrous manners, but I'm a romantic. I had seen Wallace Reid flickers, and Douglas Fairbanks in a Zorro movie and a Robin Hood movie. I read lots of books and thought this was how ladies were to be treated. Wally did not seem to mind, he knew Dawn was not about to leave him for a 19 year old drooling boy. I introduced Wally and Dawn to Jake, who was not affected by their star power.

I opened the Marmon's hood and Jake got right to work. It only took Jake a minute to determine that the Marmon had some bad gasoline, and Wally said yes, they had just filled the gasoline tank. By the time they arrived at The Village Tavern the bad gasoline got to the engine. Jake drained the tank, blew out the fuel line, cleaned the carburetor and had me pull the spark plugs to clean and check them. I told Wally about our Chicago-Indianapolis train race and how it was just like the scene in *The Roaring Road* where Wally raced a train to get across the track ahead of the locomotive so he could win the boss's daughter's hand. We sold gasoline at the shop and I filled the Marmon's tank with fresh gasoline and brought the car around to the front of the building. Just driving that car for fifty feet was exhilarating. Jake was telling Wally it was no charge on account of Wally and Dawn being my good friends, but I saw Reid slip a twenty into Jake's pocket as Dawn gave him a chaste hug and kiss while narrowly avoiding the oily spots on Jake's coveralls that would ruin her pretty yellow dress. Then I remembered the Kodak Brownie camera in Dad's office and ran to get it. I was glad to find there was film in it.

"Wally, could I ask a big favor? Would you let me take your photograph?" I called as I ran through the shop.

"You bet Danny. I appreciate your fast help today, and I feel honored that you and your friends spend your time and money to see my movies. Without you, *The Roaring Road* and my other movies would just be nitrocellulose in a can." Jake took pictures of Wally and Dawn by the Marmon, Wally and me, Dawn and me, Wally and Dawn and me, and I even got a picture of me behind the wheel of the Marmon with Dawn in the passenger seat, just to make the local girls jealous. I decided that someday I would own one of these fine motorcars. Jake surprised me by asking if he could get a photo with Wally, saying that he remembered his daughter talking about Wallace Reid and if this was the same Wallace Reid, she would love to have a photograph. It was the last picture on the roll of film.

Just before they left, Wally came up to me and said "Danny, I need ask you for a favor. Don't let any of these photographs get into a reporter's hands, OK? I like to keep certain things confidential, if you know what I mean."

"Mr. Reid, you can count on me. I will protect the pictures with my life" and Wally slipped me a fiver. Dawn hugged me, pulling me tight to her chest. Then she smiled sweetly and put her finger next to her nose and lightly tapped it, like a grifter sending a message. The lovely Dawn was an enchanting woman.

Before they left, Wally scribbled a telephone number on a piece of paper. "Danny, if you ever get to Hollywood, call me. This is my studio bungalow so if I'm not there someone will answer and let me know you called. I'll give you a tour and introduce you around the studio." I thanked him sincerely and then he and Dawn drove off. Waving as they went down the road, I stood by the side of the road until the yellow Marmon disappeared around a curve, and I saw Dawn wave one last time. Did she like me? Holy cow! I never even asked what her last name was. A real bona fide Hollywood starlet had hugged and kissed me.

Jake and I ate our lunch and talked about how nice Wally and Dawn were. Jake said he might go to see the next Wallace Reid movie. I did not tell him that Dawn was not his wife because Jake was an old-fashioned guy and he might not approve.

Jake went to the hardware store, leaving me a list of work to do. I went to put Wally's telephone number in my pocket and discovered a note already there. I opened it and was glad that Jake wasn't there to see as my heart began to race. It was from Dawn, who wrote that if I was interested in meeting her tonight to be at a certain corner in a nearby town at 9 o'clock. I went to work with a purpose and finished every job to Jake's satisfaction by the end of the day.

After work I went home to dinner with my sister and mother and then went to my room to get ready for my date with Dawn. I shaved and cleaned up, putting on my best jeans, my dress-up boots and a nice shirt. I borrowed some of my father's cologne and put on a couple of dabs like I'd seen him do. On the way out Claire was near enough to smell the cologne. She looked at me and asked who my victim was tonight. I told her I was just going for a ride with someone and she snickered and told me to be careful and not get the girl pregnant. *Smartass sister.*

I arrived on time. It was a downtown area and people were taking pleasant summer evening strolls. I got out of the Elgin and watched and waited. After ten minutes I began to think it was a joke and Dawn wasn't going to show when I felt a hand on my shoulder and Dawn pulled me around, put her arms around me and gave me a kiss. "Act like we are meeting for a date, I don't want anyone to think I'm a streetwalker" she whispered. After we kissed she asked me if I would like to come up to her hotel room. Speechless, I simply nodded. She took me by the hand and we went across the street and into a small hotel lobby, where the clerk was asleep, or pretending to be. Dawn put her finger to her lips for me to be quiet and led me down a short hallway. When we arrived at the last door, we went in and Dawn locked the door. She turned to me, we kissed passionately and my dick responded. She reached down, put her hand on the front of my jeans, and gave me a sly smile. Dawn led me to the bed and we sat. "I wanted to see you tonight because tomorrow Wally and I get on the train to return to Hollywood."

"What about Wally? Will he be angry?"

"Dan, I work for the studio. They hired me to go everywhere with Wally, and although I have been his lover, I'm not at this time. Wally is in his hotel room, probably getting ready to go to bed."

"Why does the studio want you to accompany him?"

"It's good publicity for Wally to have a young woman assistant, and I keep an eye out for those who might want to bother him."

"But you're a girl. What could you do if someone bothered Wally? And why can't he defend himself?"

"He can defend himself but I'm there if there are more than one. And I have these." Dawn pulled her dress up to display a thigh holster with a small pistol in it and the other lovely thigh with a knife strapped to it.

"Um, those are beautiful legs" I said without thinking.

"Thank you Danny, I'm glad you are appreciative. You see, in my job I go for long periods of time without male company and sometimes I see a man who strikes my fancy and know he probably won't ask me so I have to be bold and ask him. I have not been with a man for a while and when I saw you, I knew you were just what I needed. But if my being bold is not to your liking, you are free to leave. I've lost a few prospective lovers that way, but I'm just a girl with normal desires."

"So – I mean what – happens now?"

"What would you like to happen?" Dawn stood up and asked me to help her with her dress. I did, then removed her gun and knife holsters. She removed my clothes and pulled me down to the bed. I don't remember what time it was when I left Dawn's room, but my sexual education had been considerably advanced. Although I had been with girlfriends, I think of Dawn as my first woman.

Dawn saw me to the door and put her arms around me. "I want to see you again. It may be in the future, but we will make love again. Goodnight, dear Dan."

I had a premonition that we would meet again, but no idea how. I also knew I would someday call the telephone number that Wallace Reid gave me, but since I never expected to be in Hollywood I gave it no more thought.

SUMMERTIME BLUES

It was one of those gorgeous early summer days with lush sweet smells of trees and blooming flowers and the sounds of birds singing. I was underneath a 1919 Series 9 Franklin Roadster that my father bought from Widow Carlisle. Her husband purchased the motorcar for her just before he passed away. She continued to drive it until she backed it into a tree, left it there and called Marvin. He told her he could fix it for a reasonable price. My dad was always fair with his customers but she decided not to drive again so my dad bought the car from her. My job was to remove the rear bumper, straighten it and inspect the underside of the automobile for other damage so we could fix it and sell it. Dad told Widow Carlisle that he would split the profit from the sale of the Franklin with her. He often did things like that and had become one of the most respected people in the village. It was one of the best lessons I learned from him.

We finished our lunch and beer a half hour ago and I was getting drowsy. I had been out late last night with Gina in the old Elgin that my dad received from the factory for beating the locomotive, which became mine when he won another Elgin. Gina called it the struggle buggy because that's how we often ended up in the car at the lake, except I don't recall her struggling all that much as we were laying in the back seat. Gina was a hot Italian biscotti and I thought I was in love with her. Nancy was not happy when she found out I was spending time with Gina and she started dating someone else. I didn't care, Gina was hot and free with her favors and she filled my every waking moment.

Gina was fiery and cute as a bunny, but her family did not like me because I wasn't Italian and Catholic. One day her two brothers found us walking together holding hands and threatened me, telling me to leave Gina alone or they would see that I got what I deserved. I told them that what Gina and I deserved was to be together. The brothers wanted to give me some chin music. Punches were traded and I knocked one down before Gina could stop the fight.

Gina was the apple of her stepfather's eye and could do no wrong but if her stepfather found out what we were doing down at the lake in my struggle buggy, he would come after me with his 10 gauge shotgun. He would not use the shotgun to force me to marry Gina, because murder would more likely be on his mind.

It was warm and comfortable on the grass under the Franklin and my eyelids felt heavy. I was on my back, dreaming of Gina next to me. I woke up to the roaring voice of my father, who grabbed my coveralls at the ankles and pulled me out from under the Franklin and began giving me hell.

"I'm not paying you to dream about girls, we have too much work to get done before I have to leave for my truck job tomorrow. And I've told you to stay away from Regina Coniglio. She's not the girl for you, believe me on this even if you don't believe anything else I tell you."

I was still dazed and I must have looked rather stupid as he kept up his tirade. Why didn't he like Gina? How did he know who she was? I had never brought her to the house, but Dad had told me several times not to see her. With both our families telling us not to see each other, we wanted nothing better than to sneak around and profess our love as physically as possible.

I stammered an apology and Dad began to quiet down, but I was not going to give up Gina. However, right now was probably not a good time to discuss that. Dad needed me to deliver two automobiles to their owners and I hopped to it. I washed the cars, finished invoices for the repairs and drove Mr. Cole's Dodge sedan to deliver it to his house in town. I walked back to the shop and we delivered the other car on our way home.

Dad seemed to be troubled at dinner and did not talk much. My sister Claire was talking about getting a horse. She had learned how to ride from her friend Cindy Hutfilz, and thought that having a horse would be the best thing ever. She had even won me over to champion her cause, and I thought a horse might keep her busy so she would not spy on me, after which she would tell all her friends about watching me kiss girls. She had once caught me with my hand between Nancy's legs and it had cost me many favors to buy her silence.

The next day Dad left for his truck job after lunch. Jake would be here the day after next so I had to hold the fort until then. We had several customer motorcars in the shop, and Dad left instructions on the work I should accomplish while he was away. Then, he surprised me by apologizing for yelling at me yesterday. He never apologized for things like that, especially if I deserved it.

My thoughts turned with sadness to my hero, movie actor and racecar driver Wallace Reid. He died of morphine addiction withdrawal on January 18, 1923. I thought back to the day Wally and his studio girlfriend Dawn had shown up in Long Grove in his new yellow Marmon roadster. Before Wally and Dawn left, I took several pictures, which were now in a picture frame on the wall of my bedroom. Less than two years later, Wallace Reid was dead. The news reports said he had been addicted to morphine since the major injuries he received in a train wreck in 1919 while traveling to a movie location. My friend Chester Foust, now a full-fledged reporter for the *Chicago American,* told me that what the newspapers did not report was that the studio had given Reid morphine to get the movie finished. The studio continued to give him morphine because he was a profitable movie star, and they did not want him to take time off to overcome his morphine addiction. When he died, they mourned his loss as a drug addict without telling the public that it was the studio had caused his addiction. I felt like I lost a friend even though I only knew him for two hours back in July of 1921. I often ran the memories of that afternoon through my mind and could never recall any clue that Wally was a drug addict, but he was an actor and addicts often do very well at convincing others there was no problem.

I had to pull myself out of my depression. After Dad left for the truck job I called Gina but she couldn't go out tonight, something to do with family, she said. On an inspiration I called Nancy but she hung up on me, still upset that I was dating Gina. I called Suzie, a sometime girlfriend and she seemed happy to go out with me tonight. I liked Suzie and knew that she could brighten up my evening. After dinner with Mother and Claire I drove over to pick her up. We went to the Village Tavern for a while and visited friends. On the way home, I drove to the lake. I did not even have to ask Suzie, she was easy and always eager for a petting party. When we arrived at the lake I put the convertible top up and Suzie and I got into the back seat and popped open the bottle of wine I stashed under the seat. Suzie and I took turns drinking from the bottle and I got down to business.

Suzie and I had been lovers and she was warm and ready for a romp. I knew wine had that effect on her. We had plenty of time and when we got our clothes off I took out my last sheath and Suzie installed it on my hard dick. We took another couple swigs of wine and after adjusting or removing certain items of clothing, Suzie straddled me and guided me in. We were going at it when I thought I heard footsteps and then there was a loud banging on the car's rear fender. It sounded like someone was beating it with a piece of wood. I looked up and there was Constable Sherman getting a good look at Suzie's open blouse and bare breasts, then he looked at me and said "Having fun, son? Move it somewhere else" and walked away. My hardness disappeared as Suzie and I could not keep from laughing.

We heard the constable stop at each of the other cars and rap on them with his nightstick. Then I remembered that Hutfilz at the Village Tavern had warned me that the Long Grove elected officials were complaining to the constable about the unsavory activities taking place almost every night at the lake and demanded that he put a stop to it. Constable Sherman was a young man, and he sometimes brought his girlfriend to the lake for the same reason we did. He told the village elders that the lake was outside his jurisdiction, but one of them was prepared for that objection and obtained a special deputy badge from the sheriff. So Sherman went to the lake that night to let us know that the heat was on. He didn't arrest anyone, it was his way of telling us to fade from the lake for a while until things cooled down. Damn, now I would have to find another place to have fun with my girlfriends. Some of the other cars scrammed, but Suzie did not want leave, so she got me up again and we finished what we had started.

Afterward I took Suzie home and she made it obvious she was hoping to become my regular girlfriend again. Her father had to come to the door to break up our kissing contest. I liked Suzie, she was cute and kind of wild. She was not fat or skinny, kind of in between and she had big breasts. Some of the guys called her Crazy Suzie but she knew the moves. Suzie told me I was her favorite guy and she liked doing me, as she called it. I was holding back from her because I was dating Gina, and while Suzie wanted to get married and start a family, I didn't. I left her house thinking that if I had to give up Gina, I could fill my time with Suzie if I could slow down her ambition to get married.

Next morning I needed some hair of the dog and borrowed a flask from Dad's desk. After work I called Gina again but one of her brothers answered and said she wasn't home and hung up on me.

Claire was excited because she found a good horse at a reasonable price and wanted me to go with her to look it over. I knew something about horses so Claire and

Mother and I went to see it. The horse was a good-looking gentle gelding, brown with a white blaze and stockings. We told Claire that we would talk to Dad about it when he returned. Claire had already talked to Hutfilz and made arrangements to board her horse at his place. Hutfilz lived next door to the Village Tavern and for a monthly fee Claire's horse would share the pasture and barn with his daughter Cindy's horse. Claire had to groom and care for her animal, and pay for its feed and veterinarian care. Claire's nineteenth birthday was next week, but she was giddy as a first grader over that horse. I ribbed her and told her it would be cheaper to get a car, but she ignored my smart-aleck joke.

When my father returned from his truck job the next day, Claire talked him into going to look at her dream horse. I drove my parents and Claire in my perfectly maintained Elgin. Dad was impressed at how well I took care of it, but it was my first car and I either kept it up or I could walk, or get a horse.

Dad looked over the horse and the owner saddled it for Claire to ride. The gelding was a about four years old, in good health and the price was reasonable, so Dad bought the horse and tack and Claire rode her horse over to the Hutfilz place. It was about 2 miles and when she arrived we were waiting for her. Claire had a big smile on her face and Sandy the horse looked happy with his new owner. We took photos and my mother commented on how beautiful and self-assured Claire looked. We got the horse settled in and the tack put away. Claire earned some money the last few months babysitting and housecleaning, and she paid the first month's boarding bill.

Claire was becoming a woman and a heartbreaker. She was a cute kitten, her tall gawky body was developing and her movements were becoming elegant. She dated but none of her boyfriends lasted very long. I laughed when she told me it was because they had 'Russian Hands and Roman Fingers'. She was going to wait for the right man, implying that I was not waiting for the right girl.

The rest of the summer went by slowly. Jake came up every two weeks and worked with us. We took in more business as automobile ownership was growing and there were not enough good mechanicians. Dad was making plans to rebuild and enlarge the shop. The building was drafty and cold in the winter, and we needed more space to handle the increase in business.

MY FATHER, THE RUMRUNNER

My father had been gone on his truck job for five days and Mother was getting worried. He never called when he was driving. Several times I heard my mother tell him that he should quit that job since the shop was getting busier by the day and the money he made could be more easily made in the shop. He listened to her but said he couldn't quit just yet, and for some reason that ended their discussion. I did not understand it and when I asked, Mother told me to "talk to your father" which I decided to do when he returned from this trip.

Jake had left the shop to go home to Argo to do some work for Elgin. Late in the afternoon the shop telephone rang. It was my sister Claire and she sounded upset, telling me to close the shop and get home right now. I asked why but she repeated "Right now" and hung up. I had a car to deliver so I drove it to the customer's house and walked home. There was a strange car parked in the driveway and as I got closer I saw it was a sheriff's Chevrolet sedan.

As I ran up the front stairs my mother opened the door. She was crying. I went inside and a sheriff's deputy was sitting at the kitchen table talking with Claire and writing in his notebook. He asked me to wait in the parlor and he would talk to me in a few minutes. As I walked to the parlor, my mother put her arms around me and cried softly on my shoulder. "It's your father" she said. "His truck overturned on an icy road along the Fox River and he was seriously injured. A farmer came by and tried but could not get him out of the damaged truck so he called the local firemen. They cut the truck to get him out, but by that time he had died from his injuries. They are bringing him here tomorrow and we have to make funeral arrangements."

"Why does the sheriff want to talk to me?" I asked.

"He is investigating your father's death because there are suspicious circumstances, and he has to get a statement from each of us" she replied.

Claire came from the kitchen about ten minutes later and motioned for me to go talk to the deputy. Her face was red from crying too. I had a difficult time keeping the tears from my eyes. I had just turned 21 years old. Dad and I were working on plans to build a new shop building. This could not be happening. We had so much to do. I sat down at the table and the deputy identified himself as Deputy Sheriff Carlson and began to tell me about my father's accident, then shocked me by saying that my father had been driving for the Coniglio family, running booze for them. "No, that cannot be. My father would not do that. Are you sure it was him?" I asked, feeling a tremble in my voice.

"We believe it is him. A Fox Lake fireman knew him and identified him but to be sure, the body will be here tomorrow morning and you, your mother and sister can confirm or deny it then."

"But my father was an excellent driver. He would not overturn a truck. He is a fast but careful driver. It just does not sound like something he would do."

"Dan, your father's truck was carrying a heavy load of contraband booze. In fact it was overloaded. He was driving quickly and began to slow down for a sharp curve. There was ice on the curve and the truck began to slide. He tried to correct it but the overloaded truck went over and down an embankment. A farmer who came along saw it happen from a distance and hurried to get there. He said there was a car load of men chasing and shooting at the truck. I verified there are bullet holes in the truck body and contraband in the back. When the truck went off the road, the shooters drove away fast. We think they were gangsters from another mob trying to hijack the truck" the deputy told me. "I'm sorry Danny, it's not good news. I am telling you what we know so far. I'm trying to get all the information to investigate and find out who was chasing him. What do you know about your father driving for the Coniglio family?"

"I don't know anything about that. He never told me who he worked for when he drove truck. It was a part-time job to make some money so we could build a new repair shop because our old building is worn out and too small. And what's this about the Coniglio family? Is that Gina Coniglio? She's not mixed up with the mob."

"How do you know Gina Coniglio?" the deputy asked.

"She was my girlfriend. She never told me she was mixed up with the gangs."

"Have you ever been to her home?" the deputy asked.

"No, her brothers didn't like me and they offered to beat me up for dating their sister, but Gina stopped them. That doesn't mean she's in the mob" I replied, a bit angrily.

"She's not in the mob, just related to Don Coniglio, the local mob boss. He is her uncle and stepfather. When she and her brothers were orphaned, the Don took them into his family and formally adopted them. The brothers are in the gang and known to be bag men. As far as we know, Gina does not play a role in the family business."

I had never paid much attention to the gangsters. I wanted nothing to do with them. Gina certainly had not told me who her family was. "Their business is running booze?" I asked.

"Yes. The family controls liquor distribution in the northwest suburban area. The Don's only son is Joey, a mean son of a bitch, a real bad apple."

"I guess that's why my father told me to stop seeing Gina, but he didn't tell me who the Coniglios were. Now I wish he had told me why."

Suddenly the fire bell sounded to call the volunteer firemen to go to the fire station. I was a new volunteer, not fully trained but the chief told me I should answer fire calls to get experience, assigning me to an experienced firefighter for training. When I told Deputy Carlson, he said I should go and he would follow the fire truck and give me a ride back to finish our talk.

I ran to the fire station, put on my gear and was ready and waiting as the other firemen arrived. When we had a crew we jumped on the old fire truck and our driver pulled out. I had not asked where the fire was, but as we turned down the road toward the auto repair shop I saw a cloud of thick black smoke and I knew right away it was our shop that was burning. The driver brought us up as close as he could and we jumped off. There was another carload of firemen and Deputy Carlson's car arriving right behind us. I looked at the building and knew it was hopeless. It was burning from end to end, as if the entire building had caught fire all at once. The fireman that I shadowed told me to stay back. He said no one was going inside because of the intense heat and there was nothing we could do to stop it. The only thing we could do was wet down the area around it to keep the fire from spreading and let the fire burn itself out.

I stood there in shock. A hand took hold of my shoulder. It was Deputy Carlson. "I talked to your chief and he will investigate but thinks it was arson, set to engulf the building immediately so there would be nothing left. He estimated that it started about a half hour ago. It's a good thing you were with me, otherwise someone might think you started the fire for the insurance money. Even if you had, insurance will not pay for an arson fire." I informed him that we did not have insurance on the building. He wrote that in his notebook.

The fire burned hot and fast, the old wooden building collapsing into a fiery heap in less than an hour. Inside were hulks of four vehicles still burning, an old flivver owned by Farmer Schultz, a Dodge touring car, a Ford pickup truck and an Oldsmobile. We could not go in to inspect the wreckage until the building cooled down and the chief directed the firemen to spray the embers. Darkness was approaching and the chief said it would not be cool enough for inspection until morning. The deputy

THE ROARING ROAD — BOOK 1   35

asked the chief to leave a couple of firemen at the site until he could send a deputy to guard it overnight. We would meet again in the morning and inspect the remains.

Deputy Carlson drove me home and said he would pick me up at 6 o'clock in the morning. I went inside to tell my mother and sister, but they already heard the news. Cindy brought food from the tavern, but none of us could eat much. My mind was racing with so many thoughts.

My mother began tell me more. "Your father was forced to drive for the Coniglio family. They threatened to harm you and Claire if he refused. Your father and I talked about moving away, but we owned the shop and the house. And where would we go that could shield us from them? That is why your father agreed to drive and they paid him a lot of money for the job, so we saved it for a new shop building. His only concern was to protect his family from harm. He was only going to drive for them for a year, but they threatened him again and he had to stay on, finally getting an audience with the Don who agreed that after the second year he would be allowed to quit. He told me he thought the Don's son Joey would threaten again, and there was no one he could turn to for help. Constable Sherman would help but it would be suicide for him to go up against the Coniglios. He thought about going to the sheriff, but there have been rumors that many deputies are on the pad for the Coniglios, taking bribes to turn the other way."

"That's why he tried to stop you from seeing Gina. We do not believe she was bad, but you would never have been allowed to marry her. The Coniglio brothers would have killed you first. Your father made one of the conditions of his driving for them that they would not harm you just because you were dating Gina, but they kept pressuring him to make you stop. They got tough with him and he took a few punches. When that didn't work they began pressuring Gina to stop seeing you. She did not want to stop but finally the Don ordered her to stop seeing you. I know it sounds rough, but you are better off not having any association with that family. I got more worried when I found out that you were having sex with Gina. Don't look at me like that, I knew."

I looked at my sister Claire and she blushed. So she was the one who blabbed. Mother went on "If the Don or his son Joey found out about that, they would make you dead. They finally got to Gina by telling her they would kill you if she saw you again. She told them she loved you, but the Don said she would never have you and if you ran off together they would hunt you down and kill you. We were told that she screamed and raged but the Don was firm. That is why she stopped answering your telephone calls. Please Danny, do not even think about her again. Gina may have loved you, and she may not be involved in the business but these people are bad news."

The next morning Deputy Carlson was at our door promptly at six o'clock. We got into his Chevrolet and went to the shop. The chief had sent the fire truck over to spray the embers and brought my fire boots and a pair for Deputy Carlson. We carefully stepped into the still warm ashes, Carlson asking me to look carefully at the remains of the cars. Tires and wood spoke wheels had burned and collapsed so the bodies were on the ground. Deputy Carlson and the fire chief opened trunks and I opened the hoods to check for anything unusual.

"Chief! Deputy! Take a look at this" I called out. They came and looked at the gasoline cans shoved under the Oldsmobile. "They wouldn't go off all by themselves, and my father would have had a fit if any of us put gasoline cans under the automobiles."

"No, I think they were thrown under there after the contents were poured out. The perpetrators could have taken them, but didn't bother because we would figure out right away that it was arson" said the fire chief. "The fire started all around the shop. That could not happen except on purpose." The chief said he would have to leave soon to open his store. Deputy Carlson thanked him for his help and they arranged to contact each other if anything helpful to the solution of the crime was discovered.

Deputy Carlson drove us back to the house to pick up my mother and sister. He drove us to the funeral home where they had taken Dad's body. Claire was not sure if she could look, but finally tightened up her courage and the three of us stood there while the funeral director removed the sheet over the body. Mother and Claire cried immediately, and I gave in to my tears a few seconds later. It was my father Marvin. He had cuts on his face but the coroner said he died of internal injuries. He looked peaceful, disturbingly so. We each responded to Deputy Carlson's necessary question "Is this person known to you?" There was no doubt in any of us. We went to the funeral home's office and arranged for his funeral to be held three days later. Deputy Carlson expressed his condolences and drove us home. He told us to contact him if we thought of anything else that could help the investigation and promised to let us know if and when they solved the crime.

The three of us sat in the parlor, unable to speak. Claire went to the kitchen and came back with a bottle of whiskey and three glasses. She poured each of us a shot of whiskey. I drank mine down in one swallow while Mom and Claire sipped theirs. I had a second shot but Mom and Claire never finished theirs, so I did. It didn't help.

The next morning Jake arrived to work. He was not aware of the fire or my father's death. Jake went to the shop and saw the charred ruins, then rushed over to our home. Over coffee, I told him what happened and at the end he turned away from me. The normally stoic Jake had tears in his eyes, for he and Dad had been best friends. Then he brought up a subject I was not ready to think about yet.

"Are you going to rebuild the shop? What are you going to do to support your family? You are the man of the house now, and ready or not, the responsibility is yours."

"Jake, I don't know how to answer that. We just arranged for his funeral. I don't know our financial status, but I have to do something, don't I?" which was a dumb question since I knew the answer. "I don't know if I can build a new building or not, or how long it would take. You saw the place, it's nothing but ash and junk metal."

Jake looked unhappy, as if he did not like what he had to say. "Danny, the Elgin factory is moving to Indianapolis. My wife and I do not want to move because it is a last ditch effort to save the company and they may go out of business anyway. I would be out of a job where I do not know anyone, and I have to support my family. You would not be able to pay me for several weeks, maybe months while you build a new shop. I'll help in any way I can, but I have to find other work." I knew he spoke the truth. Things looked bleak and I did not know what to say. Yesterday I had a father, a job, a life. Today I had to grow up, ready or not. I said "I understand what you have to do Jake, and thank you for being direct with me. If I can call on you for advice or to run ideas by you for your opinion, I would appreciate it very much."

"You certainly can Danny, call me any time. I'll be glad to help. If anyone can rebuild, you can. You are a chip off the old block. After the funeral I will go home and start looking for work. Do not hesitate to call. I will be disappointed if you don't." Jake and I shook hands. We understood each other and I respected him just as my father had. I took a walk to think. When I returned my mother had composed herself and said she would gather the family documents and we would talk tomorrow morning so we all knew our situation. Claire had gone to her room to cry. She also had to grow up too soon. I had just turned 21 and felt like I was going on 40.

WEIGHT OF RESPONSIBILITY

My mother asked me to help her get the documents. I went into their bedroom and was surprised to find her working a combination dial on a wall safe behind a bland landscape painting that I had always wondered why they had kept in their bedroom. "Mother I never knew this was here!" I said in amazement.

"Your father was concerned with family safety and security. He installed this safe just after you were born." She turned a small lever and pulled the door open, removing several envelopes and accounting journals. I noticed there were three banded bundles of cash and a small jewelry box. Mother handed me the envelopes and took everything else out of the safe and we brought all of it to the kitchen table. Claire was washing the breakfast dishes. "I want both of you to be fully aware of our circumstances." Claire's eyes were red, and seeing her that way my eyes began to get wet too, but Mother took us by our arms and looked us both in the eyes. "There will be time for that later. I'm sorry to be tough with the both of you, but this has to be done as soon as possible so we can make decisions." I took strength from her strength and noticed that Claire did also.

I made a fresh pot of coffee and helped Claire finish the dishes, then we sat at the table. Mother passed the documents to us as she explained. "Your father was also concerned with our future if something happened to him. I have good news and bad news to tell you."

"First, your father had a life insurance policy in the amount of $5,000. The death certificate says he died in road accident, so there will be no question that the insurance company will pay on the policy. The bands of cash total over $3,000. The jewelry box holds the beautiful diamond necklace that your father gave me on our tenth anniversary, and a string of good quality pearls. Marvin saved money over a long period of time and it might have been more if he had opened a savings account, but your father did not trust banks. However, I started a savings account and here is the savings book showing it has over $1,200 in it. We owe less than $1,000 on the house and land, so our home is safe. You know I was bookkeeper for the shop but now I don't have a job. If I am careful with money, you do not have to worry about supporting me for now, but if I am going to send Claire to college I will need to find a job to make sure we can do that. As for you Danny, if you want to go to college I'll do all I can but you will need a part-time job to help out."

She continued, "We own the land that the shop was on free and clear. Now that the shop building is gone, we could sell the land, but we should not sell below market value. I can help with analyzing a purchase offer but I'm not a good negotiator and you two are sharp so maybe you can work together on that."

"Claire? A good negotiator?" I blurted out. Claire glared at me and kicked me under the table. Mother looked upset at my outburst as well.

"Danny, your sister is a lot smarter than you give her credit for. Did you know she negotiated the price down and made a good bargain for her horse? Not only that, she talked the owner into including most of the tack she needed. She did that without any help from your father. She also negotiated her horse boarding deal with Hutfilz. One of the things you need to learn is that your sister is not just an empty headed little girl, she gets top grades and had done a lot more than you think."

Claire was grinning now, but Mother was right. It would take me awhile to fully realize that Claire was a smart kid. "OK, sorry Sis. I never noticed. Let's talk before we get approached by someone to sell the property."

"I knew I liked you for some reason besides your being my brother" Claire smiled as she said it, happy to see I was beginning to accept her new status. I started to see Claire in a new light that day. We liked each other, albeit with the usual brother/sister problems like her spying on my love life. "What's the bad news?" Claire asked.

"As Deputy Carlson told you, your father was driving for the Coniglio mob. I do not know what they are going to do about it, but the deputy said their usual mindset is that the driver is responsible for the truck and they will believe that we owe them for it. That is what they have done to others in similar circumstances. We made a serious mistake by not having insurance on the building and tools. Your father said he would get insurance when things got better, but by then the building was falling apart and wasn't worth insuring. Everything in it is lost, Jake's tools too. I talked to him and asked him to give us a list with purchase prices and we will reimburse him. For Jake, it is his source of income and I will not deprive him of that. He was your father's best friend and I will not have him remembering us for being cold-hearted."

"I agree that we fully reimburse Jake. I think he might feel sorry for us and give us low replacement costs. We should make sure he gets the full amount for what he lost. It wasn't his fault that the shop burned" I said. Claire agreed.

"Regarding the Coniglios, they are wrong about our family owing them money for the truck, but they are bad people who take advantage of others and they follow their own business code. I believe that they set fire to our shop. What I don't understand is why they did it so soon, taking away our source of income" Mother said.

"Probably because Dad already told them to go to Hell" Claire replied, and Mother and I both nodded in agreement. "But now, will they come after us? Without Dad, we don't have a chance at paying them and rebuilding the shop" Claire said. "Do they know about the insurance policy? Maybe they think we will give them that money."

"Your father told no one about any of this, and you two did not know about it so you couldn't have told anyone. Jake knew nothing about it and he would not have anything to do with those thugs. He was after your father to quit driving for the Coniglio family and told him that nothing good would come of it. He was right."

"Should we try to rebuild the shop?" Claire asked.

"We have to do it quickly and take out a building loan, or our customers will go elsewhere. We could try to find a new location with an existing building but it has to be close enough to the village and suitable for an automobile repair shop. Most of the land here is farmland and farmers will not sell a piece of their land for an automobile shop, especially after our shop burned" Mother said.

"It's also going to be tough with Jake gone. I know a lot and probably know how to do 90% of the jobs we get, but Jake knows everything. There is no one else around here with the knowledge and experience, not even my friends Otto and Fritz who know a lot about motorcars. We can talk about it more but I am concerned that we will not be able to rebuild the shop in time to keep Jake. We might have to move to a larger town to lease a property with a suitable building on it. That means higher rent and we would have to raise our prices, and that could cost us customers" I added.

"This is all happening so fast, maybe we should think about what we can do. I do not want to move, this has been our home since your father and I married. He bought the land and built most of the house himself, with some hired help from a local carpenter. I cannot imagine not living here. He told me once that he carved our initials inside hearts on some of the beams and wall studs." I knew Mother was right about that. Mother and Dad had been dearly in love with each other, often holding hands and whispering things to each other, making each other laugh. They went out on dates a couple times a month and when they got dressed to go dancing they looked perfect together. Sure, now and then they quarreled, but it was almost always resolved in a day and never with any threats or anger. And many a time I had heard the sounds from their bedroom that showed they loved to love each other. I decided that I would have a relationship like my parents shared or I wouldn't get married at all.

As if she was reading my thoughts, Claire said "Oh Mother – I do so hope that my future husband is a man as good and trustworthy and loving as Father."

"Well then you should look to improving the quality of the boys you date" and I immediately recognized that I had shoved my shoe in my mouth.

Sure enough, Claire threw it back at me. "Yeah Danny, like your girlfriends? It appears that you choose them for their easy morals rather than their good characters."

"Stop your bickering! We need to work together and neither of you should worry about getting married yet. Worry about getting your lives organized so that your father will look down from Heaven and be pleased with what he sees. Get married too soon to the wrong person will just add problems. You know, I didn't even let your father kiss me for almost six months after we began dating."

"Dad told a different story about that." Claire was hot with comebacks today and Mother's face turned red. Dad once hinted to me that things between him and Mother had been so hot they moved up their wedding date to be sure the birth of their first child wouldn't be less than nine months.

"I think we are done with this conversation for now." Mother returned to her businesslike attitude. "Dan, there were a few things in the shop, tools, parts and so forth but they are probably ash or twisted metal. But Jake suggested that as soon as the ashes cooled you should go through the site to see if there is anything salvageable."

"I'll go over and take a look right now. Hey Claire, want to come with?"

Claire was pleased to be included and we got into the Elgin and drove to see if my friends Otto and Fritz would be able to come and help. I knew that Claire had a crush on Fritz, so she readily agreed. We stopped at the fire department to get my fire boots and three more pair of fire boots so we could walk in the ashes. I did not have gloves so we stopped at the general store and bought heavy gloves for each of us.

As we pulled up to the shop I could see we were unlikely to find anything. It was still warm but we sifted through and there was little to be found. All the tools and machinery were ruined. Fritz found the remains of Mother's bookkeeping record books. They were charred but partially readable so we brought them back. Claire found the twisted metal remains of the heavy cash box Dad used to put the money that people paid for their repairs. I saw the burned hulks of the cars sitting there looking forlorn, and wondered who could have done this.

After the funeral my father was buried in the small Long Grove Church cemetery. I was surprised at how many people came to the funeral. There wasn't enough room in the church or at the gravesite for everyone so people watched from farther away even though they couldn't hear the words very well. Even some managers from the Elgin Motor Car Company came up. My mother's friends organized a reception and Hutfilz offered the use of the meeting room at the Village Tavern, and provided the food.

Over the next few days I asked around and learned more about the Coniglio family. I was told they were dangerous people and to stay away from them. Joey C. was the mob chief's son, and well known as a hothead. When Prohibition began they ran booze and beer from Wisconsin, Michigan and Canada to supply the speakeasies. There were a few people who made their own beer, wine or booze but if they were smart they only made enough for their own consumption because if you tried to sell it, you were inviting a visit from Joey C. and his sluggers. Even Hutfilz at the Long Grove Village Tavern had stopped making his own beer and was buying from the Coniglio family. It was rumored that the Coniglios were allied with Johnny Torrio and the Chicago South Side Outfit.

I asked Jake why no one would stand up to the Coniglio mob. "Dan, the townspeople don't have enough guns to face the mob, and even if they did, they aren't hired killers and thugs, they're farmers, store owners with families. They respected your father but no family man worth his salt is going to go into a losing battle and leave his family homeless and penniless." Jake spoke softly and I realized I had to grow up right now, stop thinking with anger and start making plans. It was a turning point in my life. What was I going to do? Sell? Rebuild? What was best for my family?

TAKEN FOR A RIDE

At first I thought the fastest way to get the shop open was to find a property with an existing building that could be converted, but after two weeks of morning to night searches I had no success. I tried to think of what I would do if I could not re-open our automobile shop. Not too many ideas there, either. Hutfilz told me I could work as a bartender for the summer, but I wanted something of my own. I went down every street and every road in the area covered by the circle I drew on a map. I got home, tired and discouraged at around seven one evening. My mother had gone to visit her sister for a few days, and while she was away Claire stayed at the Hutfilz house with her friend Cindy, working on training their horses. Those two were thick as thieves but I was glad Claire was safe. The Hutfilz family lived next door to the Tavern and there were always several people there for lunch or beer. Hutfilz had turned the front of the tavern into an ice cream parlor run by his wife, but all the locals, including Constable Sherman, knew the password to get in the back door.

I pulled into the gravel parking area behind the tavern and walked toward the tavern door. As I approached, a Cadillac sedan pulled up and two guys got out – Gina's brothers. *Oh crap, I didn't need this on top of everything else.* They ran up to me, one in front and one behind me. "Get in the car" the one in front of me shouted. I didn't want anything to do with them so I told them to go fuck themselves. It didn't help. "Get in the fucking car asshole" was the response. The one behind me tried to grab my right arm and push me to the car and I turned to punch him in the mouth but instead was greeted by a flash of sharp steel pointing at my face. "We're not supposed to hurt you but if you resist you're gonna get cut. Now - get -

into - the - fucking - car" he repeated, emphasizing each word.

"You need a new speechwriter, I don't know what you're talking about" I replied. The knife moved up to my right cheek and I felt a tiny prick from the point. I had the surreal idea of telling him that he had a little prick, but decided against it for now. Then he made the mistake of taking the knife far enough away from me so he could show me the droplet of blood at the point. As he did that he loosened his grip on my arm. He was momentarily surprised when I elbowed him in the gut, grabbed his wrist and twisted as hard as I could. He went down on his knees, howling in pain. His grip on the knife loosened and I pried it from his fingers and pushed him further down. But I wasn't quick enough to deal with his brother, who dived on me and body-slammed me to the ground. He wasn't a little guy and his weight dropped on me like a load of bricks. The air in my lungs was forced out fast and I dropped the knife, but recovered enough strength to roll him off me. I had to raise myself up to get some room to swing at his ugly face, but now the first brother grabbed me from behind and they wrestled me into the back seat. One of them got in with me, the other ran around and sat behind the wheel. I heard someone yell "Stop" and a shotgun fired, but it had been aimed high. The Cadillac threw gravel from its rear tires and started moving. As I lay on the seat, I swear that the voice that shouted "Stop" was a girl's voice, but my head was ringing so maybe I imagined it. Anyway, the Cadillac was speeding down the road now, making random turns to shake off any pursuers.

I tried to sit up but was pushed down and this time I saw the business end of a handgun pointed at my face. "You stupid rats, don't you know I'm not allowed to see Gina?"

"Shut up" was all I got for a reply. About 30 minutes later we turned into a long driveway and the car came to a stop. The brothers jumped out and pulled me out of the

Cadillac and threw me on the ground, each of them giving me a kick. A door opened and a commanding voice called "Enough. I told you the Don said no damage, just bring him here. You two feeble-minded idiots have trouble understanding that? Pick him up and bring him inside. Now!" It was Joey Coniglio. He was bigger than the two meatballs and his contempt for Gina's brothers was clear. He was the Don's only son and was being groomed for the day he would become the Don.

Joey took me by the arm and said "Listen, if we wanted you iced, you would be dead by now. I will let go of your arm if you promise not to give me any trouble or try to run away. The Don wants to talk to you and then we will take you back with no injuries unless you do something stupid." I nodded my acceptance. "Come with me" he said as he opened the door, motioning for me to go in first. I was directed down a long dark hallway, through a couple of doors and down a set of stairs, then through another door guarded by a big guy in a brown suit a size too small and a gun bulge under his coat. We went to the end of a large room. I did not see anyone at first because the light was dim. As we got close an old man sitting in a big leather chair came into focus. He wore a black suit with a white shirt and no tie, and on his feet were bedroom slippers. He looked like a retired undertaker. I decided that this must be the Don and he did not look happy. I immediately worried that he had found out what I had been doing with his stepdaughter Gina and he was going to give me a fair trial before I was slowly and painfully hacked to death. "Stand up straight" Joey C. barked. "Show respect. This is Don Coniglio. Don, this is Daniel Lindner, Marvin's son."

"I should show respect for the man who killed my father? You might as well kill me now because I don't have any respect for you, not now, not ever." Joey C.'s fist hit me hard in the kidney as I croaked out the word 'ever'.

It was silent in the room, the only sound from a grandfather clock tick-tocking on the other side of the room. "I did not kill your father" Don Coniglio said so softly I almost could not hear him. "Why do you accuse me of this crime?"

"You ordered someone to chase my father on an icy road, causing his death when the truck rolled over. Then your gang firebombed our shop, burning it to the ground. Maybe you did it to put pressure on me. But that won't work." My voice was shaky but as disrespectful as I could make it sound.

"Is this true Joey?" the old man asked, his voice firm and dry but somehow also menacing. It was a voice that could give orders to kill people.

"No father, we did not burn his shop. We take our cars to Dino's shop in Arlington Heights, those are your orders. His father's truck rolled over and he died from his injuries. We did nothing to kill him. He wanted to quit driving for us and probably thought if he lost a load we would fire him, or else he had slipped word to the North Side Outfit who were waiting to chase and catch him. Either way, the Lindner family owes us over twelve thousand dollars for the truck and the merchandise."

"Why would he tell the cops?" I asked angrily. "My father would have gone to jail but you guys would have your lawyers tie things up in court and never serve a day. He was driving fast because a car was chasing and people were shooting at him. The overloaded truck was top heavy, the road was slippery and on a sharp curve it slid off the road and rolled over. That's what happened."

The old man stared at me, Joey C. standing next to me and Gina's ugly brothers along with the big goon in the brown suit were blocking the door. The Don softly said something in Italian and a small old man in a white servant's jacket appeared from nowhere and filled the brandy glass in front of the Don. "In the spirit of civility, would you have a brandy with an old man?" he asked. I decided it would be a good idea for me to say yes, so I did. The white jacketed servant produced a glass and Don Coniglio had two chairs brought over, ordering us to sit. I drank a little. It was high quality stuff. Why wouldn't it be? The Coniglio family were bringing in hooch of all kinds and supplying it to bars and clubs in northern Illinois. My father might have delivered this brandy.

I politely thanked the Don for the brandy and waited for him to speak because I could not think of anything else to say. I noticed Joey was not offered any brandy. That seemed rather curious.

After what seemed like several minutes of reflection the Don spoke again. "First, I express my condolences to you and your family for the loss of your father. I didn't know him well, but he seemed like an honorable man and even though he didn't like me or what I asked of him, he did it and I respected him as a good, hard-working family man." The Don stopped briefly, took a sip of his brandy. "No one in the Coniglio family burned down your shop. I do not know how that idea came to you, but I am sure of this fact. Is it not so Joey?"

"That is the truth, father" Joey C. replied solemnly. I knew he was lying.

Again the Don waited before he continued, the grandfather clock counting out the seconds. Conversations in this family must be long drawn out affairs, I thought, my mind confused by what I had just been told. I wondered if they sang 'Happy Birthday' to each other this slowly. "I would have given you time to pay because I know your only income came from the repair shop. But even though your shop is gone, I must demand that you reimburse me for the cost of the truck and the merchandise. Why would it make sense for us to burn your business down?"

"With the shop gone, you could try to force me to work for you and take it out of my pay" I shouted so loud that I could hear brown suit and the goon brothers reaching inside their jackets for their pistols. Joey C. scowled angrily at me. Disrespecting the Don was not tolerated.

"Father, let me take him for a ride. You don't have to listen to his wild and baseless accusations" Joey said.

"This young man is upset and angry, and you would be too if you thought you were facing someone who had harmed me" he said.

"Yes Don" Joey C. replied entirely without sincerity. Take me for a ride? Wasn't that the euphemism for someone to be taken out and killed in a remote place where the body would not be found anytime soon, if ever?

Finally the Don spoke again. "I understand you are a very good driver. The idea did come to me to ask you to drive for me. I pay well, immediately in cash upon receipt of the shipment in good condition." So that's why I had been brought here. He wanted me to work and pay off the debt they thought my father owed. But then after that, what would they do with me? It was a job where I wouldn't need to worry about getting a pension because I would never live long enough to need one.

"No sir, I would not, for two reasons. One, I do not agree that my father owes a debt to you. It was something that happened. He did not plan to have an accident or sabotage the truck. Second, my future after the alleged debt was paid would be rather bleak."

A long silence ensued. We both sipped some brandy, our eyes locked on each other. I thought I picked up a flicker of amusement on Don Coniglio's face. It must be amusing for him to toy with me, like a cat playing with a mouse before killing it, not a pleasant analogy in this situation.

"There is no reason for your future to be cut short, if you are providing good service to us. It would be foolish for me to do otherwise. I have several employees outside of my family who have worked for me many years and will continue to do so. I am disappointed that you think I am so crude and barbaric." Another sip of brandy, and the small white coated man appeared instantly at the Don's wave to refill the brandy in our glasses.

"Sir, I don't know what to say. I do not believe we owe you any debt, and I will not work for you. I want to leave now." Better than taking a long ride with Joey C.

"No Daniel, if I say you owe, then you owe us. That is my final decision. Under certain circumstances in the future I may order you to be taken for a ride, but for some reason I like you and don't want to do that today. It would be better for you to think about my offer, talk it over with your family, and come back in, let us say, three days. Just come to the gate and give them your name. I will have you on the list to be brought to me immediately." So Don Coniglio wasn't quite ready to give the orders to send me on a ride yet. Ah, yes, my old charm saved me once again. And I was glad that the Don did not seem to be aware of the body positions Gina and I were in together on a regular basis not so very long ago. I was sure that I would not be served fine brandy if that were the case, unless it was my last drink.

"Don, permit me to offer a solution" Joey C. spoke up. "I will work with Mr. Lindner to find a way to clear up this debt and you need not be troubled with it. I will keep you informed of what we do to resolve it. With so much else going on now you have more important things to attend to, and you have been telling me that I should step up and take more responsibility."

More silence. "Yes Joey, I like your idea. I turn Mr. Lindner's debt over to you, but I expect you to be diligent and not let this slip away without repayment. You will be responsible for the money should you not collect it in a reasonable time. Report your progress along with your other reports each week. Good night Mr. Lindner, my people will see you get home." He glared at the ugly and stupid brothers at the door. "Safe and unharmed, is that understood?" They sullenly nodded their understanding.

I was led back upstairs and through the building to the front entrance. On the way, Gina appeared in a doorway and smiled at me, then turned away without saying a word. I wondered if she knew what had just happened.

Probably did, she was a sharp cookie. Suddenly I had the feeling that, young as she was, Gina was the brains of the family. I knew she had a very good brain, along with other delightful body parts. Maybe I should be scared.

I was pushed into the rear seat of the Cadillac sedan, this time without being kicked or threatened, but now I wasn't resisting either. As Gina's brothers drove me home, the one in the front seat, the leader of the two, said "Look Lindner, we don't like you. Nobody here likes you. But you got a break, so don't fluff it."

"Go fuck yourself" I replied, very politely, and added "You idiot."

"See, even after getting a reprieve he disrespects us. Here is what we wanted to say to you if you survived the evening. After you stopped seeing Gina, she took up with a Greek cake-eater and we learned he has taken sexual advantage of our sister. He talks to Gina of marriage and took her to his Greek church, which is a great disrespect to us. We like him even less than we like you. We want you to call Gina, make up to her and have her be your girlfriend again. We will pay you so you can take her out to nightclubs and restaurants until you get a job. We will be your bodyguards when you are with Gina and will make sure she gets home safe. We would be very grateful and in return, we will not beat you to death. We know you are an honorable man, and we cannot stand the thought of that bastard fucking our little sister. You can do this for us? No? Then do it for Gina."

I almost broke out in laughter. As for doing it for Gina I would much rather be doing it to Gina. These knuckle-draggers did not know I had been bopping Gina almost every time we got together. Now, they disliked the Greek more than they disliked me and wanted me back because I was the lesser evil. Maybe I should have been more impressed that they promised not to beat me to death. But eventually, after the Greek had moved on they would revert to wanting to beat me up. How could Gina be so pretty, so sexy, so smart, and be related to these morons?

But then thoughts of being found out and taken for a ride took over. We arrived at the tavern and I told them "Sorry guys, but the Don has forbidden Gina to see me, and what makes you think I'm an honorable guy? Tell Gina I said hello. She can call me if she wants. Tell her I think that a Greek/Italian baby would be cute. And thanks for the ride." The brothers were silent but the looks on their faces were murderous.

The brother who sat next to me whipped out his knife again, and I said "Don't bother. I've seen your little prick already" and laughed.

He tried to stab me in the chest but the brother in the front seat grabbed his wrist. "No. We promised the Don he would return safely" and he turned to me and said "But we will find you another time and you will be made to pay for your disrespect."

I opened the car door and got out. Claire and Cindy came around the corner of the tavern building toward the Cadillac. Cindy carried a shotgun and Claire had Dad's M1911 Colt. I recalled Claire telling me that Cindy knew how to use a shotgun better than most men in the village, and Claire had practiced with the 1911. The brothers left the same as the first time, with gravel shooting from the rear tires. I felt lucky that was all the shooting there was.

When I saw Cindy and Claire with guns I told them they should never pick a gunfight with the Coniglio family. They could have killed the two brothers but the aftermath would have left all of us dead.

Later, Claire told me that after I was kidnapped someone called the Village Tavern and told Cindy that I had to attend a meeting and that I would not be harmed. It was a female voice but they did not know Gina's voice. I suspected Gina called to keep my family from worrying, but it confirmed to me that Gina was possibly involved with the mob if she had the ability to influence my safety with the Don.

LIGHT AT THE END OF THE TUNNEL

My search for a location to rebuild the Lindner Motor Car Sales & Service shop continued to be a dismal failure and the estimates of the cost to rebuild on our own property were coming in much higher than expected. I decided to see Hutfilz the next morning and accept his offer to bartend at his tavern. It would bring in some money and give me time to figure out what to do. One thing I knew for sure, I was not going to drive for Don Coniglio.

In the morning I went to the tavern. Before I could ask about the bartending job Hutfilz said "I think you've got some good news coming and it's about time. Guy named Scott McLanahan called here asking for you. Says he wants to talk to you about your shop. Left an address and said if you're interested to come over anytime today. If this is the McLanahan family that lives up the road to Lake Zurich, they got big bucks. If I was you I'd get in your car and head over there quick as you can. Claire said she will go with you. Here she is now." Claire was just coming through the door. She was dressed as a businesswoman in a long dark skirt and a jacket similar to a man's suit coat but cut for a woman, allowing just a hint of her figure underneath the jacket. Her hair was up, light makeup on her face. Claire was a very pretty girl and I would have to watch over her to make sure some guy wasn't taking her to the lake for a petting party. Funny how it was OK for me to take a girl there, but the thought of some guy taking my little sister to the lake to get his hands on her made me angry and protective. Hell, Dad would have shot the cake-eater who took advantage of Claire.

I told Claire she didn't have to go, I could handle it and immediately got a face full of Claire's wrath. "You agreed that we would work together to rebuild the business. Now you treat me as if I'm a kid who doesn't know anything.

Did you forget I was helping Mother with the bookkeeping, actually doing most of it under her supervision? What do you know about that? You may know how to fix cars but you don't know beeswax about running a business." She went on and on until I agreed she should come along and all the way over to the McLanahan ranch she continued to tell me that I needed to take her more seriously, that she was not just some dumb country girl. There was a lot of our mother in Claire.

We arrived at the McLanahan ranch, turned in at the gate and drove up the long driveway. It was a large farm and horse ranch, and Claire was obviously enjoying the fine looking horses in the pasture on her side of the car. We were wearing dusters and hats to keep the road dust off our clothing and before we walked up to the front porch Claire took a minute to brush off her dress and check her face in a small mirror from her handbag.

McLanahan saw my automobile and came out to greet us. Scott was tall and handsome, about my age, maybe a year older. He was casually dressed in riding clothes and leather riding boots. He looked very dashing and Claire was giving McLanahan a big smile. The McLanahan family owned manufacturing and distribution businesses in the Chicago area and several Midwestern states. They did well as evidenced by the beautiful new red Packard Twin Six roadster in front of the large ranch house. Hutfilz had said Scott was an only child and heir apparent to the McLanahan business empire, but he seemed young to be a businessman.

"You must be Daniel Lindner and who would this lovely lady be?" Scott beamed at Claire. We made our introductions and Scott asked us if we would like to sit around the table on the covered porch since it was such a beautiful day. We agreed and sat down, Scott holding the chair for Claire. He called a maid to bring iced tea and cookies. When they arrived he got right down to business.

"Thank you for coming over and I'm very glad you did. I recently purchased a Curtiss JN-4 aeroplane and planned to fly it over to Gauthier's Field this afternoon to see if anyone could go over it to tighten up and fix a few things. Aviation is a fast growing business and there is a shortage of mechanicians who know a spanner from a hammer when it comes to fixing the Jenny's Curtiss OX-5 V-8 engine. I called because I read in the newspaper about your shop burning down, and remembered one of your mechanicians, name of Jack, or Jake, who has done repairs for airmen over at Gauthier's and they speak highly of him. Does this man still work for you?"

"Mr. McLanahan, unfortunately our shop was completely destroyed and we are unable to conduct business. Our tools and equipment were ruined in the fire. Jake was our master mechanic but he has gone to his home south of Chicago to work at the Elgin Motorcar Company. I have been searching for a location with a suitable building but have not found anything. I can rebuild on our land but that will take longer." I decided to just lay it out for McLanahan. I saw no sense in trying to pull the wool over his eyes.

"Please call me Scott, Mr. McLanahan is my father. Would this Jake fellow be willing to return if you had a suitable shop? And tools?"

"Yes sir, when we last talked Jake told me to let him know if I found a building or decided to rebuild, and he said that he might be willing to relocate his family here since Elgin is moving its factory to Indianapolis."

"Yes, I heard that about the Elgin car company. Mr. Lindner, I would like to make you an offer" Scott said, and Claire immediately pulled out a pad of paper and a pencil from her handbag. "I see Miss Claire came prepared for business. I applaud you for your diligence. I know you are not a secretary, but if you would be so kind, please write down the particulars so we are fully aware of what is on the table. If we arrive at an understanding, I would be pleased to split the cost with you to for Miss Claire to develop a business agreement and contract of our understanding for us to review and sign. May I ask, does your family own the land the shop was built on?"

"My sister is experienced in all aspects of a business office and I can't speak for her but I would share the cost of having her develop the agreement" I responded.

Claire added "I would be happy to draw up the agreement and contract. The shop is a family business and all of us have a stake in its future."

"Then we are agreed, thank you Miss Claire" he said.

"To answer your other question, yes we do own the land, and it is of sufficient size to build a larger facility, possibly even an automobile dealership because next to our land is an acre with a house on it owned by Widow Carlisle. Her son died in the war and her daughter married a successful businessman in New York. The daughter is not interested in the property except to sell it when her mother passes. Mrs. Carlisle offered to sell her property to us with the understanding that she would live rent free in the house until she passes away. We would provide exterior maintenance and pay the taxes, she would keep up the interior. The house is in excellent condition so I am favorable toward her offer but until we decide what to do, I have to pass. Mrs. Carlisle said she would wait until we decide whether or not to rebuild, and she has offered terms to make payments so we can acquire the land and pay from income. But without a reliable income source, I cannot in good conscience ask my family to purchase more property at this time. I am in favor of rebuilding but it would be a major strain on our financial resources."

"Yes, your land is well located for the future because you are on the road to Lake Zurich. Here are my thoughts. I will build a shop and furnish it with the equipment and tools you need for your motorcar repair business. With that as your income, you can decide if you want to enter into an agreement with Mrs. Carlisle for her property. If the price is fair, it is a good plan to acquire additional land for the business. If we enter into an agreement, I would like to offer you the services of my architect, who is located at one of my factories in Chicago. He's a good man to work with and has experience in designing automotive repair facilities."

"Scott, let's explore a partnership, our land and your financial help with the building. But we would like to own our facility, perhaps we can add a buyout framework."

"I like that. Miss Claire, please work that into the agreement. When can we meet again? Let's see, today is Monday – my father and I will be here this week and next but after that we go to New York on business. If we have our agreement and contract in place before we go to New York the architect can start immediately. Funding is not a problem" Scott informed us.

My brain was running fast with ideas, most of them good, but how would I know if I can trust this man? Claire summed our meeting up. "Mr. McLanahan, I will be pleased to make a written record of our discussions and I thank you very much for your offer."

"Miss Claire, since we may become partners both of you should address me as Scott and if it is acceptable I would like to call you Claire, and your brother Dan. Now, there is a second part of my offer." *Aha, there's the catch – here comes the part where we will owe him everything we ever earn in the future. I thought this sounded too good to be true.*

"When you visit my architect, tell him to come up with a building design that meets your needs today, and is expandable for the future. You see, I knew your father. A few months ago he and my father had a discussion of our making an investment with him in an automobile dealership. I was impressed with Marvin Lindner, and I am glad you and Claire were able to come out today." Scott smiled, mostly at Claire. "I can understand now the reasons for his pride in both of you. My father, like yours, wants to build solid businesses to secure a future for his family. He prepared me for managing these businesses and

I intend to continue growing them. Like my father, I am delighted to help an industrious family, the same way my father got his start. I was pleased when my father asked me to be the contact for Marvin to develop our business relationship. That being said, I would like it to be part of the agreement that the site planning is such that the building can be expanded to become an automobile dealership." Scott took a break to let Claire catch up with her notes and sip some of the iced tea, which was the best I had ever tasted. This all seemed to be too good to be true. I planned to talk with Claire afterward and find a way to check up on this guy to see if he was on the up and up.

"That sounds very interesting Scott, and I will make sure all of this is in the agreement" said Claire smartly. I was proud of my sister and sorry that I told her she did not have to come along, and now I saw Claire as an important asset to our family business.

"Certainly so. There is yet another, optional part of my offer. I have a small airstrip and hangar here at the ranch for my JN-4. The airframes are good but the Curtiss engines are notorious for needing frequent maintenance. Many companies have sprung up to make reliability and performance modifications for the engine, and I need someone who can evaluate which are real and which are useless. Since I cannot fly it to your shop for that, I would build a small shop facility here and furnish it with aircraft maintenance tools, parts and equipment. For now, it would not require a full time technician, but I intend to add other aircraft in the future. I would like to have someone like Jake come over and perform the maintenance and repair of the Jenny here and he could split his time to work at the automobile shop. Or he may wish to eventually go to Gauthier's Field and develop his own aircraft business, because Gauthier has informed me that an application is in process to establish it as an official airport and when that comes to fruition it will attract more aircraft."

"I offer to pay your business for Jake's time and travel to my ranch when he works here, and you and Jake can develop what you want at Gauthier's or we can partner on that when the time comes. I have the contacts to purchase parts and tools directly for my aeroplanes. When the day comes that I need a technician here full time, we can work out an agreement for Jake, or maybe he could train and supervise an aircraft technician to work here. If we did that, I would pay the mechanic directly since he would be full time on ranch property, but I would also pay Jake to come out and inspect the work. A supervisor technician usually inspects aeroplane work since mechanical failure while airborne is something to avoid. The exact details I leave to Claire to write and I hope we can come to an agreement because after meeting the both of you I am positive that we could enjoy a mutually beneficial partnership. I look forward to our meeting again, how does next Monday sound?"

I was rendered speechless. I had to go see Jake as soon as possible. If this was all true and we worked hard, Jake and my family could be on our way to success. Now I needed to get rid of the Coniglio albatross around my neck, otherwise they would suck all our profits for years to come.

"Next Monday will be fine, Scott. I will have copies of a draft of the agreement typed up when we return. Would 10 o'clock be suitable for you?" Claire was taking ownership in developing the agreement and now I knew that I needed Claire to be a partner. Mother was right, Claire was a pretty sharp kid for a little sister. And we would get Mother involved in this too, because she couldn't live on the insurance policy proceeds forever and she had already told us she was going to find a job, but most of all she knew bookkeeping for an auto shop inside and out. My spirits, dashed to bits in the recent weeks, were now soaring. I felt confident to leave it to Claire and my mother to draft the agreement while I went to talk with Jake. I hoped that he was not going to move to

Indiana with Elgin or had found other work. There was no time to lose so I would go to Argo first thing tomorrow morning.

"I invite you both to stay for lunch today, and plan to stay for lunch after we sign our agreement next week. By the way, I have a fine typewriter and an office here in the house should you need it. You can come over any time to use it" Scott offered, looking at Claire. I was sure that Scott was developing an interest in Claire that went beyond business.

"We also have a typewriter and all will be ready Monday" responded Claire in a strictly businesslike voice. We stayed for a delicious lunch of chicken and vegetables from the McLanahan farm and gardens. Scott's mother Elaine, a very gracious lady who reminded Claire and me of our mother, joined us at lunch. Afterward, Scott took Claire out to see his horses. Since I was not a horse person, Elaine offered that I could stay with her on the front porch. She sent the maid for more iced tea and we had a nice talk. She knew that Scott was making us an offer and approved of it, so I knew that Scott's family would be OK about their part in our relationship. She was also very up to date on current events and I discovered that she had seen some of Wallace Reid's movies. He had made many movies other than the auto racing movies. He had been in 'The Birth of a Nation' and 'A Yankee from the West'. Reid was credited in over 200 movies from 1910 to 1922. Mrs. McLanahan and I were in complete agreement that the studio had treated Reid badly and without regard to his health by giving him increasing supplies of morphine to keep him working to make movies that were very profitable for the studio.

I had sensed there was some spark between Scott and my sister but Claire denied it as we drove home. We were in a joyous mood and Claire was driving. She recently learned to drive but needed road experience to build up her confidence. Like most things Claire did, she was good at it. I could not have asked for a better sister, except for that time she caught me with Nancy and our hands were where they should not have been.

When Mother returned from visiting her sister we told her the news of the meeting. She offered to help Claire draft the agreement. One thing surprised me – she did not know Jake's address or telephone number. His family had not wanted to move north while Jake worked for Elgin. They lived in a house in Argo, a small town south of Chicago and although my father had been there, our families had never gotten together because of the distance and until recently the roads were poor. Our only record of his home address and telephone was in the ashes of the shop. Mother remembered the street name and since Argo was a small town I could go there and ask around.

That evening Mother asked us to go with her to visit Dad's grave at the churchyard. We stopped to pick some flowers to leave at his headstone. Mother stayed to talk to Dad at his graveside while Claire and I waited by the car. We made ourselves a fine dinner, and opened up a bottle of wine that a customer gave to us from somewhere called Napa in California. I went to bed in high spirits, eager to get up early for my trip to Argo to find Jake.

HOW TO MAKE A GOOD FIRST IMPRESSION

That evening I checked over the Elgin Six, topped up the fuel tank and strapped on two full gasoline cans so I could leave early in the morning.

Morning came with the aromas of a hearty breakfast welcoming me as I bounded down the stairs from my room. In the dining room, my mother and sister were busy setting up for their work. Mother's Remington #12 typewriter was sitting on its stand, freshly cleaned and polished. Strategically arranged on the table was a stack of paper, carbons, a white eraser, notepads, pencils and spare ribbons. Claire held her notepad containing the outline of our agreement with Scott McLanahan but when I came into the room their conversation abruptly stopped. Mother looked up at me. "Breakfast is waiting for you in the kitchen, help yourself. We've got work to do today." She smiled as she said it. I headed for the kitchen but it was obvious Claire was telling our mother something that I was not supposed to hear. My guess was that it had something to do with Scott McLanahan.

Breakfast finished, I filled a lunchbox with leftovers from last evening's dinner along with a canteen of water. After hugs and good luck wishes from Claire and my mother I was on the road. It was a beautiful spring day in northern Illinois, a perfect day for a road trip. I arrived at the town of Argo after lunch and drove around town to look around. Argo was larger than Long Grove, and I inquired at a general store. They remembered Jake but not the street address number. The lady at the counter told me Jake's house was a well maintained white two-story house with green shutters and flowerbeds across the front.

I went to the street and found two white houses with green shutters and two other white houses with different color shutters. I knocked on the door of the first green shuttered house but there was no answer so I went to the next. As I walked up to the door I heard a Victrola playing inside so I knocked a little harder than usual to be heard above the music. The door moved slightly and I waited, but it was not opened by anyone, so it must not have been shut tight and moved because I knocked hard on it. I tried looking through the narrow opening but I could not see anyone. I pushed it open a little more and called loudly if anyone was home. No answer but the singing had stopped and I heard the sound of an electric motor and rushing air. It must be one of those newfangled vacuum cleaners. I called again but whoever was there could not hear me over the noise of the machine. I did not want to enter without an invitation but I thought Jake would understand when I told him why I was there.

I pushed the door open and stepped inside, again calling if anyone was home. The vacuum cleaner was still humming so I walked in two more steps and called as loud as I could "Hello! Anybody home?"

A switch clicked and the sound of the vacuum cleaner stopped. The house became very quiet. I was ready to call out once more when the loveliest vision I had ever seen came through a doorway to the right of the parlor. My breathing came to a halt as I looked at this most perfectly beautiful girl. I can honestly state that it was not because she was dressed for a night on the town. Quite the opposite. She wore a shapeless plain gray housedress and had a maid's mobcap over her hair to protect it from dirt and dust, but I could see blond hair peeking out. She was tall and slender. Even though her dress covered her almost down to her shoes it was obvious from the way she moved that she had long legs. I thought of the old joke about a long-legged pretty girl having legs that "went all the way to the floor." Although her legs were long, under her cap her hair appeared to be short, like a flapper's bob. She was a modern girl. Her hands and face were smudged with dirt so I thought she must be the cleaning maid. Even with a surprised look on her face, I was so enthralled by her beauty and poise that I failed to notice her growing distress and anger.

"Get out of here! Get out of this house right now! Go! Beat it you bum!" She lifted her arm to point to the door, but to my besotted brain her angry words did not register. I'm a romantic guy, I read books and I've seen Wallace Reid movies where he won the girl. In the chivalrous ideas of my mind, a man should kiss a lady's hand upon meeting her. I mistook her pointing to the door and thought she was offering her hand for me to kiss. I took two steps toward her and took hold of her hand, removing my cap and bending down to kiss her lovely hand. Yeah, that was not a modern thing, but I had it in my mind that we would be married, take road trips in my yellow Marmon roadster, and make babies together and...

I was surprised by her ear-splitting scream. As I bent to kiss her hand the girl kicked her knee into my face, took hold of my wrist and pulled me forward. I thought she was pulling me to her for a kiss so I did not resist, even though my mind failed to ask why she would kick me in the face. My brains, so scrambled by this vision of loveliness, did not see her foot kick out to trip me. I went sprawling forward and bumped into a table. A vase came crashing down next to me, shattering into small sharp pieces. Or maybe she picked it up and tried to smash my head with it. This was not turning out at all like my dreams of how I would meet the love of my life.

I started to tell her who I was and why I was there but before I could say anything she shouted "I said get out! Get out now or else!" I was flat on my face and felt something hit me real hard on my shoulders and upper back. I rolled over just in time to see a large broom coming down fast again, this time at my head. I rolled back face down and started to crawl toward the door and felt a shard of the vase cut me on the right cheek when the broom came down again and whacked me hard on the back of my head. This beautiful girl was tough.

I pulled myself up on hands and knees, eyeballed the direction of the front door and felt her kick me in the ass. She may have been trying for my balls, which might make it difficult for her to have my children. My mind was turning into mush as I began to scrabble on hands and knees as fast as I could to get the hell away from this crazy young woman. As I got to the door I grabbed the doorframe to lift myself up, and saw that the lovely vision had vanished. Relaxing for a brief second, I moved to the door and hoped she might come to her senses so I could tell her who I was looking for and that I was not a robber or a bum. I waited for a few seconds. Then I heard an unmistakable sound – a sound I knew very well, the sound of the slide of a Colt M1911 racking a round and when she appeared she was in a two-hand shooter's stance with the fire-breathing business end of the Colt aimed at me. She was oblivious to my dream, my vision of us together, laughing, playing and rolling in the grass and...

B-A-N-G!

What? She shot me?

I felt no pain, but maybe I was in shock. They say gunshot victims often had a delayed reaction. My ears hurt from being so close to the gun. But that was it, she wasn't going to be my partner in life. We broke up after a very short and tumultuous affair. I ran like my butt was afire to the curb and leaped over the side of my Elgin Six without opening the door. I looked back as I hit the starter button and saw her standing in the doorway, the cap on her head had come off and her beautiful flapper style blond bob cut was all tousled and sexy looking like we had just made love. She still had the 1911 in her hand and I saw it had pearl grips, just like my father's 1911, but at the time that did not register in my brain. I still thought she looked beautiful and sexy standing there with the gun but decided to put the Elgin in gear and vamoose from there as fast as I could vamoose. Except for stopping to make sure I didn't have a bullet hole in me and refilling the gasoline tank from my gas cans, I did not stop until I got home.

All the way home, my mind was tortured with the vision of the beautiful girl in the doorway, smiling because she was happy to have chased me away. The thought of her lovely smile, even though it was because she had put me to flight, made me feel weak inside. If that was the love of my life I sure made a mess of introducing myself.

I had no idea how I was going to find Jake now. If I failed, I could lose McLanahan's backing for the new shop. If I went back to the street where Jake supposedly lived, the police might be looking for me with an accurate description given to them by the maid. My head hurt, she must have hit me harder than I thought. I was a mess, a line of dried blood on my cheek, my back and butt and head bruised and hurting, my ears ringing.

I finally made it home, thinking I was an utter failure but Claire and my mother jumped up to hug me when they saw me come in. "Hey, this is nothing to laugh about. I failed my mission to find Jake. What the hell is so funny?"

"Claire, get me a clean washcloth and some warm water, I want to clean up my son upon his triumphant return." They both giggled like I was extremely funny looking.

"I'm wounded and permanently disfigured and you two are laughing like you're listening to one of those comedy shows on WJAZ radio at the Edgewater Beach Hotel." There must be something going on that I didn't know about.

"Danny, I don't know how or what happened because you're not talking sense. Jake called and said he will be here by lunchtime tomorrow. There was a lot of noise in the telephone line and we couldn't hear him very well. That was all we heard before the connection was lost."

What? What did I do? The entire time after I ran from the beautiful girl was a confusing mess. Mother cleaned my face, Claire applied some burning antiseptic stuff to clean the wound on the right side from the broken vase shard. "Might be just a small scar when it heals, less than an inch or so. But women like guys with manly scars. The girls will all be chasing you now."

Huh? "Well Claire, the girl that caused this was not chasing me because she was motivated by happiness or an insane desire for me, except maybe to kill me" and I related what happened, which made them start laughing again.

When I was done with the story, Claire said "Do you realize you told us what happened in about a minute, then spent ten minutes telling us what this vision of a girl looked like and what a beautiful smile she had and how she was going to be the mother of your children?" Claire was hardly able to keep a straight face. "My dear brother, I do believe that you are in love!"

I have no remembrance of saying all that crazy stuff about the beautiful modern girl, but Claire and my mother swore I did tell them all that.

FLAPPER WITH A GUN

When I awoke the next morning every cut and bruise screamed at me. My head hurt and my butt hurt, but I did not have any bullet holes in my body. I was happy because Jake would be here and we would find out if he wanted to join us in the new business, even though I could not stop thinking about the girl who tried to kill me.

It was a beautiful day, light fluffy clouds decorating the sky from horizon to horizon. Mother sent me to the store for some grocery items and upon my return I saw a strange car in our driveway. I figured it was one of my mother's friends stopping by to make sure she was doing OK so soon after Dad's funeral. I brought the groceries into the kitchen and what I saw there almost made me stop breathing. The Modern Girl. She was standing at our kitchen counter working on something – I thought she had not seen me but then I heard once again the distinctive sound of a 1911 slide being racked. I felt chills run up and down my spine. The chill turned icy cold when I saw her turn around to face me with a pearl handgrip Colt M1911 in her hand. She smiled, started to say something but I could not hear it. *How the hell did she find me? What has she done with my mother and sister?* There was no blood on the floor that I could see. I wanted to turn and run but she would easily be able to shoot me before I got to the door.

Then I saw that big smile, the one she had when she shot at me. Thinking fast I casually set the groceries on the table and jumped for the door. Not hearing any gunshots I took the porch stairs in one leap and began running toward the village when I saw Jake, Claire and her friend Cindy and my mother and another woman who looked like an older version of the modern girl walking back from the Village Tavern with a cold pitcher of beer. "Run!"

I called to them. "Get away while you can. She tracked me down and she's here to kill me!" They were all smiling. They didn't get it. "I said get down, she could shoot us all." But it was too late. The love of my life, as I thought of her even though she wanted to murder me, walked over calmly and stood next to Jake, who started roaring with laughter. I failed to see the amusement.

I took my mother's arm and pulled her toward the tavern. Maybe the constable would be there. "Get back here you fool!" yelled Claire while my mother looked embarrassed. The blonde modern killer girl was standing next to my family with the Colt in her hand. Still laughing, Jake walked over to me, the girl watching him. *Oh no, I thought. Jake is in on it and wants to kill me too.*

"Dan, you have a strange way of welcoming people but I'm sure glad you came down to find me yesterday" Jake said. "My wife Vera and I were taking a walk to talk about selling our house." He turned to the blonde girl and said "Laure, he's acting a little strange but maybe it's because you shot at him yesterday and now here you are holding a gun. I guess that might make a guy think twice when he saw you again." He turned back to me.

"My daughter Laure was cleaning the house and did not hear you come in. When she saw you, she thought you were an intruder, a hobo from the rail yards, although she did say you were dressed well and were much better looking than the average bum. They have been coming into people's houses in town more often lately. She thought you might try to hurt her or steal things. You were looking at her funny, she said. Laure defended herself as I taught her. I want my daughter to be careful and to take care of herself in any situation. When I heard the sound of the shot I came running. I saw your Elgin rounding the corner almost on two wheels. Had I been a few seconds earlier I could have waved you down. By the way, she aimed high so she wouldn't kill you. The bullet is lodged in my parlor wall above the door. When she described you perfectly I knew it was you." I stared at Jake as he explained how I had almost been murdered by the loveliest woman I had ever set eyes on.

"Laure was looking at your father's 1911 because she wanted to see it after I told her The Story of the Colts. I suppose you must have thought she had come over to finish you off." They all roared with laughter. "Come over here Laure, but give me the gun first. Daniel Lindner, I would like to introduce you to my daughter Laure-Marie, even though you two have already met under a somewhat unusual circumstance. Laure, this is Dan. There. Now you two know each other so you won't try to shoot each other next time you meet" said Jake and he laughed so hard he had tears in his eyes. Mother and Claire joined in too. I thought they were going to fall down with laughter. My embarrassment was complete.

I was about to say something I would have regretted but in the nick of time I heard Laure's real voice, not the angry voice I heard yesterday, and it was as if the heavens opened and angels were singing. I had not held my hand out during the introduction, remembering how she took hold of it, pulled and tripped me, but now she took my hand in hers, not shaking hands but simply holding it. I swear an electric charge from her hand ran up my arm and spread through my entire body. "I'm sorry that I shot at you, Mr. Lindner, Pa taught me to shoot to kill but I lifted because there was something that made me decide not to shoot you, and I'm glad. Pa would have been most displeased with me" and Laure started laughing. This time it broke the ice and caught me too and we all laughed. Claire and Cindy looked like they were enjoying watching me play the fool. I knew the story was soon going to be all over the village within the hour.

"Imagine the stories we can tell our grandchildren" I said and everyone stopped laughing and stared at me. *Damn – why did I say that?*

At least the rest of the day went well. Jake showed me his new used car, a 1922 Nash Model 697 Sports Touring car. It had a very deep red color with black fenders and a trunk, step plates, beveled glass, steel wheels, Motometer, dual side mount spares, wind wings and a spotlight. There was bright chrome plating everywhere and the upholstery was real leather. The Nash had a 248 cubic inch inline six under the hood and it seemed expensive for Jake's tastes, but he explained that Elgin had announced they were reorganizing and moving production to Indianapolis in an attempt to save the company. One of the managers had bought the Nash new in 1922 but it had become a source of mechanical problems for him so he sold it to Jake for $175. Nash made reliable automobiles and new in 1922 it sold for over $1,600 so Jake couldn't pass up the bargain, knowing he could fix the mechanical gremlins.

Then he laid his big news on me. "Laure was giving the house a thorough cleaning because we were thinking of selling it and moving to something less expensive. I was worried about being able to find a suitable job now that Elgin is moving out and I might be making less money. But when we arrived here I learned from Claire that we have a fresh opportunity and I'm as excited as you are about it. My wife Vera and I talked it over and we decided to sell the house since the town was becoming more industrial and the bums were moving in and breaking into homes. That's what Laure thought you were doing. I'm glad she didn't follow my instructions to shoot for effect this one time. I'll be delighted to join you in the new enterprise if we come to an agreement. For a long time I have wanted to get into aeroplanes and this is a great opportunity for all of us. You can rebuild the shop and get a dealership started while I finish teaching you what little you don't know and I will get more aviation experience, maybe open up my own aeroplane shop at one of those new airports popping up everywhere. For now, our family will move to Long Grove so I can spend more time at the shop and on Mr. McLanahan's aeroplane. I'll teach you aircraft repair if you're interested. I'm really looking forward to this Dan, it's a dream come true for me." I was listening to Jake as my mind filled with a new vision of Laure, smiling at me without a gun in her hand.

"That goes for me, Jake. I was almost ready to be a bartender when this came up. We should know Monday if McLanahan accepts the agreement Claire is writing. All of us should go through it so we know what we are getting into. I asked around and the McLanahan family is known to be good business people and fair in their dealings. We will be good and fair business people too, like you are and like my father wanted his business to be. Jake, let's do this and do it right." We shook hands, and Dad had told me the day before he left for the last time to go to his truck job that Jake's handshake was as good as gold. I vowed that mine would be too.

Claire drove Cindy and Laure in my Elgin to Cindy's house to show Laure the horses. The girls were giggling when they returned. Why do girls giggle? It must be because they think guys are funny. Mom and Jake's wife Vera were working on a masterpiece dinner. Jake and family were staying with us until the meeting with McLanahan on Monday. If all went well, they would pack their furniture and things and get their house ready to sell. Jake could borrow a truck from the Elgin factory to move all their household goods up here if they found a house to rent temporarily.

I apologized to Jake's wife Vera for breaking her vase but she said not to worry, she didn't like it anyway. Vera was a very happy and friendly person. Everyone who knew her adored her. Laure had two brothers and a sister who were off at college and they were OK about selling the family home. The brothers asked Jake to ask me how the girls were around here. I told Jake to tell them they didn't shoot their boyfriends here, but saw that I had embarrassed Laure. She seemed sincerely sorry about our misunderstanding and I did not have any bullet holes in my body, so I decided to accept it and stow the bad jokes so long as she did not try to shoot me again.

After dinner, Claire, Cindy and Laure went to Claire's room and all I heard from them that evening was laughing and giggling. Claire asked me to move the Victrola to her room and they played music and practiced new dance steps. I tried to imagine how Laure would look while she danced but my thoughts failed to stay very gentlemanly and I knew Jake would not miss if he shot me for what I had in mind to do with his lovely daughter. But I kept going back to thoughts of Laure in a short flapper dress, her long legs stepping and kicking, her cute little butt wiggling and I decided that I should get out of the house. For some reason I did not feel like calling one of my girlfriends so I called Otto and Fritz and they met me at the Village Tavern.

Otto and Fritz were brothers, Otto about a year older than me and Fritz maybe a little more than a year younger. They were sons of the owner of the general store but they were as hot over cars and aeroplanes as I was. Dad had said if they learned enough about repair work and things got busy in the shop he would hire them. We sat at the bar and talked about baseball and how Constable Sherman had to hassle the lovers down at the lake. I did not tell them about Laure and that she was going to have my children someday. Those two would have hooted and hollered for days afterward and would never have stopped teasing me. I also did not tell them that Laure was gorgeous and sexy. I didn't want the competition.

When I finally returned home, there was still some music in Claire's room but it was at a low volume and they were talking softly. Girls could talk forever, it seemed. What did they talk about? My mother's room was next to Claire's so I could not listen through the wall but I was tired so I went to my room and lay on the bed. That's when I noticed something on my movie poster for *The Roaring Road* I had paid the movie theater owner fifty cents for after the movie finished its run. There, next to Wallace Reid's picture in the poster, a feminine hand had drawn a small heart with an arrow through it and the letters

"LMW+WR" inside. Laure-Marie Winiarzski plus Wallace Reid? Then the thought hit me on the head like a brick swung around on a rope. Laure had been in my room, maybe right here next to my bed. Maybe she had even touched my bed! I ran my fingertips over the heart on the poster, making a wish that someday Laure would be drawing hearts and arrows of my initials with hers.

KEEP BOTH HANDS ON THE WHEEL

The next day was Sunday and around mid-afternoon we were having iced lemonade in our back yard. It was getting warm in the sun and I must have started dozing off. Cindy woke me up by telling me "Why don't you take Claire and me to my house so we can take care of our horses and you can take Laure for a ride in your Elgin. Show her around the town."

My right eye popped up and the girls were sitting there trying to hold back their giggles. But my mother didn't raise any stupid children. Well, maybe my sister but she was starting to become wise and mature. "OK, let's do that." I said and we piled into the Elgin – now I wished I had washed it instead of dozing off – and I drove them over to the Hutfilz place. Claire and Cindy said they had to exercise and groom their horses and since Laure wasn't a horse person they thought I should be a gentleman and take her for a ride. I sensed this was a setup for me to have time with Laure and I was not at all sure I could remain gentlemanly. Although Laure seemed like a modern she had a sharp wit and there was no doubt it would be a challenge to get to first base. Laure changed into traveling clothes for the ride on country roads in my open car. The plain gray dress went almost down to her ankles, but open cars and gravel roads were a sure combination for getting dirt all over a person. I wore jeans and my cowboy boots and a comfortable light blue shirt. Sporty, I hoped.

When we got to the Hutfilz place Claire and Cindy got out and Laure moved up from the back seat. The Elgin was not a wide car but there was room for three up front if they were friendly. Laure sat by the door, but not hard up against it like she might if she didn't like me. It only took a couple of minutes to show her the village of Long Grove but she listened with interest as I described it. I drove by our burned shop and Laure seemed sad to see it. I started down the road in the general direction of the lake.

"Long Grove is a very pretty village. My father likes it but my mother did not want to move until Elgin announced they were moving the factory. She doesn't want to move to Indianapolis and I don't either. I'm glad she likes it here because I do too" Laure said.

It thought that was a good sign so I pushed ahead. "I noticed that you like Wallace Reid. Have you seen many of his movies?"

I saw Laure blush as she realized that I found out she was in my room. Aha! So I could rattle her. "Oh yes Danny, I like Wallace Reid a lot. He does wonderfully romantic movies and good automobile racing movies too, like *The Roaring Road*."

Now that she knew that I knew about her being in my bedroom, she said "Danny I'm sorry. I should not have written on your poster. I saw it on the wall as Claire and I walked by your room and I ducked in to look at the poster and I wrote on it. I am so sorry Dan. I'll get you a new one."

"No! I mean, no you don't have to get me a new one. I'm not upset that you wrote on my poster. I'll just draw a Colt 1911 next to it." I did it again. Laure looked embarrassed. "I'm sorry Laure, I didn't mean to embarrass you. I was just a little surprised." I laughed as I said it to show it was not a big deal.

"Surprised at what? That I went into your room? Claire was there with me the entire time. And I'm used to going into a guy's room." She stopped, realizing what that sounded like. Laure looked at me, her smile missing. "I meant that I have two brothers, not that I make a habit of going into men's bedrooms. I am a Wallace Reid fan and wanted to look at the poster up close. I acted on impulse when I drew a heart on it and I am sorry for that."

"It's OK. I will treasure it forever, even if the heart was for Wallace Reid and not me." I was chewing shoe leather now, my boot going deeper into my mouth with every word.

"Are you jealous of Wallace Reid? He's not even alive, how can you be jealous of him?"

This was not how I thought it would be, driving down a nice country road with a lovely girl sitting next to me arguing over Wallace Reid. "No, not jealous. I'll stop teasing, I'm OK with your writing on the poster. It makes it special. Besides, we're both Wallace Reid fans so we have that in common."

She gave me a funny look. "Oh Dan, you're such a guy."

"Well that's a good thing, right? That is, if you like guys." Oh boy, I'd better just head over to the doc's office to be treated for chronic hoof-in-mouth disease.

"As a matter of fact I do like guys. Guys who do guy things but are gentlemen, especially towards the woman who he thinks should be desirous of having his children" she giggled as she said it.

Now I was blushing. "Who told you that? My sister? How could she make such a statement?"

"Because that's what you told Claire when you got home. Just remember Mr. Daniel Lindner, you are not the first guy to have those kinds of thoughts about me. I will have to keep an eye on you, so don't be expecting to act out your ideas. I am a modern woman but I'm particular about some things, and one of them is that I don't give away my favors."

"I would never try such a thing without your consent and enthusiasm. I am not that kind of guy. So yes, truth be told, I was struck by your beauty, poise and charm. I may have mentioned something foolish to Claire, I don't remember. I may have to re-think it. You seem to be a bit prickly and that dampens things just a bit. Although I do offer my thanks that you raised your aim so as not to injure or kill me."

"I didn't raise the gun. I was aiming for your manhood and missed. I'll have to spend more time practicing my shooting. A girl never knows when she might need that skill" Laure said rather grimly.

Total silence. Then Laure put her hand in front of her mouth in an attempt to hide her giggles. I could not help it as I burst out laughing and we both laughed so hard I had to pull over to the side of the road. Luckily there were no other cars around.

"Truce?" I asked and held out my hand.

"Truce" she replied as we shook hands. "And I'm sorry your face got cut when I broke the vase on you. Claire thinks you may have a small scar on your cheek. But it's very manly looking, in fact it makes you look quite dashing when you smile."

"Like this?" I flashed a toothy grin.

"Just like that. Now all the girls will be fighting over you."

"They already do, you just haven't seen the battles yet." The uncomfortable ice block between us had melted. I checked the road and pulled out slowly, and as I did so I casually – at least I thought I was being casual – put my arm across the top of the seat behind her shoulders.

She looked thoughtful, but a minute later she asked "When you came into my house, why did you grab my hand? I didn't know who you were and it frightened me."

"I have this chivalric notion that a gentleman kisses a lady's hand when they meet. But they say chivalry is dead" I replied.

"That's what Pa thought you were trying to do. He said you're that kind of guy. I've never had my hand kissed and I was afraid of you. But I could get used to it and a girl does like a touch of romance from a guy she likes."

Laure was hinting that maybe she liked me! I moved my arm from the top of the seat to over her shoulders and gently pulled her closer to me. She did not move more than a quarter of an inch, but she did move toward me.

Laure looked at the road and my one-handed grip on the steering wheel a couple of times. "Dan, don't you think you should be using both hands?" she asked as she stared at the road and the steering wheel.

I squeezed her shoulder just a bit and said "Oh yes, it's much more fun when I use both hands, but I'm driving so I have to keep one hand on the steering wheel." I clamped my mouth shut and tried hard not to laugh. I could tell she was too. "If you like, I can stop the car and give you a demonstration of how I use both hands." Silence. The first one to laugh loses.

Finally she let out a small girlish snicker and that did it. I couldn't see straight to drive and had to pull the car over again. We got out of the car and laughed. When we calmed down I put my arms around her and we held each other for a minute. Our bodies fit together perfectly, she was tall so that I didn't have to bend down to her like I had to for Gina. Her breasts felt full and wonderful pressing against me as I held her close. My body was clearly beginning to enjoy the sensation of her body close to mine and she did not try to push me away. I moved a hand down and placed it on her cute little butt, turning my face to hers, our lips an inch apart as we were coming together for our first kiss when an old black Dodge touring car went by at a high rate of speed. The driver jammed on the brakes and slid to a stop in the gravel road ahead of my Elgin, then backed up until it was next to us. Before the Dodge got there I knew who it was – my mischievous friends Otto and Fritz who sported big shit-eating grins on their faces.

"Whatcha got there Danny, a new girl in town and you aren't going to introduce her to your friends? Danny, you always want us to share with you."

"OK guys, thanks a lot. This is Laure-Marie, Jake's daughter. Laure, the big one is Otto, the very slightly shorter one is Fritz, my best buddies. However, I do not subscribe to the idea of sharing my girlfriends with them. They're so ugly they scare girls away."

The guys got out of the Dodge and came over to shake her hand and pulled her into a hug. She gave them her sweet smile and I saw it had the same effect on them as it had on me.

"Dan, your friends are handsome devils and you should treat them better. Come here boys" and she gave them a sisterly hug and a kiss on the cheek.

"Hey, that's more kiss than I got!" and I took Laure in my arms again and this time did not waste a second and my lips were on hers. I think she was surprised and at first she kissed me but then pushed me away.

"You'll have to forgive Danny, it seems that he's never kissed a girl before" she said, which caused my friends to roar with laughter.

The boys said they were making deliveries and they had to get going or their dad would yell at them for taking too long. They made their good-byes, giving Laure one last hug each as I watched with some dismay. Then we waved as they drove off.

I tried to kiss Laure again but she was quick and got into the Elgin before I could get my arms around her. Laure was sharp and I was not going to fool her with my usual bag of tricks that worked on Nancy, Gina and Suzie.

TAKING CARE OF BUSINESS

Monday arrived and a feeling of happiness came over all of us. The newspaper weather report said it was going to rain, so I went out early to put the tops and side curtains up on my Elgin and Jake's Nash. When we left for the McLanahan ranch it was raining sunshine as if we needed proof that forecasting weather was an imperfect science. Last night we made the decision that all of us should go. Claire said the McLanahans had a strong respect for family and our united families would increase their confidence in us. I wondered when she had learned that.

Claire and Dorothy offered to trim any of us who wanted to have our hair trimmed, which turned out to be everyone. My mother wore black because she was still in mourning. Jake and his wife Vera were nicely dressed and I noticed they often held hands and remembered Dad saying how much in love they always seemed to be. Claire wore a smart looking blue below-the-knee dress with a demure and delicate lace collar. I wore one of my two suits, the same one I wore to Dad's funeral, a dark gray three piece with a light gray pinstripe, white shirt and one of Dad's ties.

Laure was the last one downstairs and when I saw her my heart jumped. Knowing what this meeting meant to both families, she looked businesslike with a dark blue below the knee length skirt and a rose-colored blouse with a silk scarf tied around her neck. Her shoes matched the blouse. She did not wear any makeup except for lipstick. I drank in the look of her legs, slender waist and lovely breasts. I could tell she was wearing a brassiere, which was now fashionable. At that moment all I could think about was grabbing Laure and removing that brassiere but Jake was watching me watching her with a sly grin on his face, so I decided that ravishing Laure would have to wait. We went out to the automobiles in our driveway and I was happy that Laure voluntarily got into the front seat with me, Claire in the back seat with Dad's old briefcase and a knowing smirk on her face. My mother Dorothy rode with Jake and Vera in the Nash.

It was the right decision for all of us to come. Scott greeted us at the front door and Claire made the introductions all around. When Scott met my mother he got a huge smile on his face but I had no idea why. He also had a special smile for Claire, and they kissed cheek to cheek. *Have to keep an eye on those two. Had they met since our first meeting?* Scott brought us into the dining room and went to tell his mother and father that we were here. Good thing they had a huge dining room with a table big enough for twelve because there were going to be nine of us at the table plus our papers and notepads. We were standing at the dining room table when Scott's parents came in from the door at other side of the room, and what a handsome couple they were. Mr. McLanahan had on a perfectly tailored gray business suit and Mrs. McLanahan looked simply gorgeous in a white blouse with a lace collar and a dark green ankle-length skirt of very luxurious material. She wore very little makeup, her pretty auburn hair swept up. Scott McLanahan obviously came from good stock.

"Dorothy!" Mrs. McLanahan cried out in surprise.

"Elaine!" My mother and Mrs. McClanahan ran to each other and hugged for a long time, tears coming down their faces. "I was so sad that I have not been able to locate you – and here we are living just a few miles from each other. Oh I am so happy to see you again. We have a lot of catching up to do."

"Dearest Dorothy, we certainly do." Scott had briefly left the room and returned with two handkerchiefs, giving one to each woman.

"Dan, Claire, when I was introduced to your mother I recognized her as the person in a photograph that my mother she keeps on her dresser. She always talks about her dear childhood friend Dorothy that she had lost contact with years ago. I wasn't going to spoil the moment by saying anything so I let the surprise happen on its own." That explained the funny smile Scott had on his face when he met my mother.

Elaine explained "Dorothy and I were best friends since we learned to walk and our families were neighbors in a little town in Wisconsin called Arpin. We went to elementary school and graduated from high school together. We were inseparable until the day I went to Milwaukee to attend a secretarial school for girls. After that I found a job at one of the McLanahan offices where I met Thomas. We fell in love and married. I learned that Dorothy had moved to Chicago for a job. Over the years we lost contact. I cannot believe that we lived so close, and yet so far from each other. We won't let that happen ever again."

My mother laughed "No we will not let that happen again. This is such a wonderful and happy day for us. We are together because our children found each other before we did. I think this is a good omen for our families and future business relationship as well."

Thomas McLanahan, Scott's father finally got a word in. "This is a great beginning and I'm so happy for Elaine and Dorothy. Scott gave me the word when he recognized Dorothy from the photo and I am joyful of the pleasant surprise of your reunion. Elaine has told me so much about you Dorothy, that I feel as if I know you. Let us sit down and work out our business agreement. The maid is bringing in iced tea and our chef is preparing a summertime lunch to celebrate our business partnership, and now we have a reunion to celebrate as well."

"From what Scott told me about his meeting with Dan and Claire, I have no doubt we will put together a mutually beneficial arrangement. Let me say I am personally pleased that Jake and his family are here, after all he is very important to our new business venture. I like to know the people I do business with, and family is important to me. The fact that Jake and his family are here speaks volumes about the sense of family in all of us. McLanahan Enterprises is unique in that Scott, Elaine and I share in the management of our businesses each according to our individual talents. I'm also very pleased to learn from Scott that Dan wants Jake to be an equal partner, which speaks well of his relationship with Jake and their ability to work together. So let's have at the details and then celebrate this beautiful day."

We all applauded as Dorothy and Elaine sat down to begin the meeting. After my mother, Jake, Vera, Claire and I had gone over the agreement last evening, Claire was chosen to run the meeting, mainly because she wrote most of it and could best explain it. Scott and Claire sat next to each other at the table and exchanged knowing glances. It occurred to me that he and Claire had worked through the agreement in advance too. This was something new for me. Claire was indeed becoming a woman and had a few boyfriends, but this had the appearance of a strong mutual attraction developing between them. She began by handing each person a copy of the agreement and proceeded to read and explain each section, asking for questions or if clarification was needed. There were only three minor questions, and each was resolved to everyone's satisfaction. When Claire asked for comments at the end of the last section of the agreement, after a few seconds of silence signifying acceptance we all stood and reached across the table and shook hands all around. Dorothy and Elaine jumped up and left the room, asking Jake's wife Vera if she would like to join them, but Vera knew it was a special time for them and said she would like to stay with Jake and look at the gardens. Vera was a classy lady. She spoke excellent English with a slight but unique accent and the effect was quite elegant. Scott and Claire slipped out of the room together while Thomas McLanahan went to let the kitchen staff know we were ready for lunch.

I stood and looked at Laure, who had been quiet during the meeting but she had a bright happy smile and came over to kiss me on the lips. "Dan Lindner, I just might be starting to like you. Just a little bit so don't get excited. You are a good man, just as my father told me. You gave him a full partnership without him asking for it. This business arrangement has a good feeling about it and I'm happy for all of us. My father is not openly emotional but I know he is pleased. He was worried about being able to support us with the Elgin plant moving to Indiana, and here we are, in business together with excellent prospects. You're a sweetie."

"Does this mean you'll bear my children?" I tried to make it sound like a joke but probably came across as too serious.

"Is that a marriage proposal? I am not having any man's children unless I am married to him. Don't ask me yet Dan. I'll let you know when I'm ready to make that decision. Just don't let the wrong head do your thinking when we are alone." Laure let out a sweet little laugh and flashed her smile. What's a man in love to do? The relationship was progressing well considering that only a few days ago Laure was trying to kick me in the balls, beat my brains out and shoot me.

The day was getting warm so the McLanahans had lunch set up under an arbor in the yard to shade us from the sun. Elaine McLanahan told the butler to bring out some chilled white wine, and like my mother's wine it was also from California, from a winery called Sebastiani in a place called Sonoma. It tasted good and I decided that I might like wine. Scott and Claire quietly disappeared shortly after lunch. I took off my suit coat, folding it on the chair and Laure and I took a walk in the gardens and orchards. We met Scott and Claire walking together, holding hands. Somewhere along the way, Laure had taken hold of my hand without my noticing because it felt so natural. I stopped worrying about Claire holding hands with Scott. They made a smashing looking couple and you could see their attraction to each other in their eyes. Laure and I stopped and kissed twice when we thought no one was watching. It was a special day.

Before we said our goodbyes, Elaine had the maid come out with a Kodak Brownie camera to take pictures to record this amazing day. She took photographs of each family member, all of us together, Dorothy and Elaine together, Thomas and Elaine, Jake and Vera, Scott and Claire – now that their relationship was out in the open – and Laure with me. The photographic pairings seemed to be mutually acknowledged without anyone saying a word. We said goodbye, Elaine inviting Dorothy to stay over the weekend at the ranch so they could catch up on old times while Thomas and Scott were in New York on business. I was so happy for my mother. I had been worried about her, losing her husband and the family business suddenly, but now she had her dearest friend to lean on. On the way home Laure again sat in front with me, this time just a smidgen closer than before. Seeing this, Claire decided to ride back in Jake's Nash with Vera and Dorothy. Small steps, I decided, were best so as not to scare Laure away.

We had traveled a mile or so when Laure took my hand and pulled it up and around her shoulder, snuggling up close to me so that I had to tell her when to shift the transmission. Jake's Nash had gotten well ahead of us and I turned into a quiet lane and pulled to the side of the road, shutting off the engine. Before I could make my joke about 'this is how I use both hands' Laure turned to kiss me, so I put both hands to work. I got a little carried away and slowly moved my left hand to her right breast. She let it stay there for about a half minute but when I whispered "I love you" and started to caress her breast she removed my hand and told me we should get on our way so no one would think we were making out. This day was the beginning of great change for us, in ways neither of us could imagine.

The next few months went by quickly. Jake and I met with the McLanahan architect, who designed two shops. One was the repair shop for the aeroplane hangar at the McLanahan Ranch airstrip. The other was the new Lindner Automotive shop, and I was glad to get Jake's advice on the layout and equipment. The draftsman was a small fussy man but he knew his onions about automobile repair facility design and his drawings were first rate. For my automobile shop we made a flexible building plan that could be expanded if – no, not if, but when – we became an automobile dealership. Scott said that there would be no problem getting funding for it, also suggesting that it would be best if we became a dealer for a high end automobile manufacturer. Available to us were dealership appointments for Packard, Pierce-Arrow, Locomobile, Marmon, Stutz, Peerless, Cadillac, Duesenberg and European automobiles like Hispano-Suiza. Others would get in line, because with McLanahan Enterprises behind us the manufacturers would be bidding for our representation.

Jake was extremely happy with the design for the aeroplane facility at the ranch and they decided when the ranch shop was established they would begin another shop for Gauthier's Field, which would become a busy airstrip for business and personal aircraft when it gained official airport status.

Jake and Scott went on a trip to visit some of the aircraft manufacturers, who were very impressed and indicated they would give them appointments as service and sales agencies. Jake attended two aircraft engine manufacturer's schools and another for airframe repair. Word came back from Jake that the engine manufacturers tried to hire him immediately after he was in training for only a couple of days. Jake's natural ability with engines was quickly evident to them and they needed qualified technical people. But Jake, Scott and I wanted our own operation and Jake said his family liked Long Grove and wanted to stay. They bought a beautiful two-story house, and soon Jake and family had many friends in the village. Laure and I continued to dance, go to the movies and picnics at the lake with friends. Sometimes we went to the lake later in the evening for some kissing, but my hands were not allowed to get under her blouse or up her legs. She was always cheerful and happy when we were together and every second of every minute with her made me fall more deeply in love with her, if that was possible.

Our agreement with the McLanahans had fair buyout arrangements for both Jake and me. As with any business plan, changes were made along the way. I was amazed how quickly my new shop building construction began. I asked Jake to help me watch over it because he had construction experience. He would stop by the building every day on his way home to look at the day's progress and reported that he was pleased with the work. I checked out the contractor that Scott recommended and they had excellent references. I went to inspect some of their other construction projects, taking Claire with me as I had come to value her insight. I looked at the buildings and Claire talked to people. Outside of some minor issues, the building owners and workers liked their facilities.

When our new shop equipment and tools began arriving, I hired my friends Otto and Fritz to work for me part time so they could still work for their father at the general store. They were already good mechanics and Jake agreed to help teach them while the aeroplane business grew until it became a full time job for him. We had decided that Jake would be in charge of the aeroplane businesses and I would be in charge of the automobile side, and we would work together as much as we could. Scott was pleased with the ranch aeroplane shop construction and Jake's list of tools and equipment was approved for purchase without question. Jake had plenty of work at Scott's hangar and at Gauthier's Field and my automobile shop was profitable right from the start.

We celebrated with a grand opening picnic. There were so many guests we almost ran out of food. The mayors of several surrounding towns and villages were present, along with many local business owners. Chester Foust had become a good friend, and I invited him to the grand opening. Chester brought a photographer from the *Chicago American* newspaper, and wrote a nice article about our shop opening for the northwest Chicago edition. Long Grove residents were glad to have their only automobile repair shop open again. Farmers were increasingly turning to machinery and we started to accept farm tractor and machinery repairs, and that grew so fast that I began to talk with Scott about expanding to open a farm equipment dealership.

I asked Claire to make the deal with Mrs. Carlisle to purchase her acre, which upon the surveyor's report turned out to be almost one and a quarter acres. She had the property appraised and we paid Mrs. Carlisle what she asked because it was a fair price. We signed the contract for her to live in the house rent free for life. She was a sweet and thoughtful lady, often bringing cookies and treats to the construction workers, later doing the same for the shop employees. I added into the agreement that we would provide free maintenance for her automobile after she decided to drive again when she purchased a one year old Buick sedan that Jake and I inspected to make sure it was in tip-top condition.

Claire and Cindy rode their horses often, sometimes coming to the auto shop to bring lunch. Claire and my mother were taking care of all our bookkeeping and reported that we were doing better than expected. I ruefully thought about the day that Wallace Reid came to the shop, wishing he could see it now. Thoughts of Dawn receded into the background now that my relationship with Laure was growing.

THE GREEN MILL GARDENS

Come September, Laure and Cindy announced they were going to Moser Secretarial School in Chicago. They planned to share a room in a women's residence at the school. Jake was pleased that Laure wanted to improve herself. He told me it would be a good thing for the family businesses. Laure had an ambition to start her own business and wanted to learn accounting. It meant that we would not be able to see each other for a few months, but I knew she wanted to do this and I was happy for her. I asked her to be my girl and not date other guys while she was away. By now I was seriously stuck on her. Hell, I was stuck on her before she shot at me on the day we met.

"Oh Dan, you know I'm a modern, an independent girl and do what I want to do and if I want to be your girl, I will be and that's that. You will have to trust me without demands, as I will have to trust you. When I return, if we both want to, we will be together again. I do like you. In fact I like you a lot and I think you're a great guy. You are considerate, smart, ambitious and fun to be with, a great kisser, a handsome sheik and tall so I don't have to look down on my boyfriend. You have a lot to offer a girl." Then she gave me a long, sloppy wet kiss, holding me tight and despite her bold statement I saw that her eyes were moist. Laure was always straight up with me and I made the decision to trust her.

I decided to roll with it and be the guy she wanted to come back to. Saying that was easy. Doing it was tough. That night I talked to Claire about it. She said she was sure that Laure was in love with me but had not come to the point of being able to acknowledge it because of something about a previous boyfriend. Claire said Laure was having difficulty making a commitment and if I gave her time, with no pressure, she would come around.

Not wanting to appear too worried, I waited for over a month after Cindy and Laure went to Chicago. By then, I missed her something fierce so I devised a plan to see her. I got through on the telephone to the women's residence where she and Cindy lived. At first Laure sounded annoyed with me, but said yes when I asked her out for an afternoon picnic by Lake Michigan and a night on the town in Chicago this Saturday. That morning I got in my freshly spiffed up Elgin Six and drove to Chicago. Claire had given me a small suitcase for Laure, with strict orders that I was not to open it.

I arrived in Chicago early to check into a hotel recommended by Scott. After carrying my overnight suitcase into the modest but clean and pleasant room, I drove to the women's residence, and asked the desk clerk to send a message up to Laure's room. Men were allowed only in the lobby.

It was a beautiful Chicago October afternoon, perfect for a lakefront picnic. When Laure came down the stairs she looked like a dream, dressed casually for our picnic in a long tan skirt and white blouse with a colorful scarf artfully wrapped around her neck. She took my arm as we walked out. I could tell that other guys who came to pick up their dates were checking her out as we walked by.

When we got to the car Laure threw her arms around me. We did not need kissing lessons. The afternoon was beautiful as we walked and talked and kissed and ate the picnic lunch my mother prepared for us. To our surprise, Dorothy had packed a bottle of California wine from someplace called St. Helena. I opened and poured each of us a glass of wine, and asked Laure why she seemed upset with me when I called.

"You took long enough to decide to call. I was beginning to think you had forgotten about me. I even called Claire one night to see if you had run off to Mexico to get married to that old girlfriend of yours, Gina or something. And by the way, did Claire send along anything for me?"

"Not possible in a thousand lifetimes for me to forget the loveliest girl in the world who kisses like an angel. And yes, Claire sent a suitcase for you." I guess that was the right answer and we had a lovely afternoon by the lake. When I got Laure back to her room I gave her the small suitcase from Claire. She wanted to have time enough to freshen up and change into her evening clothes and I went to my hotel room to do the same. I declined to tell her where we were going for our night on the town. She pretended to pout so I knew that I had tantalized her.

I was surprised that Laure was worried that I had not called earlier. It seemed to be a difference from her attitude when we talked about our continuing relationship before she left for Chicago. I took it as a sign that my determination to not pressure her for a commitment was beginning to bear results.

When I returned to pick her up for dinner, Laure came downstairs and the women's residence matron looked displeased at the sight of Laure's short white beaded flapper dress and her stockings rolled to show her knees. She accented her dress with white shoes and a white headband around her blonde flapper bob cut hair, with a white feather at the right side. Her curves were so delicious that I gave serious thought to carrying her back up to her room and ravishing her, but under the merciless glare from the house matron I came to my senses and we took our leave. I was sternly told that Laure was to be back before midnight, with emphasis on the word 'before'. I wore a new black pinstripe suit in the latest style with black patent leather shoes and a white shirt and a real spiffy tie. Cindy came down to see us off and take a photograph. She told us all the swells in Chicago would be envious when they saw us.

Laure snuggled up next to me in the car as I drove to Pete's Steaks at 161 N. Dearborn St. Not having been here before, I was a little worried because from the front it did not look like a place to bring your favorite girl. It looked like a very plain lunch counter room. Laure didn't say anything but I could tell she was wondering if I knew what I was doing. However, Scott's father Thomas had given me instructions to go around to the steps at the rear. After the steps we entered the restaurant, which was a long narrow room. But this was no ordinary dining room. It was plush and nearly full, the wait staff scurrying around the tables. On the walls there were autographed photos of famous guests with the restaurant's owners. We saw a waiter carrying plates of sizzling steaks, thick, juicy and dripping with butter, surrounded by cottage fries, peas, radishes and sliced Bermuda onions. The aroma made us hungrier. Thomas McLanahan said the owners were friends and made the reservation personally. The hostess seated us at their most intimate table for two.

Our waiter appeared immediately with menus. I ordered a Pete's Special while Laure ordered a smaller version. I asked about wine, since Thomas said it was discreetly available, but the waiter put his finger to his lips.

Laure and I held hands under the table and smooched when we thought no one was watching. We were more than ready when the steaks arrived. With the first savory bite, we agreed that the steaks were the best ever. Occasionally some juice and butter would drip down from our lips and we made good use of the white linen napkins. We had only begun to eat when the waiter reappeared, placed two glasses on our table and poured wine for me to taste. I thought it tasted great and told the waiter to pour it for us. Up until now we only had eyes for each other but as we ate our dinners, we began to look around the room.

Laure recognized Paul Whiteman, the bandleader sitting on the other side of the aisle with a good-looking woman. Laure told me his band made a recording of The Charleston that was the cat's meow. We tried to be discreet and not stare but Paul noticed us – or maybe he noticed Laure, and he raised his wineglass to us. We raised ours in response and took drinks of our wine.

The restaurant owners, Bill and Marie Botham, had purchased the restaurant from the original owner but kept the original name. Marie stopped by our table to ask if everything was OK and we both told her it was more than OK, it was excellent. I asked her to send my compliments to the chef for the perfectly done steak. Marie was lovely and gracious and after she talked to us she turned to talk to Paul Whiteman. She was back to our table a minute later, asking if Mr. Whiteman could speak to us as they were just ready to leave. Of course, we both said at the same time. Paul and his wife Mildred came over and we made our introductions. We chatted for a moment and Whiteman said "I overheard you mentioning my orchestra's recording of The Charleston and I am pleased you like it. I just happen to have a few copies in my car and I want to send one up to you, if you would like."

I thought Laure was going to jump out of her chair and kiss him, but she maintained her classy behavior and accepted his offer. Paul said "Mildred and I usually sit at this table but I was happy to see you two enjoying it, and I couldn't help noticing how perfect you look together and how much in love you appear to be. We wish you the best in life." We shook hands and told him how pleased we were to talk to him and thanked him for the record. Mildred smiled but did not say much. They went down the center of the dining room, stopping to talk to other patrons, many of whom were local celebrities. Later, our waiter came to the table with a large white record envelope. Inside was Whiteman's recording of 'The Charleston' on the Victor label. Paul had autographed the envelope *'To Laure and Dan, May You Dance and Love Each Other Forever, Paul and Mildred Whiteman'*.

We had been dating since April and Laure had not yet said 'I love you' to me even though I told her often. I did not push it, but I wanted her to know my feelings for her. As we enjoyed the fabulous steak dinners and read Paul

Whiteman's note on the record envelope, she took my hand and said "I love you Dan. I'm sorry it took me so long to say that. I'll tell you why some day, please continue to be patient with me."

"Whatever time you wish, Sweetie, I'm here."

The waiter brought the check and it was $7.00, a lot of money for two dinners. But these were exceptional dinners, and feeling on a high from Laure telling me she loved me, it was worth every penny. I gave the waiter a ten spot and told him to keep the change. He thanked us, wished us a good night, and invited us to come back to Pete's Steaks. His name was Phillip and Laure said we would be sure to ask for him when we came back.

We began walking down the room when it struck me that the check had not included a charge for the wine. I found our waiter and asked him. He smiled and said Mr. Whiteman had paid for our wine because we looked like perfect lovebirds. I decided that having a date with a lovely woman worked wonders for my self-confidence.

At the Elgin, I carefully put the record under the seat, wrapping it in a blanket for protection. Laure said I would have to play it for her often, but I told her she should have the record and play it for me because Paul Whiteman had heard her talking about the song and that's why he gave it to us. I earned a juicy kiss and a squeeze for that. Life was good and getting better.

I drove us to the Uptown neighborhood, where at the corner of Broadway and Lawrence the most infamous nightclub in Chicago was located, The Green Mill Gardens. Laure let out a little shriek of surprise when she saw where I was taking her. The Green Mill was known for many things, including its alleged ownership by Al Capone. I turned the Elgin over to the valet and gave him a decent tip so he wouldn't make a smart remark about having to handle such an inexpensive old car compared to the new Cadillacs and Packards that were pulling up to the club. I did not need to do that because he was staring at

Laure, who flashed him some leg when he opened the door for her. I think he liked that better than my tip.

When we got to the nightclub's front door there was a long line. I took Laure's hand and walked us past the line to the doorman, took a note from my suit pocket and gave it to him. After reading it, he motioned us to follow him and opened the door with a flourish. A floor host met us and showed us to a prime table next to the dance floor. We ordered martinis made with high quality gin. The waiter said the orchestra would begin playing in about 20 minutes so we had some time to talk.

"Dan, how did you arrange this? People do not just walk up to the doorman and get into The Green Mill that easily. The girls at school talk about this place and how they would love to come here but they say you have to know someone in the mob to get in on a busy night like tonight. I will have stories to tell that will make them insanely jealous, especially after they got a look at my handsome boyfriend that picked me up tonight. That's you, by the way. What was in that note that you gave the doorman? I didn't see you give him any money."

"Laure, you will have to get used to the fact that your man Dan can accomplish many things that mere mortals cannot, because I am motivated by wanting to maintain my privilege of holding and kissing you." Then I added in a mysterious voice "Many things. I have my ways." At that moment a handsome man and beautiful woman came over and without being asked sat at our table. The man introduced himself as the manager, Jack McGurn, and his girlfriend Louise Rolfe. They had a drink with us and Jack seemed interested that Laure and I were being served promptly and having a good time. I assured him that the service and drinks were great and we were ready to dance. Jack and Louise moved on to visit another table. At the time I had no idea what that was all about.

Laure was impressed that I was important enough for the manager to personally ensure everything was jake. "Oh

Dan you are the very definition of a sheik. When are we going to dance?" The band was arriving on stage.

Fortunately I learned ballroom dancing because my mother was teaching Claire and I was her partner for the lessons. Claire wanted to learn so she could dance with Scott and my mother said I needed to learn too. I told Laure "Yes sweetie, we will dance the first dance. I may not be as smooth as an expert but I'll give it a try."

We held hands and talked like lovers together again after a long absence. I noticed several men walking around the room to pass by us and each one turned to check out my girl. "Laure, you are so beautiful and lovely tonight. I have missed you terribly. Life has become boring without you in it, without your smile to brighten my day."

"Thank you sweetie. Of course I could tell by how you have been looking at me, but I didn't realize until now how much it meant to me to hear you say it." After a minute Laure commented "It seems that several women have strolled across the room to look at my handsome man. I hope I don't have to fight them off. I don't share my man." I had not noticed that, but now I saw both men and women giving us the eyeball treatment. The orchestra was on the stage, and began with a foxtrot.

"May I have this dance, Miss Laure?"

"Yes, I would love to dance with you, Mr. Lindner." We went out for our first dance of the evening and I managed to turn in a good performance. Laure loved to dance and her beautiful smile worked magically to make me a better dancer. We rarely stopped dancing. Occasionally, men asked Laure to dance but she thanked them and said that she only wanted to dance with me. She said it so sweetly that no one was offended.

When the band started a Charleston and I did not know how to do that dance. Laure looked like she really wanted to dance and as a crowd of people came down to the dance floor from the tables behind us, they pulled others out of their chairs. Laure was one of them who was pulled up. Then a cute girl who looked like she was still in high school tried to pull me up but I stayed and she stomped off to find easier pickings. Through the crowd I saw Laure doing the Charleston and damn, she was good. Her long legs were kicking and she had that big smile going for the benefit of the lucky duck who was dancing with her. I marveled at the luck of the string of pearls that bounced on her breasts while she danced. The dancers on the floor gave way to her and her partner, circling around them, watching, clapping and cheering as they danced. He was a good dancer and my heart was thrilled at seeing her dance so amazingly well, but not so pleased that she was dancing with another man.

After the Charleston finished she disengaged herself from the man, who seemed determined to kiss her but she came straight back to our table. "I'm sorry Dan, I assumed you knew the Charleston. If you want to learn it I will teach you." The song was popular and in the next set the band played it again. Laure began to teach me how to Charleston, and the way she did it was energetic and lots of fun. Not wanting to watch her dance it with another man, I was an eager student and learned fast.

After that we danced and drank until it was time to get Laure back to her residence when a familiar but unwanted face with an evil sneer appeared in front of us at our table.

"Say Danny, I heard you were dating a new girl, a very pretty bit of fluff and here you are." He held his hand out to her. "I'm Joey and I'm pleased to meet you, Miss..."

"Laure." She said, but did not take his hand.

"Well Miss Laure, I insist on having the next dance, I'm sure Danny Boy won't mind, will you?" He gave me the look that reminded me that he still thought I owed him.

"Thank you Joey, but I'm sorry, I only dance with my man and this is our first date in a long time. I hope you will understand, and anyway it is time for us to leave" Laure had not met Joey C. before and I hated him for insinuating himself into our big night. She had intuitively picked up that he was not a friend.

"Nonsense Laure, we will dance. Come with me." He grabbed her arm and rudely pulled her out to the dance floor before either of us could object. He tried to hold her close during a waltz but she handled herself well and did not give him a chance to grope her. Joey must have been telling her jokes because he got her to laugh a couple times, but her beautiful smile was missing. Jealousy and fear flooded my senses. I knew that if Joey Coniglio was here, I dare not make a stink or he would have his thugs take me out back and throw me out with the trash while Laure was kept for him to play with.

Laure did not wait until the final note of the last song. She simply turned and walked back to our table. Joey made to come after Laure but Jack McGurn stepped in front of him and gave Joey a dangerous stare. Joey C. showed a brief look of fear on his face, then grinned at me and made a gun with his finger and thumb and 'shot' me as he turned and walked away laughing. "He is loathsome" Laure said. "He reeks of garlic and is a bad dancer but thinks he is hot stuff. He kept trying to grab me and rub his body on me while we were dancing." Now it was too late to get Laure back to her residence, but she said not to worry. She had arranged with Cindy to cover for her. "So where are we spending the night Mr. Lindner?"

I signed the check and we walked out. The valet brought up my Elgin, grinning at Laure. I checked and the Paul Whiteman record was hidden exactly as I had left it. I took Laure to my hotel room and the desk clerk was sleeping so we got past the front desk without being asked if we were married. I wondered if this was going to be my lucky night, but alas, it was not to be.

"Dan, how did you get out without paying the bill?"

"Like I told you Laure, I can make things happen."

"OK Mr. Mysterious. I had a wonderful, fabulous time tonight. You're really good out on the dance floor. Maybe you are good in bed too, but I'm not ready to have sex yet. I hope you understand. I want you to understand. I did not plan on being a tease, I thought we would be able to get back to the residence in time but then that awful Joey came over. You have me at your mercy but I ask that you just hold me tonight and not take advantage of me. I promise that when the day comes I will make you very happy that you waited."

"I will honor your request and just hold you tonight. Let's have a nightcap drink and go to bed." I was playing her game and betting that the big payoff would come soon. A girl who could move like that on the dance floor had to be great at horizontal bed dancing.

I usually slept naked or in pajama bottoms and I had brought some. Laure had nothing to wear to bed so I gave her one of my cotton t-shirts which was long on her but not long enough and I thoroughly enjoyed the view of her legs and cute little butt. The sight of her breasts moving unhindered under my t-shirt gave me an immediate erection when she walked in from the bathroom. I know she noticed because she was looking right at it. We pulled back the bedcovers, got in and kissed, facing each other, holding tight. "Dan, you remember when you asked me to be your girl? Well, you should not worry. I have had more offers than you want to hear about. One night Cindy and I and some of the girls from school went out to dance. I had lots of men ask me for a date, but I didn't want any of them. None of them measured up to you." Then she realized what she had said as she casually moved her hand to my erect penis trying to poke through the fabric of my pajama bottom. "Oh Danny, you know what I mean. I did not go out with any of them. I don't want to be with anyone else."

We spent about a half-hour in a makeout session, with me taking every advantage with my hands that she would let me take. She allowed me to feel and play with her breasts and run my hands over her body but whispered "that's as far as we go tonight, OK?" I kissed her breasts through the shirt fabric and she did not object. She put her hand down to my erection again but kept it outside my pajama bottom, then smiled and removed her hand before we went to sleep. I sensed that she desired more but was holding herself back with admirable self-control. We drifted off to sleep holding each other, spoon fashion. I felt very comfortable and fell asleep breathing the scent of her body, her hair and everything about her. My hand cupped a breast and she left it there. It was obvious to me that she also wanted more, and I don't know how we kept from going at each other on that incredibly sexy night.

In the morning I woke and Laure was already up and taking off my t-shirt. When she saw that I was awake she moved to cover her body but I got a glance at the side of the lovely breast that I had held last night. That picture became permanent in my memory ever after. Then she asked me if she could keep the shirt to sleep in because it was comfortable and it would remind her of me. She smiled at me, knowing I could not say no.

We called Cindy and she came out to have breakfast with us at the hotel coffee shop and listen to our stories. Cindy said there had been no problem at the residence, she had an extra pillow and a rolled up blanket arranged so if there were a bed check it would appear that Laure was asleep. Cindy said she could bring Laure inside through a kitchen door that was unlocked during the day.

Our weekend date finished with a hug and a lingering kiss. I felt good that Laure and I were on the right track. That night back at home, I fell asleep dreaming about Laure wearing my t-shirt in her bed.

ROAD TRIP DOG

Cindy and Laure decided that the school was too slow paced so they decided not to return for the spring semester. My mother offered to finish their bookkeeping and administration education.

Jake and Vera hosted a delicious Thanksgiving dinner for my family and Scott since his parents were in New York. Laure made pies and they were excellent.

They invited Claire, my mother and me over for Christmas morning and we opened presents together. I gave Laure a long string of high quality pearls and matching earrings. She gave me a sharp black Fedora. I had not worn hats very often but Laure said I would look great in a Fedora. I wore it Christmas Day as we walked around the village and I received many compliments. Jake said I had a 'hat face'. I became quite fond of that Fedora and wore it for many years.

We were invited to the McLanahan Ranch for Christmas dinner and went to the ranch in two cars. It was another excellent holiday dinner, served with wine from Napa and Sonoma in California. After dinner it was snowing lightly so we put on our coats and boots and took a short walk around the ranch. A half hour later the snow stopped so Thomas McLanahan invited any of us who wanted to go out and shoot clays at his shotgun range. Elaine, Dorothy and Vera decided to stay inside by the fireplace to talk and drink wine. Vera, Elaine and my mother were now a trio of best friends.

Claire and Laure went to the shooting range with us. Claire and I were good at shooting clays. Jake was an excellent rifleman but had little shotgun experience. Thomas and Scott were very experienced and in a class by themselves. The big surprise – although maybe it should not have been – was Laure. She had very little experience shooting clays but took to it fast and improved faster, becoming almost as good as Thomas and Scott and I was in third place. Laure clearly won fourth place with a strong finish. I took a photograph of Laure shooting and I thought girls with guns looked sexy except when they were pointing them at me. When we weren't shooting she came over and sat on my lap, saying she was cold and hugged me for warmth. Jake did not seem worried about it and I wasn't complaining. We passed a couple of flasks around to help our inner warmth. I noticed Claire sat on Scott's lap when they took a break from shooting and commented to Laure how happy they looked together.

"You just noticed?" Laure asked. "They've been like that since last summer. They look good together, don't they? A lovely couple. I wonder when they will get around to announcing their engagement."

"I know another young couple that looks good together, a stunning young blonde modern girl and her handsome boyfriend, especially when he's wearing his new Fedora" I replied.

Laure looked at me. "You noticed that too? You are observant as well as handsome and smart. Let's see if we can take some photographs of Claire and Scott and get ours taken together too." And so we did, with poses of us standing together, arms around each other, standing with our shotguns, and photos of us shooting. Since Elaine, Vera and Dorothy were back at the house Thomas and Jake took the photographs. Claire said she would take the parents' photos by the fireplace at the ranch house. Altogether it was a comfortable and happy Christmas day for everyone. Our families were becoming a tight knit business team too.

Scott rented the Village Tavern to throw a New Year's Eve party and invited everyone. Along with the usual decorations, he put up a large map and some architectural drawings on the walls. Scott announced that he had bought out a real estate investor who had been buying up land around the village for a housing development. He showed drawings and plans for the S Bar C (Scott/Claire) Ranch and the villagers were pleased with this rather than a housing development. Scott and Claire were going to build their new house and stables, training areas and other facilities for a bangtail ranch. They also announced that they would lease out some of the extra acreage to local farmers and would not develop all the land. By now Scott and Claire were deeply involved in Long Grove activities, even attending the Long Grove Church together.

"They're announcing that they are building a home together." Laure said excitedly. "Is that their engagement announcement?" And sure enough it was. Later when the band took a break, Scott called out that he was making another announcement and everyone turned in rapt attention. Scott and Claire stood together, holding hands.

"Tonight we happily take this opportunity to announce that Claire and I are engaged to be married. Since we have not been together long, and Claire recently lost her father, we will have a long engagement and set the date later, but we want everyone to know that we plan to spend our lives together." Everyone applauded and Hutfilz, helped by Otto and Fritz came out carrying trays of champagne flutes for everyone. We toasted our friends. I don't remember how many times but it was enough so that we ran out of champagne. The band started playing again, with Scott and Claire dancing together like they were already at their wedding. I was astounded how Claire had gone from gawky teenager to a beautiful and graceful woman, poised and confident, in just a year.

I took a chance and gave Laure a hopeful look but she shook her head. "Not yet Dan. I'm not ready to make that commitment. Don't take that wrong, you're the only guy in my heart. I'm just not ready. You have been so good with no pressure about marriage and I wouldn't blame you if you left me if I couldn't decide, but don't leave me just yet. I feel good about us. OK Sweetie?" She looked at me with those beautiful blue eyes and her smile that made me so happy.

"You are my main squeeze. We won't talk about marriage, just give me a hint when you're ready."

"I better be your only squeeze" she laughed. "And I promise when I am ready you will be the first to know."

Laure and I had not had sex yet. In fact she had not even let me touch her body since the night of our big date in Chicago in October. However, she was perfectly able to read my mind.

"Dan, I'm not blind. I can see how you look at me and I know you want me. I want you too, I want to feel you in me. Hold your horses, don't get excited now!" She must have noticed my pants stretching in front. "But I'm an all or nothing kind of girl. I know, modern girls are supposed to be sophisticated and easy. Most modern girls smoke too, but I don't, I got sick when I tried it. I am an independent modern girl. When I decide to have you I may let you know by attacking you. I know for sure that I could not hold off if we had another night like when we went to The Green Mill. I wanted to just pull you up on top of me."

"I know how you are when you make up your mind. I'll try not to resist!" I smiled. "Buy say, that's an idea. How about we go back to Pete's and The Green Mill? I'll reserve the same hotel room."

"Better not, or I'll have to re-think it, and you don't want to start waiting all over again" Laure said with a pretty laugh and pulled me to her for a kiss that must have lasted longer than we knew, because Claire came over and told us to break off or go get a room. I realized my hand was holding Laure's cute little butt and she had pulled me tight to her. I felt her breasts pressing into my body and I had no doubt she felt the bulge in my pants. "I'll have to be more careful talking about attacking you" Laure said, slightly out of breath.

"I'm just practicing for the great event!" I exclaimed.

"OK big boy." Laure slipped her arm around my waist. "Well Mr. Daniel Lindner, you continue to make a good impression on me" and I was just going to ask which impression of me she was getting. I think she was ready to say something about what my reward might be but Jake came up, probably to see if we were getting ready to elope. But he came to tell us that Scott was going to give him flying lessons. He would then be able to test fly repaired aircraft and ferry them back when the repair or maintenance work was completed, or when an aeroplane was purchased by one of his customers. The look on Jake's face was as happy as I had ever seen. He had often said how much he wanted to learn to fly aeroplanes but time and money were never around in sufficient quantity until now.

Even Mrs. Carlisle came to the New Year's Eve party. She was well respected in the village and had been Scott's liaison with the local landowners. Mrs. Carlisle was so happy with all the good news that night, she broke her rule to not drink more than one glass of wine and after three she was getting tipsy. I arranged with Constable Sherman to make sure Mrs. Carlisle made it home safely.

Laure and I celebrated our birthdays, mine on February 6 and hers on March 21. We were both born in 1903, the year the Wright Brothers first flew their aeroplane at Kitty Hawk, and in 1925 we turned 22 years of age.

A couple weeks later I received an unexpected present. Returning home on a rainy night from a movie date with Laure, I drove up to the house, turned off the Elgin's lights and motor and got out. When my foot stepped on the first porch stair, I found myself looking into the big brown eyes of a large German Shepherd Dog. It wagged its tail and seemed glad to meet me. I sat on the top stair and offered my hand. The dog sniffed my hand and wagged his tail as I stroked his fur. We are off to a good start, I thought. Just then the front door opened and Claire came out. "Sure is a nice dog. Who does he belong to?" I asked.

"Isn't he beautiful? He was hanging around at the tavern for a couple of days. Cindy said someone told her that a car had stopped, opened a door, closed it and drove off. When the car was gone the dog was watching the car leave, and he whined and barked. They already have three dogs so she asked if we would like to have him. He's very friendly, doesn't bother the horses or the cats. Seems protective, tried to run off the mailman this morning and this afternoon he raided a garbage pail. I called Scott and he said they would take him but they already have several dogs. This fellow is adorable. See how his left ear is straight but the right ear folds? It makes him look like he is questioning everything. Do you think it would be OK to keep him? We called Constable Sherman and he had no lost dog report, and anyway it was obvious that someone dumped him. How awful, but good for us." Claire gushed.

"I don't know that we need a dog, but he is a friendly fellow and looks healthy. Wish I knew why someone would dump a nice dog."

"Mother and I fed him and gave him water. He was hungry and thirsty. Constable Sherman said that if no one came to claim him in 30 days we can keep him. Otherwise he would take the dog to the pound but that's a horrid place. They kill most of the dogs that end up there. Please Dan, let's keep him. I don't want him killed. I think he already likes you." The dog was lying next to me, comfortable as could be. I wondered if he was dumped because something might be wrong with him.

"Yeah, we can see what happens, but I think we should take him over to Doc Atkins for a checkup. He seems too nice for someone to just abandon him. Maybe they opened the car door for some reason and he got out, and now they are looking for him."

We went inside, the dog eagerly following us. "He was inside for a while in the afternoon and seems to be housebroken since he asked for the door just before you arrived."

I didn't think much more of it, except when I looked at the kitchen calendar and saw it was April 1, 1925. April Fools' Day. Was the joke on me? But when I looked at him sitting next to me, his big brown eyes locked with mine and his tail thumped the floor vigorously.

I named him Raider because he liked to raid garbage cans. But what he liked even better was riding in my automobile. He would wait by the Elgin and get in without an invitation when I opened the door so he could be sure to go along for the ride. Laure gave him a second name – Road Trip Dog. He always rode in the front seat unless Laure was with me, then he would move to the back seat without being told. She had bonded with him as well.

No one claimed him and Doc Atkins said he was about two years old and healthy. Now I had a dog.

ROADSIDE CONFRONTATION

A couple weeks later on an unseasonably warm day in April, Laure and I went for a ride in the evening and parked in our favorite spot by the lake to practice kissing. Our private party was rudely disturbed when Joey C. and Gina's thuggish brothers drove up and parked nearby. They got out and walked over to us. As they neared my Elgin I got out, the better to defend myself. The brothers, dressed identically in dark suits watched around the area when Joey C. started to speak to me. I had almost forgotten about him. A year had gone by with no word from Joey C. about the money the Don falsely claimed I owed and I was not going to bring it up.

"Joey how not so nice to see you again. You always pick the worst times to show up. Why don't you write me a letter or something, instead of being a pest?" Joey and Gina's brothers laughed. I heard the passenger side door of my Elgin open and Laure got out.

"Y'know Danny, I just wanted to see if you were still going out with the same sheba, that pretty little piece of fluff. I think that I should make a move on her and show her what a good time is like with a real man. She will forget about you soon enough after enjoying all the good things in life that I can give her. What was her name, Loretta?"

"I'm right here and don't speak like about me as if I wasn't. My name is Laure, and giving me things to get me to like you will not work. Dan is a gentleman and I am his lady. Calling me a little piece of fluff guarantees that you don't have what it takes to attract me." Laure usually said what was on her mind but I wish she had been a little more tactful. Joey C. could be nice or nasty, whatever mood possessed him, and I wanted to get his visit over with as soon as possible.

"Well Miss fluffy Low-ree, someday you will get to know me intimately and appreciate my talents" Joey exaggerated her name and moved his hips as if he were humping air as he said 'talents'. His sluggers laughed, we did not. Joey was standing right in front of me, the brothers by the Cadillac sedan. Before I could stop her, Laure took a step forward, reached out and slapped Joey in the face. On one hand I began to be very worried, on the other I noticed she had slapped him so hard there was a red mark on his face. I should have listened to the first hand because Joey C. turned ugly and pushed Laure to the ground. He started to say something but I launched myself at him and even though he had forty pounds on me, my surprise move caught him off balance and he went down on his fat ass. The thugs were momentarily stunned, not expecting their boss to get anything but respect from me. I jumped on Joey and got one good hit to the side of his face before the thugs grabbed me from behind and dragged me off him.

"Stand him up. Stand him up against the car" growled Joey. The thugs did as they were told. Joey C. took two steps toward me and sent his fist into my stomach. I saw movement in the background but Joey hit me again. "Stand him up. Brace him, don't let him fall down." Joey C. roared and I saw him winding up for another body blow.

Laure shouted "Stop! Stop it! Is that what you are, a bully who needs help from his goons to beat up men to prevent them from defending themselves and their women? You're a disgrace to your family, you're... "

Joey shouted "Shut up bitch, shut the fuck up or I'll shut you up" and he pushed her to the ground again. He looked like he was going to kick her and I became enraged, pulled myself free from the thugs and gave Joey a good solid hit to a kidney when the familiar blast of an M1911 sounded. Everyone froze. Laure held her pearl-handled 1911 in a shooter's grip and aimed at Joey C., who suddenly acted like a frightened child, holding his hands in front as if that would push the bullets away as he babbled "Don't shoot, don't shoot! I was just playin' around." His voice was pleading and wavering in fear. I knew very well seeing the business end of a 1911 modifies a person's behavior and Joey was showing the classic signs of being a bully – mean when he had control, cowardly when he didn't.

I saw Joey getting ready to jump at her and I yelled "Step back Laure, you're too close to him." Laure jumped back before Joey could make a grab for her gun. The goons grabbed me again and one of them held my arms behind my back while the other lined up to slug me.

"Hey greaseballs – I'm going to kill your boss in three seconds unless you let Dan go – 3, 2..."

Joey C. growled "You idiots – I ain't getting iced because you palookas don't got no brains." The thug lowered his hand to his side but it was clear he was going to try again.

"Leave us alone" Laure calmly told them while keeping her gun pointed at Joey. "So it takes three guys to harass one man and one woman. Some tough guys you are." I wished Laure was not quite so direct, even though I agreed with everything she said. I went closer to Laure and Joey C. moved back a couple of steps toward the Cadillac. One of the stupid brothers reached inside his coat. Laure kept the 1911 aimed at Joey and calmly said "Keep your hands where I can see them or your boss gets a bullet in his fat face. I shoot fast and accurate and you will get the next bullet before you can pull your gun."

"All right, hold on there, Fluffy. I got something to tell Dan" said Joey. "Let me tell him now or I'll be back."

"Laure, you don't have to stay and listen to this, take the Elgin and go home" I said. "I don't think they'll try anything again. I think I know what Joey wants to talk about."

"I don't trust them and I'm not leaving. You can't tell me what to do." *That's a fact*, I thought.

"At least get in the car and I'll talk to Joey, then we can leave."

"No."

"Laure, I..."

"I said NO. If I'm your girlfriend I want to know how you're mixed up with these thugs. I'm staying right here, right next to you." I opened my mouth to tell her again and she stopped me. "And don't try to order me around. I make my own decisions." *Yeah, I knew that very well.* "You may not have noticed, but the mug on the left has a sap in his hand. If I were to leave, he would use it on your thick skull. You wouldn't like that and neither would I." Laure was observant.

"OK Joey, talk. What's so all important that you had to skulk around with your thugs to threaten and harass me and my lady?" I noticed that Laure steadily held the gun pointed at Joey C. "Hurry up about it or we're leaving."

"I haven't brought up with you the money you owe the Don. I thought you were an honorable guy and would voluntarily pay the debt, especially after your rich sugar daddy fronted money for your business. You gotta pay your debts or your shop won't stay open much longer. You know I can make that happen, just like I took care of your old shop, and no one can protect you from us. Don't be stupid, pay up while you still can."

"I should just shoot him right now" Laure said. She clearly made Joey nervous, and I was surprised that Joey admitted he had burned my shop after he had denied it to the Don's face.

"Let me finish, little Fluffy. I have a solution, a small task that Danny can perform and I will forgive some of what you owe us. Then, for just a few bucks a month for insurance, you will never have any trouble at your shop. You ready to listen?"

"No" said Laure, and I said "Yes." Laure gave me a look of dismay. "Laure, let's let Joey say his business so we can leave."

Joey's smirked, thinking he had won that round. "Our mother loves wine. She used to drink Italian wine but it is hard to get, even for us. What comes off the boats in New York is taken by local families and doesn't get to Chicago."

"Joey, that sounds like your problem, not mine" I said. Laure was calm as she held the gun on Joey C. and the longer Joey saw the 1911 pointed directly at him, the more nervous he got.

"Yeah well, smart guy, I'm making it your problem. Someone gave my mother some wine from California and she liked it, God help her. She said to get her some of it."

"So what? I don't know anything about wine or how to make it or how to get any. Why don't you send your boys out to steal some?"

"I need all the guys here, we got lots of work to do with you merchant types who refuse to pay a modest monthly fee for insurance and the other families trying to poach on our business. I told the Don that you would be grateful to go get some. The Don liked the idea and agreed to wipe maybe ten per cent of the money you owe us off the books if you were to bring back a few barrels of wine from California."

"Why don't you just get your family relations in California to send it to you on the train?" I asked.

"The families out there are aligned with other families and are not likely to help us, and the wine won't be safe on the railroad. Those thieves will deliver empty barrels and say it leaked out." Joey C. was losing his patience. He must have thought I would jump at the chance to do this.

"How the hell am I supposed to bring it back here? A 50 gallon barrel of wine is probably 400 pounds. I couldn't fit one barrel in an automobile back seat and if I could and someone discovered it I wouldn't be able to outrun them. That's a loser of a deal Joey. I'm screwed before I even start. And how do I buy wine, assuming someone out there will sell it to me? Not to mention I don't have money for expenses or trucks."

"Like I said Danny Boy, that's your problem. It's you that owes us. Don't ever forget that."

"I don't take assignments from you. I don't owe the Don anything and I want nothing more from you except to leave us alone."

"We already discussed that and you lost. Now you know what you need to do, and you should take it if you know what's good for your family. I'll keep Fluffy company while you're away, just to make sure you don't get any funny ideas. She can stay at the Coniglio compound with me" and he let out an evil laugh.

"Forget it Joey. I'm not your errand boy. And next time you want to talk to me, don't go bothering my lady or you and I will be facing off. Alone, without your goons."

"I'll remember you said that so I can remind you while I'm beating the crap out of you. I thought coming to see you would be easier. You should think about this, because if you refuse, you, your sister, mother, your friends could all get hurt when we put the screws to you rubes. And then your little sheba will have no choice, she will be grateful to be done with a loser and she will come to me. I know how to show girls like her who's the boss. She won't sass me."

"Says you" Laure replied. "I don't skate around, especially with a bumfuck like you."

Joey C. sneered but told his boys to get in the car. Once again one of them reached inside his suit coat. Laure let a round loose two inches over Joey's head. It was so close Joey ducked and the front of his pants began to show a large wet spot.

"Hey fat boy, your pants are wet. Remind your friends to keep their hands in the open. Next time one of them reaches for his gun, I'll give you a third eye, no warning" Laure was almost growling.

Joey glared at the brothers, then turned to me and said "I'm gonna give you some good advice Danny Boy. Don't let her get away with talking crap like that. You gotta be a man. When a woman gets mouthy like your fluffy little bitch here, knock her around, take the belt to her. She has t'know her place, y'know what I mean? Teach her some respect." Laure's gun hand held steady and I thought she might take it into her mind to shoot the bastard. I almost wanted to take the gun and do it myself.

"I respect real men, not cowards and bullies" Laure replied. Joey just laughed as he and his thugs got into the Cadillac.

"I didn't know you were carrying the gun" I said to Laure after they left. "Why did you have it?"

"I've seen those creeps hanging around lately and thought they were watching us. I didn't know why so I started carrying it. Let's go, take me home." She said nothing more all the way home. I walked her to the door and put my arms around her for our good night kiss, but she pushed me away and said "No kiss. I'm disappointed in you. How can you even think of getting involved with them after what they did to your father? I don't want another dead boyfriend because of the mob. Good night." Before I could ask what she meant by that, she was inside, closed the door with a bang and slid the deadbolt home. I went home with a sinking feeling in the pit of my stomach, and it was not from being hit by Joey C.

CANNON BALL BAKER

I did not see Laure the next day, or the next. She was not at home when I called. I kept busy by seeking advice about my dilemma. I talked to my mother and Claire. I talked to Hutfilz, who seemed quite nervous talking about it. He probably was paying insurance to the mob and could be in trouble if they found out he was helping me. I talked to my friends Otto and Fritz, but they didn't know much about the gangster world. They just told me they were with me no matter what. When I told them it would be extremely dangerous they replied "that's what friends are for." I decided not to talk to Constable Sherman or Deputy Carlson. Next on my list was to talk to Jake. I went over after dinner and knocked at the kitchen door. Jake opened it and asked me to come in. He called up the stairs "Laure honey, Dan is here."

"Tell him I'm not home" came the reply.

"Why don't you come down and tell him yourself? He's right here at the kitchen table." Jake gave me a grin as if nothing was wrong but I'm sure he knew what had happened. Laure talked to her father about almost everything. Laure appeared a few minutes later. I noticed her eyes were red.

"I came over to talk to Jake, but even more than that I wanted to see you, Laure. I want to know what's wrong and if you have any ideas about how to handle this" I said.

"I don't know what to tell you. I thought you would stand up to that horrible gangster and just tell him no. Sometimes I think I should have shot him. Or you."

"Shooting Joey wouldn't make the problem go away. The Coniglio family would come after you, me and our families."

"Dan when you decide what you're going to do, let me know. I don't know what I will do except think about it for now. I hope you don't do what he wants you to do."

"I understand. I don't want to do it, but there are serious consequences to saying no. I'm here tonight to talk to Jake too."

"Yes, you should. I told him about it. Let him know what you're going to do." She turned and went upstairs.

Jake came back into the kitchen as soon as Laure left the room. We talked about it but he straddled the fence on the issue of whether I should take the job or not. He agreed that I didn't owe the Coniglio's any money, but they had it in their minds that I did and there was no one we could call to help. The sheriff would not do anything because whether I owed money or not was a civil matter. Unless I was attacked the sheriff could do nothing, which would be of little help because if they attacked me I would be dead. Constable Sherman had no firepower to back him up. Jake thought that going to California might not be a bad way out, if we could be sure they would forgive what they thought we owed them. But then he said Laure had her mind set that she didn't want me to go. She told him that if I was involved with gangsters she didn't want to be with me. I told Jake I was involved involuntarily but he said she would not admit that distinction was valid.

Next stop was the McLanahan Ranch to see Scott. I called ahead and he was out with his horses but would be home in the evening. I went out to the ranch after I left Jake, and the maid showed me into Scott's office. He was sitting at his desk using one of the new Dictaphone machines that recorded words on a cylinder to be played back by a secretary for typing. Scott motioned for me to wait just a minute while he finished dictating a letter to one of his business managers. I was fascinated by the machine but my mind kept pulling me back to my own problem.

When he was finished he showed me the machine and how it worked. A maid brought in refreshments and Scott asked me what was on my mind. He had already known about my previous contact with the Coniglios as part of our agreement that I disclose everything that could affect our business together. I explained Joey C.'s demand and presented what I thought were the pluses and minuses.

"You have quite a decision to make" Scott said. "I agree that no court would enforce a debt based on what happened, and getting a court order would have no effect on the Coniglios. Worse than that, they have judges on their payroll and if you get the wrong judge, they could make it legal. The police are powerless to stop them in things like this, and probably don't care. They might think you were in with them. Your conundrum is, to go on the mission to repay a debt you don't owe, or to ignore them and put your and Jake's families in jeopardy. I admit that the advice I give you is biased because I am engaged to be married to Claire, and we are very much in love. I would do anything to keep her from harm."

"I know it seems like my only choice is between the lesser of two evils. To my way of thinking the worse evil is to do nothing and have gangsters come around threatening us and jeopardizing our families and our businesses. Then Joey said that even if I brought the wine, we would have to buy insurance from him in order to keep our shops from being destroyed. Another concern is that if I complete this mission, will they really release me from their perceived debt? Joey mentioned forgiving ten per cent, and the Don said I would have to pay interest as well. It sounds like they are setting me up to continue to harass me to do more jobs for them."

"I'll talk to some of our people, managers with experience and dare I say, have some contact with the crime families in the Chicago area. We do not officially do business with them, but that does not mean we can ignore them either. Some of the unions and businesses are infested with them and as a practical matter we have to acknowledge their existence. It's similar to your situation – we have to do things that our conscience doesn't like, but we have employees who might be harmed or lose their jobs if we don't. I will talk to my people tomorrow. What do you think of paying Joey C. off?" Scott asked.

"I don't like it. They want over twelve thousand dollars plus interest, and if I borrowed it I would have to work a long time to pay it off. I might be better off attempting the mission."

"You're probably right, but keep that option in mind, I'll back you. Come back tomorrow evening and we will figure something out, but in the meantime it would be a good idea to start thinking about what you need if you go on this mission. Make a plan, a business plan, to determine what you need in terms of money, cars or trucks, people and resources. Let's get an idea about that before we try to make a decision."

The next day I got Claire to spend a couple hours with me and I laid out everything I could think of if I were to attempt the mission. It was even more expensive than I thought and I became depressed. Claire was of the opinion that we could use our family money to underwrite the trip. With her businesslike mind she said maybe we could turn this into an opportunity for ourselves. I told her we would be nuts to go into competition with the Coniglios but it was an attractive idea. Maybe I could make enough on the side to pay the Coniglios off. I was starting to think that the lesser of two evils might be going to California, but I didn't want to become a gangster, or lose Laure.

When I returned to Scott's office the next evening the maid brought me right in. Seated near Scott's desk was a man who looked as though he had lived outdoors all his life. He was in his mid-30s, very fit and had a calm demeanor.

"Hi Dan. My friend is in the Chicago area for a few days and I asked him to join us. Dan, this is Erwin Baker, and I thought that if you should decide to go, Erwin here has unique experience that would be of help. Claire said you worked with her on a project plan today so let's take a look and talk about the possibilities." I shook hands with Erwin, took out a copy of my plan for Scott and we briefly discussed it.

"It's not complete, Scott. I can accurately plan getting out there but how to get two or three barrels of wine back with me is an unknown. I don't think an automobile would hold up to over 2,000 miles of rough road with a payload of over a half or three quarters of a ton, and if I was chased I could not outrun a flivver. A truck would carry the load but as I well know from my father's experience I would not be able to outrun a man on a horse much less a fast car. I think Joey C. was right that shipping it by train won't work. A barrel of wine smells like a barrel of wine and those barrels would disappear along the way. I also have to worry about the government finding out and then I would be going to prison. So getting to California I can do, the return trip is the problem. I've put in some estimates for a car and trailer or a large truck. I even got freight rates for railroad shipping to estimate what that would cost. I just don't like any of those options."

"Dan, as I mentioned yesterday I am quite biased in favor of you attempting the mission, so please factor that in to what I say, but I have decided to back you 100% no matter what you decide. Claire is that important to me, and she agrees. Actually if you were to go I would go with if I could, unfortunately my father has me evaluating new business acquisitions and those evaluations won't wait. I see your proposed timeline for the mission is two months. Is that enough time? It seems short."

"It could be short but I decided that the cost goes up a lot if I don't move things along and I'm sure Joey would get anxious if I was to disappear for longer than that. I have no idea how long it will take to make a deal to buy wine, good wine, and I don't know how to evaluate what I'm buying. I'm sure there will be a lot of substandard crap for sale and not so much of the good stuff. Then, what if no one will sell to me? Joey says he will give me a contact but I don't know if the Coniglio's reach goes that far. This is all going to have to be done in secret which adds to the time and the danger of being caught."

"I have some contacts too, real business contacts, so I am going to assume that a deal can be reached one way or another. But I'm concerned that you're going alone. Is there anyone who would go with you?" Scott asked.

"No, not really. Otto and Fritz have to stay to work the shop, Jake is busy and if anything happened to him, Laure and Vera would be in jeopardy. I don't know anyone else who could help." Actually I liked the thought of Scott going along and I think he wanted to. I hoped there might be some way that he could arrange to go with me.

Erwin, who had been quiet so far and I wondered what he was doing here, finally spoke up. "Dan, think of me as a travel and transportation consultant. I've been across the United States several times and I can advise you where the law might be watching, road conditions and lots of other things." I had no idea how he could help except route planning, which I could do pretty well on my own.

But then Scott added "You may know Erwin as Cannon Ball Baker, a competition representative for Indian Motocycle and automobile manufacturers. He also...

I excitedly interrupted Scott. "Cannon Ball Baker! I've read about you, setting records New York to California, Mexico to Canada, all kinds of records. Didn't you drive a

Stutz and then a Cadillac to cross country records? And you drove in the Indy 500."

"Yes I drove a Stutz and later set a better time with a Cadillac 8 from Los Angeles to New York in 7 days, 11 hours and 52 minutes with a reporter riding along. But you may not have heard, in midwinter, I drove a stock Gardner sedan across the United States in 4 days, 14 hours and 15 minutes. And yes, I drove in the 1922 Indianapolis 500 in a Frontenac, starting in 16th position, finished 11th. I've crossed the U.S. several times on Indian motorcycles. I know all the major routes and a lot of the secondary ones. I can help you with advice on where the law hangs out and the best roads. I too would like to go with you but I have competition events that I am contracted to do. I can leave you a schedule where I'll be so you can telegraph me with questions on the road, if that would help."

Just sitting next to a legend, someone who had motored across and up and down the country not once but dozens of times gave me courage and I made the decision right then and there to go. Of course I had already been leaning toward that, but having Cannon Ball Baker's help and advice was the clincher. I began to feel like I could do this. "Thank you Mr. Baker, I would be more than glad for your advice. Scott, I'm going to do it. I still don't know if it is right or wrong but it's the best way out of this mess. Besides, Claire hinted that my mother likes California wine and would appreciate it if I brought her some wine as well."

Scott said "I'll help in every way I can including financial backing. And don't be surprised if Elaine suggests she would like a few bottles too. Since the load is becoming even larger, I will explore other transportation ideas. So let's put our planning into high gear. Erwin has to leave in five days for a competition event so get maps and we will set aside time to plan the best routes."

Erwin said "I can help with maps, I have several sets of good maps and would be pleased to give some to Dan.

Let's get together tomorrow at lunch, I can give you two or three hours every day until I have to go. I want to tell you lots of things besides the best road to take. Depending on when you leave, I might be in the area when you get near San Francisco. I could ride my Indian motorcycle to join you for a day or two, if that would help."

"I'll be glad for every ounce of help you can give me. Thank you sir, this is just what I needed. And thank you Scott. I need to talk to you about business while I'm gone."

"That will be the least of your worries. Claire and Dorothy are already managing the business side of your shop, and from the word I get on the street, your friends Otto and Fritz are well respected as first rate mechanics. Don't forget, Jake will also be available if they need him" Scott replied.

I was filled with energy and decided to stop at Jake's house to tell Laure the good news. She was not happy about me doing this, but I was sure that when I told her about the help I was getting, she would see that this was the best thing to do. Plus, the adventurous side of me was taking over. I wanted to do this road trip.

It was late when I got there and Vera opened the door, calling to Laure to come downstairs. When she came down, she looked unhappy to see me, but I jumped right in and told her, with all my enthusiasm, about meeting Cannon Ball Baker and what a good thing this would be and it would solve a big problem. But by the time I was finished she was crying.

"Well you go then. Do whatever you want, but we are finished. I don't want to be a gangster's wife. I mean, girlfriend. I'm not your girl now or ever. These are the gangsters that pushed your father to his death. How could you work for them? I thought you were hitting on all eight in your brain, a wise head, a smart man, but you're just going to be the fall guy for the thugs who killed your father and they will come up clean as a whistle. Do not come around to see me again. I don't hang around with chumps."

Laure ran up the stairs and I heard her crying. But I felt like I was making the right decision and if Laure didn't agree there was not much I could do about it. I went from excited and confident to depressed and saddened. I turned to leave. Vera took me by the hand and told me she was sorry, that she loved seeing Laure and me together and maybe when I got back things might work out. I said Laure seemed determined and if I knew anything about her, I knew she rarely changed her mind if she thought she was right. As Vera let me out the door I looked at her, a beautiful woman, and could see that when Laure was older this is what she might look like. I damn near changed my mind, but I knew the only chance I had to get the Coniglios out of my life was to go to California and bring back wine.

DUESENBERG MODEL X

The last few days flew by and I hardly had time to think of Laure except first thing in the morning and last thing at night, and most of the day in between. I spent hours with Cannon Ball Baker and he was a wealth of information. I filled a notebook with his observations. At our last meeting he gave me a schedule of where he would be in the event I needed to send him a telegram.

I had my photograph taken with Cannon Ball and he gave me a bundle of new maps marked with potential routes we had discussed. I considered taking the Lincoln Highway but he said at this time of year it still could have bad weather and recommended I take a more southern route through St Louis and pointed out the National Old Trails Association route. I would have to use other roads from Chicago to St. Louis but it was a busy route and the roads would be good. The Old Trails route took me through Missouri, Kansas, Colorado, New Mexico and Arizona and into California farther south than I wanted. Baker told me it was safer but advised me to be armed and watchful. He said in his early cross-country trips he had been chased by Indians on horseback, while he was riding his Indian motorcycle, which gave me a laugh. But it turned out the young Indians just wanted to race the motorcycle and were not out to take his scalp. But still, he told tales of highway robbers and said I needed to always be aware of my surroundings.

I had to see Joey C. too, and he took the news that I was going without much surprise or emotion. I did not tell him Laure had broken up with me, but he sounded like he was bragging when he told me when I returned she would be his girl. The asshole still called her 'that little bit of fluff'. He told me that I was to send him a telegram when I got to California and when I was on my way back. I said I would think about it and he reminded me of what he might do if I failed my mission. I tried to see Gina but she was always out when I called. Nancy was nice to me and said goodbye, she had found a new guy and had forgiven me for taking up with Laure. I didn't tell Nancy that Laure and I were now a thing of the past. I called Suzie and she said she would go with me, but I told her it was too dangerous.

Otto and Fritz had told their father that they might have to spend more time at the shop and he was OK about it. I talked to Scott almost every day. I bought some new clothing, not wanting to look too ragged when I had to go see the winemakers in California. I packed the Kodak Brownie camera and lots of film. My mother gave me Dad's pearl handled M1911 and told me to be careful and have plenty of ammunition. Even Hutfilz got into the act, saying he would pack some road food for me.

Jake told me the Elgin was too old and tired to make the trip and I should buy another car. I told him money was tight. He even offered me the use of his Nash but I told him I would be OK with the Elgin.

A week before my planned start, Scott asked me to do a small job for him before I left, but it wasn't such a small job. He wanted me to go to Indianapolis, pick up a car for him, and drive it back to Long Grove. I would rather not have gone but for Scott I readily accepted.

The next day I drove my Elgin to the McLanahan Ranch and got into Scott's Packard for the ride downtown. He drove me to Chicago to drop me off at Dearborn Station to catch a Monon passenger train to Indianapolis. Scott gave me an envelope with an address on it, told me to go there and give the envelope to whoever was at the front desk. He gave me plenty of expense money. I would spend the night in Indianapolis and drive back to Long Grove the next morning. I figured it was a business or an important person who was sending a car to Scott.

I had a lot of memories when I got to Dearborn Station. This was where we started from on that express train race back in 1919. I arrived at the station early, had a sandwich and waited until the conductor put down the little step stool and called "All Aboard!"

All the way to Indianapolis I relived that day of the race as I sat in the coach and watched the scenery that I had seen from the back seat of the racing Elgin in 1919. Some things had changed but most had not. The train arrived at Indianapolis and I flagged a cab and gave him the address. The cabbie looked at me funny, shrugged his shoulders and pulled out in traffic. We arrived at the address and the cabbie pulled over, but I just sat there in the back seat. It was the Duesenberg factory. Holy cats, was I going to drive a Duesy back home for Scott? No wonder he was tight-lipped about the errand. I paid the cabbie and gave him a tip, then walked into the factory office. There was a woman behind the front desk and I gave her the envelope. She asked me if I would like some coffee or tea and I accepted coffee while she went to give the envelope to its recipient.

I was sitting there flipping through a magazine when in walked August and Frederick Duesenberg. Like any good car guy I recognized them from pictures in the newspapers. They shook hands with me and asked about their good friend Scott and his father Thomas, and I assured them that all was well at the McLanahan Ranch. They even seemed to know Scott was engaged and were even happier when I informed them that he was to marry my sister.

The brothers gave me a personal tour of their clean, organized and impressive factory. The quality that Duesenberg automobiles were known for was much in evidence on the shop floor. I don't think I had ever seen more than two or three Duesenbergs in my life before today, and here I was in the middle of where they were manufactured. The brothers treated me like royalty, even having their secretary call the hotel and upgrading my room at no charge.

I asked questions about their automobiles and they were very proud to answer every question in detail. I was even bold enough to ask if a Duesenberg dealership was open in our area and they told me that Scott had already secured it for me. It was one of the few afternoons that I almost didn't think about Laure. No, that's not true. I did think about Laure and the emptiness in my heart from losing her was almost more than I could bear.

Near the end of the day August and Frederick took me to see Scott's new automobile. My knees weakened when I saw it – a beautiful dark red with gold pinstripes dual cowl phaeton with the most beautiful tan leather interior I had ever seen. It came with steel wheels for durability on the rough roads. A set of chrome wire wheels was being shipped to Scott to be installed when I returned. The brothers Duesenberg told me this automobile was a prototype that they planned to introduce in 1926 and Scott was going to give them reports on the car so they could fix any glitches before they began manufacturing the Model X. The current series was the Model A and I wanted to ask about the letters in between but didn't want the brothers to think I was a wise guy.

The Duesenbergs gave me all the details of this special prototype. The Model X chassis was longer than the Model A and in place of the planned 100 hp straight 8 for the Model X, this automobile had an engine developed from their racing program. It had dual overhead camshafts and four valves per cylinder. The brothers said they had tested it at 119 miles per hour, even getting up to 94 mph in second gear. It was installed in this car for testing purposes. Good thing it also had an advanced hydraulic brake system. It was a beautiful automobile in every way. I signed the documents, received the owner's tools and books and a Duesenberg factory shop manual. I thanked the Duesenbergs sincerely and said my good-byes. When I got to the hotel, the manager came out to meet me and said the car would be parked in the underground garage overnight. Dinner and breakfast were on the house and I was to let him know if I needed anything.

Then I remembered the Duesenberg brothers had said Scott was going to send them reports – that's when I realized Scott was giving me the car to drive west. It still wasn't big enough to carry wine, but I thought it possible that it could pull a trailer.

Next morning I was up early, had a big breakfast and got on the road with the Duesenberg. What an automobile! Powerful and solid, it felt like it was carved from one solid steel billet. The longer wheelbase gave it a smooth, well controlled ride. The brakes were amazing. The huge Straight 8 performed flawlessly. Miles just flew by and I realized I was seriously speeding. I slowed down just in time to pass a patrol car hiding behind a billboard.

When I arrived at the McLanahan Ranch, Scott and his parents came out to see the Duesenberg. Claire was there too. I blabbered for several minutes about how well the Duesenberg brothers treated me and how great their factory was and I could tell even Thomas and Elaine were impressed with the automobile.

"Well Dan, I'm glad you like it because you're driving it west." Scott announced. I had to pretend I had not figured that out. Jake arrived in the Nash with Laure at the wheel. I had been teaching her how to drive and now Jake had taken over her driver training. She was a damn good driver. My depression returned when my eyes took in her beauty, maybe for the very last time. She did not even acknowledge my presence, just turned the Nash around and left, leaving Jake to drive the Duesenberg. *For what?* I wondered. "Jake is going to check it out and make a few carefully selected modifications. He will return the Model X to you Saturday morning. Sorry Dan, but you'll have to make do with the Elgin for a couple more days" Scott said. I didn't mind, knowing that if Jake was inspecting the Duesenberg it was well worth the time.

Saturday morning Jake brought the Duesenberg back. He had added a few things. Jake had installed two driving lights on a headlight bar that turned with the front wheels, and two spotlights, one on each side of the cowl at the base of the windshield, and a second battery. There were spare tires and parts lashed and clipped down everywhere. The tires had been replaced by sturdy looking new tires. Jake made a custom leather holster to fit my 1911, using his twin to my 1911 so it fit perfectly. The holster could be mounted under the seat, next to the seat or under the dashboard, or clipped to my belt. Extra ammunition magazines were within easy reach. I would have a hard time shooting and driving, but it was better than spitting at an adversary.

Joey C. made an appearance to give me two envelopes, one for me and one to give to a contact in California. He held out his hand but I turned around and did not shake it. He spit on the ground and left, wheels spinning. I noticed he had a brand new Stutz Bearcat. The Bearcat was a fine automobile but the design was getting a bit long in the tooth. Still, the little yellow speedster looked spiffy.

Scott told me that the Duesenbergs had called him to ask if I could make a side trip to Indianapolis on the way out. They had just finished a stronger transmission to handle the more powerful engine and decided to install it for the testing of the Model X. Jake said it was an excellent idea and he had been concerned about the big engine with the standard Model A transmission. Scott advised me that if I got to Indianapolis by noon, the Duesenbergs had two of their best technicians ready to swap out the transmission and put me up at the same hotel at their expense, and I would be on the road the next morning. The only other person I told about this detour was Claire. It did not seem important enough to tell anyone else.

Sunday evening came. I was excited for the adventure and confident that I had a good chance. I was depressed because I was leaving and Joey C.'s words stuck in my mind about how Laure would turn to him. I couldn't take thinking about him kissing her and did my best to get it out of my mind. I went over to see my best friends and employees Otto and Fritz and I knew they would have dropped everything if I asked them to join me. As I walked back to my house, the little yellow Stutz Bearcat came tearing by at full speed. Idiot driver, I thought to myself. But then I saw the worst of it - Laure was next to Joey in the car. The Stutz had two bucket seats so she wasn't close to him but it looked like she was laughing. That's all I needed to know. It was definitely over, no hope. My dream of life ever after with my love was gone. I was so devastated that I couldn't even cry. It just hurt. I don't think she saw me but Joey did and he waved a finger at me. I vowed that the next time I saw him I would punch him in the nose.

Claire tried to talk to me that night, not knowing what I had just seen. She said I should go over and talk to Laure before I left, try to reason with her one more time. Don't give up and all that horsefeathers. Claire was more serious than I had ever seen her, but I couldn't take it any longer. "Claire, I just saw Laure. She was laughing and riding with Joey C. in his new Stutz Bearcat. Now why should I go see her? She made her choice. I don't know why Laure would tell me she didn't want to be a gangster's girl and then be with Joey Coniglio. I just don't understand women."

Claire looked shocked at what I told her and she became angry. "Fools! Both of you are fools. You two are crazy in love with each other but you're both stubborn jingle-brained fools. I've tried to help both of you. Go live your lives filled with regret that you couldn't stop being stubborn long enough to see what's real and what's baloney." Claire turned and ran up the stairs crying. My life was falling apart and there was nothing I could do about it. Laure had left me and told me never to come around again, and now she had a new gangster boyfriend to keep me away from her. Well, good luck to her with that.

Next morning I was up early loading and checking the Duesenberg. It was a superior car in handling, power, braking, comfort and it had the strength for rough conditions. Duesenberg was a tough, durable performance automobile with superb engineering and reliability proven at the racetrack. Scott had chosen well.

By seven in the morning everyone was there to see me off, even Joey, and I wondered why he wasn't with his new little bit of fluff. Joey stayed in his automobile and everyone ignored him. He did not look well, in fact he looked like he was in a lot of pain. He probably showed up to make sure I was leaving. I held my temper and didn't punch him in the nose in front of my family and friends. He soon left and a few minutes later Jake's Nash drove up with Laure behind the wheel. Jake had come to make some final checks and adjustments. Out of the corner of my eye I thought Laure, still sitting behind the wheel of the Nash, had turned to look at me. I put a smile on my face and turned to wave, hoping to get a fleeting moment of recognition to give me hope that maybe, just maybe, we could work things out when I returned. But it must have been my imagination. Laure was looking the other way.

Raider enjoyed the attention he was getting and Claire took our photo. I fixed Raider up with a couple of blankets on in the back seat and a dish of water on the floor. When I opened the back door he hopped in and sat on his blankets, looking like he knew all about traveling. His eyes followed me wherever I went. I lost a girlfriend and gained a dog friend. At least the dog was loyal to me.

The Roaring Road beckoned, and I was on it. Go West, Young Man! Horace Greeley supposedly wrote that in 1865 although some claim that was not exactly what he said or meant, but it worked for me. The adventure began on May 18, 1925 as I started down the road to my first stop at the Duesenberg factory in Indianapolis.

IF YOU DON'T DANCE, NO ROMANCE

The main road from Chicago to Indianapolis – not the road that ran next to the railroad that we raced on in 1919 – was in good condition, some of it gravel outside the towns but reasonably smooth with a few areas where the ruts were troublesome. The long chassis of the Duesenberg Model X handled the rough stuff easily. Raider and I established our routine. I would talk, Raider would listen politely and agree with me. I was happy to have his company for the long road ahead, but sometimes my sadness at losing Laure overcame me and tears would reach my eyes. I alternated between being angry that she was willing to throw away our relationship after all the good times we had enjoyed together – then I would turn to sadness because our relationship was over and done. I couldn't put my thoughts of her out of my mind.

I made it to Indianapolis before noon and as promised the Duesenberg factory shop manager took the car in right away and had the new transmission installed by the end of the work day. I decided to spend the night as planned and go on to St. Louis in the morning. It was about 250 miles to St. Louis from Indianapolis with a good portion of the route paved or hard gravel.

The next day on the road was warm and cloudy but no rain threatened. Following Jake's advice I drove slower than usual to break in the new transmission properly. After St. Louis I would step up the pace. Raider and I talked and I knew he felt my sadness, Once when we stopped I put my head in my hands and tears overflowed my eyes. He licked my hands and face, as if he was trying to comfort me. We stopped to share my lunch and I threw a ball for him to get some exercise. With the convertible top down there was no shade for him so I rigged a coat to provide shade at the right rear seat. Both of us felt better when we got back on the road. I liked the new transmission, it shifted with smoothness and precision while the Duesenberg engine and chassis rolled up the miles. This automobile was the caterpillar's spats.

About fifty miles from St. Louis on a long gently rolling stretch of road I heard the sound of an aeroplane engine approaching. I did not see it until the aeroplane flew low over the Duesenberg. No one else was near me on the road so I watched as the pilot waggled the wings, pulled up to gain altitude, then turned on a long arc to come up behind me again. This time the pilot flew to the right of the road and waggled the wings. *Must be some country boy learning to fly.* The pilot climbed again to come around in a big circle, closer this time, about two hundred feet from the automobile.

I pulled over and Raider and I got out to look before he came around again and gave me a propeller haircut. Raider barked at the aeroplane. It was a familiar looking two-seat biplane – then I saw it had S Bar C Ranch markings on the tail. It was Scott's JN-4 aeroplane and I recognized him in the front cockpit, but who was in the back? The pilot usually flew from the rear cockpit. The pilot waved. Raider barked, but this time at me and not the Jenny. Claire was in the back cockpit – flying the aeroplane? She waved again and even under her leather helmet and goggles I recognized her. She took the aeroplane around on another pass, this time coming right over the Duesenberg. About 100 feet ahead of me Scott dropped a small package tied in a piece of yellow cloth. Raider and I ran up the road, he was faster and got to the package first, picked it up and brought it to me. "Good dog. Good dog." I unwrapped the yellow cloth, put it in my pocket and took the plain butcher paper wrapping off the cardboard box. Inside was a small rock to weigh it down and a note:

Dan –
Very important. Be at St. Louis Union Station at 5PM and
wait for special package arriving on the Alton Limited from
Chicago. If you are late, get there as soon as you can and
wait at the station.
Love,
Claire and Scott

It was in Claire's handwriting and they had both signed the note. I waved, then got Raider to sit while I held a front paw up and waved it. The plane made one more pass, Claire blowing kisses to me and Scott waving.

Claire was a pilot? I didn't even know she was taking lessons. Now what was this all about? Did I forget something? Wait for a special package? Well, I would find out soon enough. I looked at my map and located Union Station in St. Louis. Damn, I would have to drive in city traffic, but I was curious and the note said it was important. The little aeroplane flew away in the general direction of Chicago. "Well, Raider, I guess we're going to meet the Alton Limited." He wagged his tail in agreement. The Chicago & Alton was one of several railroads with a Chicago – St. Louis route and the Alton Limited was the fastest daily passenger train. I must have forgotten something, but I could not come up with any idea of what it might be. I wondered why Scott and Claire did not drop it to me, then realized it might be an automobile part and they would not want it to get damaged.

We arrived at St. Louis Union Station just before 4:30. I took Raider for a walk, picked up a newspaper and sat on a bench near the station platform to read and wait. The Alton Limited was only three minutes late. I put a leash on Raider because I did not know if he would be spooked by a noisy, steam-hissing locomotive. Turns out he wasn't, he sat next to me and watched like he was interested in what this was all about. The Alton Limited took only 6-1/2 hours from Chicago to St. Louis and it was a beautiful train, pulled by a Pacific 4-6-2 locomotive and tender followed by a post office railcar, then four coaches and a dining car, all painted a deep red with black roofs and trimmed with gold lettering and pinstripes.

The conductor stepped down, set out the little step stool and people began to disembark. I did not know what to look for, so I went towards the conductor to ask if he knew about a special package. I watched several people get off and then my brain froze. Cold. Icy cold. Frozen. Paralyzed frozen. There, just 20 feet from me, Joey C. was getting off the train. Raider began to growl. How did Raider know to growl at Joey? Must be a dog's natural sense of good and evil. I got angry. No, I was enraged. I wasted time to wait for this mug? What the hell did he want? To travel with me? To gloat that my girl was now his? Whatever it was could not be good. I decided to send a nasty telegram to Claire about this. How could she do this to me? Had Joey threatened her to force her to deliver the message?

Joey C. turned to face the passenger car as a woman's gloved hand came out from the entryway. Joey took the hand and the woman came down the steps. My brain unfroze and I saw red. Deep red. Blood boiling red. This was too much – Laure and Joey C. coming to St. Louis and making me wait for them. Why? Were they going to announce their wedding? I heard Raider growl again but I had only one thing on my mind, just one damn thing. I was focused. I was enraged. I knew exactly what I had to do. With Raider at my side I pushed through the crowd to Joey C. and before he knew I was there I put my hand on his shoulder, spun him around and punched my fist into his fat face as hard as I could. I quickly hit him again, square on his nose and blood spurted. Raider growled, wanting his chance. Joey, obviously afraid of the large angry German Shepherd Dog tried to turn away but tripped over the conductor's step stool and spun around backwards, falling on his ass. Raider moved quickly to stand guard and Joey wisely did not move a muscle when a full set of big canine teeth were bared, saliva dripping, a deep growl coming from the large dog.

Laure held her gloved hand to her mouth. I wanted more blood. Someone tried to get in front of me and I roughly pushed the person aside to get at Joey, who looked terrified of the growling big dog. I decided to get Raider a steak bone tonight for his reward. Hell, I'll get him a big juicy steak. I set myself and aimed my right foot to kick Joey C. hard in the ribs. He tried to roll. The conductor yelled for me to stop. Laure began to laugh. Gina stepped in front of me and put her hand on my chest saying "Don't kill him Danny, or I will not have an escort back to Chicago. I will have to go with you two to California." Gina? Where the hell did Gina come from? Who were the two people going to California? I did not see Gina get off the train but that was the only possible explanation. Then I realized it was her that I had shoved to get to Joey.

Gina? Laure? Joey C.? Who else will show up? Santa Claus? The conductor was shouting for the police. I asked "Will someone please tell me what the hell is going on here? Where's the special package I came to pick up? What are you three doing here?"

Gina was talking to the conductor as two cops ran toward us. Why was Laure laughing? Gina turned to me. Not caring about the consequences, I wanted to beat Joey to a pulp.

"Calma Danny. Stop! Non più scontri! No more fighting. OK? Calma now, listen to me. Are you listening? Do you hear me what I am saying?" Her Italian accent seemed more pronounced than usual. Everything crazy, people crowding around to watch, the cops talking to the conductor. They were trying to decide if we were inmates from an asylum or gangsters trying to kill each other. Laure was laughing, but she smiled at me. For a moment I was completely unmanned by her beautiful smile.

Gina shouted "Danny, stop, listen. Listen to me! Joey and I bring Laure to you. It is not safe for a woman to travel long distances alone. There are bad people who take advantage. No one else knows Laure comes here to you. Joey said he would accompany her as guard but Laure said she did not like that. So I come along to chaperone and I need Joey in one piece so he can escort me back to Chicago. Capisce?"

"I capisce what you're saying Gina, why are you going to California with me? Why is Laure here with Joey?"

"You must ask that of Laure" Gina said with a sly smile.

Laure turned to me. "Daniel Lindner! I came here to be with you. WITH YOU! If you do not want me I'll go back to Chicago with Joey and Gina. They came as travel guardians because I could not ask anyone else. Listen to me, Dan, listen real good. I - WANT - TO - BE - WITH - YOU" she said each word with emphasis. "I'm sorry for breaking up with you and if you'll take me back, I'm going with you to California!" Then she laughed, using a silly imitation of Gina's Italian accent "Capisce?"

The crowd around us was listening, laughing, talking all at once and confusion reigned supreme. The conductor did not know what to do and the cops were beginning to laugh. I was speechless. *Laure, here to go to California with me? After breaking up with me because I was going to California?* "But what will Jake say when he finds out?"

"I am over 21 years of age and I left my family a letter. They will have to understand. After you left, things happened. I talked with Claire and made my decision to catch up with you, and you do not appreciate all the trouble I have gone through to get here!" Laure turned around and motioned for the conductor and told him to have a porter put her luggage in the station until the next train to Chicago arrived, then stormed over to the train station. Gina and the cops were trying to help Joey C. get up but he seemed wobbly and unable to stand straight. I moved into position to hit him again, cops or no cops, just for being next to Laure and touching her gloved hand.

Joey was holding a bloody handkerchief to his nose. "Hold on Danny. There was a misunderstanding and Laure came over and got an audience with the Don. I don't know how because nobody gets to see the Don without an appointment. Gina came in with her and the two of them ganged up on the old man. Afterward he seemed angrier than I had ever seen him before. He called me in and told me in no uncertain terms to get her to you today, to not ask questions and to not touch her. No excuses. I knew you would be angry and I should have expected you to take a poke at me. Look, I'll forget about it just this once, there will be no retribution. If Laure wants to go with you, then good luck to both of you, she's a mean bitch." Joey C. turned around unsteadily, told the coppers who he was and that he would not press charges, then walked with a pronounced limp to the station to clean up. His nose was broken and it looked like he was going to have two black eyes. Good. I would do it again, with pleasure. I thought of running after him and hitting him again.

Gina turned to me. "That's what happened. It is the truth. So believe it or not Danny, we did this for you. Laure came over, like Joey says, and after I heard what she say I join her to demand that the Don guarantee her safety to get to you. Your sister Claire offered to deliver a message to come to this station. That is all there is to it. The Coniglio family wants the wine and you get Laure. Looks like a good deal for both of you. Capisce? Are you on the trolley now?"

Gina is one of the smartest and toughest people I have ever known. The Don thought of Gina as the daughter he always wanted so he indulges her. Gina is about 5'1" but she makes mob hit men cower in fear because she sounds tough and she has the Don's backing. I guess I should be glad I'm not marrying her – even though she is cute and sexy as all get out, and a hot pleasure in bed.

Raider seemed just as confused as I was. He seemed to want to bite Joey as much as I wanted to punch him again. My mind slowly began to grasp what Laure and Gina told me. I ran to the station with Raider right behind me to stop Laure from buying a ticket to Chicago.

The station's waiting room was half-full of travelers, but to me they didn't exist when I found Laure in line to purchase a ticket. "Laure – Laure, wait! I didn't understand. I saw you riding in Joey C.'s Stutz and you were laughing. I thought he had won you over and decided the next time I saw him I would punch him in the nose. Well, that's just what I did and dammit I'm glad I did it, even though my hand hurts like hell. I had no idea you were on your way here. Claire dropped a note wrapped in this" I pulled out the yellow cloth and it dawned on me it was Laure's scarf that I had seen her wear – Claire had wrapped the note in Laure's scarf as a hint that Laure was the special package. Hindsight now struck me speechless.

We put our arms around each other, holding each other tight as people started to cheer. Some of them figured it was a boy-gets-girl-back story and looked around to see if a movie camera was filming the scene.

"I am never leaving you again, Daniel Lindner. I'm yours if you'll have me. And I want to go to California with you and Raider, because he's a real cute guy" she smiled at her joke. Raider protectively watched us with that quizzical look on his face. "So what do you say big guy? Do you want to keep me or dump me in St. Louis?"

"I'll take her off your hands if you don't want her" a man's voice shouted and everyone laughed.

"No thank you, I'm keeping her. She's the love of my life." The crowd cheered and applauded and we kissed, then went to find a porter to put Laure's luggage on his cart and take it to the Duesenberg.

This was an amazing turn of events, but I still wanted to go back to the station and apologize to Joey for sucker-punching him, then sucker punch him again, but Laure talked me out of it.

"How about some dinner?" I suggested. "All this punching of noses and capisce-ing makes me hungry."

"Yes, a celebration dinner and a nice hotel for tonight. I know you plan on camping and I brought clothes and things for that but tonight I want to clean up from the train trip and celebrate being together with you. I missed you so much. I brought a couple of my dancing dresses and don't deny it Dan, I know you like them." I nodded my agreement. Oh yes, Laure as a flapper with her gorgeous body and long legs definitely caused a reaction in me. "So let's find a good hotel that accepts dogs and Duesenbergs. Then we will dine, drink and dance. You do dance, don't you?"

"I danced with you that night at The Green Mill. I just didn't know the Charleston. But I am tired from driving all day and my hand hurts from punching Joey. Maybe we can just have dinner and watch the other dancers tonight."

"Why, do you do handstands when you dance?"

"No, to hold you when we dance and my hand..."

"And it would hurt to put your arm around me with your hand on my back?" I saw the look in her eye and knew that she was leading up to something. Laure had a sharp wit and loved to use it.

"No, that shouldn't hurt too much, I guess."

"Well, then you should remember how the song goes" said Laure with her beautiful smile that signaled I had been disarmed and she was closing in for the win. There was nothing to do now but play along.

"No, I don't know. What does the song say?"

"If you don't dance, no romance." She looked me in the eyes. "If you won't dance, that means that your hand hurts so much you will be unable to hold me, touch me and make love to me tonight. Capisce?"

Well this was a fine kettle of fish I had gotten myself into. The thought of Laure naked in bed with me swept through my body like a raging fire. "There's really a song that says that?"

"Yes, there is. You can have a nice quiet evening and watch me dance with someone else and sleep alone on the couch, or you can dance with me and then we will have a special private dance in the hotel room. I told you I am an all-or-nothing kind of girl and I would attack you when I was ready. Now I am ready. The choice is yours."

"You really mean that? It's not gonna be like how it was that night in Chicago after The Green Mill?"

"Why would I come all the way to St. Louis to ask you to take me back and travel with you and live like a nun to California and back? That sounds really boring."

"Hey, I'm the happiest guy in the world, but this is an unexpected change from last time we talked and I'm trying to understand. What happened for you to change your mind?"

"I'm not going to explain everything now, it would take too long. Tonight I want to drink Champagne, dance and then I want you to make passionate love to me. Tomorrow on the road we will talk" she said.

"OK. I'm on the trolley. Let's have fun tonight."

"And to make it even better, I know where we can dance and have real drinks too."

"Lead the way Laure. But how do you know where to go in St. Louis for dancing and booze?"

"Easy squeezy. It may be Prohibition but I know where to find the best speakeasy in St. Louis." Laure put her arm in mine and we went for a walk. Raider ranged a few yards ahead of us, ready to protect us from trouble or squirrels, whichever came first. Like I said, Raider is a very intelligent dog. He knows to never question a woman who is offering something very special. Dogs capisce.

CAFÉ LULU SPEAKEASY

We drove to a new hotel that allowed us to have Raider in the room. The desk clerk looked at us strangely but Laure smiled at him and I signed the register. Many hotels did not allow unmarried couples to stay in the same room but some big city hotels and the fleabag flophouses winked at it. We weren't in a fleabag flophouse and the bellboy loaded our bags on his cart, took Raider's leash and led us to our room. It was a very nice corner room.

We cleaned up and dressed for dinner and dancing. Laure came out with a black flapper dress that combined elegance and sexiness with gold threads interweaved that sparkled in the light. The hem was above her knees and rolled stockings allowed glimpses of her sexy legs. Her blond bobbed hair was accented with a black headband featuring gold threads and a black feather edged in gold. I smiled at the thought that her attire might scandalize some of the old people in the restaurant.

The picture of Laure and her sexy modern dress, her curves, long legs and big beautiful smile lit up the room. "You're so beautiful" I said as she came over and we wrapped our arms around each other. She kissed me and told me I looked very handsome as she straightened my tie. I wore a dark blue suit, white shirt and a striped tie. After taking Raider for a walk and feeding him I made arrangements with the bellboy to check on him and take him for a walk later since Raider liked the bellboy. We left the hotel and walked to the restaurant that the hotel concierge recommended. It was delicious and we were hungry. At first it seemed too reserved a place for alcohol but I noticed other patrons discreetly sipping from flasks so I brought mine out. We finished it off with dinner.

After dinner, we walked to the Duesenberg and I drove to the speakeasy following Laure's directions. We arrived in front of a small cafe that appeared to be closed. The words *Café Lulu* were painted in script on the front windows. It looked like a place to get pancakes for breakfast or soup and a sandwich for lunch. After the Duesenberg was parked, I followed Laure down a narrow walkway to a side door where she knocked on the door in an odd fast/slow combination. A small window in the door slid open and a pair of eyes scanned us. The window slid shut, the deadbolt was drawn and the door opened, closed and bolted immediately once we were inside. The doorman had a big revolver on his hip but said not a word as he motioned for us to follow a narrow hallway. At the end was a room with a large and scary looking guy standing there. He was a huge cat, tall with big hairy arms crossed in front of his barrel chest. His shoulders looked wider than the door and he had a scowl on his face. Like the doorman, this guy didn't say anything but it was obvious that something had to happen or we were not going to get past him.

Laure stood there looking at the guy for a minute. It got real quiet in the room. He looked like he was going to pick us up by the scruff of our necks and throw us out, and I had no doubt he was capable of doing that. Laure opened her small nightclub handbag and took out a photograph. She stepped up to the big man and held it out to him. He did not look at it but he was watching Laure with a curious look on his face. "Uncle Viktor" Laure said softly, then stood on her toes and kissed him on the cheek. He did not move, but he now looked at her with greater interest. He took the photo from her, inspected it carefully, looked at her, then looked at the photo again.

"You must be Laure" he growled in a deep rumbly voice. "I haven't seen you since you were a little girl. You've grown up to be a beautiful woman. Jake and Anna must be very proud of you."

"It's Jake and Vera, Uncle Viktor." It had been a test, to make sure she really was his niece. Laure stood on her toes again and threw her arms around him as best she could because his shoulders were so wide. He did not move for a moment but then put his arms gently around her. Another person came into the room, a young sheba who did not seem happy that Laure was hugging the big guy. She looked like a college girl and wore an exquisite flapper dress.

Now that I knew Viktor was her uncle, his resemblance to Jake became clear. It had been hard to see it at first because of his scars and grim countenance. A small smile crossed his face. "Evelyn, come over here and meet my niece Laure-Marie from Chicago." Evelyn seemed happier now. Was this young girl Viktor's girlfriend? An unlikely combination, but Viktor did have a powerful presence that filled the room.

Laure said "I remember you Uncle Viktor, and my father talks about you often. He told me that you were living in St. Louis and had some association with an establishment named Café Lulu. So I asked around when Dan and I were coming to St. Louis because I wanted to see you, and we would like to have cocktails and dance."

"Yes." Viktor was a man of few words. "Evelyn, please seat them a table near the dance floor. And you are Dan?"

Viktor held out his hand and we shook hands. Or rather my hand, already hurt from punching Joey C. in the nose, was crushed in his huge paw. I thought he knew I was going to use that hand to intimately touch his niece and he meant to disable it. "Yes, I am Dan Lindner, Uncle Viktor. I am very pleased to meet you." Viktor gave me a small smile.

"Did you arrive by car?" Viktor asked.

"Yes sir, a red Duesenberg."

Viktor pressed a button and a young guy came into the room. Viktor told him to add the red Duesenberg to the list for the outside guys to keep an eye on. I remembered there were a half dozen luxury automobiles out front when we arrived. Viktor reached into a vest pocket and pulled out two small black four-leaf clover cloisonné pins outlined in gold and gave one to each of us. "Put these somewhere discreetly on your clothing, like in the inside pocket of suit coat" he told me. "Laure, you can fasten it inside your handbag. These will get you into Café Lulu if I'm not on duty. Do not tell anyone where you got them or what they are." I nodded my acknowledgement. He turned to Laure. "If it is slow later I will come to your table and visit." He motioned for Evelyn to take us through the next door. Laure gave her Uncle Viktor another hug and he responded with a slightly bigger version of his little smile. The big guy didn't show much emotion but when he let his guard down, it wasn't too hard to figure out that he was pleased Laure had come to see him.

Evelyn took us down a stairway and through another hall to a room that was much larger than the cafe upstairs. There was a bar and a five piece band supplied the music from a small stage. Evelyn sat us at a table next to the dance floor and a young kitten came over to take our drink order. The lighting was low and people filled the room around the cocktail tables. Laure showed me the photo. It was of her as a little girl, with Jake and Vera and a handsome and carefree young Viktor in his Army uniform.

With the supply of good booze diminished because of Prohibition, there were more and more stories of people being poisoned by bad hooch. I whispered to Laure "Do you know if the whiskey here is safe?"

She nodded yes, she had been told by a reliable source that they used good Canadian whiskey so I ordered a Manhattan and Laure ordered a vodka martini. Our drinks while I was wondering if this was a dream that Laure had left her family to take this nutty adventure with me. We looked into each other's eyes, clicked our glasses. Laure smiled and said "Na zdrowie" which came out sounding like "nah zdroh-vee-eh." She said it was a Polish toast 'to health'. I liked that.

The whiskey was indeed good and Laure said the martini was perfect. The band switched into a dance number and I asked Laure for the dance. We went out to the dance floor. We had only danced a few times since that night many months ago at The Green Mill, but we took up right where we left off and soon we were gliding around the floor. I had already forgotten that my hand hurt as I felt her body moving close to mine.

The night went by with one fabulous scene after another as we drank and danced. Laure got me out on the floor for a Charleston. She had to show me some moves again but I did it. We danced waltzes, quicksteps, foxtrots and jives. I was dazzled by her sweet, lovely smile as we danced. She enjoyed every second of every dance, which in turn made me happy. Off the floor, we met some of the other people when Evelyn took us around for introductions. One was a tall, lean cowboy-looking fellow named Bill, who vaguely said he was in distribution, which could mean any number of things.

Viktor came to our table later and hugged Laure. I asked him about Bill and he told us that he was a guest passing through St. Louis, just like us. Laure filled him in on how Jake and Vera were doing and that they had moved to Long Grove Illinois. She told him that Jake was repairing aeroplanes and was going to learning how to fly them. "Yeah, that's Jake. He was always a good hand with a wrench. I'm not surprised he would be attracted to aeroplanes, he loved to fly kites real high when we were young. I'm glad they are doing well. Your mother is a sweetheart. I would have stolen her away from Jake but the two of them were already tightly wrapped up with each other. So what are you two doing in St. Louis?" Laure told him, giving him an abbreviated but complete enough account of our mission. He said "I don't know the name Coniglio, but there are many outfits competing for business these days. What family are they aligned with?" I said to my knowledge they were aligned with the Chicago South Side Outfit.

Viktor gave Laure a piece of paper with a telephone number on it and told her to call and leave a message if she needed anything in St. Louis and he would get the message and handle it. Then little but oh-so-cute Evelyn arrived and pulled Viktor up on the dance floor. It was amusing to see little Evelyn taking Viktor by the arm and pulling him up as if he were no bigger than she was. Viktor was a good dancer, graceful for his size. Viktor and Evelyn were an odd combination, Evelyn so small and cute and Viktor so big and menacing but cuddly when Evelyn was nearby. Evelyn was full of fun and laughter and Viktor somber and stoic, but there was an electric undercurrent between them that led me to believe they liked to have fun. I liked them both.

A lovely young lady stopped at our table to introduce herself as Maybelle Manx, owner of Café Lulu. Maybelle was curious about Viktor's niece Laure from Chicago. Maybelle asked how things were up in Chicago these days, and gave us some advice about the blind pigs of St. Louis and Kansas City, telling us what to watch out for so that we could avoid those that were dangerous. Maybelle told us that in honor of our first visit to Café Lulu and being related to Viktor, our drinks were on the house. We thanked her and told her we would probably be back in a month or so when we returned from out west. She asked where we were going and Laure told her. She hesitated but asked if we might be able to bring a couple dozen bottles of California wine and she would pay cash on arrival. Laure said yes. I thought we were already going to have trouble with all the wine orders we were getting but being in a good mood I agreed. My mind was fixated on what was going to happen in our hotel room soon.

Visiting with the band during their break, I complimented their musicianship and song selections and put a fiver in the tip hat. After that, Laure and I danced until midnight when we decided to go back to the hotel. We made our goodbyes to our new friends at Café Lulu. We had a great time there and I looked forward to our return visit. On the way out we chatted with Bill for a minute. Bill seemed to know what we were up to and casually mentioned he would be in the San Francisco area next month and gave us a San Francisco telephone number with no explanation why we should call it.

I gave a buck to the boy watching the Duesenberg, opened the car door for Laure and was rewarded with a flash of her shapely leg. It was all I could do to drive at a reasonable speed to the hotel. I took Raider out for a quick walk and when I returned the covers on the bed were turned back and Laure was watching me, wearing nothing but her sexy smile. Raider's blanket and water dish were in a corner and he went over to it and went to sleep.

I took off my suit, hung it in the closet and got in bed. I asked her if she was really Laure or someone pretending to be Laure. She took my hand and placed it on her breast and asked "Do you remember this?" I had to fondle it and pretend to search my memory until she laughed and pulled me to her. I moved my hand to her leg and pushed her on her back for better access to her body. She let out a sigh and said "Dan, I want you to know that I'm not a virgin. I was engaged to be married and thought I would not need to worry about virginity. My fiancé died in a train wreck three months before we were to be married." I looked in her eyes and kissed her. She continued "I brought sheaths that I want you to use. I know it's not as much fun for you, nor is it for me, but I don't want to become pregnant, so please?"

"I'm sure you know I'm not a virgin either, so let's not have that get in our way, and it will feel better if you will do the honors of installing one of those at the appropriate time." Without another word, Laure and I pulled each other close as our lips and tongues and fingers began the dance of new lovers touching and tasting, seeking discovery of every part of each other's body. We played with each other and when we were ready, she put a sheath on me and stroked it down firmly, driving me wild. We closed together and I slowly entered her for the first time.

When our bodies were fully engaged it felt as though we were custom made for each other.

"Please be gentle with me" she asked. As we made love our passions took over and I finished faster, harder and less than gentle and apologized.

"Don't be a goose. I would have told you if I was uncomfortable. I like being taken passionately, but I didn't know if I could handle you. It has been a long time for me. Let's have a glass of Champagne and do it again if you're up for it." Maybelle had presented us with a bottle of French Champagne and I had the night porter bring up a bucket of ice and two flutes when we got back to our hotel room. We talked and I did not feel tired after the long day of surprises. Finishing our second glass of Champagne, all Laure had to do to arouse me was kiss my dick and it jumped to attention. We took our time as we engaged in the preliminaries, exploring and enjoying every little touch, every movement and every wave of passion. After an extended foreplay session Laure installed a new sheath on me and this time we made long, smooth and delicious love. "Oh Laure – Laure – Laure" I gasped during our ecstasy as we climaxed together. As we fell asleep, on the other side of the room Raider looked up for a moment, saw everything was copacetic and went back to sleep.

I woke up to a knock at the door. Laure was up and had ordered room service coffee and food. I dressed quickly, took Raider out for a relief break and we had breakfast together. "You said something about Raider deserving a steak bone last night, so I asked the waiter at the restaurant to wrap one up and send it over to the hotel. I left instructions with the night clerk to put it in the cooler overnight, and to warm it and send it up with our breakfast." Laure took the cover off a dish with a nice juicy bone on it. If Raider had any doubts about Laure, he lost them all and forever with the receipt of the savory smelling steak bone with a lot of meat still on it. He took it over to his blanket to work on it, watching us carefully to make sure we were not hiding another one somewhere.

After breakfast Laure took me by the hand and led me back to the bed, pushed me down on my back with surprising strength and climbed on top.

"I like to make love in the morning. Do you?" Laure asked. There was no need for a response, my answer was standing up in front of her.

JOEY GETS A KICK OUT OF LAURE

After breakfast we packed and called for a bellboy to bring down our baggage. Laure came out of the bathroom and I let loose with a low wolf whistle. She was wearing brown riding pants and leather boots that showed off her long legs and cute rear end, with a light tan shirt I recognized as one of mine. Over it she wore a short jacket. "I decided this would be comfortable on the road so I borrowed the pants and jacket from Cindy and the shirt from you. You should get used to me wearing your shirts. They smell like you and feel good, although not as good as you make me feel" she said with a sexy smile.

"Please turn around so I can see how you look from every angle."

Laure turned around slowly in front of me. "We must be officially in lust now" she said.

"Well then, I'll just have to do my best to uphold my side of things" and I went to grab her but just then the bellboy arrived to load our bags onto a cart. It was the same bellboy as yesterday and Raider seemed happy to see him as he clipped a leash to the dog's collar. We exited the room and got on the elevator. When we arrived in the lobby I noticed the bellboy had Raider riding on the cart and they both seemed to think it was funny. Most hotel people liked Raider and we never had any problem getting someone to walk him or check on him if we went out for an evening.

The clerk sent for the Duesenberg to be brought to the front door and we waited for it to arrive. A heavyset man and woman walked into the hotel on their way to the coffee shop. The woman saw Laure and turned to the man saying "Oh my goodness. I've never seen such a girlish looking boy. These moderns are ruining the moral fiber of our young people."

I could not resist giving this intolerant woman a lesson. I took off my flat driving cap, held it in my hands in front of me and said as if I were in an English drama "Dear madam, I give you greetings of the day. I feel that I should clear up a slight misunderstanding. Last night, and again this morning, after a thorough and complete physical examination and exhaustive testing of this young lady, I can vouch for the fact that every one of her body parts are of the highest quality gen-u-wine female variety." Out of the corner of my eye I saw the men sitting in the lobby had picked up newspapers and were holding them in front of their faces with just their eyes showing above the paper. The hotel clerk at the front desk turned away and pretended to be busy putting mail in the cubbyholes behind the desk. The hotel concierge picked up the candlestick telephone and pretended to be talking into it. I knew he was faking it when I saw his finger holding down the hook. A waitress at the podium in front of the coffee shop was having a difficult time controlling an attack of the giggles. I glanced at the bellboy and his face was as red as his bellboy jacket. A fat old man wearing a tall hat walked by and smiled.

Laure smiled sweetly at the older woman who appeared to be swooning into a faint. The large man caught her and held her upright since she had not completely passed out. He was chuckling and then started guffawing quite loudly.

I looked the large woman in the eye and added "Thank you ma'am, for allowing me to correct any misperception you may have had about this fine young lady." I put my cap on and noticed that the Duesenberg awaited us. I turned to Laure and asked "Miss Laure, may I escort you to the motorcar?"

Laure flashed her brightest smile, batted her eyes at me and put out her hand for me to take. "Why yes, young man, you are a most kind and chivalrous gentleman to clear up my reputation. Please show me to your fine automobile." We turned and walked out the door, our backs straight and our heads held high, although I noticed Laure sashaying her feminine walk with some extra wiggle. It was a good thing we heard the room break out in laughter behind us as we went out, because we could not hold off our own laughter any longer.

The car valet and our bellboy loaded the Duesenberg and we were ready to go. As I put the transmission in gear the concierge came running out the hotel's front door, waving to us. *Oh oh*, I thought, *we are in trouble*. My little show in the lobby must have displeased the hotel staff and we would be informed that we were not welcome there ever again. But the concierge just grinned and gave me an envelope. I opened it and he waited in the event a reply was required. It was handwritten in a large scrawling style on hotel stationery. I held it so Laure and I could read it together:

> *Dear Mr. and Mrs. Lindner,*
> *I hope you enjoyed your stay at The Mayfair and that you will return soon. Please give this letter to the desk clerk on duty when you check in on your next visit. It is good for two free nights in one of our top floor suites as a token of our appreciation for making our day more pleasant and interesting.*
> *Your Humble Servant,*
> *Ambrose P. Wolfinger, General Manager*
> *The Mayfair Hotel, St. Louis Missouri*

Well now, they thought – or maybe wanted to believe – that we are Mr. and Mrs. Lindner. I thanked the concierge as I gave him a tip and told him "Please tell Mr. Wolfinger that all the hotel staff provided superb service. We will be pleased to stay at The Mayfair upon our return from our western vacation." He smiled and assured me he would pass my compliments on to Mr. Wolfinger.

We finally got under way, Laure and I laughing as we recounted our morning. Her laughing would start me laughing again. Finally, she put her face in her hands and said "Oh it's time for a new one." I asked her what kind of new one she meant. She said it was time for a new boyfriend but her smile told me she was joking. At least I hoped so.

"Why Miss Laure" I said "you haven't fully trained your current boyfriend yet. Whatever do you mean by that comment?"

"Dan, you keep me laughing, and if you stop doing that, then I will know it is time to find a new boyfriend." She moved over on the seat until she was snuggled close. "I hope you know that I am teasing." Laure reached behind my shoulder and gently massaged my shoulder and neck and played with my hair. It was a very pleasant sensation and it began a routine we used on our road trips. When she drove I would do the same for her. The day was bright and getting warmer. Later, when Laure was driving, I gave her a hand to help her out of her coat and was careless with my hands. She told me to save it for later when we could better enjoy it. I replied "Oh, that's OK, I'm enjoying it pretty good right now." We were on the road west and Laure had a big smile as she set the Duesenberg to work eating up the miles. It was a marvelous motorcar, the engine required hardly any oil, the chassis tight, the bodywork dusty from the road but still flawless, the driver beautiful. There had not been a flat tire yet, and although these tires were a harsher riding, Jake had done us a big favor by installing the tougher tires.

When I took over the driving again, I decided to ask. "I am curious as to what happened to change your mind about me and going on this mission. You don't often change your mind unless something significant happens." My curiosity was overwhelming.

"I cried every day over my decision to break up with you, but I was stubborn and determined – in your sister Claire's words – not to have a mobster boyfriend again. When I drove my Pa over to the ranch on the morning of your departure, I didn't want to see you, but couldn't stop myself from looking in your direction. I was immediately overcome with a dreadful sadness that I was wrong, very wrong. When you drove off, about a minute later I wanted to catch up to you. I didn't know what I would say, I just wanted to tell you that I love you. I didn't even wait for my father, I just drove off as fast as I could. For a couple miles I could see you ahead, but you were driving faster than I could in the Nash, and soon you were out of sight. When I got back to the ranch, I started to explain to my Pa, but he just took my hand and said 'You don't have to explain, Laure. I understand'."

It took her a minute before she began talking again. "When we get home I'm sure Joey will have spread nasty rumors so I want to tell you the true story. I decided to try to save our relationship and after consideration I called Gina and said I wanted to talk to Joey. I was naïve and had it in my mind that I could talk him out of making you go to California. Gina tried to talk me out of talking to Joey but I was insistent. Joey called back minutes later and asked me out to dinner. I accepted, in spite of what he did when he and his thugs stopped us, thinking he would listen to reason, but I was horribly wrong."

"How did he convince you of that?" I asked.

"I only wanted to talk to Joey, that's all, trust me on that. But Joey thought I was sending a message that I was interested in him. I was not and am not in any way interested in him. He is revolting. Joey picked me up in a yellow Stutz Bearcat. He drove like a madman, as if that would impress me but it had the opposite effect and I began to fear for my life. Claire told me you saw us and thought I was laughing but I was screaming for him to slow down. He did not take me to dinner; he drove to the lake and said we could talk there. I told him we could talk over dinner in a restaurant but he ignored me. He told me to get out of the car and we would take a little walk. He took out a blanket and a bag with two sandwiches and a flask. I guess that's his idea of taking a girl out to dinner, or he thought I had the hots for him and did not want to waste money on me."

"He led me to secluded area and I began to worry. He spread the blanket out and told me to sit next to him and have a sandwich. He took a drink from his flask and offered it to me but I did not want to drink where his lips had been nor did I want a stale sandwich, nor did I want to sit next to him. On the ground I would be helpless; at least standing I had a chance to evade him. He just stood there and laughed, saying how I asked for dinner but it was obvious that I just wanted him. He was already a little sozzled. He grabbed me and tried to kiss me. His hands were all over me. I did everything I could to stop him but he was fast. I had been naïve but realized what a terrible mistake I made. Please don't be angry."

"No Laure, I am upset but not at you. Now I want to punch Joey again, and kick him like I wanted to kick him before Gina stopped me." I was upset with her for not being aware of what Joey C. was like after our confrontation with him and his thugs. But telling her that after she had taken the big step to come to me would be useless and confrontational. She had already learned her lesson the hard way.

"I kept telling him no but he had a tight grip on my arm and I couldn't get loose. He said that he knew what I wanted. He tried to put his weight on me to get me down on the blanket. I knew if he got his weight on top of me I would have no chance to fight him off and he would rape me, so I said something that you may not want to hear. He will claim I meant it, and my resistance was just teasing. I decided to act like I was going along with him and suggested that I might give in if he would not be so rough. I hoped by doing that I could escape and run to the other cars." Laure paused, and I knew this was tough for her to talk about.

"Don't be afraid to tell me what that jerk did to you. If I get mad it will be at him, not you" I told her. She took a couple minutes to regain her composure. I kept quiet. Laure would continue when she was ready.

"Oh Dan, I was acting, but I am ashamed to admit that I told him I would take him in my mouth if he would stop grabbing me. He had already torn the front of my dress. That surprised him but he looked at me and wanted to believe me. He let go of me, loosened his belt and let his trousers fall. He wasn't wearing underwear. He held his penis and told me to kneel in front of him." Laure put her face in her hands in shame.

"I did not kneel but I moved closer to make him think I would be easy and he let his guard down. He started to stroke his penis, saying I should feel privileged to pleasure him because so many women wanted him."

"I acted as if I was hesitating so I could get my footing just right. Joey told me to suck it and tried to push my head down, so he wasn't ready for what I did next. I slapped his arm aside, took a step and with that momentum and all my strength I kicked between his legs as hard as I could. I mean really hard, my father taught me how, and I felt his balls squish. It made me feel sick. He face showed surprise, then anger, then pain. He screamed and held his crotch, dripped to the ground and rolled into a fetal position. You can imagine the names he called me and you would be right, and then he threatened to beat me. If the whole thing hadn't been so awful I might have laughed but he was enraged and his threats scared me."

The thought of her kicking his balls made me want to laugh too, but I held it back. "What did he do then?"

"His body was shaking as he whimpered. I ran toward the cars parked nearby, calling for help. All three cars started up and drove away. I started to panic. I thought Joey might not be able to rape me now, but if he recovered enough to get hold of me he would beat me. I didn't know what to do so I ran back up the road toward the highway."

"Joey recovered enough to crawl to his car and he started driving up the road. I could not outrun his car so I went into the trees to hide. Joey drove back and forth but he did not see me hiding in the trees. He must have been in too much pain to get out and search for me. He stopped the car several times and shouted threats at the trees on both sides of the road that he was going to find me and kill me. He finally drove off. I waited in the trees not knowing if I should run or hide."

"I began cautiously walking up the road again until I heard an automobile coming. I went back into the trees but the headlights of the car had caught me on the road. If it was Joey I would have been in trouble, but it was Constable Sherman. One of the drivers who had left the scene had enough sense to go to Long Grove and tell the constable about my calls for help and Sherman came out right away. I recognized his car and waved him down. He was very kind, first giving me a blanket to cover myself and asked if I wanted a doctor but I only had scratches and bruises from fending Joey off and running in the woods. As he drove me home, Constable Sherman asked what had happened and I told him. He said I was fortunate because Joey had raped at least two women there. That's why when I called for help the other drivers drove off as fast as they could. They had seen Joey and me walking and were afraid to get mixed up in whatever was happening. I think Constable Sherman was nervous too, but he did his job and asked if I wanted to press charges. I told him I would decide in the morning. The other girls had not pressed charges because their families did not want to tangle with the Coniglio family. So he got away with raping women, and I would have been another victim if my father had not taught me how to defend myself."

"How did you get Gina and Joey C. to travel with you?"

"I sneaked into my house because my parents were asleep. In the morning Joey telephoned and fortunately I was home alone and answered the call. He screamed at me, called me names and told me in horrifying detail what he was going to do to me, describing brutal and humiliating sexual acts and beatings. I suspected he was too hurt to actually do them but he scared me. I called Claire and she called Cindy and told her to bring her shotgun and pick her up, and soon they arrived. Claire had the idea to call Gina, so I did. Gina must have sensed what happened and said she would meet me at the Tavern and Cindy drove us there. I told Gina what happened and she became extremely angry and told me to come with her. I was not sure if that was a good idea. I didn't know if she would just hand me over to Joey. She said no, she wanted me to tell the Don what happened. She said it was time that the Don knew what Joey was doing. I told Gina I would tell him if she would be there with me."

"As Gina drove, I began having second thoughts, but Gina assured me that she would stand with me and took me in to see the Don. He was unhappy about my being there but Gina has influence with him. She told him to listen to me, that I was not the only one this had happened to. I told him exactly what I told you. The Don became enraged, shouting at his people in Italian. Gina translated, telling me he said that was not how a man should behave, and told them to find Joey and bring him in immediately. People jump fast when he tells them to do something. He told Gina to drive me home and apologized to me, telling me to call Gina if there was anything he could do for me. He seemed shocked at what Joey had done and his apology sounded sincere."

"When I got home I called Claire and told her about my meeting with the Don. I told her that I missed you so much and that I was foolish to break up with you, but Claire assured me that you still loved me. I said I wanted to go to California with you. Claire said if I was serious about going I could catch up with you by taking the Alton Limited express to St. Louis. Claire is learning to fly and could not fly on her own, but Scott would fly with her. She offered to fly over the roads to find you and drop a message that you should go to the train station. I worried about traveling alone and Claire came up with another good idea."

"So I called Gina again and told her I had decided to go to St. Louis to meet you but I did not want to travel alone.

She went to the Don, who told her that Joey should chaperone me to St. Louis, but Gina said no, she did not trust him, so the Don said she should go along to watch Joey if I promised not to press charges. I thought of going through an ugly courtroom scene, humiliating myself while Joey sat there and laughed because there were no witnesses. He would have the best lawyers and I would be shamed as a whore. I was failing the girls that Joey had raped, but Gina said no, the Don was angry and he would take care of Joey. So that's why the three of us were on the train. Joey was angry when the Don told him that he had to guard me but he had no choice, it was part of his punishment. Dan, I was so glad that I laughed when you punched Joey. I'm sorry Gina stopped you from hurting him, in fact I would have given him a few more kicks to his balls if I could. I wanted Raider to tear into him too."

I said "I'm so sorry you got dragged into my problem with Joey. If I knew what he did to you, instead of leaving I would have found him and shot him, if Jake didn't get to him first."

"Dan, that's the problem. Gina told me that would be the worst thing to do, because no matter what Joey had done, the Don would kill anyone who killed his son. Gina was right, it is better that the Don be angry at Joey than have the Don angry at us. It will be interesting to talk to Gina when we get back to find out what happened. No one else knows, not even my parents. I swore Claire and Cindy to secrecy."

"If Claire knows, Scott knows but he won't talk."

"Yes, that's OK, I trust Scott. I did what I thought I should do, only it turned out to be wrong and I was lucky to escape. When we talked earlier, Claire told me I was as clueless as you. She made me aware of the Coniglio mentality and that you were not joining the gang as I mistakenly thought. Now I understand why you are on this mission. Claire doesn't like it either but said that no one came up with any better ideas. I'm so sorry I acted like a goof and broke up with you. But there is more that I want to tell you about me."

"And that is?" I asked.

"I told you that I had been engaged. His name was Patrick and he was killed in a train wreck. Dan, I was sure we would be married or I wouldn't have given myself to him. Later I began to have serious doubts about Patrick but that's a story for another time. When he died I still had feelings for him and his death caused me so much grief that I became afraid of being in love with the wrong man again. Then you came into my life. I liked you the first moment I saw you, even though you were breaking into my house."

"Breaking into your house? The door was open and I was looking for your father. I fell in love with you on first sight, but then you tried to shoot me. Jake told me you were a good shooter, so I admit to being confused as to how you missed."

"I was scared when you came in. I had no idea who you were. At first I was going to shoot you but something told me that I might be making a mistake so I lifted the gun just before I pulled the trigger and shot the wall above your head. My father figured it out, because he knows I can hit what I aim at when I'm that close, and if I missed by that much it was deliberate. I told him it was because I thought you were cute and he laughed. By my description he knew it was you."

"Before you came along, I told myself I did not want to be in love because of the grief and because sex with Patrick wasn't good or satisfying. But you excited me with your devilish look that seems to attract women. I found out about Gina, Nancy and Suzie when Claire and I had our girl talks."

"Despite all that, I knew that I was in love with you, so when Claire convinced me you were still in love with me I needed to get you back and begin a physical relationship. You were a very enthusiastic lover last night and it was obvious that you enjoyed having your way with me. You did take me harder than I expected, but your passion increased mine and I liked it after I got comfortable with you inside me. Now I know that sex with the right lover is wonderful and I want more. Claire's a very smart woman, she helped me work out my problem of being unable to love. By the way, she thinks you are the world's best brother. Don't tell her I told you that or she will never tell me any secrets again. Which brings to mind, where are you going to take me tonight?" She reached over to touch me and my mind flashed on Joey C. doubled up in pain.

"Don't squeeze them! Don't hurt me!" I yelped in mock terror.

"Trust me, you've got I want and your family jewels are safe in my hands." We rode quietly together for a few minutes as I let it all sink in, when Laure asked "Capisce?"

"Capisce."

Raider woke up from his nap on the back seat. He thought capisce meant a comfortable night in a hotel and his humans would make happy noises in bed, and there would be another juicy steak bone for him. His thoughts were correct on all counts.

BANK WITHDRAWAL

The next day the road looked smooth so I let the Duesenberg stretch its legs and we crossed into Kansas. I noticed a motorcycle gaining on us. Five minutes later the motorcycle pulled up next to me, the rider flashing a badge and motioning for me to pull over. I stopped off the road and turned off the motor. A young officer parked his motorcycle behind the Duesenberg and walked up to us. Cannon Ball had told me that highway patrols were being established all over the country. They were becoming necessary since automobiles were traveling in greater numbers on the highways but this was a deputy sheriff and his brown uniform appeared similar to what Laure was wearing, with brown pants, tan shirt, and a leather jacket. He removed his goggles and introduced himself as Montgomery County Deputy Sheriff Keith Aldridge.

"Where are you folks going to in such a hurry?" he asked with an authoritative tone. I immediately remembered Raider was with us when he sat up in the back seat at the sound of the deputy's voice. I hoped he did not dislike cops, as some dogs did. But the officer was very friendly and a natural with dogs. Raider sniffed his hand and jacket with great interest. "He probably smells Sheba, my German Shepherd."

"We are on our way to California on vacation." I replied.

"You are going a little too fast, but the reason I stopped you is that we are advising motorists to take special care because there was a jailbreak in Jefferson City Missouri two days ago. We believe the escapees are headed in this direction, and I want to ask if you have seen anyone suspicious. There were five jailbreakers. We don't know what they are wearing now, they wore jail suits when they broke out, but probably have stolen other clothing by now. We do not have any reports if they have guns or a car or truck. That's usually the first things jailbreakers steal. They may have someone helping them, so there may be more than five. Do you have any guns with you?"

"We have seen hardly anyone since we left St. Louis. We each have a Colt 1911 and I have a rifle and a shotgun under the seat. I hope I shall not have to use them but we both know how to use them if necessary."

Deputy Aldridge said "I advise you not to stop for anybody. They may have accomplices or have split up, or some of them might be hiding by the road to trick drivers into stopping so they can take their automobile and I expect they would like to bag a Duesenberg. Sure is a beauty. May I see the engine? I've heard that Duesenbergs have beautiful engines."

"Sure, let me show you the motor." I got out of the car and opened the hood. "This is a prototype for a new model that Duesenberg plans to put in production next year. It has a longer and stronger chassis and a more powerful motor. It will be called the Model X." Deputy Aldridge was impressed with our elegant and powerful machine. Seeing he was riding an Indian motorcycle I asked "Have you ever heard of Cannon Ball Baker?"

"Well my goodness, yes I have – I stopped him for speeding but after talking to him I did not write him up. He is an interesting man and we talked for quite a while. When I was a kid I read a lot about him. That's why I joined the Sheriff's Department, so I could legally ride a fast motorcycle and carry a gun. I would sure like to have a beer or two with him some day." Realizing what he had just said, he added "If it ever becomes legal again, of course."

Laure smiled and asked "How far is it to the next town?"

"Next town is Cherryvale, about 20 miles, and the road is good until you get near the railroad depot where there are ruts from farm and factory trucks.

My poorly attached shade for Raider was loosening up and I went over to fix it. "Say, when you get to town, my father owns the leather shop at the corner of the block with the bank building in the middle. He's made shades for dogs riding in open automobiles. He could fix you up with a real nice leather shade with fasteners and everything. I see you take good care of your best friend and usually people who take care of their animals are good people. If you stop in, tell my father that I sent you."

"I sure will, and thanks for the information. We will be stopping in town for food and supplies and to send a telegram to a friend in Chicago."

"The telegraph office is in the hotel across the street from the bank. There is a grocery store and a new store, Newton's Hardware on Main Street on the next block." We shook hands with Deputy Aldridge he got on the Indian motorcycle, stomped the starter lever and with a friendly wave was soon a cloud of dust down the road.

A few miles later Laure said she would like a relief break. I pulled over and stopped where there was no one around. On the road, people often pulled over and went into the trees to relieve themselves. There were a few trees by the road where I parked and about 100 feet further off the road there was a larger group of trees. Laure went for the farther trees. I got out the leather bound logbook that the Duesenberg brothers had given me to record information related to the automobile for their analysis of problem areas. I sat under a tree by the car and began writing. Raider was having his relief break too, sniffing and peeing on every bush and rock that looked interesting.

A minute later Raider began acting strangely, running up to the edge of our roadside trees, looking at the other tree line then running back to me and whining. I looked at my watch and noticed that Laure had been gone longer than expected. Something told me we might have inadvertently found the jail-breakers. Or rather, Laure had. Maybe they had been hiding in the trees and grabbed Laure. They might not have seen the Duesenberg because I parked next to the roadside trees. The field between the road and the farther group of trees had corn over three feet tall. I crawled low through the cornfield to the patch of trees. Raider followed silently. We got to the tree line and I tried to peek in, seeing nothing at first. We crept around a few more feet and I heard a man talking. Crawling to the sound I saw a clearing with the remains of a campfire, food and whiskey bottles carelessly thrown around and three men laying on their backs motionless as if they were drunk and sleeping it off. I was about three feet from a boulder so I crept up to it, motioning Raider to stay down.

Then I spotted Laure sitting on a log near the campfire. Her hands and feet were tied with strips of cloth and they had gagged her. Two men were standing, their backs to the campfire and keeping watch while the others slept it off. The two men were saying something about Laure. One of them argued he wanted to do her now while the other said they should wait until the boss woke up since he always demanded to be first. I did not want to wait for the others to wake up so I began to crawl slowly around the tree line to get closer to Laure. I told Raider to stay and he seemed to know to stay low and quiet. It took a few minutes but I got to within ten feet of her and behind her so she could not see me. Then I got a break. The man who wanted to wait until the others woke up walked to the other side of the wooded area to relieve himself. The other man began walking along this side of the tree line and if he kept that line he was going to cross right in front of me. I took my 1911 out of its holster but left the safety on. I did not want to shoot unless I absolutely had to because that would alert the others, even if they were drunk. The walker came along about four feet in front of me, hidden behind a thick bush. He stopped and turned to look at Laure. He set his gun down, a snub-nose .38, and stepped over to Laure with a stupid smirk on his face.

This was a small window of opportunity for a one-on-one fight and I took it. The man reached to grope Laure's breasts but she squirmed away from him. He was getting angry. That's when he made his mistake, turning his back to me so he could get his hands on Laure from behind her and she would not be able to squirm away. I jumped up and slammed the butt of my gun on his head and he went down like a sack of coal. Raider stood by him, quietly baring his teeth but the man was out cold. I pulled my knife and cut the cloth binding Laure's hands and feet and pulled her up, telling her we had to run fast. I forgot the gag in her mouth but that did not stop her from running like the wind, with Raider protectively running next to her while I ran a few steps behind to watch our backs. None of the three sleepers moved, nor did the one I had whacked on the head. The other man was now coming out of a clump of bushes on the other side after having done his business. He did not see us until we were almost to the road and he let out a shout, waking the others except for the guy I had just clocked. Laure scrambled over the door on the passenger side, pulling the gag from her mouth. Raider leapt clean into the back seat and I jumped into the driver's seat. The Duesenberg started right up and I got it in gear. We were rolling when the first shots came.

"Laure, get down – Raider, down!" Laure had already slid way down on the seat and Raider laid low on the back seat. I slid down as low as I could and still see the road. More shots came. It sounded like one rifle and three or four handguns. If they had .38 snub noses I would be out of their range fast but the rifle would be a problem. I heard bullets hit the Duesenberg's body. The pistol sounds stopped but the rifle kept firing, scoring another hit on our car. I had the accelerator floored and was thankful for the big engine as the Duesy gained speed. The firing stopped so Laure peeked behind and reported a Model T had come out from somewhere and five guys were in it, trying to chase us. I was not worried much about that, the Duesenberg would easily pull away from an old flivver with five passengers. The rifle fired once more and I heard the bullet zip past. Now the Model T was out of rifle range but I kept going fast until we got to town. The ruts outside of town were bad but I managed to swerve around them.

Laure called out when she saw the bank building and the leather shop. Across the street was a hotel with a café. Keith's Indian motorcycle was parked next to a row of cars by the hotel. I pulled up behind an Oakland automobile across from the bank. We ran into the cafe and found Deputy Aldridge having a piece of pie and a cup of coffee. I ruined his break with the news that the jail-breakers were right behind us. Deputy Aldridge asked us to go to the hotel desk and have the clerk call the sheriff in Independence for backup. The sheriff's office was about eleven miles away. Laure ran to the hotel manager's office and was able to get a telephone line to the sheriff immediately. I asked if there was a town policeman and Keith said one of them was the bank guard who doubled as a town constable. Laure ran across the street to the bank to warn him. She was so fast I could not stop her.

Laure ran into the open bank doorway just as shots were fired. She ran right into a bank robbery in progress. The real jailbreakers were robbing the bank. It was like a Keystone Kops movie. From the outside it looked like Laure ran in the door and ran right back out. What happened was when she ran in the masked bank robbers had just pulled their guns and demanded money. The bank guard pulled his gun but there were too many armed robbers and that was not a good thing to do. The robbers shot the bank guard and took his gun. Laure had come partway through the door but stopped fast when she heard the shots and surprised the bank robber who had just shot the guard. None of them expected to see a pretty girl running into the bank. The bad guys were armed with large caliber six shooters so she backpedaled out the door, pulling her 1911 from her holster behind her back and fired at one of the robbers, wounding him. The bank had a stone front rather than the wood fronts like the other buildings and as the robbers fired wildly at Laure their bullets ricocheted off the walls. I watched as she fled down the street and into the leather shop. Despite the danger, I admired her long legs that covered the ground fast. It was a good thing she wore pants today. I wanted to go back to St. Louis and tell that ignorant woman what Laure had been able to do because she wore pants.

I pulled my 1911 but from across the street it would be risky to shoot. The robbers were under cover and I had no clear shot at them and did not want to risk hitting bank employees or customers. Deputy Aldridge joined me at the boardwalk side of the Oakland four-door convertible with its top up in front of the hotel across the street from the bank. He had a .44 Magnum Colt in his hand, but we were clearly outgunned until help arrived. Laure, not wanting to be a target while crossing the street, was in the leather shop. I hoped and prayed that she stayed there and out of any shootout. Just then the old Model T filled with the five highwaymen rolled into town. They were the ones that had tried to grab Laure, but these were not the jail-breakers, they were just road bums. They were angry as hell and wanted blood. They did not know there was a bank robbery going on, or that the deputy sheriff and I were on the other side of the Oakland in front of the hotel. I felt like I was an actor in a Wallace Reid movie.

I wondered what the hell I'd gotten us into, between two separate gangs. Deputy Aldridge said his father had a sweeper, a sawed-off 10 gauge shotgun in his leather shop and knew how to use it but it was useless except at short range. Aldridge said his father would have his sweeper out but would stay in the shop and lay low. I hoped Laure would also stay there. I thought that if he and Laure were behind cover in the shop they could take care of any bums or bank robbers that came into the shop.

The highway bums stopped in the middle of the street near the corner and began shooting up the town, still unaware of the bank robbers inside the bank and Deputy

Aldridge and myself behind the Oakland. They must have been very drunk or very stupid and were firing wildly at both sides of the street. From a shop a couple of doors down on our side of the street a rifle shot rang out and a bum dropped to the ground. Deputy Aldridge said that was old Betsy, who kept a rifle under the counter of her general store. She was a good shot but he had warned her not to use her rifle in town. Betsy obviously had not listened. I silently thanked old Betsy for removing one of our assailants. I looked for Raider and could not find him, nor could I go looking. I hoped he was OK and not lying alone and wounded somewhere.

It became quiet in the bank and we could not see what was happening inside. Deputy Aldridge could not enter the bank alone with armed robbers inside and the drunk road bums outside. After a minute of quiet, the drunken road bums started walking and shooting up the town again. They were passing a bottle around between shots. The town's citizens had long since disappeared if they had any sense. Now the bums were walking directly toward Deputy Aldridge and I on the other side of the Oakland automobile. There were now four of them. The one Betsy shot lay deathly still in the street and I recognized him as the one I hit on the head with my gun back in the woods. It just wasn't his day.

We heard sirens approaching the town from the west. The sound of the sirens brought the bank robbers out of the bank in a hurry, carrying bags of bank cash. They were dragging two women hostages. The bank robbers began crossing the road toward the Oakland. *Damn, this really was like a Wallace Reid movie, with me and Deputy Aldridge using the other side of the getaway car for cover.* The bank robbers must be real dummies, parking their getaway car across the street from the bank, and they couldn't see us yet. I took my knife and cut the rear tire, crawled over and did the same to the front tire.

All of a sudden Laure crawled up behind Deputy Aldridge and me, along with Raider. She had doubled around the block and through an alley and the hotel to come behind us, thinking if she could get to us she could help. But it was a case of jumping out of the frying pan and into a hot fire. Laure had not listened to Aldridge's father, who sensibly had taken cover to stand off anyone who came into the store. *Oh Laure – what am I going to do with you?* But there was no time to think about that, the bank robbers and their hostages were almost to the Oakland and we would be exposed. They left the wounded member of their gang in the bank. The bums were quiet now after seeing the heavily armed gunmen coming out of the bank. They were exposed in the middle of the street between the bank robbers and Betsy in the store. One of the bank robbers turned and saw the bums, got off a shot wounding a bum and a second crack from Betsy's rifle wounded the bank robber in the arm, giving further confusion to the bums and the bank robbers. Who was shooting at whom? Good ol' Betsy sure could shoot, but the angle to take a shot at the bank robbers was now too sharp for her with the hostages so close to the Oakland. Two of the highwaymen were still uninjured and they took off running the other way in fear of the bank robbers.

Laure, Deputy Aldridge and I were crouching below the side at the back of the Oakland when the first bank robber got into the car from the street side. The others clambered in from the street side, not noticing us low on the boardwalk side of the Oakland. After Betsy had shot their companion, they clubbed and threw the hostages to the ground in the middle of the street, abandoning them in their rush to get in the car and out of town. Then Deputy Aldridge made a very brave – or stupid – move. Jumping up, he put his .44 in the ear of the jail-breaker sitting in the front passenger seat and told the bank robbers in the car that they were under arrest. I did not want to do this, but the other bank robbers could just turn and shoot Deputy Aldridge in the face and drive away. They would not care if the guy in the front seat had his brains blown out. Aldridge needed a diversion but the sirens were still not close enough. I crawled to the street side at the same time Laure got behind the Oakland and popped up to put her 1911 on the back of a robber's head in the back seat and he froze. I came up with my 1911 pressed to the driver's left temple. Raider growled his presence. Betsy came rambling up the boardwalk towards the Oakland with her rifle and Aldridge's father arrived with his shotgun, thinking Keith needed help and unaware that we were backing his son. I hoped Deputy Aldridge's father would not fire the shotgun because if it was loaded with buckshot he would take us all down.

Fortunately Aldridge's father and Betsy were fast thinkers and could see that we were helping Keith. The robbers looked at three big handguns, a crabby looking old lady with a rifle and the huge barrels of the sweeper in their faces and surrendered. Deputy Aldridge ordered them to get out and lay face down on the boardwalk. At first they wouldn't move but Betsy didn't approve of their disrespect and clocked one of them in the face with her rifle barrel. They got out. Clem and I kept them covered while Deputy Aldridge searched them to remove their guns. Seconds later, the sheriff arrived with a carload of deputies and two more on motorcycles.

What a sight we must have been with Deputy Aldridge, his father Clem, Betsy, Laure, Raider and I standing guard over the bank robbers in the street. Raider wanted to tear into one of the bad guys but he waited for me to tell him it was OK. I told him I was sorry, but not this time. He obeyed but kept up the occasional growl so we would know he was on the job, no doubt hoping for another steak bone reward. Then Raider saw the hostages, a young woman and a lady who was a bank teller, motionless in the street. He went to them, carefully sniffing and licking the face of the young woman. She felt his wet tongue on her face, woke up and began to giggle. Raider sat down to watch protectively as townspeople ran over to help the women to their feet, unharmed except for bruises and the teller had a bump on her head. Raider took an interest in sniffing Sheba, Clem's German Shepherd Dog.

Sheriff's deputies took custody of the prisoners, handcuffing and chaining them together. The sheriff told the telegraph operator to send for the Jefferson City jail wagon to come get their inmates. The two road bums who tried to run away were caught by citizens who brought them back at gunpoint. The bank guard was severely wounded but a doctor went into the bank as soon as the sheriff's car came down Main Street. He said the guard, Egbert F. Sousa, would likely recover as ambulance attendants loaded him in for the trip to the hospital. The bank robber Laure shot was madder than hell when Deputy Aldridge frog-marched him out of the bank since he had been shot by a woman and his buddies had left him behind. His wound was serious but not life-threatening. Another teller and two customers were slightly wounded but all the bank money was recovered. The bum that Betsy shot was severely wounded and died later, and the others had minor wounds. Laure told the sheriff about being kidnapped on the road and the bums were placed under arrest. The street was filling with townspeople as Deputy Aldridge, Laure, Raider, the hostages and I became the center of attention. Andy, the town newspaper editor arrived on his bicycle and began interviewing people and taking photographs.

I counted five bullet holes in our battle-scarred Duesenberg's rear fenders and body. None had hit a tire, a brake or fuel line or the gas tank. Or one of us. I wrote in the logbook that the Duesenberg had five bullet holes but remained roadworthy. I wondered what the Duesenberg brothers would make of that.

The sheriff interviewed everyone involved so while we waited to make our statements I sent a telegram to Scott. He had given instructions to send a telegram every day if possible to a McLanahan security office that was also a telegraph office. When they received a telegram from me, they would immediately send one back if Scott left instructions that he wanted to communicate with us. I went to the telegraph office while Laure went to the bank to change a $50 gold piece into smaller bills and coins while I sent a telegram saying 'A-OK', our code word if we were OK. We had other code words in case there was trouble. I did not add anything about the day's events. I would write to supply that news. No sense worrying everyone.

Over at the bank, Laure was welcomed as a hero. Her brief appearance at the door and her shot at the robbers had thrown them into confusion and they had begun arguing amongst themselves. This allowed the bank employees and a customer to get to Egbert, the well-liked constable, to stop the flow of blood from his wounds and that saved his life. Andy took Laure's photo with the bank president and his very relieved employees. The bank president gave Laure the $50 in small coins and bills that she had originally came over for, then gave her the $50 gold piece back as a reward. We did not know until several days later that Laure's photo and the story of the foiled bank robbery and capture of the jail-breakers was picked up by the wire services and printed in newspapers across the country. Laure's mother Vera almost fainted when she saw it.

A couple of minutes later, Scott's security office wired back. We were requested to meet a train, the Santa Fe's *California Limited* when it arrived early tomorrow morning in Dodge City. It only said some necessary parts would be arriving, but no description. I thought Scott was sending parts we might need for our return trip.

THE CALIFORNIA LIMITED

The sheriff, a prickly old bastard, interviewed us and asked to see our guns. We pulled the magazines and cleared the rounds from the chambers and showed him the pearl handled M1911 pistols that Col. Patton had given to our fathers for their service when he was wounded in France. The sheriff took our guns, saying he was taking them as evidence because they had been used in a crime. I pointed out that we did not commit the crime and in fact assisted Deputy Aldridge, but he just said the guns were confiscated and were now property of his department. Laure was holding the magazines and refused to turn them over to the sheriff, even when he threatened to put her in jail with the bums. I told the sheriff that he had no legal basis to take our guns, but he replied he could do anything because he was the law. I was incensed. Laure made an excuse to go to the ladies' room but instead went to see Deputy Aldridge and his father Clem.

When Deputy Aldridge came steaming into the room with Laure, the sheriff refused to talk to him and told him to leave. Without saying a word, Deputy Aldridge went over and took possession of the guns. The sheriff became angry and threatened to fire Aldridge, just as Clem and Betsy came in. Seeing them, the sheriff said we could keep our guns and left. I asked what that was all about.

Betsy explained that her husband had been the sheriff of Montgomery County for over 20 years before he died 10 years ago. Since then no sheriff was elected in Montgomery County that did not get Betsy's endorsement, and there was an election coming up for sheriff in November 1926. The greedy sheriff had taken property from other people in the past and had been forced to give it back when the seizures were found to be illegal, but as we suspected the property often vanished.

He thought he could get away with taking our guns because we were out-of-towners.

When he saw Betsy he knew he had to give the guns back or she would not endorse him. He did not know it yet, but Betsy wasn't going to endorse him anyway since he was an ass and a bad sheriff. In fact, Clem Aldridge was rounding up support for his son Keith to run for sheriff and Betsy said she would back him because he was a fine young man who had grown up in the county and now had law enforcement experience, and she would serve as advisor. Keith was well liked by his fellow deputies who also said they would support him. Laure and I profusely thanked Deputy Aldridge, Clem and Betsy. I privately gave Keith Aldridge a $10 campaign contribution. He did not want to accept it but Laure told him it was from both of us, and she kissed him on the cheek and told him sweetly that she wanted him to be the next sheriff. He accepted it with the condition that he got a kiss on the other cheek when he won the election.

Betsy smiled and very graciously thanked us for helping the town capture the bad guys. She especially seemed to like Laure, saying that she recognized her as an independent woman and told her she was very brave, just like Betsy herself had been back in her younger days when she helped her husband clean up the town. I thought Betsy was still brave, plunking two of the bad guys, but she brushed it off. Before she left, she pressed $20 of her own money into each of our hands. Betsy said she was encouraged that young people like us were out in the world and told us to repay her by making lots of babies and teaching them to grow up like us. Later, I asked Clem about her, telling him that if the money she gave us put her in need we wanted to give it back. Clem said no, Betsy may be eccentric but knew what she was doing. She came from one of the town's wealthiest families and could easily afford it. She loved Cherryvale and when someone did good for the town, she felt kindly toward them.

We needed to get some food and supplies so we went to the grocery store and hardware store. When we returned Deputy Aldridge politely asked if he and his father could take a short drive in the Duesenberg and I gave him the key, telling him to go ahead. He and Clem left and I heard the Duesenberg drive off. A few minutes later it was back but it went over to Clem's leather shop across the street. Hoping this wasn't another property grab, Laure and I strolled over there. Raider was in the car, he was The Road Trip Dog and if someone was taking the Duesenberg he was going to be in it. Clem and Keith were measuring Raider and the back seat of the Duesenberg. Deputy Aldridge's Shepherd Dog Sheba appeared and when the measuring was done the dogs went outside to the fenced yard. I don't know why, but later both Laure and I had the impression that Raider and Sheba had recently lost their virginity, if they had been virgins. But no one was talking, especially not Raider and Sheba.

Clem said he was not a metalworker and couldn't do anything for the bullet holes in the bodywork, but he would like to make Raider a sunshade at no charge to us. He selected some leather samples and held them to the seat for comparison. He found one that Laure said was such a perfect match that it could have come from the Duesenberg factory. Clem got to work and Deputy Aldridge explained that they appreciated people who took care of their animals as we did with Raider, and because of that and how we helped capture the robbers, Clem wanted to fix Raider up with a nice sunshade. When he was done it really did look like a factory accessory. The leather edges were finished beautifully, and the shade was attached behind the second windshield divider and the leather pulled out to snap onto sturdy fasteners behind the rear seat to hold it in place. He even made vents for airflow through it. Clem showed us how easy it was to attach and remove the shade. We tried to pay him but he refused, saying we may have saved his son's life by jumping in to create a diversion. The hotel manager came in, said that since it was late in the day we might not want to travel far and offered us a room at The Leatherock Hotel at no charge, and said Raider was welcome to stay in the room with us. Deputy Aldridge said the Leatherock was the best in town and urged us to accept, so we did.

The state of Kansas had voted itself dry back in 1880 and the local bootleggers had been active for many years. We found a small speakeasy behind Betsy's general store that she must have known about and were invited in for a drink. We surprised Keith Aldridge and his pretty girlfriend Amy Andersen cuddled in a corner, each with a glass of wine. They seemed a bit embarrassed to see us but we told them we were not Prohibitionists. To back that up we bought drinks for them. Afterward, Laure and I took a nice evening walk and then went back to the excellent Leatherock Hotel.

Afterward Laure said "I think Deputy Aldridge will be a good sheriff. What he lacks in experience can be made up with good counsel from his father and Betsy." I agreed.

In the morning we were up, had a good breakfast and loaded the Duesenberg behind the hotel, thanking the manager and Deputy Aldridge, who had come to wish us a safe journey. Laure set the sunshade and Raider hopped into the seat. I drove down to the end of the block and turned right and then right again at the street. It was a little after 9 in the morning when we turned to Main Street, but there were about 200 people on the sides of the street waving to us. There was the town's small brass band, a Girl Scout troop to give Laure a flower bouquet, and a Boy Scout color guard stood at attention with the United States and State of Kansas flags. Raider sat in the middle of the back seat looking like the King of England being chauffeured in a parade. We stopped and thanked everyone for coming out to see us. Laure hugged and thanked each Girl Scout, Deputy Aldridge and I saluted the flags held by the Boy Scout color guard. As we drove away I waved, Raider and Sheba barked when they saw each other and Laure blew kisses to the crowd. It was a royal send-off. Laure wrote thank you notes to express our appreciation to the town and the Scout groups and the businesses who gave time off for their employees to honor us. We mailed the notes from Dodge City.

Back on the road we talked as we traveled west, grateful that nothing unusual happened for the rest of the day and we easily made Dodge City in the afternoon. We did not have to meet the *California Limited* until tomorrow morning and we had no energy for camping so we found a dog friendly hotel and put up for the night. We went for a walk and found that there were speakeasies almost everywhere in Dodge City.

After an enjoyable evening we were engaged in pleasure back at the hotel after which we snuggled together for the night. I felt like the happiest guy in the world, with a lovely and loving woman, a good dog, a Duesenberg and financial backing for our adventure. All we had to do was transport a large load of wine illegally and undetected over 2,000 miles of rough road to get home. What could possibly go wrong?

We were up, bathed, breakfasted and looked forward to the Duesenberg burning up the miles after we picked up the parts from the *California Limited*. Arriving at the station, we heard the whistle of the Baldwin 4-8-2 Mountain-class locomotive at the head of the Santa Fe's *California Limited*. The Railway Express Agency car would have the package for us, so I stood back to watch for the packages to be unloaded for Dodge City. Raider noticed something first and he went on the alert. I looked and my brain froze. Was this a déjà vu thing?

I couldn't believe my eyes. I said "Laure, in the last three days you surprised me in St. Louis, I punched Joey the mob boss in the face, we met your Uncle Viktor, danced at a speakeasy, made love for the first time, were stopped by a deputy sheriff, you were kidnapped by bums and we were shot at, then you walked into a bank robbery and were shot at, we helped apprehend dangerous armed robbers and fortunately didn't get shot, then a sheriff tried to steal our guns. Last night we visited the best known Dodge City speakeasies, but when all this happened I was not scared. I'm not scared now – I am frightened out of my wits. Laure, always remember that no matter what happens to me, I love you. I have from the first moment I saw you and I will always love you until I die, which will probably be just a few minutes after your father sees me."

Laure, who could usually come up with a witty comeback was as speechless as I was, for she had also seen her father Jake getting off the train. He did not look happy, but then Jake did not often go around with a big smile on his face. He was a solid, stoic, hard-working Polish man who was brilliant at fixing anything mechanical. He was a big guy and a war hero. His daughter and I were standing there holding hands when he saw us. Laure had left home, leaving only a letter to explain she was going to travel unchaperoned with me on an illegal and dangerous mission to bring a supply of California wine back to Chicago. I was convinced that my life was over. Jake had found us and came to Dodge City for the sole purpose of killing me for violating his daughter and I couldn't blame him if he did.

A few seconds later, apropos of nothing I said "Laure, I think that last night was my last supper" and we looked at each other. Laure, remembering how I pleasured her last night, started laughing. She was still laughing as her father approached us. I love her laugh and her smile, and told her that just so I could see and hear it one last time before my lights went out. Raider sat there and did not lift a paw or growl or even bare a canine tooth to protect me. "I thought German Shepherd Dogs were protective" I muttered but Raider just wagged his tail. He liked Jake.

Laure believed a good offense is a good defense. She stepped directly in front of her father, threw her arms around him and hugged him. He stopped but did not return the hug. She took a step back and told him "Pa, I am here with Dan because I want to be with him. You know what Dan's mission is, so you know where we are going and what we intend to do. It is dangerous but we know that. I love you and Ma, but I am 22 years old and legally can decide for myself. Please accept that. I know it was wrong of me to leave without talking to you first, but there was no time and I was afraid you would try to keep me from leaving. I'm sorry I left the way I did. But I am very happy being with Dan and I ask your permission to stay with him." She stood up to Jake, not giving him an inch and we all waited. It felt like we waited several hours but it was probably less than a minute because there were still people getting off the train. Jake looked at his daughter. He looked at me. He looked at Raider, who wagged his tail and came forward so Jake could scratch his ears. *Traitor dog. See if I give him that bone for lunch.* I would probably be maimed or dead by then.

Finally Jake spoke. "Laure, this is an unusual day, because this is the first time you ever asked me for permission to do anything. You two look like you just saw the Ghost of Christmas Past, but it's just me and I'm bringing some parts that the Duesenbergs sent, parts that are unavailable except from the factory and you will need them sooner or later. I decided to bring them to you and see how you are doing and check the car over. I knew where you were going. Claire told me and I didn't even have to beat it out of her." Jake gave one of his rare smiles at his little joke.

"Claire took the same defiant tone as you and said it was what you decided to do of your own free will. I told her that I knew better than to try to change your mind, I've been trying for all these 22 years I've known you, with very little success." Jake turned to me. "And now Dan, you get to do the impossible. Laure is a very intelligent woman, determined to do what she believes is the right thing to do. Laure is extraordinarily stubborn when she makes that decision. When she decides to do something, she will do it with everything she's got, and then keep on doing it. Dan, your father was a great man and a good friend, and I know you've got good character because you didn't fall far from the family tree. But you've got the toughest job of your life standing next to you now, and her name is Laure. Good luck Dan."

I was again rendered speechless. Jake was approving us traveling together, unmarried? Laure let out a whoop and kissed her father, kissed me, kissed Raider, who gave me a look that said he knew everything would be fine. Her glorious smile melted my fears. Even Jake was smiling, satisfied that he had foxed us and given us a good scare.

Jake added "I didn't get breakfast on the train, so I'm hungry. I expect you two have already eaten but if you'll spare me the time I'll eat quickly and we can talk. Is there a greasy spoon breakfast joint nearby?" We walked over to a diner next to the train station. I got Raider a bone and told him to stay by the door out front, which he did while happily gnawing on the bone.

Laure whispered "Last night wasn't your last supper, so you'll be able to have it often" she giggled. She rarely giggles so I knew she was relieved.

Jake told us that not much was happening back home. Otto and Fritz were doing great in the shop. Jake only had to help them once with a troublesome electrical problem. All the families were doing well and hoping to hear from us and sent reminders for us to write. He said Scott had a plan for our return trip, but in the tight quarters of the little restaurant he didn't want to say anything. Jake told us about the parts he had brought that were unique to the Model X. Then he asked how we were doing.

Laure and I took turns. She told him about meeting Viktor and dancing at Café Lulu, and Jake was very pleased to hear his younger brother was well. Jake said he'd had a rough time after the war, like so many soldiers, and Jake was worried about him. We told Jake about our day yesterday and he had a hard time believing what we had done. He tried to admonish Laure to be more careful, but he knew that Laure was going to do what Laure wanted to do. Later I slipped up when I called her my lover. We struggled to find the right words to explain that we were in love and enjoying each other sexually.

"Well, I expected that. I need to tell you two something. I knew you are in love. Vera and I – well, we know how it is. Don't pretend you're the first generation to enjoy the pleasures of someone you love." He stopped to let that thought sink in. "I only ask you to be careful and not get pregnant. That would break your mother's heart, Laure. She already hopes that the two of you will have a big wedding when you return, and you know she is very traditional. She does not want to see you with a big belly in a wedding dress. You may think it limits your enjoyment, and from experience I know it does. But it's all I ask of you and I'll help you in every way I can. Vera and I are happy for both of you. We knew you two loved each other before you knew. It was pretty obvious the way you both looked and acted. I don't think I'll be able to get Vera to accept that you're sexually active, but she is an intelligent woman and knows, but for appearances might not admit it." He winked at me. I have seen people get fooled into thinking Jake is just a regular guy, but then he stuns them with an insightful analysis. Jake has a whip-smart brain and knows how to use it. The phrase *just like Laure'* came to mind.

We found an automobile repair shop where we could rent a work stall and some tools for the day and Jake went over the Duesenberg with loving care. He stopped and stared at the bullet holes and I could tell it bothered him. Not for the car, but those could have been holes in his daughter or me. He said he could fix them when we returned and that I should drive it to Indianapolis so August and Frederick could inspect the car and hear our experiences firsthand. I told Jake that I had kept up the log every day and so far we had no problems with the Model X. It was strong and solid, handled and stopped well. The power and torque of the sophisticated Duesenberg

Straight 8 gave it the ability to go up most hills without downshifting. Laure showed Jake the dog sunshade and he agreed it looked like a factory job.

Jake planned to work on the Duesenberg himself but Laure had worked on automobiles with her father and was a good technician. Jake knew I was too, so he gave us tasks to work on. Laure borrowed a shop coverall that almost fit her and by the end of the days' work she had dirt smudges on her face. Those smudges reminded me of the day we met, when she wore a maid's simple dress and had dirt smudges on her face. It drove me wild with desire and I whispered to her that I would have to bathe with her to make sure she got properly cleaned up. She had to pretend to be working real hard to stifle a laugh.

Jake was done with the Duesenberg in plenty of time to have dinner with us before he embarked on the eastbound *California Limited* that evening. Jake paid the hotel for our room, which we found out the next morning when we went to check out. Before Jake got on the train he gave me a box of sheaths. It was a timely gift since our supply was running low.

That evening we found a store that sold us a bottle of wine after we talked to the shopkeeper's wife. It wasn't from Napa or Sonoma, but it was decent and we drank it. We enjoyed our bath together and felt very clean that night since we had spent plenty of time washing each other. I felt like the luckiest guy alive. As we fell asleep like spoons together, Laure whispered to me that she was the luckiest girl in the world. We were starting to think alike.

GRAND CANYON TO WINE COUNTRY

A couple days later we stopped in a town in New Mexico to send an A-OK telegram to Scott and another to Cannon Ball Baker telling him when we expected to arrive in Arizona. I wanted to see him and tell him about our adventures. Laure and I enjoyed two days of pleasant travel free of highwaymen, bank robbers, sheriffs, gangsters, fathers or anything else to worry us. The roads were good with more paved miles than I expected. Raider alternated between dognapping under his new sunshade and sitting up in the middle of the seat to enjoy the wind on his nose. When we stopped he amused himself sniffing around or chasing rabbits. He seemed to be enjoying travel and we often talked to him while we drove. He was a good listener, and if he had any differing opinions he wisely kept them to himself.

Laure was driving. She was an excellent driver, smooth and fast. I was napping while Laure drove, waking up now and then when she moved suddenly to avoid a pothole or an animal. I liked to look at her behind the Duesenberg steering wheel because she looked as if she was driving a racecar and leading the pack. She could really make the Duesenberg eat up the miles. Today I had put the top up for protection from the hot sun. The Duesenberg was a phaeton model so it had a removable windscreen behind the front seat to protect the backseat passengers from wind and dust. Raider did not seem to care for it; he preferred the wind on his nose.

One of the new accessories Jake installed was a small mirror to watch behind us. A mirror that enabled us to see behind without taking our eyes too far from the road ahead was a real benefit. Laure woke me saying a motorcycle rider was coming up fast behind us, worried that we might have a highwayman after us.

I had my 1911 ready and looked at the motorcycle. As it came closer I recognized Cannon Ball, so I told Laure to pull over at the nearest place where we could get off the road. Two minutes later I introduced Laure and Raider to Cannon Ball Baker. He told us there was a small town just ahead with a nice park where we could have lunch, so we followed him there. It was a lovely park where several families were enjoying picnics. Some children came over to ask if our dog could play with them and it didn't take long for a good time to develop. We told Erwin about our adventures and he remembered Deputy Aldridge. He asked us if we had a couple extra days to spend. We were already behind my original schedule, but there was no set time we had to be in California so I asked what he had in mind. He wanted to show us the Grand Canyon National Park that Theodore Roosevelt had signed into law in 1919. He said it was incredible and worth the detour. We both said yes at the same time and set a meeting point in Flagstaff. Baker gave us road directions and then sped off to pick up his wife Elnora.

A day later we stood in awe at the rim of the Grand Canyon. It was amazing beyond our imagination and well worth the time, and it felt good to get off the roaring road for a rest. We camped with Erwin and Elnora for two days while we explored and hiked and we vowed to come back. Baker was planning and resting up for one of his next record breaking runs from Vancouver, British Columbia down to Tijuana in Mexico driving a Rickenbacker automobile for the manufacturer. The manufacturers paid him well for these events. They liked his terms – no win or new record, no pay. Needless to say, Erwin "Cannon Ball" Baker almost always got paid, and since he gave news reporters good interviews and photograph opportunities he often got a bonus for the good publicity he brought to the manufacturer.

After a well-deserved rest we went back on the road bound for California. Since I had chosen the southern route we had an extra day of traveling north to get to San Francisco. Baker reviewed the route with me and I appreciated getting an update from someone who had been there recently. Cannon Ball had a restless spirit and a need for competition that kept him on the road most of the time. Elnora understood and sometimes traveled with her husband.

Arriving at Martinez, California where the *City of Seattle* ferry boat carried automobiles across the bay to Benicia, we decided to take the earliest ferry crossing to Benicia the next morning, then drive to Napa, arriving around noon. We had a restful afternoon in a park. Laure was reading *The Great Gatsby,* a new novel by F. Scott Fitzgerald, while Raider took a protective role to chase away any squirrels that dared to come near Laure.

The next day provided bountiful sunshine and the ferry boat was on time. Our excitement took over as we approached our destination. We talked about how we should go about our task to acquire wine. Cannon Ball told us that since so many people wanted wine, beer and booze, a lot of bad stuff was made to sell to uninformed buyers. We did not intend to be among them.

The first thing after finding a hotel to stay temporarily was to find a knowledgeable winemaker and learn how to taste and evaluate wine properly. We also had requests for distilled spirits. I knew good whiskey and could evaluate that for myself before we made any purchases.

Our plan had been to get there, buy wine and bring it back so we could move on with our lives in Long Grove. But almost immediately after we arrived in Wine Country we both were impressed by the countryside and the people we met.

As it became obvious that this was not going to be a quick in-n-out purchase, we decided to find a house to rent for two or three months and scout the area, with special attention to learn everything we could about the transportation options available by rail, water and road.

Prohibition forced many wineries to take out their vines and bring in other crops or cattle, or struggle to stay open selling grapes or grape juice. We rented an abandoned winery estate south of St. Helena from a Napa bank for an absurdly low cost. There was a huge main house with furnishings, a guest house and three small cottages, along with almost new production and storage facilities. The bank was happy to rent to us because there were few buyers for winery property. Exploring the buildings, we found a dozen barrels of good wine that the revenuers had missed, or so it seemed, because later on we chased away several people who were nosing around as if looking for something. Raider earned his dog food giving us warning when someone came near. Twice we shot over the heads of trespassers to encourage their departure.

The first winemaker we met was Georges de Latour at Beaulieu in a small village called Rutherford. He was most gracious and gave us our first lessons in wine tasting. His winery was licensed to produce sacramental wine so Beaulieu remained active but he could not sell us wine because if it were discovered he would lose that license. Over in Sonoma we met Samuele Sebastiani, an energetic and gifted winemaker where we learned about Zinfandel and other Italian varietals. He and his lovely wife Elvira invited us to dinner often, each dinner becoming another chapter in our education about wine and food. Our only complaint was that we gained a couple of pounds but with more hiking and other work around our winery property we got back into shape.

We also got to know William Nolan who continued to make and sell excellent wine. His winery was way up in the hills where the Prohis never found it and the local residents did not volunteer information about one of their own. Another connection was made in St. Helena at the Leunberger winery. Although the winery itself was closed for Prohibition, Laure worked for them by putting her secretarial and management skills to good use to help manage the property and whatever grapes or other crops they could produce and legally sell. They could not afford to pay her much but she suggested that if they had any good wine she would gladly accept it in trade some of her pay. Nothing was promised but Laure sometimes found a case of good wine under her desk, and when it was time for us to head back east the Leunbergers made a large contribution of wine to our inventory.

If we were asked, we offered references from Scott McLanahan, Erwin Baker and a few others. Some of the winemakers who had transported their wines east knew of the McLanahan business empire and a couple of them even knew who Cannon Ball Baker was and were amazed that we knew him personally.

We hoped our cover remained good until we had to go home, but after a couple of months neither of us wanted to leave Wine Country and all the wonderful people there. So many of them had been hurt financially and personally by Prohibition, and many others moved elsewhere or eked out a living with fruit orchards and other types of farming. Some managed to stay in business. During the first years of Prohibition, enforcement had been left to local law enforcement, many of whom did little or nothing to stop the manufacture, transport or sale of alcoholic beverages. In Napa, the sheriff, Joe Harris was more diligent in his attempt to enforce Prohibition but leaks from his own department to those being raided often resulted in the raiding party finding little or no contraband.

Wine was a big part of Napa and many people were involved it, or had family or friends in the business. This network kept us in good cover and we were accepted into the Napa and Sonoma winery society while keeping our real mission out of view. For all most people knew, we were wealthy tourists spending a summer in Wine Country. We weren't exactly rich but with Scott's backing and the generally depressed market, and a Duesenberg to help complete the picture, we lived well.

Our contraband was stored at our winery in the outbuildings and a hidden cave on the property. Since the vineyards had gone wild it was obvious there was no wine production here so Sheriff Harris left us alone. We participated in an underground winemaker network, passing on any leaks or tips about forthcoming raids we received. A few times we helped with fines and bail money for those who had been caught. Our reputation was a shell so we were careful to maintain our outwardly neutral appearance.

Laure was irrepressible when it came to dancing and we regularly frequented the speakeasies in Yountville, north of St. Helena and down in Napa Junction. One evening especially stands out for me. We were going dancing and as usual, Laure came downstairs looking absolutely smashing in a new dancing dress. This one was really short, at least six inches above her knees. It was black with a red trim line and decorated with beads. It had a short fringe that covered about three inches of the bare leg above her knee but when she was dancing she showed a lot of leg. She had a very pretty matching beaded headband with a single black feather, this one in the front. When she came downstairs I was speechless. I was also aroused.

"Is that dress just to tease me or are you really going to appear at Molly's like that?" I had to laugh, because it would not make any difference if I approved or not. Laure was the most independent thinker I had ever met, and I knew better than to try to tell her what to do.

"Tease you? I don't have to tease you, you get turned on if I come downstairs wearing a potato sack. You are, as you have heard me say often, such a guy."

"And it would be a lucky potato sack to have you wearing it. So you admit you like teasing me and any other red-blooded males in the room? I'd better bring some boxing gloves or brass knuckles if I'm going to have to fight off a couple dozen guys."

"Oh Dan." She came and threw her arms around me. "You know very well that it's only you that I want. OK I admit I like to tease but not to cause fights. I always leave with you, don't ever worry about that. I like to dance, and this dress happens to be the most current fashion. You wouldn't want to see me dance in a floor length dress now would you?"

"You even turned me on in the floor length dress you wore when we met."

"You're an animal." She pretended to be exasperated. "Oh well, I just don't want any complaints tonight about my new little black dancing dress being too short. It arrived by Railway Express for me at McCaulou's store in Napa yesterday. I ordered it sight unseen because your sweet sister Claire wrote to me about it and included a little sketch of it. I simply had to get it – just to see the look on your face when you first saw it."

"And you got the expected reaction, see?" and I pulled her close so she could feel my reaction. She had learned not to put on her lipstick until just before we were leaving because we often engaged in some passionate kissing and fondling at the bottom of the stairs.

"Well, you know how the old poem goes." She started a familiar line to reel in a fish, the fish being me.

"No, what old poem should I have known this time?" I followed her lead and asked, fully knowing that I was walking right into her joke. She recited:

"If the skirts get much shorter,
Said the flapper with a sob,
There'll be two more cheeks to powder,
And one more place to bob."

I made us drinks to calm down from laughing.

"You are such a guy, letting me get you with that one."

"Where do you get this stuff?" I asked.

"I make it up, just for you."

Laure was the center of attention at the speakeasy as we danced late into the night. Someone had brought several bottles of decent French Champagne. "Champagne and dancing until dawn" was Laure's attitude. I did not have to fight off anyone, but that was only because everyone there knew Laure and I were a team. The first time we went dancing in Napa I had to take an obnoxious man outside to give him a lesson in manners after he began to insult and threaten Laure when she rejected his request to go out to his automobile for sex. I won the fight early on and did not want to hurt him, but he kept getting up and coming at me so I had to knock him down until he finally stopped getting up. The next day, he went to the sheriff's office to file a complaint. The deputies knew Laure and me, and they told the guy he had picked on the wrong couple, and that he should consider himself lucky that Laure hadn't shot him.

Since then, no one bothered us at the speakeasies although that night Laure received many compliments and a few wolf whistles. When we danced I could tell every eye in the room was on her. Laure loved to dance and I loved to watch her long legs along with all her other moving body parts. It was a wild night, we danced almost till dawn. At home we fell asleep, exhausted from our evening of dancing. We slept late the next morning, something we rarely did. Refreshed and ready, we made up for not having sex the night before.

WEATHER FORECAST: CHICAGO LIGHTNING

Claire wrote to tell us that she was coming to visit and asked if there were any airports nearby. We knew she didn't want to call because sometimes the operators were listening. I remembered a recent conversation with a winery owner who also was an aeroplane pilot. We were discussing how some wines were getting out and he said if there was a local airport, small quantities of wine could be shipped out that way. I did not think much could get out because any significant amount of wine would be too heavy for most small aeroplanes. The winery property Laure and I were renting covered over three hundred acres. I called my winemaker friend and asked him to stop by to 'talk about the weather'. We often said something like that to avoid saying anything over the telephone lines that might be incriminating.

Charlie came by the next morning. Laure, Raider and I drove him to a long, narrow but flat grassy field I had found, shielded from the roads. I asked Charlie if it would be long enough for a small aeroplane to take off and land. We paced it off and Charlie said it was, so we made a plan for him to fly his aeroplane in the next day to check it out. After Laure and I returned home, we hired some local boys to walk the field to remove rocks and fill any holes they found. As agreed, at ten o'clock the next morning Charlie came in flying low to inspect the field. Laure held up a flag so he could see the wind direction. After crisscrossing the field a couple times, he lined up and came in for a smooth landing and proclaimed the airfield suitable for use. In fact, he said, with some tree trimming at one end the field, it could handle a bigger aeroplane. I wrote Claire back, sending a map of the field.

About ten days later we heard an aeroplane circling low overhead. Laure and I drove over to the airstrip and Raider barked at the aeroplane like he usually did when they were flying low. As requested by Claire, I installed a wind flag on the field. We got there just in time to see a very pretty new aeroplane make perfect landing with Claire in the pilot's seat.

When the aeroplane's engine was turned off and the propeller stopped we ran over to see Claire pulling her leather helmet and goggles off and climbing down to the ground. Raider kept barking at the aeroplane and I saw another person preparing to disembark. When the passenger took off her helmet I saw it was Gina Coniglio. After helping Claire tie down the aeroplane, we unloaded a trunk and a large carryall stashed in the third cockpit. Other than some brief hellos and hugs, we didn't say much at first. I think our flying visitors were getting their hearing and other senses back after several hours in the air. At the house, we made sandwiches and iced tea and served them to our guests from the covered porch which had a nice view of our property. Our guests were hungry and began to tell their story. I noticed that Laure did not seem very happy to see Gina.

"Sorry for the surprise but we had to leave Long Grove with as little fanfare as possible. Gina will tell you about the trouble back home" said Claire.

Gina took over. "My stepfather, the Don is dead, assassinated by his son. The Don was ill but Joey decided not to wait for the Don to die of natural causes so he made a deal with Hymie Weiss, leader of the North Side Outfit to kill his own father and turn over the Coniglio family operations to them, with Joey made *capo* and kept in charge. Weiss is a vicious man and made the deal with Joey since the Don was allied with the South Side Chicago Outfit, and Weiss was at war with the South Side Outfit because they killed his friend and mentor Charles Dean 'Dion' O'Banion, leader of the North Side gang."

"Joey lured the Don to travel to Chicago, telling him it was for a peace talk between the North Side and South Side outfits. The Don wanted peace and never thought his son would betray him. But there was no peace talk, it was an ambush. My brothers were guarding the Don the day his car was riddled with machine gun bullets, what the newspapers call 'Chicago Lightning'. Everyone in the car was so bloody and torn apart that it was hard to identify the bodies."

"The Coniglio family operations were shattered. A few members who would not turn traitor were allowed to join other gangs, others were killed. Some turned traitor and joined Joey when he promised them power and money. They paid for their treachery because Joey's promises were empty, and now they are stuck with Joey because the other gangs will not allow traitors into their family operations. It is even worse for Joey. Traitors are intensely disliked and Weiss treats Joey with disdain. Weiss kept the agreement to name Joey a capo, but instead of gaining power, Weiss doesn't trust Joey. That, combined with Laure injuring Joey's manhood, has made his irrational behavior become much worse."

"To avenge the Don's murder I have taken a blood oath of vendetta to kill Joey. I have never told anyone of this, but another reason I must do this is because Joey raped me many times when I was younger and could not get away from him, and Joey threatened to kill me if I told the Don. Now I regret my failure to tell the Don. Even though Joey would have killed me, the Don would have killed him. Therefore I have promised to fulfill my oath, even at the cost of my life. I had to leave Chicago when I spurned Joey's offer to join his new gang, and by doing so I became next on his hit list. I need time to train and plan for my vengeance. My only worry is that someone will kill him before I get to him."

Laure and I were stunned. It was hard to believe that even Joey could be that stupid. Claire told us "The McLanahans secretly took Gina into hiding and even I did not know where they hid Gina until arrangements were made for her to travel. Scott and Claire asked our mother Dorothy to move to the McLanahan Ranch for the time being, and she is being trained to use a gun."

Gina added that "Years ago when our parents died, the Don took us in and cared for my brothers and me as if we were his own children. He was good to us, and made arrangements for us to have a life outside the family business. Fortunately, Joey was not aware of those arrangements, and with my brothers gone I have substantial resources."

Gina continued "If I can impose on you in the name of old friendship, I would stay here a few days to make contact with people the Don told me to go to in San Francisco in case of trouble. I will pay for this and do not argue with me about it. Claire has agreed to stay with me until I go to the city. I will be safe when I get to the city under protection of the Don's loyal extended family and friends. When I am trained and ready with a plan I am going to kill Joey. Do not try to stop me. But listen to me, even without me here, you are in danger. Since that night when Joey tried to rape Laure, he has become obsessed with getting his hands on her, and he has threatened many times to do bad things to her, terrible evil things. She hurt him bad. That is why he did not try to fight when you punched him, Dan. She hurt him so bad that he could not move to fight. I think he's recovered some now, but he is angry because after Laure kicked him it is difficult for him to have sex. Laure also humiliated him when she told the Don what he tried to do to her, and the word is out on streets now about how Joey treats women."

"Do you think that we were a factor in Joey's decision to betray his father?" I asked Gina.

"No. Joey was already trying to negotiate with Weiss. He wanted sexy Laure with him when he went to the other family because he thought it would make him look like a big boss with a pretty woman submissive to him. But he learned Laure was not submissive, and now women laugh at him. He is frustrated and angry."

I tried to get Laure to take a walk with me and talk about this but she jumped in with her decision. "Gina and Claire should stay here until Gina is ready to go to San Francisco. We are well armed, but someone could still come here and surprise us. I think we should get some help to watch the roads in the area and report any strangers. If Gina has a picture of Joey we can show it to people so they know who to watch for."

"I have Chicago newspapers I brought here, his picture is in the papers" Gina said. "You can use them."

Dan said "I'll ask a fellow I recently met by the name of Sky Wolf, if he can bring some of his family to help us watch. He is a full-blooded Wappo Indian and is teaching me how to move in the woods so quietly even the deer don't notice. There are several Wappo families in wine country and they live in poverty since the wineries are not able to offer jobs."

"I will pay them well for this service" Gina said.

Our house was huge so we gave Gina and Claire their own rooms. I talked to Sky Wolf to see if they would patrol the area on horseback. He quickly agreed, glad to provide his people an opportunity to earn money even if it was for a short time. Gina was true to her word and paid them well. We made the rounds of our neighbors and they also offered to tell us of any unusual visitors.

I could tell Laure was not happy with Gina in the house, but not because of the danger. Laure knew that Gina and I had been lovers. She usually wasn't the jealous type but decided that Gina was a woman who might try to rekindle the relationship.

Later, when we had time to talk about it I told her "I know you worry, but don't. Laure, you are my partner, my best friend and my lover. I don't care if Gina throws herself at me – although I don't think she will – that is all in the past and I will not let it into the present. Gina was a young man's desire, but when I met you, even before we became lovers, I lost my desire for Gina. I can keep my dick in my pants around her."

"That's all nice to say, but things can happen. I'm not going to throw a jealous fit because if you want to fuck her it won't make any difference. Being jealous won't make me more desirable. I have nothing more to say. I agreed that Gina should stay here. That's my decision and I will not talk about it again." I knew Laure was worried to have Gina there because I was surprised to hear her talk that way. Laure only talked like that when we made love.

At first it seemed like things went well. Claire took Laure and me up for our first aeroplane rides. Her new aeroplane was an engagement present from Scott, a brand new 'New Swallow' made in Wichita Kansas. It had cockpits for the pilot and two passengers. Scott had talked to Waverly Stearman, the designer, and found out that they were already planning to upgrade the standard 90 hp Curtiss OX-5 engine to a more powerful and reliable 225 hp Wright Whirlwind. Money talks, and just like Scott talked the Duesenberg brothers into selling him a prototype Model X, he talked Stearman into selling him a new Super Swallow with the Wright engine. Scott insisted that Claire be fully trained to fly it by the factory's pilots since the engine is much more powerful than the aeroplanes she had flown. Claire was a natural pilot, among her other talents. She loved her new aircraft and was an avid learner. Before Claire and Gina left Long Grove, Jake had gone over the New Swallow thoroughly to make sure it was in the best possible condition. It proved to be a very stable aeroplane capable of carrying three passengers, or as we calculated later, a pilot and a few cases of wine.

Around this time Laure and I started a company to provide business management, transport contracts and negotiation services. Even though most wineries were out of business, some of them had changed over to other agricultural products. Our customers were pleased to find that Laure was an excellent negotiator for shipping and sales contracts. She continued to help at the Leunberger winery and we soon had several clients. Laure and I incorporated our first business partnership with each of us owning 50%. We also combined our first names for the business to name it The LaureDan Company.

Laure needed an assistant and we hired a young woman named Enid Hanlon. Enid had some office experience and we told her it was likely to be a temporary job. With so few jobs available in wine country, at first she seemed happy to get the work. Enid also helped Laure manage our household, supervising workers, repairs and improvements. Enid told us she had lost her home when she lost her last job so we put her up in our house. Even with Enid, Gina, Claire, Laure, me and Raider, the place still seemed empty, although it was obvious that Raider did not like Enid. We gave Enid a room in a wing of the house where Claire and Gina each had their rooms. We still had another wing closed off, unused.

Our business office was set up on the first floor with a separate door for business entry. We were settling in, which was something we had not planned. The mission was to buy wine and spirits, but Laure and I were falling in love with the Wine Country although we still planned to leave. Now, with Joey C. wanting to grab Laure and Gina we decided to stay here until things cooled down.

We hired a chef since there were so many of us and Laure was too busy to do much cooking. She was an excellent chef, but preferred not to have to do it, except she did love to make pies. We found an excellent home chef, a young lady named Sunny who lived in St. Helena and had a name that fit her disposition perfectly. She had an ambition to open her own restaurant some day and was working to make some money to do it. Laure thought I should have a butler, but I turned that down and instead we hired a maid, an Englishwoman named Elsie Rutherford. I thought it seemed that we were getting rather posh.

Because of all the events going on, and that we were going to be here for a few months, I set up a gun range at the base of a small hill on our property for all of us to practice shooting.

I was in the office one afternoon when Laure and Enid were out getting contract signatures. Claire was at the landing strip working on her aeroplane. She checked it out every day and flew it twice a week to make sure it would be ready the moment it was needed. And as often happens, what you don't expect to happen, happens.

Gina entered my office wearing a dark blue robe. I felt a suspicion that this visit was going to be trouble, and my sense was correct. Gina made some small talk but then just said "Danny" and her robe dropped off her shoulders. She was completely naked except for her shoes.

I have to admit that I admired her sexy body for a few seconds but when she moved around the desk toward me I told her "Stop Gina. Put the robe back on." She kept coming toward me and put her hand on my shoulder, her other hand taking my hand and placing it on her breast. I took my hand away. "No Gina. Put your robe on. Look, Gina, I know we have a history but that is over. I appreciate what you did for Laure when you chaperoned her to St. Louis, and I'm glad to help you get to San Francisco. But our affair is over. I love Laure now and forever if she will have me. I'm sorry Gina, I really am. You are a beautiful woman and there will be many men competing for your affection. But I cannot be one of them. Please Gina, put your robe on."

Gina slowly moved away and bent over, showing me her sexy ass as she picked up the robe. She slowly slid it over her shoulders, trying to make sure I saw every move and curve of her body. It was tempting, but I began looking out the window and filled my mind with thoughts of Laure. Gina left the room.

Later that night just before Laure and I got in bed, I decided that she should hear from me what had happened. "Laure, I have to tell you something and it may not be pleasant, but you need to hear it from me. This afternoon, Gina came into the office and..."

Laure hushed me and smiled. "I know all about it. Gina felt so bad that she told me how you refused her. Gina said how impressed she was that you were loyal and hoped someday she would have a lover who would be as devoted to her. I had a woman's intuition that Gina might try something and it worried me. I trust you but now I know my trust is well founded. Put your arms around me and take me, take me right now." I always found that in moments like this it was best to do as I was told.

GINA GOES TO SAN FRANCISCO

A few days after the naked Gina incident, her people in San Francisco wrote to say they were ready for her. I loaded Gina's luggage – she had gone shopping often and had considerably more clothing than she had upon arrival – and with Laure, Claire and Raider along we drove to Sausalito to take the car ferry *Eureka* to San Francisco. It was an all day trip because we also wanted to see the city.

Following Gina's directions we found the driveway to a gated, walled compound. At first we did not see anyone, but suddenly four men armed with Thompsons surrounded the Duesenberg. Gina talked to them in Italian and someone came to open the gate. The people in the compound offered strong Italian roast coffee and sweet delicacies, which we gratefully accepted. The boss was not there but would be arriving later and they wanted Gina settled in prior to his return. We said our goodbyes to Gina, who looked very elegant in a color-coordinated skirt and jacket combination. I asked her to write to us so we would know everything was OK. She gave us a letter marked "To be opened only upon Regina Coniglio's death" which seemed rather ominous and made us nervous.

We drove around to see the sights of San Francisco after we left the compound, finding a small restaurant where they packed up a lunch for us. We paired the lunch with a good bottle of Napa wine. At Golden Gate Park we enjoyed our picnic lunch while Raider made friends with the local children. We were back on the ferry and on our way to Napa in time for a late dinner after which we went to our office to make up for being gone all day.

The next day Laure packed Claire a lunch and other travel food. Claire took off in her beautiful New Swallow aeroplane, glad for the extra power of the 225 hp Wright Whirlwind motor behind the propeller instead of the 90 hp Curtiss. She calculated the weight and balance carefully to decide how much she could carry and where to place it. Claire sent us an A-OK telegram when she arrived at Gauthier's Field, and our families wrote to thank us for their cases of Napa and Sonoma wine.

We cautioned Claire to make sure word of our little bootleg operation did not get to Joey. Gina told us that with the death of Don Coniglio, and our help getting her to San Francisco, she considered the alleged debt to the Coniglios to be erased. Gina said that Joey had not even told Hymie Weiss about it, because he planned to pocket any money collected from me. That was all the more reason for us to help Gina accomplish her vendetta, because as long as Joey was still alive, he was still dangerous to us, maybe even more so than before because he would be desperate to look good to Weiss.

Laure and I talked it over and decided that since we were here and our project was in process, we should finish what we started and the proceeds would be ours.

"Laure, doesn't that make me a rumrunner?" I asked. "If that is true, you are in a relationship with a gangster. I hope you won't break up with me again."

"Being an independent minded modern girl, I am comfortable adjusting my attitudes as I see fit. And my attitude is that we are in this together so I am a gangster too. Take me upstairs and prove that I made the right choice."

"You're talking like a gangster now."

"You gonna keep on flapping yer gums, or you wanna take me upstairs?"

Scott called us for our monthly conference. When Claire was here she told me that Scott purchased a new, larger aeroplane. My curiosity was piqued and I asked him about it. Scott said it was a Fokker F.VIIa/3m, manufactured in The Netherlands and powered by three 9

cylinder Wright J-5 Whirlwind 220 hp radial engines, one in the nose and one on each side under the wings. Jake already performed his magic, making several performance and reliability modifications. It had seats for eight passengers but if Scott planned to carry wine and distilled spirits back instead of passengers he could remove the seats. Scott said this was an interim plane because he had seen the new designs that were going to be built in the next couple of years, including Ford's new all-metal Trimotor.

We told Scott that Laure and I decided to finish our project and bring our contraband to Chicago and St. Louis where we could turn a nice profit.

Scott's other news was not so good. The Chicago gang wars were heating up again and his contacts reported there were no signs of peace in the near future. Al Capone who became the South Side boss a few months ago, was quick to send out his gunmen. Rumor had it that the North Side mob was intercepting the South Side Outfit's liquor convoys, and mob guys on both sides were going down under storms of Chicago Lightning. We did not care, that was their worry. If Joey contracted a case of Chicago Lightning, that would solve a major problem.

Scott asked about the San Francisco, Napa & Calistoga Railway that ran up the middle of Napa Valley to Calistoga and down to Vallejo where there was a railroad ferry to the city. It was an electrified passenger service that also carried small freight on tracks parallel to the Southern Pacific freight rails, but during Prohibition they mostly shipped grapes east for home winemakers. I asked why he was interested in the railroads.

Scott told me that his father Thomas held a large investment in the Chicago & North Western Railroad. The railroad made a connection with the Union Pacific at Council Bluffs Iowa and was the basis for "The Overland Route" claim for C&NW and UP passenger service. Carl Gray, President of the Union Pacific Railroad and a friend of the McLanahan family had encouraged Thomas to make an investment in the Union Pacific Railroad. This investment had recently been completed.

Thomas signed a contract with the Streator Car Company in Streator Illinois, to build a heavyweight private business railcar. Scott said there would be plenty of room for our products, with very slight risk that a railroad magnate's business railcar would be searched. When it got near St. Louis though, Prohibition enforcement was more aggressive. We would have to unload and forward our contraband in small shipments by car, truck and aeroplane. As long as we remained in Napa, whenever Scott or Claire flew out they would bring back small shipments, but so far we had sent no wine to Joey C.

"I don't want to make trouble for Thomas, should our contraband be discovered" I told Scott.

"He knows what we're doing, but I am insulating him so that he can claim he did not know about it." Scott would be taking the big risk. I didn't like that either, so Laure and I would have to be careful to help maintain their shield of innocence.

Since our business was growing and we were staying for at least a few more months, I began searching for a second automobile. A Packard cost more than we wanted to spend, even though we could afford one, but it would not make sense if we might be leaving it here. I was driving on Highway 29 near Calistoga when I saw the perfect car with a 'For Sale' sign. It looked almost new, a 1924 Dodge Phaeton Touring, black with red leather interior.

It was in front of a closed winery and I knew that the sheriff had caught the owner selling wine. Unfortunately, the winemaker got the wrong judge and was fined $1,000 and sentenced to six months in jail. His family had to sell almost everything to pay the fine and continue living until he was released. The wife offered the Dodge for a ridiculously low price because she needed cash. Her children were too young to work to help the family. I offered her $100 more than she asked for the Dodge, and she thanked me as she tearfully accepted the money. I told her to call us and not let the bank take the winery.

I went home to pick up Laure to bring back the Dodge. I did not tell her what it was until we got there and she was surprised. She drove the Dodge home and was so happy with it she informed me that it was her car and I could keep the Duesenberg. The Dodge was not as powerful or comfortable as the Duesy, but it was quick and sporty. Having learned performance modifications from Jake, I made some modifications to the Dodge's motor and Laure liked it even more.

THE RAID

Laure and went to separate meetings with two clients. I was going to see Bill Nolan about renewing his contract with The LaureDan Company, and Laure had a meeting to discuss arrangements for distilled spirits with Mrs. South for her Yountville speakeasy. We departed just before four o'clock in the afternoon with the plan to meet afterwards for dinner and dancing. We kissed and hugged and my hands got a little frisky on her. "You have the fever and I have the cure. But if I stop to take the cure we will not get anything done. Sorry, Dan, the bank is closed" she said.

As usual, she was right. Laure drove her Dodge and I drove the Duesenberg to my meeting with Bill Nolan. It went quickly; we understood each other and trusted our handshake deals. I was back at the house earlier than expected so I had a glass of wine and must have dozed off because Sunny came in and woke me. "Mr. Lindner, wake up. It's after 6 o'clock and Laure has not returned from her meeting with Mrs. South. I was worried when I could not get through on the telephone so Elsie went over to check with Mrs. South. She told him that there had been a sheriff's raid and they arrested all the girls for prostitution, including Laure and ripped out the telephone lines. Mrs. South is worried because she did not recognize the sheriff's men, and she knows all the Napa deputies." I jumped out of the chair and splashed some water on my face. I checked my wallet and made sure I had a couple hundred dollars in case I needed to make bail for Laure. It was ridiculous. The sheriff knew Laure was not a prostitute. Even if he borrowed some deputies from Sonoma, many of them knew us and would not arrest Laure. I left Raider with Sunny. I asked her where Enid was and she said Enid had taken the afternoon off since we were going out tonight. I asked Sunny if she would stay by the phone, and she said she would stay by the phone until we returned.

I arrived at the South's speakeasy a few minutes later. Mrs. South and her people were working to repair the damage. The sheriff's men had needlessly smashed everything, but that was not Joe Harris' style. Something was wrong about this. I asked Mrs. South to tell me exactly what she remembered and it worried me more and more as I heard it. Then Mrs. South remembered something, reached under her bar and gave me a pearl handled 1911. It was the twin to mine. Laure had slipped it to her just before the deputies arrested her. I took the 1911 and thanked Mrs. South, heading down to the sheriff's office in Napa. I had the Duesenberg barreling down Highway 29 at over 80 miles per hour. As I went by a group of trees near the road, a cop car pulled out, a red light came on and the siren started its wail. I did not have time to talk so I opened the Duesenberg's throttle. The speedometer rolled up to 100mph and never went below that until I got to Napa.

I had little confidence in the sheriff but I had to start somewhere. Sheriff Harris and I got along at first but our relationship deteriorated. He was becoming more aggressive in raiding wineries and speakeasies, including the one Laure and I liked to go to in Napa Junction run by a woman they called Dago Mary.

I remembered the night Sheriff Joe raided Mary's speakeasy. When the deputies came in through the kitchen, Mary was cooking and began to throw things at the deputies. She threw utensils, pots and pans, food, dishes, everything she could get her hands on until she ran out of things to throw and the deputies were able to seize her. But the racket she made told her customers that Dago Mary was buying time for them to vamoose.

The sheriff stationed men outside but in the darkness they only caught about 15 of the approximately 100 customers and employees of the speakeasy. We found out that many deputies had family and friends there who were not caught. That's how Laure and I got away. One deputy saw us and looked the other away. We got far enough from the speakeasy, then hitchhiked the rest of the way upvalley with an amused Calistoga family who thought they were picking up a flapper and her date with car trouble. I think they knew who we were but did not ask questions. I knew the husband was out of work and gave them a twenty for their kindness in picking us up. We went back to Dago Mary's the next morning to retrieve the Duesenberg. The sheriff's men had not bothered to make a list of automobiles parked there, probably because they would have had to separate their friends' cars from those who were captured.

However, our red Duesenberg was conspicuous and Sheriff Harris knew we had been there. After that our relationship went rapidly downhill, especially when I bailed Dago Mary out and paid her fine.

I went into the sheriff's office but before I could speak, Sheriff Harris told me that his office had not made any raids today, and that they received the reports and were on the lookout for the impostors. Evidently the phony raids caused a lot of unhappy people to call. The sheriff said they would probably find the perpetrators tomorrow.

Steaming at the sheriff's casual attitude, I cornered him. "Probably? Tomorrow? That's not good enough, Harris. Laure's been taken and who knows what they might do. Who are those guys claiming to be your deputies? I think you know and you don't want to tell me. I'm thinking you're in this up to your neck and when I find out, I will expose you to the citizens of Napa County."

"You're right, I won't tell you" he said. "Because you'll want to go after them and if you do you'll wind up dead. But I'll tell you this. Go to Mare Island and see Col. Mosby of the Marines. I'll call him and tell him you're coming."

Minutes later I was steaming down to Vallejo. The Duesenberg ran like it knew there was an emergency. I remember thinking how much my dad would have loved to drive this automobile. But I didn't think that for long, I wanted to find out who had taken Laure and where she was right now.

I arrived at the Mare Island gate and the sentry motioned me to halt. A Marine lieutenant jumped in the passenger seat and the sentry raised the gate. The lieutenant gave me directions to Mosby's office. He said that the sheriff was so worried that he called twice. I carried a little too much speed into the parking area and nearly wiped out two Dodge staff cars. Surprisingly the lieutenant remained calm. We got out and he told me to follow him to Col. Mosby's office. Laure and I had met the colonel at a dinner event in Napa a few weeks ago.

"I am glad to see you again Mr. Lindner, but not under these circumstances. First, the lieutenant is my aide-de-camp Lt. Griffin. He is also my chief intelligence officer. I asked him to check with his sources about these phony raids and he received information that it was the Cranston Gang, a Central Valley gang of horse thieves who posed as sheriff's deputies and took about two dozen young women. They rarely work in wine country because we have been aggressively working with police agencies to catch them. We work with the police because not only does the gang kidnap young women to sell into forced prostitution, our reason for jurisdiction is that they shanghai Marines and Navy sailors and sell them to foreign agents and ship captains, who force the men and boys to work as crew on their ships."

"They put the victims on a ship just before it is leaving the pier. Lt. Griffin got a good lead this time because a lot of people were willing to talk. He says that the gang is holed up in a warehouse in the city. They are probably waiting for their contact on a ship that is leaving tonight, but they could take the women to a ship or several ships at any moment. Time is of the essence. I'm sending four squads of Marine MPs to the city to find them. I want those bastards caught and I don't care if we have to break a few rules to do it!" and he pounded his desk with his fist for emphasis.

"I'm going with your best squad" I told Mosby. "I don't give a shit about rules and if you don't authorize it I'll follow them anyway. Laure is one of the women. She is not a prostitute and I'll give every last drop of my blood to get her back. You will not be able to keep me from it, sir."

"She is a wonderful young lady and I expected you would say that when Sheriff Harris told me you were upset. Lt. Griffin is taking my best squad over on a fast patrol boat. Go with him. Are you armed?" I lifted my coat and Mosby saw my pearl handled M1911 in my shoulder holster and another in my waistband. "Good grief Lindner, I guess you are armed. But look here son, I can't have you going with an MP squad and shooting someone. When you go ashore in San Francisco, give your weapons to Lt. Griffin. The MPs know their stuff, they are my best men at this sort of thing. Good luck and good hunting. I want this Cranston Gang captured and unofficially I do not care if they are dead or alive. They have been a scourge on the waterfront for a long time. Griffin has my authority to get the job done as efficiently as possible and to use deadly force if necessary, and I expect it will be necessary. If I get cashiered from the Marines for this, it will be worth it if we can put paid to the Cranston Gang. Griffin, you have your orders. Move out."

Griffin was already at the door and we took off at a run, leaving the Duesenberg at the Marine HQ. Griffin had a Marine driver in a Dodge staff car with the engine running and he drove us smartly to the pier. We ran down the pier and when the boat captain saw us coming he gave orders to cast off, engines rumbling and ready to go. Griffin obviously knew how to make things happen. We jumped aboard and the patrol boat's commander began accelerating before we landed on the deck. "Permission to come aboard sir" Griffin called to the deck officer, even though we were already there. "Permission granted" was the immediate reply.

I learned that Lt. Griffin had earned a reputation as a hardass officer who got results, and with Mosby's authority there was no military officer on the San Francisco waterfront who could overrule him. He also knew his way around The City and knew how to get information from his many contacts there. I felt fortunate that he was on the job tonight. Griffin introduced me to the squad and I almost fell overboard at first glance. There were only eight men and a sergeant, none of them much over average height.

Griffin saw the look on my face. "Mr. Lindner, when Col. Mosby told you this was his best squad, he wasn't pulling your leg. These men and I have been on some hair-raising raids and I trust them with my life. Every one of them is hand-picked, a top-ranked shooter and they are armed to the teeth, experienced in hand-to-hand combat, knife combat, night combat, explosives, hostage rescue and they are smart. If these guys find the Cranston gang, we will do them damage even though we are undermanned. Last week, a squad member was ambushed and killed by the gang. We found three of the killers a couple of days ago and the gangsters are officially listed as missing. However I know they became fish food. They may even have been alive when the fish started to eat."

I looked at the men who had lined up to meet me. They were in Marine battle uniform but they looked like pirates. Sgt. Reilly shook hands with me and introduced me to his men, and with each one I became more confident that these guys were, in fact, Mosby's Best. For some reason each one was a different nationality. The sergeant was Irish, the corporal Italian. The others were a German, a Swede, a Frenchman, a Spaniard, a Dutchman, a Scot and an Englishman. They were a grim looking bunch to be sure. Besides their M1911 sidearms and various wicked looking knives, between them they carried four Thompsons, five rifles and three street sweeper shotguns, with bandoliers and pouches of ammunition and grenades.

The Irish sergeant was the shortest of the bunch, but he had a wiry strength and I correctly guessed he was a formidable bantamweight boxer. He was the sparkplug of his squad and they obeyed him instantly. Sgt. Reilly eyed me up and said "Mr. Lindner, we can't have you on a raid with us in civvies. With the lieutenant's permission I will get you something else to wear, if you don't mind, sir." Lt. Griffin made a slight nod of approval, in less than a minute Sgt. Reilly and the Italian corporal went below deck and returned with a Marine field uniform that was exactly the right size for me. "Cpl. Maranello was a tailor before he joined us and he knew what you needed. Unfortunately, the only uniform in our storage locker in your size is for a Marine captain. We have no idea how that got there, do we Luigi?" Luigi smiled silently. I went below to put the uniform on. Back on deck, Luigi looked me over and smiled again. Lt. Griffin pretended not to notice I had become a captain.

Sgt. Reilly asked me if he could have a look at my 1911s, so I handed them over, hoping it was not a trick to take them from me. He inspected them both carefully. "Mr. Lindner, these are government issue, how did you come by them?" I gave him a condensed version of my father's story and he seemed impressed. He held them and then asked if I knew how to use the guns. I simply took a 1911 and field-stripped it, then put it back together. "That's fast enough to qualify you as a Marine" he said. "If you know how to shoot as well I'll draft you as a semi-official member of the squad." I assured him I was intimately familiar with the guns, so he ordered one of the squad to throw a tin can in the air. I hit it with my first shot. The light was fading but my mind was screwed down so tight that my eye and hand coordinated themselves for the shot. I pulled the magazine and added one round to replace the shot.

Sgt. Reilly looked at me and said "OK sir. I'm going to say something so you just say 'I swear' after it, OK?" and he mumbled something that might have been a swearing-in oath although it sounded like there were some Irish words thrown in.

"I swear" I said.

"Well, this is highly irregular but you are a Marine for tonight's mission." Sgt. Reilly held out his hand and we shook on it. "But even though you got those captain's bars, I'm the boss on this mission, understood?"

"I capisce" I automatically responded and Luigi looked at me and grinned. He went below and came back with a double holster officer's rig for my matched M1911s. He gave me a pouch of loose .45 ACP rounds and four more loaded magazines that I put in leather belt pouches and one more in my pocket. I wondered what else Luigi had in the storage locker. I was reminded of what my father and Jake had done in the Great War, acquiring things that were officially unavailable.

When I put the rig on, the Navy gunboat commander, who had been watching the entire time, came down from the wheelhouse and looked me over. "By golly captain, you really do look like a damned Marine officer!"

At this, even Griffin laughed and he took me aside to say "I'm going to the command base at the pier to co-ordinate all the squads and you're going with Reilly's guys. As soon as I get positive word of the location of the gang I'll direct the squads there and I'll get there fast. I have my own personal Indian motorcycle stashed at the pier. Since you're wearing Marine captain battledress you can pretend to be an officer in front of other people but don't give orders, just agree with the sergeant and tell him to 'carry on' or 'make it so' or something like that. Sgt. Reilly is devilishly smart and experienced so listen to him, because I do. Col. Mosby is taking quite a chance sending a civilian on a raid but I understand why. Your Laure must be something special."

"Yes she is, Lt. Griffin. Very special. I'll play the part and do nothing to embarrass you or the colonel. I hope Sgt. Reilly's squad finds the gang first. I have the impression there won't be anything left of the gang for the other squads."

"We don't know how many gang members might be there, but we have been told they have twenty to thirty or more armed men, all ruthless thugs. Do not try to be brave. Let Sgt. Reilly carry out the raid. And for heaven's sake don't shoot anyone." Griffin looked me in the eye and I knew he knew he was supposed to take my guns, but after my display of 1911 knowledge he was letting me keep them.

I liked these guys. But I was scared. I was scared for Laure, scared for myself, but there was not a shred of doubt in my mind that I was going on the mission. I wondered what I would do if harm had come to Laure, or if we did not find the women in time. Before I could think about it for very long we closed up to a San Francisco pier and disembarked. The gunboat commander shook my hand and told me he wished he was coming along, and that all of the MPs under Mosby as well as all the Navy men at Mare Island wanted to get their hands on the Cranston gang. On the pier, Lt. Griffin told us to get going on the double and we took off at a fast trot. I was in good shape and easily kept up with the squad. Evidently Sgt. Reilly knew where he was going so I just tried to look like an officer letting the sergeant run the operation, sort of like a regular military officer.

Something inside, some inner sense kept telling me that we were getting close to Laure. My senses, already straining to notice everything, tightened up another notch. I decided the best way to help rescue her was to stick close to Sgt. Reilly.

The squad inspected two darkened warehouses without finding anything and I was getting worried. Sgt. Reilly sent Cpl. Maranello off on a task while we looked at another warehouse. Luigi came back, whispered in Reilly's ear. Reilly signaled us to gather around. "Corporal Maranello got a tip from one of his countrymen that the gang is aboard a tramp steamer and are getting underway, and word is that the women are on the ship so we will go back to the patrol boat and give chase. Keep quiet, follow my hand signals and check your weapons. Remember, if we find the women we will likely have a hostage situation. Let me handle it, I have the Irish gift of gab." The squad chuckled.

Without another word Sgt. Reilly turned and we hot-footed it down dark streets and alleyways while two and four-legged rats scurried away. We made it back to the patrol boat, its engines running. Lines were cast off and our boat moved out smartly. Sgt. Reilly told me that it wasn't officially a Navy boat, it was a captured rumrunner that they used for its speed. It was manned by a Navy commander and a volunteer crew who were itching to get in on the action.

The corporal gave the description of the tramp steamer to the Navy men, who must have known which ship he was talking about because a few minutes later we were following an old steamship that was just past the Golden Gate. It looked like only the rust was holding it together. The patrol boat was gaining on the ship and there did not appear to be any watchmen, but it was dark and the gang probably thought they had gotten away. The Navy commander detailed a dozen sailors to board the ship with the Marine squad. They looked as piratical as Reilly's Marines, armed to the teeth and ready.

Sgt. Reilly said we would board the steamship, the Navy sailors would take the bridge and engine room and the Marines would conduct the search and rescue of the women. "We are the Marines, so we get the women" Corporal Maranello told me. "If we lived a couple centuries ago we would have been pirates – we know how to board and take a ship." We were moving with as much stealth and speed as we could towards the rusty old freighter.

"Dan, I don't know if you've ever killed a man, but this promises to be nasty business. We are going to climb up the side of the ship using these knotted ropes with grapples to throw and hook on. That's the dangerous part, if they see us they can kill us like fish in a barrel. You can stay on the patrol boat and no one will think any less of you" said Sgt. Reilly.

"No, I have not killed anyone, but my Laure is one of the captured women. I will do anything to get her back safe. I want to go aboard, and I will follow your orders" I told him.

"You must have some Irish in you, Danny Boy. Stay close to me or Corporal Maranello if we get separated. Just be careful to shoot them and not us."

"Yes sir" I replied.

"I'm a sergeant, a working man, not a sir. Call me sergeant, or Reilly like the officers do."

The patrol boat was about 100 yards from the ship now, and Reilly had all of us arranged in order.

"Dan, when we get to the ship, three sailors were going to throw and test the grappling hooks. We begin climbing immediately. Can you climb up the rope?"

"Yes sergeant. I learned to climb a rope when I was a volunteer fireman" I replied. Reilly nodded and placed me in the middle of the boarding party.

There was no shouting or loud voices now, all commands were by hand signals as the hull of the patrol boat was at the starboard quarter of the ship when Reilly signaled for the grapplers to throw. The sailors knew their stuff, as each of the three grapples went up and held fast. The first three sailors began climbing up the ropes when a gangster above at the rail of the ship appeared and began shooting a Tommygun down on our crew. A sailor was hit and he fell back to the patrol boat deck, dropping his

Springfield rifle. Being closest to it, without thinking I grabbed the rifle, worked the bolt, took aim and fired. The gangster with the Tommygun fell down the side of the ship and screamed as he was caught between the patrol boat and the ship's hull when a wave pushed them together. When the hulls came apart there was only a red smudge with some skin, blood and body parts where he had been.

"Next time someone asks if you've killed someone, you'll have a different answer" Reilly said. "You've earned your place here tonight."

MARE ISLAND PIRATES

I put my arm through the Springfield's shoulder strap and over my shoulder, took hold of the rope and climbed up just as fast as the Marines. As I came over the rail, a gunman on an upper deck began shooting at us. I had seen the flash of the shooter's rifle. I dove behind a ventilator, worked the bolt on the Springfield. Moving slightly I got a bead on the shooter and fired. He went down. Reilly called "Good shooting Dan, give us covering fire until everyone is on deck then join us."

More gangsters arrived. I shot another one but with most of our crew now on board, they got the others. Ahead, a knife flashed in Reilly's hand and another gangster splashed into the water. The thugs began to retreat when they saw the squad advancing toward them and I ran to catch up with the Marines. The sailors divided into two groups, one to secure the bridge and the other to take the engine room. Reilly split the Marines in two groups, one going below on the starboard side and the other going to the port side. I got right behind Maranello, went down a hatch and climbed down a ladder.

As we silently moved in a passageway, the sergeant went ahead, stopping at each bulkhead door to listen. At the third door, he gave the signal for us to silently approach. I don't know how Reilly heard anything with the noise of the old steamer's engines and the creaks and groans of the old ship. Reilly tried the door and found it was not locked so he signaled his orders. He pointed for Helmut to open the door and take the middle, Lars to go in and cover left, Reilly covering the right. I was right behind Lars.

As Helmut began to push the door open, first one gunshot, then another, then the sounds of multiple gunshots erupted. Women and men were shouting, some screaming in pain. I recognized Laure's voice. My blood ran cold. I would not hesitate to kill whoever it was that harmed her.

At the sound of gunfire, Helmut stopped trying to be stealthy and kicked the door the rest of the way open. Reilly went right and Lars left. Reilly went in and I took his place at the door. Several handgun shots were fired to my right and I saw Sgt. Reilly go down, blood coming from his arm. I already had my rifle to the right, saw the gunman, shot him. He had a .44 caliber revolver in his hand so I went over to kick it away to be safe, but he was dead. I picked up the revolver and went to Sgt. Reilly. He was conscious and asked me to help him sit with his back to the bulkhead so he could hold his handkerchief against the wound to slow the blood flow.

After getting Reilly settled I gave him the .44 revolver. That's when I saw a gangster holding a girl by her hair, his big fist coming up to hit her in the face. I had one chance for a clear shot and took it. He hit the deck dead, but had fallen on top of the girl. It was the last bullet in the Springfield and I did not have any clips for it, so I dropped it, pulled my 1911 and went move him off the girl.

Before I got there, I saw Laure running to help the girl, she had a revolver in her hand. She had not seen me. In an instant a large gangster leapt to her, grabbed her and roughly threw Laure to the deck. She tried to shoot him but the revolver just clicked. Empty. He rolled her on her back and straddled her. He was too close to her for me to risk a shot. I was behind and moving fast, but his knife was in his hand. He took hold of her blouse and cut it open, then pulled on her brassiere and sliced it open. She tried to push him away but he was too heavy, but he made a mistake by stopping to leer at her breasts. Sgt. Reilly saw it too, recognizing Laure from the photo I had showed the squad. Reilly couldn't risk shooting him directly but fired over them high enough to avoid shooting Laure, shouting "I'll cover you, go rescue your girl!"

I was three steps from Laure but Reilly's shot had his attention so I launched myself at him. He turned his knife toward her, intending to stab Laure. As I landed on him, I got my arm under his knife arm to pull it up and away from Laure. He slashed the knife at me and I felt blood coming from a cut in my midsection. As I rolled him to get farther away from Laure, I felt my knife being pulled from it sheath. I got on top and landed two solid punches to his face before he pushed me over and now he was on top of me. I got both hands on his knife hand, and it took all my strength to keep him from pushing the knife into my ribs.

Suddenly his face constricted and he screamed, followed by a gunshot that was so close my ears rang. I pushed him away before he and his knife fell on me. Gunshots came from the other side of the compartment and I moved over to Laure to protect her. I saw the girl who had been trapped under her attacker got free, and I pulled her over next to Laure so I could shield both of them. That's when I noticed the girl had my knife in her hand, dripping with the gangster's blood.

With fear in my heart because Laure had not moved I looked at her. Laure smiled at me and said "Hi sailor, nice of you to come and see me. What's that hard thing in your pocket?" It was a 1911 magazine, and I breathed a sigh of relief. Laure was alive and looked lovelier than ever, as if that were possible.

"Hi Sweetie, I'm not a sailor, I'm a Marine and I brought some new friends to the party." I don't know why we tried to be funny, maybe it was the release of tension. The gunfire became intense for a few seconds and stopped. I looked up and Corporal Maranello was moving past us with the rest of our squad while Lt. Griffin stormed in with a newly arrived Marine squad.

"How did you stop the thug?" I asked.

"When you held up his arm, it gave both of us an opening. Josefina pulled your knife and stabbed him, I shot him with your 1911 that dropped next to me when you jumped the guy."

"Remind me never to get you two angry at me."

"No, I tried to shoot you once but then you swept me off my feet, so I won't shoot you now." Josefina looked at Laure curiously. "I'll tell you the story." The girls laughed. "Dan, this is my friend Josefina. Josefina, Dan."

I got on my feet and helped Laure up. Cpl. Maranello was there helping Josefina and we saw their eyes meet. I don't know what it was, the adrenaline from the fight or the release because it was over, but I saw something pass between their eyes. Could love at first sight be visible? Had my eyes looked like that the first time I saw Laure?

Laure put her arms around my neck and we held each other tight. She kissed me and put her head on my shoulder. "I love you" she said softly.

She noticed the blood dripping from my stomach wound. Sgt. Reilly had been moved to the passageway but he stumbled back into the compartment, still holding the .44 revolver. He looked around and took in the situation which was now under control of his Marines, saw Laure and me, smiled and passed out. A Marine and a sailor got hold of him and set him down gently on the deck.

"Does anyone have a medical bag?" Laure asked. A Marine gave Laure a medical kit from his belt. She looked over Sgt. Reilly and found the wound under his arm. He must have raised his right arm to be shot there. It was bleeding again and he was barely conscious. The compress had come loose when he passed out and the blood flow from his arm needed to be stopped, if left any longer it would be fatal.

Laure turned around, removed the brassiere that the gangster had cut, turned back and took Reilly's knife to cut a length from it, tying it around his arm above the wound and tightening it. The blood leaking from Reilly's arm stopped. She sat me down and inspected my wound.

"The sergeant's wound was critical, that's why I took care of him first. Your wound is a long shallow slice, looks worse than it is, but I will take extra good care of you" she said as she cleaned my wound and put a dressing on it. "Now I'll kiss you and you'll feel better."

Sgt. Reilly was conscious again and added "If you kiss me, I'll feel better too." Laure turned to him but stopped and looked to me.

"Carry on, Nurse Laure" I ordered. She gave him a little kiss but Sgt. Reilly had his Irish wits about him, pulling her to his mouth to give her a kiss that was more than casual, but I didn't mind. Without Sgt. Reilly, Laure might not be alive.

A sailor came to report to Lt. Griffin that the Navy had secured the bridge and the engine room, and the ship was returning to the dock. My Marine squad proved they were pirates and I was calling them 'my' squad. Maybe I was a pirate in another life.

When the ship stopped at the dock I carried Laure up to the main deck. Nigel assisted Sgt. Reilly and Cpl. Maranello carried Josefina, who was holding on to Luigi like she was glued to him. I ordered my squad to get all the girls outside on the main deck with the ship's metal bulkheads at the girls' backs, and then form a defensive perimeter in the event a gangster got loose. I detailed Lars to watch for anyone on the deck above us. I was barking orders like an officer, but Sgt. Reilly nodded his approval and the squad followed my commands.

The wharf filled up with San Francisco policemen and firemen, Marine MPs, Navy sailors, newspaper reporters, photographers and civilians. Ambulances, SFFD fire trucks and SFPD paddy wagons arrived, their sirens spinning down. First to board when the gangway was secured were two more squads of Marines and when they got to the deck I told them to report to Lt. Griffin to search the ship for gangsters. They did, and found more gangsters hiding, attested to by the sounds of several shots from inside the ship.

Medical personnel boarded Marine medics put a loudly protesting Sgt. Reilly on a stretcher and into an ambulance. Its siren started its wail as the engine roared to take him to the hospital. Soon the deck was crammed with people. A doctor looked Laure over but other than a couple of minor cuts and bruises she was OK. Even so, she was looking pale and weak like she was going into shock. Now that the Cranston gang was neutralized I carried her down the gangway. At the bottom of the gangway a weasel-faced photographer's flash bulb went in Laure's face. I was carrying her so all I could do was glare at him and he ran away, probably seeing the expression on my face that I was going to beat the crap out of him.

Our Navy patrol boat was tied up next to the ship, Lt. Griffin's Indian motorcycle parked on the dock nearby, its motor ticking as the heat dissipated.

A few minutes later Sgt. Reilly emerged from a taxi and came aboard. He told us that he had jumped out of the ambulance. "I don't want to go to a hospital. People die there." Unfortunately five of the rescued girls had been wounded by the thugs badly enough to require hospitalization. The doctors treating the girls reported that they would completely recover.

Lt. Griffin reported that his interrogation of two of the thugs revealed that they had been given orders to kill the girls when Cranston discovered Marines boarding the ship. He said "Fortunately for us the stupid thugs thought they could kill the Marines and take the girls for their own pleasure. Their greed played in our favor. They forgot that we are Marines and we get the girls. The doc who treated Sgt. Reilly at the pier said that whoever applied the tourniquet had saved the sergeant's life, with a comment about the unusual tourniquet material."

The San Francisco doctors wanted to keep all the girls overnight for observation but those who did not require hospitalization were adamant that they were going back to Mare Island with their Marine heroes. Sgt. Reilly and Cpl. Maranello agreed with the girls so the doctors retreated. My squad of Marines with the rescued girls boarded our patrol boat for the return trip. Some of the girls were in the cabin but there wasn't room for all of us, so Laure and Josefina and I huddled on deck for warmth from the chilly night air on San Francisco Bay. Luigi came by, and seeing that we were chilled, went to his clothing stash to bring each of us a warm Navy pea coat and watch cap. I wished for a camera, because Laure was looking very sexy in her Navy coat, with a few blonde hairs peeking out from under the watch cap.

I noticed the squad members were still calling me captain but I thought they were kidding me because I was still wearing the uniform. About fifteen minutes into the bay crossing, Lt. Griffin and the squad came over to where we were sitting on the deck. The squad was called to attention in front of us by Sgt. Reilly, who should not have been standing up, and they presented a sharp Marine salute. I stood and returned their salute and Laure smiled. Sgt. Reilly told them what we done in the action.

Laure became the squad's darling, having charmed the Marines by stopping Sgt. Reilly's arm wound from bleeding him out by using her brassiere as a tourniquet. Each one of the squad hugged Laure and shook my hand. Sgt. Reilly told me I was now the honorary captain of the squad and Laure was declared the chief medical officer and pinup girl.

Laure promised to come back to pose for pinup photos with the squad at Mare Island on the condition that she be properly dressed. The guys began to moan but she said she would wear one of her flapper dancing dresses and show some leg for the photos, and that won approval. Sgt. Reilly asked if he could keep the tourniquet that had saved his life. Laure said "I won't be able to wear it again, and I'm happy knowing it was sacrificed for a good cause" which got cheers from everyone. On the ship just after the action,

Laure had been looking very pale and showing signs of going into shock but with fresh croissants bought by the sailors in San Francisco for the girls, and hot tea laced with rum from the boat commander's private stash, my gentle smiles and hugs, the warm Navy coat and the happy company around her, Laure's natural good spirit took over and her color began to return. She told the Marines that having the toughest squad of pirates in the Marine Corps waiting in line to hug and kiss her had something to do with it.

Sgt. Reilly was looking better and started humming a catchy little tune. Laure asked him the name of the song, and he told us it was an old Irish drinking song called *Garryowen*. We had worried about Sgt. Reilly not getting checked out at the hospital, but we knew he was going to be OK when he disappeared down to the lower deck with a girl on each arm, supposedly to help him walk in his weakened condition. When the boat arrived at Mare Island, Reilly came up the ladder on his own power with a big happy smile on his face, still humming *Garryowen*.

"We proved tonight that the Marines really do get the girls" I told Laure.

"Yes, but tonight I'm getting the Marine captain" she replied and her beautiful smile was back.

DOG ROBBER

Laure and I were exhausted when we finally got back to our house in the early morning. It was almost daylight and we needed sleep so we left a note that we were not to be disturbed and then went upstairs to our bedroom.

"Would you be upset if I asked you to just hold me? You know I love you, I need to get past that horrible experience and I probably wouldn't be a very good lover" Laure looked into my eyes as she asked. "I promise your reward will be most generous."

"Sweetie, my reward is just being with you. I could not possibly be upset holding you. My body is sore all over so I might not be a very good lover right now either."

She kissed me, which caused a natural reaction and she giggled. "You're such a guy, but I like that. Thank you for bringing the Marines and rescuing me and the girls, and for covering me with your body when we were in the middle of a gunfight even if your gun or something was poking me. I am very happy that I joined you in St. Louis. Just think, if I were still in Long Grove I would be doing nothing. How boring."

"Life hasn't been the least bit boring since we've been together. Good night, or good morning, whichever it is" I said. We pulled the drapes closed but light still filtered into the room. We were too tired to let it bother us.

We snuggled up next to each other and I put my arm around her but over the covers and was almost asleep when Laure whispered "I didn't mean for you not to touch me. I just meant no sex yet. I feel safe when you hold me and I need to feel safe." I snuggled up a little closer. She took my hand under the covers and placed it on her breast. "That's what I want" she said. Unfortunately my hand on her breast began causing a reaction in another part. My brain wanted to do as she requested but my dick began having other ideas. She felt my reaction and added "I'm sorry to have that effect on you. Will you be alright?"

"I'll be OK and I know you're not really sorry you have that effect on me. Just ignore that hard thing and go to sleep. It will eventually go away." She laughed and we fell asleep.

It seemed like only minutes later someone was calling my name. "Dan. Wake up Danny my dear." The sun was high so it must have been nearly afternoon.

My eyes slowly opened and my brain began to analyze what was happening. It dawned on me that I was laying on my back but there was something else. "Of course I'm awake. I often find it difficult to sleep when you are holding my cock" I responded sleepily. My eyes shot open as I realized it wasn't a dream when her hand tightened and became more aggressive. I looked into her eyes and I knew what that look meant.

"Good. I was worried that I'd have to get a new boyfriend and it's so much work to train a new one."

"Yes, I'm well trained."

She looked at my stomach wound. Fortunately it was just skin deep or it would have been a serious problem. "No more talk, we don't want the wound to reopen so I'll take care of everything." Laure said as she climbed on top.

"Oh Laure, you take such good care of me" I moaned.

"It is my pleasure because as you know, I like it on top."

Several minutes later during our mutual enjoyment session Elsie came into the room without knocking, carrying in coffee and breakfast on a tray. Elsie was unflappable and put the tray on the table by the window. Our view from the windows was of the Mayacamas, the western border of Napa Valley. We often enjoyed a quiet early breakfast with the sun rising to paint the hills with sunlight. Elsie pretended to ignore our romp and the sounds and moans of satisfaction, leaving as quietly as she had arrived. "We have a very thoughtful maid."

"Yes Sweetie, we do." After finishing our morning fun we got out of bed without getting dressed and sat at the table to have breakfast. Elsie came in again, knocking on the door this time but not waiting for a response. It was a small improvement.

She said "Beggin' yer pardon, lovebirds, but a man in a military uniform, says he is Lieutenant Griffin and you know him, gave me this letter to give to you as soon as you was done screwin' each other's brains out. He's waitin' in the parlor downstairs. Here's a newspaper he brought and said to be sure you saw the front page right away."

I unfolded the newspaper so Laure could all see it and we began to laugh. On the front page of the *San Francisco Chronicle* was the story of the raid and above the fold was the picture of me carrying Laure off the ship. "Oh don't we look a sight" Laure commented.

I opened the envelope. It was from Col. Mosby, an invitation to The Marine Ball and Commendation Dinner on November 10 at the Admiral's Quarters on the Mare Island Naval Base. In the margin, Lt. Griffin had added that a guest apartment in officer's quarters would be reserved for us for the night before and after so we could fully enjoy the festivities. "Elsie, would you bring Lt. Griffin up here and ask him to join us for breakfast, and bring more coffee, scones and jam?"

"You're both sittin' there wit' nothin' on but yer smiles. Buck nekkid is what you are. Should I warn him first or do you want to surprise him?"

"No, by the time you bring the food and Lt. Griffin up we will be presentable" Laure said. Elsie grinned as she always does. We amuse her and says she loves it. No one around here seems to have a boring life. Elsie kept our house in immaculate condition and helped Laure keep our lives in a semblance of organization. We jumped up and I pulled on my Marine pants but Laure had already put on my Marine shirt so I got another shirt from the closet. The Marine shirt was long on her and Laure sat on the far side of the table so Lt. Griffin would not be able to see she was buck nekkid down below. She smiled, and I was happy to see she was recovering from the ordeal she had been through. Laure had an inner strength that helped her overcome adversity.

Lt. Griffin looked Marine sharp in his dress uniform and came in as if a bit embarrassed to be in our bedroom with the bed looking like it had been the scene of a healthy romp. We could be sure that Elsie had told him what we were doing when he arrived. Sensing his embarrassment, Laure ordered "At ease, lieutenant, by authority of Honorary Captain Dan's Girl who wears his Marine shirt, but I allow him to wear the pants. Before we go on, I want to tell you how grateful I am to you for getting the Marines out and masterminding the operation to rescue the girls and me. I wouldn't be here today if it weren't for you and the Marines and my guy."

"Thank you Laure, I appreciate your compliment. But it was Dan and Sgt. Reilly and the men in his squad that did the hard work. I suppose I should make a report of your rather unusual variation of wearing the Marine battle dress uniform, but on the other hand I was informed that there was some sort of party going on up here, which explains it. Speaking of parties Sgt. Reilly is up and roaring about, can't keep that Irishman down for long. He made sure to tell me to thank you again, both of you, for all you did last night. Sgt. Reilly and the squad will be receiving commendations at the ball and they all would like you to be there to see it. Will you be attending?"

"We will absolutely be there." Laure told him. "We would love to see Sgt. Reilly and the boys get commendations for a job well done. Tell them I wish to dance with each one of them if Dan doesn't shoot them in a jealous rage" she looked at me and laughed as I was suddenly choking on my coffee. "Will there be dance music, like The Charleston and jazz? Or do we have to polish up our old foxtrot moves? And can I dress as usual when we go dancing, as a modern girl, a flapper? I don't want to embarrass Col. Mosby but I do like having a good time, and being dressed properly for dancing helps. Oh, and would you ask the band if they know that song *Garryowen*? I love it and Sgt. Reilly said he would teach me to dance an Irish jig to it."

Lt. Griffin must have formed a favorable mental picture of Laure as a flapper because he had a rare grin on his face. "*Garryowen* is an old Irish drinking song, well known by military bands all over the United States and the British Empire, and I've heard the Mare Island Marine Band play it. I'll tell the band to be sure to play modern dance music but that won't be a problem. The Mare Island Band already has dance jazz in their repertoire because not too long ago most of them were playing in dance bands. The younger wives on the post like to dance to the modern music and some of them would love to have an excuse to dress modern so I will pass the word that our guests of honor will be so dressed. The older officers' wives dance to the usual old-fashioned dances, so there will have to be some of that, but they enjoy watching the young people dance. Being Marine wives, they aren't the stuffy old broads like some in the Army. Col. Mosby has made sure of that on this post. One more thing – Col. Mosby will serve wine at the dinner. It might be against regulations but just between you and me and no one else, the colonel is no friend of Prohibition. However, he won't serve it if anyone will be offended."

"Dan and me offended about wine? Tell the colonel I will be offended if he doesn't serve wine. You can also tell the wives whose husbands won't dance to use this line: 'If you don't dance, no romance.' Dan responds with alacrity when I use it on him. Alacrity is good. It's a good thing in the military too, isn't it?" Our morning exercises put Laure in a fine frame of mind.

"I would be disappointed in him if he didn't respond with alacrity" laughed Griffin. "And Dan, if any of the men grabs Laure inappropriately while dancing with her, I'll save you the cost of ammunition and shoot them myself."

"By the way, Col. Mosby ordered me to request both of you to come see him in his office next Tuesday at 1030 hours. Col. Mosby wants to talk to both of you in private and then Cpl. Maranello is tasked with giving you a tour of the base, followed by lunch with the colonel. He wants to thank you personally and make sure you are both OK with what happened. Believe me, if it weren't for you two, the alarm would not have been raised in time. We would not have known that the Cranston Gang had struck until they were gone. That bunch was a black eye to the Marine MPs and the Navy and Marine rank and file are relieved that the gang is destroyed. The SFPD is also pleased. The harbor police captured the captain of the freighter and the ship's owner, who is accused of collusion with the gang. The captain and ship's owner will be turned over to federal authorities for prosecution. We captured or killed most of the Cranston gang, twice the number we estimated, but there is evidence that some are mercenaries hired for this job. All the girls are expected to fully recover and none of them are prostitutes so we asked the newspapers not to describe the raid as such. It will be described as an attempted kidnapping.

"That reminds me. The colonel requested me to clarify an order he gave last night. Col. Mosby wanted to be clear that he authorized you to use firearms *if necessary*, and the colonel deems that during the subsequent action to secure the hostages, it was necessary. Sgt. Reilly states this in his report. The colonel is pleased it ended the way it did and his status with the Marine Commandant in D.C. is way up this morning. But as for the order, in the military if you fire a gun in public against orders the colonel would be required to convene a military board to investigate the incident. Col. Mosby feels that there are better ways to use taxpayer money and the Marines' time. Will you both be amenable to that interpretation of Col. Mosby's orders?"

"That's exactly what I heard the colonel say, and I'll swear to it" I said. "And you were there too lieutenant, and witnessed the orders. I believe you to be an officer and a gentleman and take your officer's oath seriously. You would not have let me keep my weapons if he had ordered otherwise."

"I am nothing if not a loyal dog-robber" Griffin said somewhat half-seriously.

"What's a dog robber?" Laure asked. "Do you go around robbing dogs? What do you rob from them, dog biscuits and steak bones?"

Lt. Griffin laughed and explained. "The term dog-robber has been around since at least the Civil War and probably long before that. Commanding officers have had someone like me to help them manage their day-to-day duties. My official title is aide-de-camp. But in reality I do whatever the colonel wants me to do, with no questions asked. Meaning, he doesn't ask me how I get something done as long as I don't attract the wrong kind of attention. The legend is that a general told his aide-de-camp he wanted a certain type of dog breed that was practically impossible to find, but the aide-de-camp did it and the general never asked how. Ever since then, we have been unofficially known as 'dog-robbers'. The highest generals have dog-robbers. In fact, the higher up the officer, the more dog robbing is required."

"Yes, that description applies to what Laure's father and mine did for an Army colonel named Patton in the Great War. They somehow got things that the supply depot claimed were not available. They became well known for their special talents, with the result that other officers tried to steal them away from Col. Patton for their units. I never heard the term dog-robber before, but that sounds like what they did" I explained to Griffin.

"I think I've heard of them. I was a brand new lieutenant just out of West Point serving with then-Captain Mosby in the war. Were your fathers the ones who helped evacuate Col. Patton when he was injured? What are their names?"

"Yes, they were the ones, and Col. Patton gave them matching M1911s with pearl-handled grips. The ones you saw me with last night that I used appropriately under orders. My father's name was Marvin Lindner and Laure's father is Jake Winiarzski."

"Marvin and Jake eh? Yes, I'm sure I've heard of them. Well, that is very interesting and I'm sure Col. Mosby will like to hear about that. I'll be on my way, and all of us look forward to seeing both of you at the ball. I will place your names on the list for Tuesday so when you get to Mare Island, just tell the guard at the gate who you are. He will call me and I will dispatch Cpl. Maranello, who will show you to your quarters and take you to the colonel's office after you have freshened up. Do the same at the gate when you arrive for the ball. Thank you for the coffee and breakfast rolls. See you Tuesday" and the lieutenant departed. We heard Elsie downstairs saying goodbye to Lt. Griffin on his way out.

"That was funny, Griffin talking about our unusual variation of wearing the Marine battle dress uniform. It gave me strange thoughts about you wearing nothing under the Marine uniform shirt."

"Yes, I heard him say that. And look." Laure took off the shirt. "I am wearing nothing under it. But yes you do have strange thoughts on your mind. I felt evidence of your strange thoughts earlier this morning. Don't deny it; the proof was obvious" Laure teased.

"I alone had strange thoughts on my mind? My dear partner and lovely lady, I do believe that it was you having strange thoughts. I admirably restrained myself from taking advantage of your nekkid body last night as requested, only to be awakened and relentlessly attacked this morning until my defenses were worn down and I fell victim to your womanly wiles."

"Oh you poor boy. But defenseless? I felt something hard poking at me most of the night while you claimed to be asleep. Have you no shame sir?"

"None at all."

"You're a bad boy, but a good man." We teased for a few more minutes but I could tell when she had something on her mind. I waited for her to decide when to talk about it, because if she was having a difficult time, it wasn't going to be easy. Laure put the shirt back on and took my hand, then said "I have to tell you something I heard last night. I couldn't tell you then and we had important things to do this morning."

"What is it?" If I sounded worried it's only because I was worried.

Laure took a deep breath and let it out slowly. "I overheard a couple of the Cranston gangsters who were guarding the girls saying that it was a shame to send the tall blond with nice tits to Chicago when they could have their way with her right here and they complained about losing prize money because they couldn't get the bounty for selling her. I was the tallest blond girl there, and there's only one person who would want me kidnapped and taken to Chicago. Kidnapping the other girls was a cover so they could get me to Chicago before anyone could discover the truth. I think the gang was hired to do the dirty work for Joey Coniglio, and that would explain why they hired extra gangsters for the job."

"When they raided Mrs. South's saloon, they herded us into trucks and took us to an abandoned pier on San Pablo Bay. They took us by boat to San Francisco to an old warehouse. The guards were rude and obnoxious and kept saying crude things to the girls, but at least they didn't touch us because the gang leader was nearby. They moved us by truck to other warehouses a couple of times, probably to throw off anyone trying to find us."

She continued "The gang took us to that rusty old ship and put us in the compartment with the guards. Cranston went to talk to the ship's captain. I decided I would rather fight and die than be shipped somewhere and sold into prostitution or sent to Chicago for Joey's revenge. Some of us girls devised a plan. Two girls pretended to start a fight with each other to divert the guards' attention. While the guards were watching the fight, the rest of us, in twos and threes, jumped the guards, knocked them down and took their guns. I teamed up with two girls. Josefina hit the guard in the back of his head with a piece of wood while the other pushed him down. As he fell I pulled his gun from his belt and shot him. Many of the other girls surprised the guards, knocking them down and getting their guns and four or five of the guards were shot. I was afraid when another guard came at me, but I overcame my fear and shot him. I don't know if I killed him or not but he went down. There was more shooting and screaming, then the gangsters began hitting the girls, but all of us kept fighting. Girls began to get injured as more guards came in to beat the girls." Laure stopped for a moment.

"I was trying to get a clean shot at one of them when I saw a big thug trying to hit Josefina, that pretty Italian girl that Luigi likes. She was fighting the gangster like a demon but he got hold of her by her hair and raised his fist to hit her in the face. I pulled the trigger but the gun was empty. Just then, someone shot him but at the time I didn't know it was you. The thug fell on top of Josefina. I was trying to help Josefina get up when another gangster grabbed me and threw me down on the deck."

"You saw the rest. Just as he started to bring his knife to stab me I got the best surprise of my life when you appeared. He would have harmed or killed Josefina and me. I never want to hurt anyone but last night I was determined to kill as many of those bastards as I could before they killed me. Afterwards, I wanted you to hold me last night but my mind was racing and I was not in the mood for sex. I didn't sleep very long and woke up before you, and used the time to think it through. I decided that given the alternatives, if we had not fought the guards we might have been dead or injured before you and the Marines got there. If you had not arrived when you did, we would have been overwhelmed and I wouldn't be here today."

"This morning I thought about how good we are for each other. That turned my thoughts to happiness and I needed you, physically and emotionally. You came for me last night, but somehow I knew you would. I don't know why, but I felt your presence nearby. I did not know you'd bring the Marines, or be one yourself. Dan, I love you so much." Laure held me for so long I thought she would never let go but I am not one to complain.

"Laure, you did what you had to do, the alternative was unthinkable. I admit that I was scared as hell but all the same, I was determined to get to you. Sgt. Reilly's Marine squad was the best, he trained them well, and Col. Mosby broke military regulations by allowing me to go with the Marines and keep my guns. I think he knew I would only use them if necessary."

Laure silently hugged me close for several minutes until I added "I'm thinking that Luigi and I make a pretty good damsel-in-distress rescue team." That made her laugh again. "By the way, are you sure they were talking about you? I didn't notice, but were there other blonde girls with nice tits there?"

"It really is time for a new one."

"But won't you miss me when I'm gone?" I asked.

"Yes Sweetie, I would miss you so I'll let it pass this time. But I'll worry if you continue to insist on asking about other blonde girls with nice tits."

Laure doesn't think evil of people, which is why she tried to talk Joey C. out of sending me to California. I kept to myself the thought that if Joey C. was behind this, we should expect him to strike again.

Something else about the raid bothered me. It came to me that if the goal of the gang was to kidnap Laure, how did they know when and where to find her?

LUNCH ON MARE ISLAND

The story of the raid and the photo of me carrying Laure off the ship was picked up by the news wire services. I would rather not have that happen, but maybe it was a slow news day. We went for our morning walk with Raider and sorted through the possibility that someone had tipped off the Cranston Gang that Laure would be at South's saloon the night of the raid. The only people that knew our schedule besides us were Mrs. South, Enid and Elsie and we doubted that Mrs. South or Elsie would betray us. I felt a chill coming on as I realized that it had to be Enid. When she came to work for us she was pleasant and we naively allowed her to learn everything about us. Later, she became surly and complaining about her work and seemed to dislike everything. Laure was thinking about dismissing her.

On our return from the walk we went to our office and began going through the files that Enid had worked on. Her recent work was sloppy and needed to be re-done, and our suspicions grew because she had left work early yesterday and had not shown up for work this morning. Laure and I went to get the Dodge at Mrs. South's. Raider came along for the ride, happily wagging his tail.

We went to the address in St. Helena where Enid said she lived and it was a vacant lot. Laure and I each took a side of the street. I sent Raider with Laure and we knocked on the doors of the few other houses on that block, but no one had heard of the woman. It was becoming obvious that Enid was the gang's informant and she had scrammed last night. When we got back to the office Laure knew the local telephone operator and called her. The operator remembered placing a phone call from Enid to a number in Sacramento earlier in the afternoon before the raid. Laure called the sheriff's office and talked to a sergeant who thought he knew the woman from Laure's description, saying she went by the name of Rose and was under suspicion for theft. The sergeant said he would keep an eye out for her, but speculated that she was long gone by now.

Laure came up with a great idea to hire Josefina to work in the LaureDan office. On the way back from the raid Josefina told Laure she helped her mother with the bookkeeping for her family's winery. With so little business at the winery, she was eager to find a job to earn money to help her family. I liked the idea and we agreed to ask Josefina to come work for us.

Laure changed the dressing on my wound and said it did not look like it was becoming infected, but it still stung like hell. Later in the afternoon the calls started coming in from family and friends who had seen our picture in the newspaper and read the article. Jake and Vera were relieved that Laure answered the phone when they called and told them we were safe.

I was glad the next call was from Scott McLanahan. Laure sat on my lap and held the earpiece between our heads to listen and I held the stick, allowing us both to talk and listen, and for me to put my arm around her. We gave Scott a review of the raid and promised to write up the details and send it to him. When Laure told Scott that she had heard she was to be sent to Chicago, Scott wasn't surprised.

Scott said that Joey C. was getting out of control and the North Side mob bosses that he had allied with to assassinate his father were not happy because he was bringing bad publicity to them. That was bad for business. The mob boss was going to send an enforcer to get Joey under control, and that promised to be a difficult task. In the meantime, he would try to get some of our growing stock of wine and spirits back in his Fokker trimotor aeroplane which could handle larger payloads than his old Jenny or Claire's Super Swallow.

We took Scott's news with mixed feelings. We both missed our families, but our success with The LaureDan Company was growing and we were profitable as we added more services like property management. Winery properties had been lost to banks through loan defaults but some were still owned by a family when the owners moved somewhere else so the breadwinner could get a job or start a business, and they were able to maintain the property. We hired several ex-managers and workers to provide regular property inspections and a crew of maintenance people to make repairs as needed to keep buildings intact so they could someday be reopened.

Scott told us that he believed Prohibition would be repealed although it might take several years and certainly not before the 1928 or maybe even the 1932 presidential elections. That was the feeling we shared with many people here in California. Some of it was probably because we wanted to see it that way, but there was no doubt that many of the organizations that initially pushed Prohibition into law had lost support. People were upset by the crimes related to Prohibition happening on city streets almost every day in major cities. Some realized that since the alcohol tax revenue that had been generated before the 18th Amendment became law dried up, government turned to other fees and taxes. The repeal of Prohibition was one of the ideas behind The LaureDan Company business plan, to keep businesses and property ready for either repeal or for some other agricultural product to take over. Areas like Napa and Sonoma would not stay depressed forever, something would happen to turn it around and we wanted to be part of it.

Scott told us that my auto repair shop that Otto and Fritz were running for me was very busy and had built up an excellent reputation for honesty and good work, and it was profitable. They had just asked Scott if they could hire a third mechanic. I had not thought much about my Long Grove auto repair business and realized it would be a long time before I could run it again. By then Otto and Fritz, having worked hard to build the business might want to go off on their own instead of continuing to work for me. I told Scott to offer Otto and Fritz ownership of the business. Since it was on my family's land, they would pay us rent for the facility, and I would set it at a reasonable rate. Eventually I might want the property to build a dealership, but we would give them a long notice and provide financial assistance if they needed to relocate, or be open to some other arrangement. Scott said when I returned we should look into establishing two or three automobile dealerships. Laure and I liked that idea.

We also told him we were planning to open a LaureDan office in San Francisco. Scott offered to send us an up and coming young man in his organization that was doing an exceptional job and needed a bigger challenge. He could send the man out by train sometime early next year but Laure was shaking her head and I saw her silently mouthing the word "No". I thanked Scott but told him we had someone in mind for the job. Scott finished the phone call, advising us that his private railcar was nearing completion in Streator.

Laure was immediately inspired with an idea. "How many people could travel in the railcar?" she asked and Scott replied that it was flexible and with temporary extra beds and room dividers he thought 12 to 15 or more people would be possible. "That's it – why don't you, Claire, your parents, Dan's mother and my parents come out here for Christmas! We have a huge house here and guest cottages too. There's a railroad that runs right up Napa Valley just a few minutes from our house. It would be wonderful to have you here."

Scott said "Laure, that's a grand idea – I'll call everyone tonight to see if they are interested. Claire loved it out there, she talks about visiting you every chance she gets. I might need some temporary office space and a staff assistant."

Laure excitedly jumped in. "We have plenty of space here, and we have an extra room next to our LaureDan

Company office. I will get another telephone line brought in and whatever else you need. Oh please, Scott, tell them they have to come here for Christmas!" Privately, I was thinking the same thing, and it would be fun for everyone and good for Laure to put the raid behind her. Scott was enthusiastic about it and we signed off on a happy note. Scott asked if I was wearing a uniform of some kind in that photo and I told him I had been a temporary Marine.

Scott informed me that "I have a cousin in the Marines and I learned from him that once you are sworn in you are always a Marine, never a temporary Marine or a former Marine. They have a different way of looking at their service. For example, they won't accept being called soldiers, they are Marines."

We signed off, Laure sending our love to all and promising to write to everyone. Afterward, Laure and I talked about the future of The LaureDan Company. Even when we returned to Long Grove we expected to run the business but had not decided exactly how to accomplish that. We agreed that Scott had become a good friend, but Laure wanted to develop our own businesses, and someday we might be competitors rather than partners with Scott. She wanted separation of businesses that we built up on our own. We agreed that any business we started with McLanahan financial help would be partnerships, but LaureDan was all ours. It seemed ridiculous to think that with one small but fast growing business we would someday become competitors with the McLanahan empire that included factories, stores, construction, railroads, real estate and more, but Laure was competitive and had no doubt that we would do it.

Early Tuesday we drove to Mare Island in the Duesenberg. Arriving at the gate we found Cpl. Maranello waiting for us, having a cup of coffee with the gate guard. Luigi stood on the running board and directed us to Col. Mosby's office. Cpl. Maranello brought us into Col. Mosby's outer office and Lt. Griffin welcomed us with a smile and took us immediately into the colonel's private office. It was not fancy but it was fitting and proper for a Marine base commander. He showed us to some chairs and a table by a large window overlooking a parade ground with groups of Marines at drill practice. Lt. Griffin offered refreshments and we each accepted coffee and a warm croissant.

Col. Mosby once again thanked me for my actions on the ship and inquired of Laure if she was OK. He seemed genuinely sensitive to what she had gone through and told her to not hesitate to call him or Lt. Griffin if there was anything they could do to help. After that Col. Mosby told us a little story.

"In France during the war there was an Army captain in a meeting with two Army staff colonels to review the captain's request to have two men reassigned from another command to his unit. The colonels were about to agree. But suddenly Major Patton threw the door open with such force that it went around and banged against the wall. The major was in enraged. The Army colonels listened as he told them how the captain was trying to pull a fast one and steal two men that Patton desperately needed to keep his tank units in a high state of readiness at the front. His ability to repel German tank attacks was at stake, and if the Germans pushed through his tanks they could be at the colonels' staff HQ in minutes.

The colonels turned to the captain who made the request and told him the request was denied. The Army captain was me. I tried an underhanded trick to steal Marvin and Jake for my unit, such was their reputation for getting things done. After the Armistice I was turned out of the Army and I think Patton had something to do with that. Fortunately, I had connections in Washington D.C. and was able to get a commission in the Marine Corps where Patton couldn't touch me. From your actions I think you are both cut from the same cloth as your fathers, I am not surprised that the two of are together. You're quite a team in a fight and I would give each of you a commission if I could."

Col. Mosby continued "I'm aware of a connection between the Cranston gang and certain gangsters in Chicago. Lt. Griffin discovered what the purpose of the raid was, as I think you have also figured out."

Col. Mosby went on. "Lt. Griffin is a master at intelligence work. Not much gets past his scrutiny. Let me point out that Lt. Griffin somehow got the dubious idea that you and Laure are purchasing wine and distilled spirits in quantities far more than you can drink in the foreseeable future. Now, you know that I am not a friend of Prohibition so I officially do not know anything about that and Lt. Griffin has already forgotten whatever it was he told me. I will help you if I can but my help is limited. I trust Lt. Griffin, so keep him updated and he will decide what I need to know."

Col. Mosby stood and held out his hand to me, then Laure, but when she reached to shake hands, he lifted her hand and kissed it gently. "Dan, if I were a great many years younger I would be your rival for this beautiful young lady's affections."

Laure, as always, handled it perfectly. "Col. Mosby you flatter me. I'm sorry to say you are too late because Dan has dog-robbed my heart, but had you been around earlier my choice might have been very difficult."

Mosby laughed. "Those women's groups say that someday there will be women in the United States military and if that comes to pass I hope they are just like you Laure. Let me know if you ever need a new boyfriend" which caused Laure and me difficulty in keeping from snickering. This brought a lack of understanding to Col. Mosby's eyes until Laure told him how she sometimes teased me with the line "It's time for a new one."

"Well, then I can still hope, eh? And Laure, I am authorizing you and Dan to come to the Mare Island base at any time. Do not hesitate to come here if there is even a remote possibility of a threat to your safety. I can't run a personal protection service, but I can invite you to be my temporary guests. Lt. Griffin will provide you with gate passes. You will be safe here, just advise Sgt. Reilly, Sgt. Maranello, Lt. Griffin or myself when you arrive. I believe they are sufficiently motivated to take excellent care of your security. Something about a pinup girl? I don't know, maybe that's just an idle rumor?"

"Did I hear you say Sgt. Maranello?"

"I should not have said that. He is to be promoted but he doesn't know it yet, and I would appreciate if you kept our secret until the Marine Ball."

On the way home, I told Laure "I'm surprised they did not ask me to return the Marine uniform."

"I'm glad, because I was thinking about the opportunities I will have to see my handsome Marine Captain take off that uniform."

"I assure you that were I actually an officer I would have to be modest so as not to offend you" I replied.

"Dan, if you're going to start acting modest when we are alone, I will become offended and attack you, and you wouldn't want to cause a scene where Sgt. Reilly and his squad have to come over and hold me down would you? They might like holding me down, but do you know what I say about that?"

I knew she's springing a verbal trap on me, but I always go bravely unto the breach. "No, you have not told me. Pray tell, what is it you would say?"

"Remember that you only live one time so you have to be a little bit crazy if you're going to be mine."

"Well, I guess that I qualify. And no, I would not want to see a squad of Marines holding you down, and I am positive they would enjoy that."

"Good. I may want to wear the uniform shirt occasionally and I hope you will not turn me in to be court-martialed."

"I think you have to be a member of the military to be court-martialed, and it is illegal for a civilian to wear a military uniform. I was authorized to wear the uniform for the raid."

"I will only wear it in the privacy of our home. You wouldn't report me for that, would you? By the way Captain, I have a request for you to do something for me later. Would you wear the uniform? You won't have to take it off, I'll handle that."

"What? I'm shocked. I'm expected to behave like an officer and a gentleman, you know."

"You're not really an officer and I don't want a gentleman. I want my sexy Marine boyfriend to seduce me."

"I accept the challenge of seducing you."

"Good. Otherwise, I would have to call Col. Mosby to take up his offer when I need a new boyfriend, although he is rather dashing for an older man" Laure smiled as she put her arm behind me and massaged my neck and shoulders as we drove home.

FLAPPER, MODEL, PINUP GIRL

The next day Laure and I went to visit the Montanari family to offer Josefina a job with The LaureDan Company. As usual, Raider sensed we were going somewhere and was waiting by the Duesenberg for us. We had talked with Luigi the day before at Mare Island and he told us that Josefina's family was struggling to hold on to their vineyard and winery. That was why Josefina was working at Mrs. South's roadhouse as a cook but it did not bring in much money, and after the raid her father Vincenzo would not let her work there. Luigi said the bank was threatening to call their loan, and if that happened, Josefina's parents would lose everything. With a good job, Josefina might be able to contribute enough to her family so they would not lose the property.

Laure called to tell Josefina we were stopping by for a visit, and she met us at the door. Josefina's mother Bettina welcomed us at their big kitchen table and served hot fresh Italian coffee, dark with a good strong flavor. We liked it and learned that the Montanaris made it themselves, buying and roasting the coffee beans. I thought it might be a business opportunity for them because it was great coffee.

Laure got right down to business and made the LaureDan job offer since she would be Josefina's direct supervisor. They had gotten along great together ever since the night of the raid.

After hearing the job offer, Josefina looked to her parents who nodded their approval and she accepted by jumping out of her chair to hug us. We offered her a good pay rate to start, and Laure also said that she would have a room at our house so Josefina would not have to travel in the dark by herself if she worked late. Vincenzo made the condition that she had to call to let them know, which of course we agreed. Josefina would have lunch with us since our chef Sunny made a great lunch. She would also get dinner if she worked late. Josefina's mother was very proud that her daughter was offered a good job at a time when good jobs were scarce, and her father seemed pleased and relieved. As in many families during tough times, Josefina was going to turn over most of her earnings to her parents to help the family finances.

After it was settled to everyone's agreement Vincenzo brought out a bottle and poured each of us a small amount of clear liquid. He made some remark in Italian to his wife and daughter and they laughed. Then he told Laure and me that it was grappa and it was very powerful. I'm sure glad he told me because it was more than powerful. He made a toast to us, to the U.S. Marines, and probably the Pope because he lapsed into Italian by the end. The first taste of the grappa was rough and incredibly strong. By the second glass it had become much easier to drink. Fortunately the amounts were small and they offered us lunch so we had some food in us before we drove home.

Josefina told us that Luigi was buying her a used flivver to teach her how to drive, so she would soon be able to drive herself to work. We offered to drive her until she was ready to drive on her own. Their winery was only ten minutes from our property. We did not know it at the time, but hiring Josefina turned out to be one of the best business decisions we made.

Laure enjoyed life but did not demand fine automobiles or mansions. The fact that we had those things did not impress her, it was just how we lived and a reward for our hard work. She was more interested in our life together. We treasured our growing relationship and the way we respected each other. Living together for almost a year had tested and strengthened our relationship.

Laure's everyday clothing style was practical. When she was out in vineyard properties or warehouses she usually wore pants or jeans tailored for her in a way that always drew my attention and admiration. She wore cowboy boots, and her top was often a sweater or jacket over her shirt in our moderate cooler weather, or a nice shirt or blouse in the summer that hinted at her fine figure. For meeting new clients she would wear a conservatively tailored business suit with a hem below her knees.

I took the same attitude as Laure when it came to clothing. Daily wear had to be comfortable and rugged, not expensive or dressy, while our evenings out were the highlights of our week and I wanted to look great when I was in the company of a beautiful, sexy, intelligent woman.

When Laure dressed to go out, she dressed to kill. She favored the modern flapper style with the ever-shortening hemlines, sexy party dresses, shoes and accessories. She had a modern attitude, but not in every way. Flappers were noted for smoking and casual sex while flapper dress styles did not accent the bust. Some women wore undergarments to flatten their chest. Laure had a lovely figure and liked to show her curves. Factory made brassieres did not do that so she had them custom made for her figure. We found an excellent Italian tailor in Napa who made men's clothing and alterations. His wife was a dressmaker and seamstress who designed and made women's clothing. She blended classic and modern styles, to create a modern and sexy look. I enjoyed the results of her work every time Laure came downstairs for a night out, so lovely that my heart skipped a beat or two and she often had to slow me down so we could get out the door.

A week before the ball, Laure, accompanied by Josefina and Raider went to Mare Island to pose for photographs with Sgt. Reilly's Marine squad. Lt. Griffin hired a fashion photographer from the city and the lieutenant's wife Carole would be there to oversee the fashion shoot. Laure did not want me to go along but promised that I would see every photo taken that day. She chose to drive the Duesenberg since it was a big comfortable car and it would be safer and faster if there was any trouble. I was also relieved to find out that Sgt. Reilly and Luigi were assigned a staff car for the day, and they drove up to Napa to follow them to the base.

After the photo shoot, Laure and Josefina had dinner and stayed overnight with the Griffins at their officer's quarters townhouse. Laure told me not to worry because Lt. Griffin assigned an MP squad to patrol the area that night. Even though it was extra duty for them, no one complained because the Marines were pleased to protect Laure and Josefina. When she arrived home in the morning she told me about her first photo shoot as a model. The photographer was so impressed with Laure, he asked her if she would like to do fashion photo shoots. I old her that it was her decision to make, and that I thought she would be a fabulous fashion model.

Tuesday, November 10, 1925 was the 150th anniversary of the creation of the Continental Marines in 1775. In 1921 Marine Commandant LeJeune set November 10 as the annual holiday to commemorate the event and in 1925 the first formal Marine Ball was held. Col. Mosby followed the directive and ordered the Mare Island Marine Ball held on that day. Formal dinners were to be at the Navy base admiral's quarters and other buildings on the base so that all could attend, and the ball itself was held in the large main hall, nicely decorated for the occasion. The Mare Island Marine Band practiced several new dance numbers. This was also the occasion to honor the squad members who were victorious over the Cranston Gang. Before the dinner Col. Mosby would officiate and award the medals and promotions.

We drove the Duesenberg to our quarters on Mare Island on Monday afternoon before the Marine Ball and spent the night there. Our quarters was a small remodeled townhouse on the base and while it was not lavish it was clean and comfortable. The next morning Cpl. Maranello came to take us to breakfast at the

Officer's Club. I invited Luigi to join us, but he said it was not allowed for an enlisted man to dine in the Officer's Club. Since the promotions today had already been announced, Laure and I congratulated Luigi on his promotion to sergeant. He was happy because Josefina and her parents were going to be there to see him receive his new stripes.

At the ceremony Laure and I cheered the promotions of Gunnery Sergeant Reilly and Sergeant Maranello. Two of the squad members were promoted to Lance Corporal. Every member of Sgt. Reilly's squad received commendations for their performance under fire on a dangerous but successful mission. All of the hostages had recovered from their wounds and many of them were present. Some of the women had become girlfriends of Sgt. Reilly's Marines. Enlisted men in other MP squads received commendations or promotions.

I was taken by surprise when Col. Mosby called me front and center. I had no idea but Laure obviously knew because she had her big smile on. I received the Citizen Service Medal and Col. Mosby read the citation, which said that I had contributed to the success of the mission, had saved Sgt. Reilly from injury or death, and assisted in the battle and hostage rescue. I was most surprised when Col. Mosby stated that I had briefly commanded the squad, and had done so as effectively as if I had been an officer. I didn't remember it that way, but later both Reilly and Maranello told me how I had directed the squad after Sgt. Reilly had been injured. Col. Mosby called Laure up to have the honor of putting the medal on me and give me a kiss.

"I asked Laure to pin the medal on you so she could have an excuse to kiss you, although I understand you two never need an excuse" said Mosby. I turned to face the applause and cheers from the audience. Then Lt. Griffin was called front and center for his promotion to Captain, which had just come through by telegram that day. I was very glad to see him promoted. After his captain's bars were pinned on by his wife Carole, there were a couple of short speeches and we were dismissed to prepare for dinner. The Marines and Navy personnel marched out to the now familiar tune of *Garryowen*.

At dinner, at our request and special permission from Col. Mosby, Gunny Sergeant Reilly's squad and Sgt. Maranello and his guests were invited to dine with us at the base admiral's house. It was a very large house with additional rooms for entertaining and it could seat 140 dinner guests. Wine from Napa and Sonoma was served and I saw no one who was offended. Capt. Griffin told me that one officer on base was very pro-Prohibition and Col. Mosby had sent him to Washington D.C. that week on a temporary assignment.

The dinner was good and afterward we retired to our quarters to change into our dancing clothes. I knew Laure had something special she had purchased just for the occasion and Claire had sent it to her from Chicago. I was prepared to be very calm this time when Laure came down the stairs but once again she overwhelmed me with her combination of elegance and modern flapper fashion. She was so gorgeous and sexy that she took my breath away. I asked her "Cash or check?" and she laughed. I knew the answer had to be 'later'.

Laure was always the bees' knees when we would go dancing, but this time she really was the cat's meow and pajamas and everything else. She had on a cardinal red flapper dress with gold trim and accents, a gold headband with two red feathers. Red was also the color of her dancing shoes. I tried not to stare at how much beautiful leg she was showing. Her hem was so high I repeated that poem she had told me several months ago:

> "If the skirts get much shorter
> Said the flapper with a sob
> There'll be two more cheeks to powder
> And one more place to bob."

Laure laughed and gave me her most brilliant smile and we hugged carefully so as not to get each other too excited, although I had the usual reaction which always amused her. "If you think I'm too risqué, wait till you see what Josefina and some of the officers' wives are wearing."

We went into the dance hall and as the others arrived everyone was talking about how gorgeous all the women were. Capt. Griffin's wife Carole – they had only been married for five months – wore a very fetching gold flapper dress with a short hem and a long fringe. She could show some leg while dancing but when standing she would look demure, as befitting a Marine Captain's wife. I turned to Laure who seemed enormously amused and I knew she had something to do with all this showing of female legs. I started to ask but she just put her finger on my lips and said "Later." Except when later came my mind was full of thoughts of her legs being wrapped around me.

Sgt. Luigi Maranello came in with Josefina on his arm followed by her parents who were very proud of their daughter and her boyfriend. Josefina looked so fabulous that when they entered the room it became quiet for a few seconds as everyone turned to look. Her white beaded flapper dress was astoundingly beautiful. It was high above her knees, showing even more leg than Laure. I whispered in Laure's ear "Has she powdered and bobbed in all the right places?" and was rewarded by having Laure stick her tongue out at me, which she rarely did. Josephina was so lovely it was easy to understand Luigi's ardent attraction to her, and her for him as he was a very handsome man in his new tailored dress uniform. Josefina in a plain old worn-out housedress was a certified kitten and Luigi affectionately called her his Dolce Gattino, or sweet kitten.

"The loveliest women in the world are here tonight" I began "but you, my Sweetie, are the loveliest of them all."

She smiled and said "You are quite the smooth talking devil, aren't you? Or are you just trying to make sure you get my favors later? Well, you don't have to worry about that because I'm a sure thing for you. But if you want something extra special, there's champagne in a nook around the corner, and I am getting thirsty, if you need a hint." I immediately excused myself and found the champagne, bringing two flutes back. Laure was already surrounded by some of the bachelor lieutenants that didn't know me, and she was enjoying the attention. I did not mind as long as it was polite and gentlemanly. It made me happy to think that such a lovely woman as Laure chose to be with me and my ego was flying pretty high that night. When I came back with the champagne, the opportunistic junior officers melted away. "You scared away all my new admirers" she said.

"They can admire all they want but I get the last dance."

"You have the first and last and all the dances in between, except I promised to dance with each of Sgt. Reilly's men who were on the raid" she replied. Col. Mosby was a widower and his date was a very elegant anti-Prohibitionist lady I had seen around Napa. They came over, we chatted for a few moments until the big doors at the end of the large building opened, and the Mare Island Marine Band marched in, looking sharp in their dress uniforms. They took their positions on the bandstand and except for the uniforms they looked just like one of the famous big bands. Their musicianship was excellent. Col. Mosby, who was in charge of Marine recruiting for the Western United States, told me that he reviewed the papers of everyone who signed up for the Marines, because many musicians would run afoul of the law and be encouraged by the courts to go into the military to get their lives straightened out. That was how he kept the award-winning Mare Island Marine Band stocked with the best musicians.

The band got going right away with an up-tempo number that had most of the dancers on the floor including Laure and me. The Mare Island Band was hot tonight and featured a couple of talented singers, occasionally augmented with some of the gifted amateurs in the crowd. I was surprised when the next song started and Laure got on the stage next to the bandstand. I had no idea she could sing. She was one of the chorus line girls, which to my surprise included Josefina and Carole Griffin. That must have raised eyebrows among the older wives.

They sang a hot dance number and the words went something like 'shut up and dance'. Then the chorus line did a high leg kick routine in perfect unison, which made me concerned about their short hemlines, so of course I inspected them and found the parts that should be concealed were in fact concealed. The flash of perfectly timed chorus girl leg kicks was wildly appreciated by the Marines. That's why Laure didn't want me at the photo shoot, because it was also a practice session for the dancing girls.

When Laure got off the bandstand I was waiting for her with fresh champagne. "Thank you Sweetie, you are so well trained!" she laughed.

"I had no idea you were a singer" I exclaimed.

"I sang softly because I don't sing very well at all, but I had to be on stage because I led the high kick line. I will favor you with a private horizontal dance later" she said, giving me a sexy-eyed look over her champagne flute. She had a way of raising my heartbeat. But then, it wasn't a tease because she made sure I got the real thing. We danced again after which Laure danced with Sgt. Maranello who was an accomplished dancer. I took the opportunity to dance with Josefina and she was a real treat to dance with. She told me that her parents were good dancers and had been teaching her ballroom dancing. Josefina was so sweet, she thanked me again for the job, but I told her it was Laure's idea and we were pleased she agreed to work for us. Then in between dances with me, Laure danced with Reilly's MP squad and none of them made a wrong move. Capt. Griffin must have passed along his offer to shoot any of them who grabbed Laure's cute little butt. When the band broke into *Garryowen* Laure and Gunny Sgt. Reilly went up front to dance an Irish jig and soon several men and women of Irish descent joined them. They drew the loudest applause of the evening.

Laure and I didn't smoke but it seemed like everyone else in the dance hall was and a couple hours later my eyes were burning. I decided to sit for a moment or two while she was dancing with the MPs so I could shut my eyes to give them a rest. I spotted a comfortable chair just off the dance floor and plopped down into it. I must have sat there longer than I thought, dozing off from the dancing and champagne and cigarette and cigar smoke. I awoke to a low-pitched female voice behind me whispering in my ear "Get some champagne and tell the band to play a slow song so I can have a sexy dance with you." I did not turn to look or even open my eyes to see who it was, because it didn't sound like Laure.

"I'm sorry, but my girlfriend is here and my dance card is full" I mumbled.

"Oh I'm so sorry, I must have confused you with my boyfriend Dan. You look so much like him" the woman said in Laure's voice. Laure's voice? I jumped up and turned just in time to see Laure walking away with a little extra swing in her step. I realized my mistake. The low pitched voice was something new she was trying on me and I didn't recognize it. She was always adding something new to our lives.

I caught up to her and said "Oh I'm sorry Miss, I didn't recognize you. I'll find Dan and send him over."

She didn't turn around, saying over her shoulder "Tell him if he is still interested in taking me home, I'll be over there talking with those handsome Marine officers, and he should move with alacrity, if he's awake."

I decided to turn the tables on Laure's little joke. After talking to the bandleader I picked up two fresh glasses of champagne as I went back slowly, to time my arrival just before the next dance number. As expected, she was the center of attention in a small group of bachelor officers who were almost drooling over her. I held the cool glass to the exposed skin of her back. She jumped and turned around. I said "Oh Laure, there you are, I've been searching everywhere. I just heard that the bandleader is going to start a sexy number next and hoped you would be agreeable to dancing with me, if you weren't too busy with these gallant young Marine officers." I lowered my voice and added "Laure, I don't ever want to see you go, but I sure do love to watch you walk away."

Laure smiled and took the glass of champagne. We clinked our glasses together, took a sip and she said "OK wise guy. I'll call that a win for you."

The band started a slow sexy tango, which was a dance we had just learned so we took to the dance floor. Right at the start we interlocked our arms and put our champagne glasses to our lips and drank our glasses dry. Just as I took the glasses in hand to set them on a nearby table, I saw one of Laure's lieutenant admirers coming over looking like he wanted to break in. "Lieutenant! The colonel wants you to take these empty glasses over to the table" and I handed them over so fast he barely had time to grab them before they dropped. He gave me a funny look but did as he was ordered. I pulled Laure close to me and our sexy tango routine worked very nicely that evening. A little passion improves a guy's dancing abilities.

All things considered, it was a fun event, although both Laure and I had been thinking more along the lines of a Gatsby type soiree like those we read about in F. Scott Fitzgerald's *The Great Gatsby*. As Capt. Griffin pointed out, the Marine Ball was paid for by the taxpayers who would fail to be amused if it were overly extravagant. Only the fabulously wealthy who did not have to account for their expenditures could throw those kind of fashionable big parties.

I do not recall much of what happened after that dance, except later, when Laure's legs were wrapped around me.

The next morning the photographer brought over our set of photos with Laure and the MP squad. Some of them had funny poses and Laure did show some leg for the men. Laure was very photogenic and the camera loved her smile as much as I did. For fun I asked him how much to shoot a set of photos of our choice of poses and his price was reasonable. Laure gave me the question mark raised eyebrow, but she agreed and we dressed in our party clothes. By the end of the session some of our clothing had come off for a few intimate photographs.

After we dressed, Laure looked out the window and saw Josefina and Luigi strolling by. We called them in and asked the photographer take a set of photographs of them. Josefina was thrilled, saying these were the first professional photographs of her and Luigi together.

Luigi offered to pay for the photos, but I told him it was our present to them and they graciously thanked us. Laure quietly told the photographer to print a set for Vincenzo and Bettina, and another set to send to Luigi's parents in Italy. Laure liked to do things like that.

PARTY LIKE IT'S 1926

December saw our nearly empty home fill with family and friends. Scott and Claire, my mother Dorothy, Thomas and Elaine McLanahan, Laure's parents Jake and Vera, and even Cindy Hutfilz came out in the newly commissioned McLanahan private railcar. There was a Napa Valley Railroad siding at Rutherford near our winery property and we obtained permission to park the McLanahan railcar there. We had so much space in our main house, the guest house and three cottages that everyone had luxury accommodations. Josefina brought in her mother to help with office work for the McLanahans, and Claire also helped. Scott, Jake and I found and cut a tall Christmas tree for our high-ceilinged parlor and everyone spent a fun afternoon making decorations and placing them on the tree. Raider's liked the popcorn balls, so we had to put them higher up. We made grapevine wreaths for the doors and windows.

We introduced Cindy to our local friends who had horses and one afternoon all of us went for a ride. Dorothy, Elaine and Vera opted out of horseback riding since they were enjoying their time together so much. They made new friends in Wine Country and went shopping in Napa. I borrowed a Pierce-Arrow sedan from a neighbor and author of adventure novels and we piled into the automobiles for a trip to Napa to see the Christmas decorations in the neighborhoods and downtown. One afternoon Elaine, Vera and Dorothy went over to see Josefina's mother Bettina and the four of them opened up bottles of Montanari wine. Hours later, Elaine called and asked someone to come and get them since they seemed to have had too much Christmas spirit. There was some teasing about how the mothers were out drinking too much wine and their children had to go pick them up.

Vincenzo Montanari came over to invite us to a Saturday evening dinner. I told him how many we were but he said "Lots of room here" and when we arrived they had a beautiful setting on two long tables in the winery's stone barrel room. It was a bit chilly and we were glad Vincenzo advised us to bring sweaters, jackets and shawls. Josefina helped her mother Bettina put together an outstanding Italian family-style holiday dinner, served with excellent Montanari Napa Valley wine. We especially liked the Barbera wine with the main course. Luigi, almost a member of the family now, was a big help to Vincenzo these days and turned out to be a witty conversationalist. Josefina, always so very pretty, was a charming hostess. She was interested in horses and talked with Scott and Claire about their horse ranch. They liked Josefina so much they invited her to come for a visit, but she said after she and Luigi were married so she could travel with him. Bettina admonished Josefina not to be in such a hurry to get married, but we could tell she was pleased with Josefina's choice of Luigi as her future husband.

For New Year's Eve we converted our house into a speakeasy. Laure talked Jake into playing the part of the bouncer. Then Laure scored a coup by getting Dorothy, Elaine, Vera and Bettina to dress flapper style.

The party was remembered by everyone for a long time. Buffet food, excellent wine – bottles of wine from Leunberger, Nolan, Montanari and others. There was Champagne and locally made brandy, whiskey and gin, all checked for quality several times before the party.

Laure hired a band. Our house had a ballroom with a band stage. The band had a gig at a speakeasy that had been raided and closed so they were glad to play for our party. They were excellent musicians and singers, and during the party they blended hot dance jazz with slow and sexy belly-bumping music that got everyone on the dance floor. The party was a roaring success and the main house, guest house and cottages were very quiet until late in the morning. Even when Raider went outside in the early morning he didn't bark at the jackrabbits.

At the party Elsie had been dancing with her new boyfriend and drinking Champagne like it was water, yet she looked younger than ever in the morning. Word came around that there had been sounds of passion coming from Elsie's room after the party.

Coffee and tea, cereal, scones and muffins, fruit, bacon, eggs, along with sausage and potatoes (which Elsie told us were called 'bangers and mash') were served for breakfast by Elsie and our house chef Sunny who came up with the tasty holiday fare. After breakfast we looked healthier than when we first came down the stairs.

I asked to talk to Jake privately later that day. I knew Laure wasn't ready to talk of marriage but hoped that eventually she would be so I requested Jake's permission to ask for Laure's hand in marriage. Jake said that he would be pleased, but he told me that it would be a nice touch to talk to Vera. It took another day for me to have that opportunity and she was surprised at my question. "Of course you and Laure-Marie should get married, I do not know why she doesn't do this while we are here. Did Jake put you up to asking me about this?" I had to admit that he advised me to do so and we had a good laugh. "Jake is a good man and we make decisions together. It's one of the things that keeps us as one, and from talking with Laure-Marie she tells me you two do the same thing. I'll talk to her."

I asked her not to do that because Laure was very independent minded and would probably not appreciate anyone, not even her mother, encouraging her to get married. Vera nodded her agreement because she knew that was true. That's how the 1926 New Year arrived with song, dance, wine, laughter and hope. Laure and I were blissfully unaware of the challenges that were going to come at us in the year 1926.

On their second to last evening all of us gathered after dinner at our large dining room table. Scott had received the latest report on the Chicago mob situation and gave us the news.

Al Capone's outfit ruled most of the South Side liquor and prostitution rackets. On the North Side the gangs were mostly Irish and Polish with a few Italians, and they made their money from liquor and extortion, having decided that prostitution brought too much heat from the police. The North Side boss had been Charles Dean (Dion) O'Banion, who contracted lead poisoning by Chicago Lightning in November 1924. O'Banion had been insulting Al Capone in the newspapers, hijacking liquor shipments, then selling them back to Capone, and he reneged on a deal to sell an interest in some North Side breweries to Capone that might have brought peace to Chicago for a while.

The North Side gang had more leverage with Chicago politicians since they stayed out of prostitution and because they helped get the politicians elected through generous campaign donations and vote fraud. The North Side enjoyed protection from the Chicago PD because of bribes to many cops on the beat, and more bribes going all the way up the PD chain of command. The North Siders even got the Chicago PD to help them raid the Sibly Distillery in 1924, which was under federal guard for almost five years. The North Side mob's plunder was more than 1,750 bottles of whiskey and other distilled spirits. Both mobs began to hit their opponents hard after peace talks failed.

Scott said "The North Side gang is run by Hymie Weiss through a power sharing arrangement. Despite the Jewish sounding name, Hymie is Polish Catholic. When Joey made his arrangement to assassinate his father, he made it with Weiss."

"Why wouldn't Joey go to Capone, both being Italian?" Laure asked.

"Don Coniglio was allied with Capone. If Joey had gone to Capone, Al would have whacked Joey. We don't know for certain how close Don Coniglio and Capone were, but there were no reports of gang warfare or hits between the Coniglio and Capone gangs. So Joey had to go to the North Side gang, and Capone was reported to be furious. Several liquor routes run through the Fox River area and the Don had protected them before his death. Now with Joey in charge, the North Side mob is aggressively hijacking bootleg traveling through there. The North Siders gained more power when they pushed Johnny Torrio, Capone's mentor, out of the country. After an assassination attempt left Torrio seriously injured, he decided to retire to Italy while he was alive. Torrio gave his power to Capone, who has consolidated the South Side outfit completely under his control" said Scott.

"Recent indications show that there are problems developing between Joey and Hymie Weiss. Joey is known as being not very bright but very brutal and in their world that's saying a lot. Laure kicking him in the groin made him even more mean and dangerous. The news is that Hymie Weiss is sending a top enforcer to work with Joey, which we interpret as trying to get him under control. This means Chicago Lightning storms with no predictable outcome. The information we have on the new guy is skimpy. What we know is that he's Irish, a very cool customer and a ruthless assassin. When I get more news I will pass it along, but probably in letters unless it is urgent. Phone calls can be easily listened to so be careful saying anything over the telephone." Scott concluded his update, and we agreed to keep watching and talk again in three weeks or earlier if Joey C. was pushed out of the picture.

I prepared an inventory of all our stock to move to Chicago and it was far more than we had ever dreamed. We had a laugh remembering that the original plan was that I would take the back seat out of the Duesenberg to fit a wine barrel in, or pull a trailer all the way back to Long Grove. Now we needed a railcar. Fortunately, we had one.

Another factor in planning for our future was the Bureau of Prohibition, the agency charged with enforcing the Volstead Act. It was seriously underfunded and undermanned until 1924. The feds expected the states to enforce the law, but when Prohibition's negative side effects became apparent, many local governments developed a lackadaisical attitude toward enforcement. After Coolidge was re-elected in 1924, he increased the budget for the Bureau of Prohibition and they hired a large number of new federal agents.

At the same time public support for Prohibition was waning. People wanted their booze, and they took notice of the dangerous gangs who sought to monopolize the supply. At first many thought of the gangs as making exciting news headlines and helping them get their liquor but opinion turned against the gangs after the violence they used to enforce their liquor monopolies became widely known, and occasionally the violence caused civilian casualties.

In late 1925, several new Bureau of Prohibition agents arrived in Wine Country and that worried us. We had an easy time of it so far and were making good money but neither of us wanted to get caught. More agents meant more investigations. Although some of the new agents were caught taking bribes, the re-named Bureau of Investigation caused us to worry about our mission. Even though we had moved some wine and booze to Long Grove, we still had a large quantity to transport. Enough, we hoped, to get us to the end of Prohibition. New purchases had become few and far between, only made if some really excellent product became available.

We wanted out of the liquor business. Jake said he would like us all to be out of it. Laure and I wanted to get into normal businesses and do our own empire building. The word was if the anti-Prohibition groups could replace a few Representatives and Senators that had been elected for their support of Prohibition, there was a good chance it could be repealed.

There was also our growing love for Wine Country, wine and our new friends. We had talked about buying some wine property before Prohibition ended because land prices were sure to go up with the resumption of legal winemaking. We still thought of Long Grove as home and had not worked through the details about how to manage a winery and live in Long Grove. Since it was several years in the future, we thought there was plenty of time to make those plans. But as we learned more we were beginning to see that a winery was not an absentee owner business. Family and home meant Long Grove, and that held excellent business prospects for opening automobile, truck and farm equipment dealerships and adding aircraft sales centers should that business 'take off' as I used to pun. Everyone thought that aeroplanes would become very popular and they were, although not as popular as expectations had been right after the war.

Before their departure, Jake and Vera went for a walk with their daughter. Jake was worried that he might never see her again because of the mob problems in Chicago expanding out here with the raid. Laure was confident that we would prevail over the difficulties but she was unable to convince her father.

Two days later our Chicago guests, some with tears in their eyes, boarded the luxurious McLanahan executive railcar and a locomotive hooked up. With them we sent over two hundred fifty cases of wine and spirits. Some of our wine in barrels had been distilled into brandy by moonshiners up in the Mayacamas range to the west of Napa Valley.

The rail route home was planned and approved by the railroads, greased by the fact that Thomas McLanahan was a substantial investor in two major railroads. He had asked for fast routing based on the reasonable request for the families to spend as much time together and then return to work as quickly as possible. Thomas McLanahan said there would be very little possibility of a contraband search until St. Louis where there was a large presence of federal agents. When they got near St. Louis, Scott and Claire would travel ahead and return with their aeroplanes to bring the wine home.

Laure, Raider and I watched as the yard locomotive slowly eased the railcar down the Southern Pacific track on the first leg of its journey.

Many in our families expected that a Scott/Claire wedding date would be announced to tie the opening of the ranch with the beginning of their lives together.

We celebrated our birthdays in February and March. We were now both 23 years old and had known each other for two years. Laure was still not ready to talk marriage and I was beginning to wonder why. We were best friends, lovers and business partners. We enjoyed each other's company, loved to dance, walk, take day trips up and down the coast, explore and we even liked to read newspapers and books to each other. Our lovemaking was passionate and fulfilling. Our education about vineyards and winemaking continued and we made a couple of small casks of our own wine which we planned to open for our 1927 birthdays.

This year, we decided to take a vacation so we made a list of potential vacation destinations. Our short list included a week in San Francisco followed by another at Yosemite National Park but we had not made any reservations. That turned out to be most fortunate.

CALLING MISS DOVE! MISS BILLIE DOVE!

On a foggy Thursday morning I was working outside on a minor house repair when Laure shouted excitedly from the kitchen window. "Dan, come in and take a look at this. I just made some fresh coffee." Raider was with me as usual when I was outside and I raced him to the back door, a hopeless endeavor. He was casually wagging his tail and waiting for me when I arrived at the back door.

"You should let me win once in a while." I said to Raider.

"What was that Sweetie?" Laure asked.

"Just asking Raider to let me win now and then."

"That doesn't sound like it will happen. He's got four legs to your two."

"Thank you Laure" I said as I accepted the cup of steaming Montanari Italian Roast coffee along with the Napa Valley Register folded to the entertainment page.

She directed me to "Read this. No not that little blurb, this article here."

It was a society news paragraph about Wallace Reid's widow, Dorothy Davenport, hosting a lawn party fundraiser on Sunday April 18 to benefit her addiction rehabilitation clinic in memory of her husband Wallace Reid. All of a sudden I yelled "Wallace Reid!" as I jumped out of the chair, nearly spilling my coffee. Laure smiled at my reaction. "That sure brings back memories of when I met him in Long Grove after his car broke down in 1921."

"Yes, you've told me about it at least a hundred times. He was a handsome, daring, and he looked like a great lover and made my heart beat faster."

"Faster than I make your heart beat?"

"You're such a guy, but yes – I mean, no! You make my heart beat faster because you're alive and here with me. Now stop being difficult."

"Think about how boring your life would be if I stopped being difficult. What would you do if Reid showed up on your doorstep?" I asked foolishly.

"If it was before I met you, Wallace Reid could have carried me away to fulfill his wicked desires and I would have gone willingly. I wasn't the only girl to think that way."

It was a sad day when he died in 1923 from his morphine addiction, which had slowly taken his life. The studio provided him morphine since 1919 when he was seriously injured in a train wreck on the way to a movie location at Valley of the Giants in Oregon. The train derailed off a bridge and went down about 15 feet into a small ravine. The wreck was up in a remote mountain area and Reid was seriously injured, along with most of the passengers and movie crew. Help did not arrive for over twelve hours, and even though Reid was more seriously injured than most, he performed first aid and took care of the others. "I wanted so much to be like him, except of course for the morphine" I said, mostly to myself since Laure knew the story.

Laure moved her chair next to me and kissed me. "You are like him, you know. You're a handsome sheik, occasionally polite, devilishly funny, you have good character and you like helping others" she said "and you are also a great lover."

"Also? How do you know Wallace Reid was a great lover?"

"You have to accept the fact that women just know things and we can't or won't explain why or how. I'm sure he was a great lover because I would dream about him holding me and I would melt in his arms. He would pick me up and carry me off, and I would kick my legs and feebly cry for help, but that was a sham because I wanted him to have his way with me. All right, I admit to having fantasies about Wallace Reid ravishing me." After a moment of silence she added softly "After you came along, I stopped fantasizing about Wally." We laughed.

"Do you fantasize about me ravishing you?" Now that I was asking silly questions, I couldn't stop.

"I shouldn't admit this, but yes I have since our date at The Green Mill. You could have taken me but you kept your promise and I felt safe with you. I began to have daydreams about making love with you. I expected that you would be a great lover, and you exceeded my expectations. But stop a minute and listen. I have an idea for you to think about." I was all ears. Laure often had great spontaneous ideas.

"Does this idea have anything to do with you being carried upstairs for a couple hours of ravishing? Just give me a few minutes to clean up and I'm your man."

"Yes, that is an excellent idea but not the one I was going to tell you. But hold onto that thought. I might be able to fit you into my appointment schedule for a ravishing sometime next week" she said with that same low pitched soft and sexy voice she had tricked me with at the Marine Ball.

"Well now, I must insist on being first. I don't want to wait around while someone else is ravishing you, even if it was Wallace Reid."

"You are the first and only man on my list of ravishers. Only if Wallace Reid were here and alive would you have competition."

"OK, OK. What was this hot idea you were having before you got into a swoon fantasizing about Wallace Reid having his way with you?"

"Let's go to the party! I would love to see Hollywood. We might meet some movie stars, play on the beach and take nude photos of each other." Laure was getting excited and so was I. *She wanted us to take nude photos of each other? We had only done that once, after the Marine Ball.*

I read the article again. "It says 'by invitation only.' I wouldn't want to travel there only to find that we made a trip for biscuits." Then I thought of something. "Remember I told you that Wallace Reid gave me a telephone number? He said I should call if I ever got to Hollywood. I know he's not there, but maybe his wife is, unless she moved somewhere else and has a new telephone number."

"Why don't you try? We have nothing to lose but the cost of a long distance phone call, and we can afford that. Do you still have the telephone number?" Laure asked. I didn't reply, I was already running upstairs. I had the telephone number, remembering that when I started the journey I was alone and thought since I would be in California I might call and see if maybe the elusive Dawn who was with Wally answered the phone.

I called down to Laure "I found it – get the operator, I'm on my way down."

When I arrived at our telephone in the parlor, Laure was already chatting with an operator whom we had come to know after making so many long distance calls. "Here" Laure said as she handed me the candlestick telephone.

I gave the operator the number and she said she would try to put it through as quickly as possible. "Thank you, either Laure or I will be here" I told her.

Ten minutes later the telephone rang. The operator recited her formal "Your party is on the line" message.

"Hello?" a sexy female voice answered.

"Hello, would you perchance be Mrs. Wallace Reid?" I blurted out, probably sounding like a low-class babbling idiot. The voice at the other end immediately became hard.

"No, and if you're looking for him, he passed away several years ago. If you want a photograph I'll give you his agent's telephone number, but don't call this number again. I can't help you with anything else."

"No, no, I'm sorry, I don't want a photograph, that's not why I'm calling. Please don't hang up, allow me to explain properly."

"Make it snappy, I have to be in makeup in a few minutes." At least she didn't just cut me off. I tried to relax and put all the friendliness and charm I could muster into my voice without sounding silly. "I just saw in the newspaper that Dorothy Davenport is organizing an event to honor Wallace Reid's memory and raise money for an addiction rehabilitation clinic. My girlfriend and I would like to enquire about invitations. We are able to make a nice donation."

Her voice softened. "Wallace was quite a man. He was a gentleman in a world of impolite and not so nice people. I only met him a few times. The first time was when I auditioned with him for a role that I didn't get and always wished I had. I admit I fell a little bit in love with him then, but nothing ever came of it. We met other times at parties and industry events, we even danced a couple of times but he usually was with his wife or – well, someone. The last time I saw him he was having noticeable problems because of his addiction. It was so sad to see a wonderful gentleman, a top movie star, a handsome young man with charisma and talent who obviously did not have long to live. But I am not Miss Davenport. How did you get this number?"

I gave her a brief description of my encounter with Wallace Reid in Long Grove because of car trouble with his yellow Marmon roadster, leaving out the part about the mysterious Dawn who was with him. I told her how he gave me the number, telling me to call him if I was ever in Los Angeles and he would show me around. "I'm sorry to intrude, and I knew he wouldn't be there but I had hoped Miss Davenport would be there to give me the particulars about the event and extend an invitation. We live north of San Francisco, in Napa, so we could take the train or drive down to Los Angeles."

The woman on the other end laughed and I got the impression that she was beautiful. Her tone of voice regained its warmth and sexiness. "This telephone number is for a bungalow at Famous Players-Lasky movie studio and it once was Wallace Reid's bungalow, now it is assigned to me. I used to get so many calls from Wally's fans wanting some kind of souvenir, a lock of hair or something, and some got nasty when I told them I couldn't help them. It got to be annoying but a few months after he passed away the calls dropped off and I have not received one in quite a while. I'm sorry if I barked at you earlier, you sound like a nice sincere man." I had been holding the earpiece out so Laure could hear and she smiled and nibbled at my ear at hearing that remark. I found that very sexy and she said I tasted good.

The woman said "OK I'll do this for you. I will call Dorothy – I know her from studio events and such – and ask her about the party. Maybe my husband and I will go too. I will call you back after I talk to her. I'll need your name and telephone number."

I gave her the information. She said she would try to call back soon but she might not be able to call until after her dress rehearsal. I closed with "Thank you so much for your help. I really do appreciate it, Miss?" and realized I had not received her name.

"Billie. Billie Dove. Look forward to talking to you again." She said as she hung up.

"What was her name? I couldn't hear it." Laure asked.

"Said she was going into makeup for a dress rehearsal and her name is Billie Dove."

"Billie Dove? Are you trying to be funny? Oh, right, this is April first, April Fool's Day."

"No, Billie Dove was what she said her name was and she was in a studio bungalow that used to be Wallace Reid's."

Laure was standing there speechless. Which was something rare to behold, but there it was. She said again, in an astounded whisper "Billie Dove? You just talked to Billie Dove?" and I remembered a movie we had seen not too long ago, and one of the stars was a beautiful actress named Billie Dove.

"I doubt if it was the real Billie Dove." I told her. "It must be someone with the same or similar name or I did not hear what she said correctly."

"No Dan, listen to me. What are the chances that another person named Billie Dove lives in a bungalow at Famous Players-Lasky movie studio where Wallace Reid used to live when he was a star? And this Billie Dove is going to a dress rehearsal. She also knew Wallace Reid and his wife Dorothy Davenport, and could get in touch with her. It would one be an extraordinary coincidence that this woman is someone else with the same name yet has these connections. No Dan, you just talked to Billie Dove. When she calls back if you answer the phone put me on and introduce me. Billie Dove! Oh Dan she's so beautiful, you must remember her don't you? We saw her last November in a movie just before Thanksgiving, it was 'The Ancient Highway'. It was just an OK movie but Billie was a wonderful actress and I enjoyed it anyway."

"I remember now, Billie was great in that movie, and very pretty. Now that I think of it, we have seen her in other movies too" I said. "Since you're not available till next week, maybe I should ask Billie Dove if she is available." Laure did not think it was as funny as I did, as evidenced by the dirty look I received. We both just sat there speechless at what had just happened. We drank some coffee and grinned at each other.

Laure broke the silence. "Well, let's not overdo it when she calls. She probably gets a lot of strange calls so let's just be calm, polite and respectful. No gushing. We don't want to have her think we are creepy fans."

We jumped when the telephone rang but Laure had the candlestick in her hands before I started to move. "Hello?" she said sweetly.

She kept the ear set on her ear, so all I heard was Laure's side of the phone call. "Oh yes, thank you for calling back so soon. Yes, I have a pencil and paper here – OK, ready for the number." I held the telephone for her while she wrote.

Laure read back the number. "Thank you again Miss Dove. Yes of course Billie, and I'm Laure, L-A-U-R-E. Will you be at the party too? Oh that's wonderful. I would so love to meet you. I'm a fan of yours, although Dan said I shouldn't say it because you get a lot of that."

After a few seconds she added "Thank you, and yes Dan is a good guy and – no, we haven't set a date yet. What's that? The line had some static and I couldn't hear." Laure listened, then picked up the paper and began writing again.

"Thank you Miss Dove – I mean Billie. Yes, I can give you references. No, I don't mind, after all you're inviting two strangers into your home. I think it is very smart of you to ask. Scott McLanahan of Long Grove Illinois is a businessman and dear friend and he is the fiancé of Dan's sister" Another few seconds pass. "You know him? It is getting to be a small world. Yes, I'll get it right away."

"Dan" Laure whispered "Get Scott's telephone number. Billie knows Scott, he was an investor in one of her movies. She could get invitations for Scott and Claire too. Won't this be wonderful?" Laure was jumping around with energy and she was turning me on, but then she could stand still wearing a potato sack and turn me on. I knew Scott's number by heart and wrote it on her paper.

Laure gave Billie Scott's telephone number and our names and address, then added "Oh yes Billie, we would be glad to bring some wine!" They chatted another minute then said their goodbyes.

"No gushing, eh?" I said, but Laure ignored the remark.

"Dan – did you hear that?"

"Um, no, you had the earpiece to your ear and I couldn't hear what Miss Dove was saying."

"You'd better call her Billie. She's very nice and insists that her friends call her Billie. She will be at the party too, along with lots of stars. She invited us to stay at her cottage in Laurel Canyon. She may have to stay at the studio part of the time because she will be wrapping up a movie, and since her studio bungalow is small she invited us to stay at her canyon cottage. Her maid will have our names and Scott and Claire are invited too. We will be the only ones there unless her movie wraps up in time. We should call ahead a day or so before we get there so the maid knows when to expect us. I can't believe we will be staying at Billie Dove's cottage. Billie said her husband probably will not be there, he is the movie director Irwin Willat and is scheduled to be on a movie set during the weeks before and after the party. So Dan, you devil, you will have to forget about ravishing Billie Dove."

"I don't recall saying I would ravish Billie Dove, but now that you mention it, I could become interested if you're still swooning over Wally."

"Oh stop it. You're such a guy. But you never know with the stories I've read about those Hollywood types so maybe you have a chance. Billie seems to like you. She told me she was going to hang up but you charmed her so now she thinks we are wonderful, even with all my babbling. If she can, she will give us a tour of the studio and introduce us to people. She mentioned that she just finished her last bottle of Napa Valley wine last week. Since we are staying at her cottage for free I think it is reasonable to give her some wine and we certainly have plenty of it. Oh Dan you've fixed us up for a fabulous spring vacation. I just have to call Claire and tell her." She put a call to the McLanahan ranch and got through right away to Claire, but Scott reminded her that they were committed to a business meeting with Bessie Coleman on the day of Dorothy Davenport's event and would not be able to attend, but Scott was sending us their donation check for $1,000 to deliver at the party for the Wallace Reid rehabilitation clinic.

After she finished talking to Claire we just sat there and looked at each other. She had that look in her eyes that I knew well, and said "I, um, since I don't much like the idea of you ravishing Billie Dove, and Wallace Reid isn't here, I might be able to let you have an earlier appointment, let's see, how does right now sound?" Laure asked. "Maybe you could pretend to be Wallace Reid and I could pretend to be – me" she barely squeaked out the last word. I saw the passion in her eyes. She saw the same in mine. It was one of those times when we felt an uncontrollable desire for each other. And she offered some role play too – we had not done that before.

Laure came over and sat on my lap, put her arm around me and we kissed, softly as first, then with increasing intensity. I let my hand roam, and my growing passion became physically evident.

Without a word I picked her up, put her over my shoulder and carried her to the stairway. She pretended to be taken captive, kicking her legs as I carried her. When we got to the hallway, Josefina, Sunny and Elsie were standing there talking and got surprised looks on their faces when they saw us. I stopped. Laure was feebly kicking her legs and softly crying "Help!"

"Do you be needin' some help Miss Laure?" asked Elsie, who had correctly guessed what was happening. She knew us very well by now.

"Oh yes, this madman is taking me to his bed to have his way with me!" But I saw in the hall mirror that Laure was desperately trying to keep from laughing and giving Elsie the OK sign. Josefina blushed and turned to go to her office and I heard her begin to laugh. Sunny decided she had something to do in the kitchen.

"What are your intentions with this sweet, innocent woman, Master Daniel?" Elsie asked.

"I intend to take this wild flapper upstairs to tame her. I will require that bottle of cold Champagne in the refrigerator, and put another one in to chill. Bring up the ice bucket with lots of ice and a dish of those strawberries we bought at that farmer's roadside stand yesterday. I must keep my strength up to get the job done properly" I said with as much piracy in my voice as I could without falling on the floor laughing.

I turned and purposefully went up the stairs, with Laure still over my shoulder putting on her damsel in distress act, calling for help and kicking her legs. When I brought her into the bedroom I shut the door and gently threw her down on the bed, removed her clothing and mine and then stood there inspecting her as she lay there watching me.

"What are you going to do with me?" she asked softly.

"I've seen Douglas Fairbanks and Wallace Reid movies so I know how this is done. You will just have to trust me." I got in bed with her and the ravishing began. We ravished the hell out of each other. It got so that I didn't know who was the ravisher and who was being ravished, but that wasn't important. Nor was it important to know how much time passed because neither of us was watching the clock. I have no memory of how many times, but it was impressive even for a healthy and lustful 23 year old couple. The first round of ravishing was wild and energetic fucking rather than making love. After the first round, we found the bottle of Champagne in the ice bucket, two chilled flutes and a big bowl of strawberries in the room. Elsie had stealthily come into the bedroom while we were busy and left the wine and fruit for us. I wondered what she thought about all this, but then remembered the New Year's Eve party when several guests commented on the sounds of activities from Elsie's room. She looked to be in her early thirties and had a perky figure and attitude. She must have lured a man upstairs after the party.

"You know the flapper's poem about her maid?" Laure asked after we had some Champagne and fed strawberries to each other. She sucked my finger each time I put one in her mouth to tease me. It worked.

"No, I do not know the flapper's poem about her maid, but I have the surest of feelings you are going to tell me." She said:

"If the maid gets any quieter
Said the flapper to her lover
We'll have to spend the rest of our lives
Making love under the covers."

"Where do you hear these poems?"

"I make them up just for you" she said.

"You just make them up? On the spot?"

"Yes, on the spot, and only for you" she replied.

"What else can you think up for me?"

"How about this?" she said as she pushed me down on the bed and got on top of me.

"Oh Laure – Laure – Laure. That's even better than your poetry."

"I can't talk until you're satisfied."

"Silence is golden."

Sometime later when that round of ravishing was finished, Elsie came to the door but didn't open it, calling out "If yer be needin' any of me help let me know now 'cause it's almost time to start dinner."

"Thank you Elsie, but I think the taming lessons are going quite well, and I've got her right where I want her – or maybe she has me right where she wants me, it's hard to tell. But don't worry about dinner. We are not finished yet and I want to take Laure out for a nice romantic dinner, if she thinks she can handle more of me afterward."

Laure said "I can handle him all day and every day. Elsie, you must come to dinner with us to protect me from this insatiable madman. He may decide to throw me on the table in the restaurant and cause a scene. Call our favorite restaurant and get us our usual table."

"I won't be able to stop him. In fact, I might join in" Elsie laughed. "Especially since we're going to that restaurant with that good looking waiter." Laure and I remembered Elsie and the waiter with the thick Irish brogue checking each other out, then remembered Elsie had invited him to the New Year's party. That solved the mystery of who was in her room that night.

"Dan, next time he visits Elsie, let's go in and deliver some Champagne and strawberries while they're busy."

"Laure, how scandalous you are, planning to snoop on the maid."

"Speaking of scandalous, I'm not tamed despite your best efforts, but I'll let you give me another lesson if you think you can. I'm just getting started" Laure said.

"OK, I'll go all out and do my best Wallace Reid style ravishing. Wally told me he never left any women unravished."

"Oh he did not say that to you."

"Yes he most certainly did say that to me."

"Mmm, OK then Wally, stop talking and show me how it's done."

There was a small amount of Champagne in the bottle so I laid her on her back and poured a little between her breasts and placed a strawberry there. After feasting on the wine and strawberry I worked my way down, pouring a small Champagne trail to lick along the way. We ran out of strawberries but Laure never complained.

When I was done Laure said "That was incredibly intense. You were wonderful, Wally" she laughed. "I've never had Champagne poured on my body before, and you licked it all off, not missing a single drop. I'm so glad you like Champagne. OK, you have temporarily tamed me. But you may have to do that again if I forget." We cuddled together, not saying a word as we exhilarated in the comfort and warmth of each other's body. Early in our relationship we developed the ability to communicate our thoughts, and we did so as we lay together. I was woolgathering, thinking that ravishing is a great Hollywood sport, describing a wonderful unplanned activity to have with your lover that should be repeated often.

We took Elsie with us to dinner and she had requested her boyfriend to be our waiter when she made the reservation. When dinner was finished, Elsie asked if she could have the night off, because all the sounds of ravishing going on upstairs put her in the mood. She said her boyfriend would bring her home in the morning since he had the day off. We told her to take tomorrow off too and have fun together. As we left the restaurant her boyfriend came by to thank us. He had a grin on his face that only Elsie could wipe off. As for us, we were so spent that all we wanted to do was go straight to bed and fall asleep together. When we woke up, Laure reminded me how much she liked it in the morning. I told her I had not forgotten and would not disappoint her.

We decided to celebrate Raider's birthday on April 1 because that was the date he came to live with us. That, along with Hollywood party invitations and the best ravishing of our lives to date made it an April Fools' Day to remember.

HOLLYWOOD ROAD TRIP

Laure had an excellent fashion sense but she called Claire and a couple of other Napa friends who regularly traveled to Los Angeles to plan our clothing. Our Italian tailor and his wife put together some new party clothes and I shined up all my shoes, while Laure went to Napa to buy shoes. Laure loved almost any excuse to buy shoes and since she always looked great she never heard a complaint from me. She found a daring flapper style dancing dress and modeled it for me, which received my enthusiastic approval, as did her entire vacation wardrobe.

With just the two of us we had lots of room in the Duesenberg. I packed four cases of wine and brandy in the Duesy and four more bottles for our own personal use. We decided to take our time driving to Los Angeles. The roads were almost all paved and we wanted to see more of California while we were still here. I put a call through to Cannon Ball Baker and he gave me his always useful travel information. I checked over the Duesenberg to make sure it was in top form for the road trip.

Since we wanted to arrive rested and refreshed in Los Angeles we planned to stay at hotels or these new places that were springing up called 'motels' along the way. Instead of parking the car and walking into a large multi-storied building, we would drive into a courtyard with separate cabins or attached rooms where we could park in front of the room where we spent the night. 'Easy squeezy' as Laure said. In the years since our fathers competed in events for the Elgin Motor Car Company, the world of automobile travel had changed rapidly.

We left Road Trip Dog in the care of Elsie and Josefina, unsure of how he might be received by the Hollywood elite. Raider was not happy as he watched us load the Duesenberg. We planned to take three or four days to sightsee and travel before we arrived Thursday at Billie Dove's Laurel Canyon cottage. Billie sent us a map with directions. Friday we would rest and clean up, have a studio tour after lunch and be ready for the Saturday party. I had Scott's $1,000 donation check and our checkbook for when we decided how much to contribute.

We left Napa Valley early Monday morning. I planned our southbound route for Highway 99 with a side trip to Yosemite National Park. The return trip would be a leisurely drive north mostly on Highway 101. To begin the trip we drove to Benicia and crossed the Carquinez Strait on the Southern Pacific car ferry *Solano*. By mid-afternoon we arrived in the park and were awed with the beauty of Yosemite, just as we had been with the Grand Canyon. We went over to Camp Curry and since it was early in the tourist season they had a bungalow available so we rented it. Then we went to a ranger station and picked up maps and saw an artist rendition of the Ahwahnee Hotel that would begin construction in August and was expected to be completed in mid-1927.

After breakfast the next morning we began hiking along a lovely trail on the way to Vernal Falls. "Oh Dan, this is so beautiful! Let's come here for our honeymoon! We can stay at the Ahwahnee when it is finished."

"Does that mean I can ask you to marry me?"

"I'm sorry Dan, sometimes I just say happy things. I love you but I don't feel ready yet. You've been wonderful about not pressuring me. Eventually I will be your wife and live with you happily ever after, if there is such a thing. I think there is, because my parents are living it. That is, if you still want me after I've made you wait."

I said nothing at the moment, just savoring the thought in my mind. It was what I wished for ever since I walked into her family's home in Argo looking for Jake. I know she wanted me to say something but we kept walking up the steep and slippery trail to top of the lower falls, then we decided to keep on going up the trail to the top of the upper falls. The vistas were stunning. For lunch we sat on a rock and split a sandwich from the food we had packed in my knapsack.

I saw some flowers nearby and on a whim I picked a few, twisting the stems together to make a ring. I took her hand, kissed it, and slid my little flower stem ring on her ring finger. "Since we are not engaged but have not ruled it out either, I present you with this flower ring to show my affection for you."

Laure rarely cried but her eyes were wet as she said "Dan this is the prettiest and grandest ring ever! I shall preserve it and treasure it in memory of this day."

"I've had my eye on an exquisite ring at that little jewelry shop in Napa and when the time is right I want to present a ring like that to you, but we can celebrate our relationship any time."

"I know which ring you were eyeing. You're rather obvious, you know. I caught you looking at it and decided you were making an excellent selection. By the way, I know that you asked my parents for their permission. That was very sweet of you, perhaps unnecessary because they love you too. But the fact that you did once again proved to me that you are a careful and considerate man. That's on my list of 100 character traits I require my future husband to have."

"Only 100? I have 1,000 on my list for the perfect wife."

"See? You are careful. Have you written down the 1,000 things that your perfect wife would be?"

"No, I keep the list up here" and I tapped my head.

"Well I wrote mine down."

"OK, so how many of the list of 100 things did I score correctly?"

"All 100. I was able to check off number 100 when you ravished me for an entire afternoon" as she gave me her million dollar smile.

"There were times I thought I was being ravished."

"You were. It's best when it is a mutual activity. Now, how many of your so-called list of 1,000 did I score correctly?" she asked.

"You're still being tested but so far you have a perfect score."

I had given Laure a new Kodak No. 1A Series III camera for Christmas and we took photographs of each other. When another couple arrived we asked them to take a photograph of the two of us at the top of the falls. Laure took a photo of them and they gave us an address to send it to them. On our hike back down, Laure stopped in the middle of the trail, turned and put her arms around me, kissed me and said "I love you." And she kissed me again. A couple walked by and made a snide remark about young people kissing in public.

I laughed and said "Laure you really are shameless, shocking these people by kissing your boyfriend in public."

"Rhatz! This isn't in public. There's been hardly anyone on this trail" she exclaimed.

"Oh there are others, look over there" I pointed. There was a mother bear and two cubs ambling across a small meadow toward a creek. They were far enough away that mother bear was not concerned with us.

After a day and a half at Yosemite it was time to travel again so after breakfast we took to the road. We shared the driving, switching seats every hour or so. Arriving in Bakersfield we decided to stay there and cross the Ridge Route into Los Angeles Thursday morning. We stayed at the El Tejon, a new hotel. We had no trouble registering as if we were married. We must look like we were married because we were never challenged. I called Billie Dove's house and spoke to her maid, who said Billie was at the studio. She told us that she had errands and shopping to do tomorrow, but if she wasn't there she would leave the key at a neighbor's house and gave me the address.

Thursday morning we were on the road after breakfast and arrived in LA for lunch after which I obtained a Los Angeles road map. We used the time to look around. Los Angeles was a very large metropolitan area with good roads and lots of automobiles. Our automobile was a prototype Duesenberg Model X but it was two years old and had seen many hard miles. I wiped it down every evening and although the paint was not as shiny as when it was new, the car still looked great. But as we drove in LA we saw so many Cadillacs, Rolls-Royces, Lincolns and cars imported from Europe that even the rarity of a Duesenberg wasn't a big deal. Especially when stopped to walk and look in the stores in Hollywood. We came out of a store to find a stately and luxurious Packard Eight Phaeton parked next to us.

A couple who left the store just after us got in and when the man started the Packard I was most impressed by how smooth and quiet its engine was. I made a mental note to ask Scott to see about getting a Packard dealership. I was a fan of the Duesenberg brothers and their engineering but they were slowly losing the sales race to manufacturers like Packard.

I took a quick look at the map, easily found Laurel Canyon and we arrived at Billie's cottage. The maid left a note on the door that she was shopping but would be back about four in the afternoon and to go to the neighbor's house for the key to let ourselves in.

We drove over and Laure waited in the Duesenberg while I went to the neighbor's door. I was surprised to see it open just as I was ready to knock. There in the doorway was one of the most beautiful women I had ever seen yet she looked familiar. Then it hit me that she looked a lot like Laure, except she was shorter and had black hair instead of blonde. I must have been staring at her, because she started to laugh.

"Yes, I am who you think I am. Just call me Louise" she said with a smile as she handed me a key. "I hear we are going to the same party on Saturday. Well, that should be interesting. Are you OK?" she asked. I snapped out of my trance.

"Um, yes, if you're going to the Dorothy Davenport party." I was sure I sounded like a moron.

"You're cute, but please don't be starstruck. I'm just a girl."

"Yes, oh yes you sure are. A girl, I mean."

Her eyes held mine as she looked at me inquisitively, as if trying to make sure I had a functioning brain. "Sure. Well, see you at Dorothy's." and she laughed a very pretty laugh, gave me the key to Billie's cottage and closed the door. I went back to the Duesenberg and must have looked funny because Laure asked if I was OK.

"Yeah, I'm OK. I just saw you with black hair."

"Me, with black hair?"

"She told me she is going to Dorothy's party so you'll see for yourself." We went back to Billie's and let ourselves in. It was a lovely cottage but not small like I thought of cottages. The maid had left a note to help ourselves to cookies and the lemonade in the refrigerator. We poured ourselves some and took a cookie each, sat at a small table on the patio and talked. We were excited and looking forward to the party and the weekend.

"This neighbor looked like me but with black hair?" Laure asked.

"Yeah, and she was wearing a modern bathing suit. She did not look exactly like you, but there was a strong resemblance. Said her name was Louise."

Laure stared at me. "Did she look like Louise Brooks? You remember her, we saw her in the movie *The American Venus* a couple months ago. I knew that you liked her by the look on your face."

Now I did remember why the neighbor looked familiar. When we saw the movie I thought how she looked like Laure except for the color of her hair. They both had the bob hair style shingled in the back. "Dan? Are you awake? Is something wrong?"

I once again had to snap out of my woolgathering state of mind. "No, nothing wrong. I was just trying to remember the movie. I can't remember the name of that actress but she did have a similarity to you."

"I said her name was Louise Brooks. She's an 'It' girl, very sensual and beautiful. And you're acting quite distracted. Care to comment on that?"

"No, I don't think so. We'll see her on Saturday" and I changed the subject to talk about what we wanted to see in LA on Friday. Laure could read me like a book and she picked up on my conversation change. She just smiled at me. It was looking like Saturday would be a most interesting day.

Billie's maid arrived, a very sweet lady who showed us our room and told us that Billie's movie had wrapped that afternoon and she was expected to arrive in time for dinner. Laure and I decided to get freshened up from the road to be presentable to our hostess.

Billie arrived and we greeted each other with hugs. Billie was beautiful, even better looking than on the screen and very gracious. I brought in cases of Napa and Sonoma wine and brandy to her amazement. She had thought a bottle or two would be sufficient but we told her we really appreciated all that she was doing for us and we had plenty of wine. We gave her a shortened version of our story of how we came to live in Napa, leaving out the part about Joey C.

Billie told us that there had been a lot of wine in Hollywood but as Prohibition went on the good wines were disappearing although you could still get them at a much greater cost. There was cheap wine readily available but knowledgeable wine connoisseurs would not touch the stuff. She told us about Scott McLanahan investing in a movie she starred in, and that she had met Scott and thought he was a very handsome and witty man, and Billie said that if he lived in Hollywood he would look very good on the screen. We had wine with dinner and drinks afterward. We got along like old friends. Billie told us she had to go to the studio Friday morning to sign a contract and asked if she could see that beautiful Duesenberg automobile. She was familiar with Duesenbergs but recognized that this one was different, something most people were not aware of. We showed Billie the car and told her it was a prototype Model X with a longer frame and larger engine. Billie found the bullet holes in the rear bodywork so we told her the story. She thought it was a great story and told us we should write a book, maybe it would be made into a movie.

Billie saved the best news for last. If we would come to the Famous Players-Lasky studio tomorrow at 1:30 PM, she would be done with her business and wanted to give us a personal tour and introduce us to actors and actresses who were on the property. We all hugged and said our good-nights but just as we turned to go to our bedroom, Laure asked Billie "Is Louise Brooks your neighbor?"

"Yes, that's her. I take it you met her?"

"I didn't meet her but Dan did when he went to the door to get the key. He somehow forgot to have me come over to be introduced" Laure said.

Billie laughed. "Louise has a presence about her that affects people. Addles their brains. We are not close friends, we know each other as neighbors since she often has Eddie Sutherland at her house and he likes to entertain." Billie's emphasis on the word guest made it very clear that Eddie might be more than a guest. "Louise and I share a dislike for the Hollywood way of doing business. She is more comfortable in the New York scene, for various reasons. Like me, Louise came up through dancing for Ziegfeld's *Follies* and dancing and acting in Broadway shows. After that we worked in the New York studios but so far not on the same movie. They will be closing the New York and Chicago studios in the near future and all movie production will be moved to Hollywood. The culture in Hollywood is very different and I try to get along with the Hollywood types as best I can but Louise is incredibly independent-minded and has no trouble telling people what she thinks. I've told her that will not be good for her career over the long run, but so far she has done very well for herself and is a fast rising star, one of the hot Junior Stars at Paramount. You know Laure, you do look like her except for your blonde hair, and you're taller."

"Laure is also incredibly independent-minded and is not afraid to tell you what she thinks. I can attest to that!" I added as they both laughed.

"Louise still lives mostly in New York but is here now and then since her most recent director Eddie Sutherland is all over her trying to convince her to marry him ever since their hot affair during a movie production" which explained Eddie's visits. "Louise will be at Dorothy Davenport's on Saturday and I'll make sure you get to meet her. She will probably like talking to you since you are not in the movie business. Louise is a very intelligent woman but... oh, I shouldn't say anything. When you meet Louise, be open minded and form your own opinions. Good night."

After the travel and excitement today we fell asleep almost immediately. At least I did. During the night I sensed that Laure wasn't sleeping very well and hoped she would get enough rest for Friday.

Our association with Louise Brooks and Hollywood was going to dramatically change every part of our lives. Which, had we known that along with what other mayhem was planned for us by persons unknown, we might have turned around and gone home.

LAURE AND THE CASTING COUCH

Laure and I were up early and went for a walk. When we returned, Billie had already gone to the studio and left directions for us. Her maid served us an excellent breakfast. We thanked her and headed to Hollywood. After driving around and not really seeing much we parked and walked, window shopping and generally enjoying a beautiful day in Southern California. I had on a white pullover shirt and dark gray pants. Laure wore a cream colored shirt with black stripes that surrounded a very revealing opening in front that narrowed down to a V with a wider black border around it. It was very fashionable and served to attract attention from males and females alike. She wore a dark gray skirt that came to just above her knees. She wore a cloche hat that she later removed as it got warmer. As always, Laure was dazzling.

Just before noon we decided to get something to eat and found the Brown Derby, a name Laure heard from Claire, who read Photoplay and other movie business magazines. Claire was educating herself to become the entertainment business expert in the event she and Scott wanted to invest in a project. The Brown Derby had recently opened and was already a busy place but for some reason we were seated at a table right away even though other people had been waiting before we arrived. We wondered about that but since we did not have to wait we felt lucky. Then we found out why. A young woman came up and asked Laure if she would please autograph her photo. Laure looked at it and it was a Louise Brooks photo. The young woman said "Oh Louise, I love what you've done to your hair. It's simply lovely." Laure did not want to disappoint the woman so she wrote something on it and signed L.B. We had an interesting lunch and Laure signed a few other photographs. When we were ready to pay and leave, I left a generous tip for the waitress. All the hardworking waitstaff were women and they wore uniforms with hemlines at the knees, and they all had nice legs. We learned later that was a qualification to be hired at the Brown Derby.

At the studio, Billie had put our names on the gate guard's list, and he gave us passes and directions. The guard gave Laure a special smile. I had the impression that she was being compared to Louise Brooks. The gate guard cautioned us to drive slowly as there were people and equipment moving around between studios and bungalows. I parked, as Billie had directed, in the parking space at her bungalow. Laure had her camera and we took photos of each other standing in front of Billie Dove's – formerly Wallace Reid's – bungalow. I felt like I was in the presence of history. Billie came to the bungalow as I was taking Laure's photo and offered to take one of us together on the front porch. Then she stopped a studio messenger and had her take a photo of the three of us.

Billie took us to soundstages where scenery carpenters were building sets, some of which we remembered later when we saw a movie. Then we went to a set where filming was taking place. Billie had cleared it with the assistant director who told us in no uncertain terms that we were not to make a sound or we would be banished. We had no desire to anger a director and actors and other studio personnel so we were very careful and did not make a sound until we were outside. It was eye-opening to see actors acting and film crews filming. We did not recognize any major stars, just a few character actors. Billie told us that they were mostly doing scenes that did not require the big stars on camera. The assistant director walked us out and thanked us for being so careful. It sounded like other visitors had not been so quiet.

We told Billie about people approaching Laure at The Brown Derby and asking for autographs. She thought it was funny but said that in Hollywood, anyone who looked like a star usually was asked for an autograph and it was best to play along because some people became angry if they were refused. Billie took us to another soundstage and again cleared our visit with the assistant director. The movie people seemed to like and respect Billie Dove. We stood in an out-of-the-way place with a perfect view.

This time, Douglas Fairbanks was on the set. We watched one of the most famous actors of the day at his craft and were fascinated with every second of it. He definitely had talent and a huge stage presence. But surprisingly the director didn't like the first take and ordered the scene to be shot again. He talked to the actors personally and told them what he wanted. The scene was only a few minutes long so we watched a third and a fourth re-take. Now we understood what actors and actresses had to go through when something wasn't right. Even if you played your part perfectly, if someone else messed up the scene it had to be re-done. Later Billie told us that if it was an individual camera shot, under some conditions only that actor would have to re-do it. When the director finally called it a wrap for the day, the actors relaxed. Billie waved and Douglas Fairbanks himself came over to meet us. He especially seemed to like Laure and gave her a very close hug. We enjoyed talking to him and learned that Douglas was quite the prankster.

Douglas and Billie had just finished *The Black Pirate*, a swashbuckler pirate story that Douglas excelled at. Laure remembered seeing him in *Robin Hood* a few years ago and Fairbanks was very pleased with her compliment on his performance. He used every opportunity to stand next to Laure and try to look down her shirt. After about twenty minutes Fairbanks excused himself, saying he had a prank to set up, but he looked forward to seeing us tomorrow at Dorothy's event. He winked at Laure and made a comment that she could be in the movies if she wanted to, and he would be glad to help her. I don't think he realized that Laure and I were in a relationship and she blushed, which was one of the few times I saw her blush.

When Billie went to see someone in the costume department, she said we could walk around and check out the movie sets instead of standing and waiting. We set a time and place to meet later. Laure and I enjoyed walking down the fake streets with the fake sets, identifying those we had seen in the flickers, when a well-dressed middle-aged man stopped us and immediately began telling Laure that he wanted her in a movie he was producing and asked if she had time to do a screen test. Laure thought it was a prank but thought she should play it out and agreed to go with him. I went with the producer and Laure to a studio office building and I was asked to wait in the producer's waiting room. I was rather nervous about that, saying that some producers had reputations for using a casting couch to offer nonexistent movie roles in exchange for sex.

Laure said she knew that because Claire had told her, but it still made me nervous. Almost an hour passed and I waited with growing impatience. I finally went to the producer's secretary and demanded to know what was going on. She said it was between Laure and the producer and none of my business. I went to the corner where we were to meet Billie and told her about it. She got upset and told me to wait in the office lobby while she contacted a friend. I waited another five minutes in the lobby and then simply walked to the producer's office door and opened it. At the very same moment on the other side of the door, the producer was opening it fast, and combined with my pushing the door open hard, it smacked him in the nose and blood began dripping down on his suit. He ran from his office as if the hounds of hell were after him. The secretary was lifting up her telephone to call security.

But it wasn't the hounds of hell, it was Laure who serenely walked out of the producer's office and smiled at me. Two security guards arrived and Billie rushed in with a studio executive, who sorted out the situation.

It was obvious what had happened. Billie and the studio executive apologized profusely but Laure was not upset or angry. Since Billie had a studio car pick her up in the morning, we took her home. Billie said "I would like to hear in detail what happened with him, let's go to my cottage and talk over dinner." Since it was the maid's night off, Billie asked if we liked Chinese take-out and that she knew a good place to get some. Laure agreed since we liked Chinese food, so we stopped for Billie to order Chinese take-out.

When we got to Billie's house, she said we should have dinner first and then she wanted Laure to tell us in detail what happened with the producer. The food was superb, just as Billie promised. After dinner she offered us wine or cocktails and asked if I would do the honors of making the drinks. I went to her well stocked liquor cabinet and made myself a Canadian whiskey on the rocks. Laure and Billie had vodka gimlets. Then Billie and I sat in rapt attention as Laure described her fake screen test.

"The producer took me to a screen test room, gave me a script to read and described what the scene was about. He had an actor come in to read the male part and a photographer to run the camera. I was confident because I didn't care if I got a role or not. It went OK although the actor reading his lines kept looking at me with a mischievous grin and he muffed his lines several times."

Did you see if the cameraman loaded film into the camera?" Billie asked.

"I did not see it if he did" Laure answered.

"It could have been a fake screen test. The actor reading the male role would know you were getting a casting couch interview, and he was probably wishing he could finagle his way in on it" Billie said.

"After the screen test the producer led me to his office, and called his secretary to tell her he did not want any interruptions." Then the story turned really funny and Billie and I were rolling on the floor laughing as Laure described what happened next.

"He asked me if I had an agent and I said I was my own agent. He got a real greasy smirk on his face when he heard that. He asked me what movies I had starred in, and I told him none. He said he did not believe that, and told me he had seen me in movies and I should confess, that was the word he used. So I made up some titles from random words that came to mind, titles like *Viktor's Speakeasy* and *Carry Me to My Grave* and *Gone With The Wind*. The producer said those were stupid titles for movies and that's why I hadn't had a hit movie yet. He said a reputable producer like himself would never make a movie with insipid, meaningless titles such as those. He said if I signed to be in his movie, it would be a first-class film with a catchy title."

"Laure, you should be in the movies for your spontaneous wit as well as your looks" Billie laughed.

I made another round of cocktails and Laure took up the story again. "The producer pointed to a door and said I could use the bathroom. I was puzzled by that and told him I did not need to use the bathroom. He got the greasy smirk on his face again and said that was all right, that I could just undress right there, he liked to watch women do a striptease. I may have been naïve at first but Claire, who reads all the movie gossip sheets, told me that a screen test was often a trick for a producer to get sex."

"The producer said that he would put together my contract and began to shuffle some papers around. I could tell he was just trying to impress me, thinking I was some dumb bunny he could fool with his act. I knew there was not going to be a contract and that he was trying to hustle me to his couch, then afterward he would tell me I didn't pass the screen test. I was not going to fall for that but he didn't know it yet. When I didn't start undressing he looked up at me and asked what I was waiting for, that time is money in the movie business." Billie and I got a good laugh about that.

Laure continued "Then he tried to get tough and told me I had better take my clothes off or there would be no movie contract ever, at any studio if I didn't put out. I decided it was time to end the charade and told him I was leaving. This made him angry and he came around his desk, telling me I had better stop teasing and get naked or he would remove my clothing himself. I told him to go ahead and try."

"He said 'You're just like that Brooks bitch. She does it for everyone else but she wouldn't do it for me, but you will when I get through with you. In his anger he grabbed at me but I had my derringer hidden in my hand. I showed him the derringer aimed at his belly from only two feet away. He said 'You won't shoot me. Do you know who I am? You'll never get anywhere in this town without my help. Now put that little gun away, get your clothes off and get your naked ass on that couch."

"So I let my hand fall to my side, still holding the derringer. I moved a step towards him. He must have thought I changed my mind and was coming on to him. People often believe what they want to believe. Then his eyes got real big when I lifted my hand to press the gun at his package. I told him that it is double-barreled and I can't miss, and that maybe I should do aspiring actresses a favor and turn him into a eunuch. He yelped, jumped back and covered his balls with his hands. If the producer thought that I was going to let him fuck me for a phony movie role I had just convinced him otherwise. I didn't flinch, but he sure did. He stumbled past me in a rush to get to the door. At the moment he grabbed the doorknob Dan pushed the door open hard from the outside and the door hit him in the face."

"Laure, that producer has tricked dozens of young women into getting on his couch, and none that I know of got a movie role for it" Billie said. "I wouldn't let him touch me either but he didn't try to get rough with me. I have been with many men in my life but they were by my choice. His comment indicates he was humiliated by Louise Brooks turning him down, so maybe your similar attitude and physical appearance created a desire for revenge in him and it overloaded his little brain."

Billie followed that up by telling us "The studio was already trying to get rid of this producer, not because he made frequent use of the casting couch because that is commonplace in Hollywood, but because he was not profitable for the studio. If the executive I brought over gets approval from the board, that producer will be gone real fast. But don't broadcast the story in Hollywood for a while because the producer still had friends and could make trouble for you if you should be offered a legitimate movie role. You should tell your story to Louise Brooks tomorrow because she would get a kick out of it."

"How did you come to have a derringer?" I asked.

"My father gave it to me for Christmas. He was worried for me after the kidnapping and thought a derringer could be useful if I got into a jam. I didn't want to tell you right away because I did not want you to be upset if my father was worried enough to give me a derringer."

"Well Laure, I'm sure glad you didn't shoot me a couple weeks ago when I was carrying you upstairs."

"Dan, the way I felt that day I might have shot you if you didn't carry me up the stairs for a healthy ravishing."

We all laughed and Billie said she was tired and going to bed since we had a big day ahead of us tomorrow. She said we could stay up and have more drinks but we were tired too. Laure said "Thank you, Billie, for the interesting studio tour even though I didn't get the movie contract."

Billie replied "I'm so glad you accepted my invitation to stay here. Both of you are lovely people and have such a wicked sense of humor. You'll fit in perfectly well with the crowd tomorrow." We said our good nights and went to our room, falling asleep as soon as our heads sank into the pillows.

HOLLYWOOD GARDEN PARTY

Dorothy Davenport's event was at her home in Woodland Hills, not too far away and it started at noon so we had the morning to get ready. As usual, Laure and I were up early for a morning walk followed by breakfast with Billie.

The phone rang and Billie answered it and a moment later turned to ask us if we were up for a prank. "It's Louise Brooks. She already heard about a blonde girl who looked like she could be her sister at the studio yesterday with that producer. She came up with one of her crazy ideas. It involves both of you and Louise wants to see if you're up for a good practical joke. She loves to pull pranks on the Hollywood elite. It will confuse the hell out of them for most of the day."

Laure and I agreed to listen to her idea so Louise said she would get the rumor mill going with a few carefully planted telephone calls and then come over to talk to us. I went out to clean up the Duesenberg. We weren't going to leave until noon since no one showed up on time at a Hollywood party and Louise wanted us to make a big splash upon our arrival.

Half an hour later Louise came over. They looked at each other for a few seconds, then Louise said "You could be my cousin. Laure, there are benefits to being thought of as my cousin; certain people, like some producers, may leave you alone if they think you are related to me. I'm independent, you know. I don't do what they want me to do unless I want to do it. Billie says you have an independent streak too. Let's be cousins. What do you think Laure?"

Then Louise turned to me, looking me over. I felt her eyes take me in for a closer inspection. "I think it will be quite easy to get excited over you."

Without waiting for answers, Louise unveiled her prank. The plan was to introduce me as a producer from a Chicago studio moving to Hollywood when the Chicago studios closed. "You are the hot new cat in town, ready to dispense favors to those who curried favor with you." It sounded like I was going to dish out what the producer who tried to get Laure on the couch was offering. "Oh this will be fun!" Louise's enthusiasm was contagious and the combined brilliance when Louise and Laure smiled at the same time could blind a person. We agreed to do the prank and Louise went back to her cottage to get ready.

Laure dressed in her sexy lawn party dress that showed some leg and her curves. Just before noon I went to pick up Louise from her cottage. As before, when I lifted my hand to knock on the door it opened. This time Louise's arm came out and pulled me inside. Louise was stronger than she looked and I wasn't expecting her to put her arms around me and put her mouth on mine in a passionate kiss. But she let go just in time or I would have had a difficult time walking. "That was to get you in the mood, Mr. Dan, boyfriend of my cousin." Louise Brooks struck me as being quite an unusual woman.

Louise went over the details again when her actor, friend and lover William "Buster" Collier arrived. He would drive while Billie sat in the front seat to watch for photographers. The cousins, Laure and Louise would sit on each side of me in the back seat. When we got near Dorothy's home they would kiss me and play with my hair. We would ignore cameras, no poses, just let them take candid photos. The idea was to be natural so people would think we were the real thing.

Billie adjusted Laure and Louise's hair to be as alike as possible, which was easy since they were already very much alike. Of course hair styling wouldn't last long in the rear seat of the Duesenberg, but their bob cuts had the advantage of being easily fixed. I gave Buster a quick rundown of the Duesenberg's quirks and we were off.

Close to Dorothy Davenport's house we saw photographers along the street waiting to photograph stars on the way to the party. Buster slowed down because a small group of photographers stood in the middle of the street. Louise put her arm around me, pulled my face to hers and gave me a long wet kiss while she ran her fingers through my hair. When she was done, Laure grabbed me for her turn. William and Billie up front were waving to people and Billie turned around with her knees on the front seat and leaned toward me. I moved forward so Billie could grab my face and kiss me. She was a great kisser. One of my back seat companions goosed me but I couldn't tell which one. I looked at Laure then Louise but neither looked like they had just gotten away with something.

I decided to be very careful around Louise, which was going to be difficult because I liked being near her. But if I stayed close to Laure, what could possibly go wrong? Just as I thought that, Louise saw another pack of photographers and got on her knees in the back seat, straddled my lap facing me, held my face to her chest and ruffled my hair and waved to the photographers. She had a lovely scent and I felt her firm, small breasts on my face. Since my face was turned away from Laure I nibbled Louise's breast through the fabric of her dress while putting my hands on her butt. She just smiled.

Buster drove up to Dorothy Davenport's house and I was surprised at how large and elegant it was. But then, Wally Reid made a lot of movies in a very short time, and she made movies too. A good sized crowd was already at the party. When the Duesenberg stopped at the front entrance the cousins both kissed me at the same time as photographers snapped their cameras. Buster got out and a valet stepped up to move the Duesenberg to the parking area. Billie disappeared inside the house. Louise told us she was going to clue Dorothy in on the prank because she and Fairbanks were the only other people who would know who I really was.

I did not expect this prank would work for very long. I thought it would be obvious to those in the business that I wasn't a hotshot producer. But as I walked through Dorothy's house to the back lawn, several people stopped and introduced themselves to me, some of them stuffing pieces of paper in my pockets. Louise put her arm around me and nibbled on my ear, whispering that I should go along with it. She did this in a very sexy manner so that people would think she was playing with me. She also began introducing Laure as her cousin Laure Brooks, which at first made Laure uncomfortable but people accepted it because of their appearance and because Louise said so. Soon Laure was playing it up too. Yes, she would make a good actress. I might have to cast her in a movie. I mentioned it to Louise and she said that was a great idea. The story that I was a producer from Chicago seemed to be accepted. I was surprised that people took it all in without question. Maybe Louise was right about this prank, and that Hollywood types did not know the people in the New York and Chicago studios.

Billie brought Dorothy over and introduced us. Billie winked at me and Dorothy gave me a big smile so I knew she was in on the game. Dorothy took me around, introducing me as Dan Lindner, Chicago producer relocating to Hollywood in the near future. Louise had coached me to say I was an independent producer and not aligned with any of the Hollywood studios yet, but that I had projects in the works and would be calling on the major studio heads in the coming weeks.

I asked Louise if they would be angry at her when they found out it was all fabricated. Louise laughed and said it served them right if they believed such a flimsy story, and anyway she really didn't care because she loathed the Hollywood scene. I thought Louise's attitude strange for someone rising up as a top star, but I followed her lead.

Some people asked what movies I had produced and I remembered some Chicago productions and named them. One woman said she knew the producer of one of the movies, so I told her I had been one of many assistant producers on it, working my way up. Fortunately it was a large and successful production so that satisfied my questioner. Louise was nearby ready to jump in if needed but listened as I replied to the woman and gave me a small nod and a smile. If she had been worried about my ability to play the game she wasn't anymore. She liked it even better when I told another Hollywood studio executive about being friends with Scott McLanahan and meeting Wallace Reid in Chicago, and that they helped me get a start in the movie business.

On the way over we developed the further story that I discovered Louise's cousin Laure when she came to Chicago from Kansas, and that I had brought her to Hollywood with the intention of putting her in one of my new productions. All this was swallowed hook, line and sinker. I was astounded. I was even more astounded when Billie took me aside and told me that Scott McLanahan had not only been an investor in movie projects, but had been a partner in one of the Chicago studios that had just been bought out by Paramount. I made a note to find out from Scott if he sold his share or retained an investment in Paramount. I could drop his name carefully since people knew he was a movie and studio investor.

Our friend from yesterday, Douglas Fairbanks, arrived and came up to me and shook my hand, loudly telling me how great my project ideas were and hoped that he might be considered for one. Douglas touched his finger to the side of his nose and winked, grifter style. I told him he was at the top of my short list, which was the right thing to say and Douglas played it up in front of others. Fairbanks was a prankster extraordinaire and he was having a grand time playing the con artist. With Scott's and Wally's names and Fairbanks and Brooks spreading the bullshit, soon everyone at the event was trying to get close to Laure and me to get our attention. I had thought the gag would be uncovered in ten minutes, but now it acquired a life of its own. I saw Louise off to the side, watching and smiling.

Some people drew me aside to tell me to be careful with "those Brooks girls." I responded that Laure was fresh to the movie business and I was keeping her centered and yes she was independent minded but she would listen to me. Laure heard that and rolled her eyes but played it up, telling someone that I had discovered her and that she owed her career to my intuitive perception of her talent, thereby proving that Laure could bullshit with the Hollywood crowd. Laure was having a great time playing the flibbertigibbet as she flitted about, talking to everyone. I could see everyone was looking at her, and if she wanted to be a Hollywood star there would be no stopping her. She was already starring in her first role.

I thought that I was almost detected when the producer's secretary from yesterday's studio visit came up and told me she was looking for a job since her boss had been fired that morning. She claimed to have been unaware that I was new in town and understood why I wanted to get Laure out of her former boss' office. Had she known, she said, she would have gone in herself to get Laure out. I laughed and told her she had done the right thing by following her boss' orders because she had not known who I was.

The secretary unintentionally added credence my story, telling everyone about my physically bursting into the producer's office to rescue my client. The secretary asked if I was going to see Mr. Lasky about joining Famous Players. Louise was standing off to my left and I saw her nod yes, so I said I would be calling on him very soon. The secretary seemed relieved, and said that if I brought a project to Lasky with Laure as a star, she just knew it would get green-lighted. I didn't know all the movie business terminology but it seemed that getting a green light was a good thing, so I said that was our plan.

The secretary said she hoped I would join Famous Players and she would do everything – and she winked at me so I was sure to understand what she meant by 'everything' – if I kept her on as a secretary. Our prank continued to grow as more details conveniently fell into our game.

An hour later, Dorothy called me up to the podium to say a few words on behalf of Scott McLanahan. Billie told her I had Scott's donation check but she did not know the amount. After Dorothy introduced me, I talked briefly about how sad Scott and I had been when Wallace died of complications from his morphine addiction withdrawal. I added that Laure and I were gratified by the work Dorothy Davenport and her team of doctors was doing to bring modern research and rehabilitation treatment to those who, for whatever reason, had become addicted. Then I announced that I was proud to present Dorothy Davenport with Scott McLanahan's donation of $1,000. The crowd broke into applause.

Then I added that Laure and I were donating $1,000 and gave our check to Dorothy. The crowd gasped and broke into cheers and applause. Dorothy had tears in her eyes as she had been unaware of the size of our donations. She thanked Laure and me for our generosity. Personally delivering Scott's donation check gave more legitimacy to my claim as a Chicago movie producer.

I noticed some director/producer types – I was already getting to know who they were by the way they looked and acted and how some people seemed to be subservient to them, pulled out their checkbooks, tearing up their previously written checks and writing new ones presumably to match or beat ours. Laure and I had decided to give $1,000 of our own money because we wanted to, as our personal memorial for Wallace Reid. The LaureDan Company had been turning good profits and we hoped that future stars trapped in addiction could be successfully rehabilitated. Our prank had a side benefit since it brought in larger donations when the other big shots presented their checks to Dorothy.

Laure and I found a few minutes to get some Champagne and talk by ourselves. She said that initially the producers, directors and actors were coming on to her, but after they found out she was Louise's cousin, and that she was the one in the incident at the Famous Players studio yesterday, most of them stopped trying to bamboozle her.

So I asked "And this is a problem? Seems to me that it's a good thing. I don't have to fight off every man in Hollywood!"

"Oh you're such a guy. I'm not going to run off with any of these people, except maybe that Buster Collier who is very good looking" Laure said with a big smile on her face. As if on cue, Buster came by with a glass of Champagne for Laure and asked her to dance. Dorothy had a wood dance floor set up outside with a hot dance band. Laure gave me her glass to hold and put her arm in Collier's and they walked over to the dance floor. *I'll have to keep an eye on Buster.* Then I saw Louise surrounded by men, so I picked up two fresh Champagne glasses and broke into her group and asked her to dance. The other men, mostly minor actors, reluctantly moved aside. Louise flashed me a huge smile, pulled me to her and gave me a big wet kiss then took my arm and we went to the dance floor leaving a few grumbling guys without Louise Brooks to entertain.

As we fox trotted around the floor, Louise thanked me for rescuing her from all those wannabe actors, none of whom, in her opinion, were worthy of her favors. Then Louise startled me by saying "My experience has been that most of the nice men I like are not very good lovers, while many of the bastards are. I'm beginning to like you and think you are a good man, and Laure says that you are a great lover. You could singlehandedly change my perception of nice men being rotten lovers and I'm willing to take the chance. Would you like to sleep with me?"

To say that I was surprised would be the understatement of the year. I thought Louise was incredibly sensual, her look, attitude, posture, the way she moved and spoke, her intelligence that she tried not to let show too much, in short, everything about her added up to a very sexy, desirable woman. I think I just looked dumbly at her for a few seconds without regard for my good fortune and she added "Don't look surprised. A successful producer expects women to throw themselves at him. You don't have to agree right now. Think about it, we would have to set something up. I take it you're worried about what my cousin Laure would think?" she said with a laugh. "We've had the opportunity to get acquainted this afternoon and I like Laure, except she's too much like me and Hollywood wouldn't know what to do with two Brooks girls. She told me she's only had two lovers besides you." I was surprised that Laure would open up so quickly to Louise.

"You know, a woman needs to have experience before she gets married, otherwise after a few years she gets to thinking she never had a chance to find out what all those other attractive men are like between the sheets, and she may decide to find out. I'm not trying to take you away from Laure, I already love her like family. She attracts a lot of attention from women as well as men. She can turn on the desire in anyone without even trying."

The song ended but Louise kept me on the dance floor, as Buster did for Laure. "So how many women have you slept with?"

I was amazed at how direct Louise was and barely managed to croak out "Six, including Laure."

"Only six? Oh yeah, you two are from small towns in Illinois. I'm from a small town in Kansas myself. You might feel guilty for having five other women versus Laure's two other men. You should have had at least a dozen or more women, and she should have had a dozen or more lovers. That way when you two get married, you'll both know what you have with each other and be less likely to stray."

"Have you talked to Laure about this?"

Louise laughed. "I'm working on her and I can set it all up for both of you. Buster, who I had an affair with during and after we made *Just Another Blonde* even though he was in love with Constance Talmadge seems to be quite taken by Laure and I'm sure he would be happy to expand her sexual education. He's an energetic and talented lover, I can vouch for that."

"Well, if he's a good man and good in bed, doesn't that blow up your theory that good men aren't good in bed?"

"Dan, don't be difficult. I have never worked so hard on seducing a man as I am working on you. Accept that as a compliment. I've had a lot of experience and so far, Buster has been the only man to beat the odds. You could be the final proof."

"So you haven't talked to Buster about this? How do you know he will want to have sex with Laure?" I asked.

Louise laughed. "Don't be silly. He asked me if I could fix him up with her. He realizes that I'm getting married soon and it's not going to be to him, so he may think that being with Laure would be just like being with me. Is Laure good in bed?" Louise had a way of asking direct questions but making it seem like ordinary conversation.

After I cleared my mind for a moment I told Louise "Laure is the best lover I've ever had. But we are more than lovers, we are partners and best friends. We have a strong bond with each other."

Louise stopped and turned to face me. "Anyone, and I do mean anyone, can succumb to the temptation of an affair with the right person and in the right circumstances. You're tempted, aren't you, to have sex with me?"

"I am tempted, but it doesn't mean that I'm unhappy with Laure in any way. And I'm not sure how we would feel about it afterward."

"Think about it. You'll find, in your pocket, my telephone numbers here and in New York. I put them there with all the other women trying for your favor when I put my arm around you earlier. Throw the other telephone numbers away. You do want to sleep with me, don't you?"

"Louise, I think it might be better if I stayed awake with you."

"Oh Dan, you slay me! Yes, it would be much better if we were both awake. It is interesting, isn't it, that people talk of sleeping together when actually we are talking about an activity that could not be performed while asleep. At least by normal people."

"You mentioned you were getting married soon. Wouldn't your husband-to-be object to your playing around? And who is the lucky man?"

"Don't think of him as the lucky man. He's pushing me to get married but I don't want to. I'll be a horrible wife, staying in bed all day drinking gin and I'll be unfaithful. Eddie Sutherland directed *It's The Old Army Game* movie that will be released next month and we are having an affair and he has asked me to marry him. I'm thinking about it and he keeps trying to sell me on the idea, so if it happens it will be in May or June, depending on our schedules."

"You don't love him?" I asked.

"Love? I have loved very few people in my life. I don't think anyone in Hollywood marries for love. They marry for career, money or lust but not love. I am fond of Buster, I really care about him but he never asked me to marry him. I might marry you if you asked, after you take me to bed and become the new big movie producer. But maybe you shouldn't, remember I would be a very bad wife." Louise laughed. She had a wonderful voice and a lovely laugh to go with her radiant smile. Just like Laure. Here we were, talking about sex and love live we were old pals but Louise made it sound like it was just part of life. Which of course, it is. How brilliant, I thought.

Just then Laure came up to us. "Did I catch you two plotting something? A getaway, perhaps? So what happens next? Now that donation checks have been given some people are sneaking away. What part are you giving me in your new production, Mr. Producer?" Laure seemed a bit tipsy, rare for her and I remembered seeing Buster going to the Champagne table a few times. Or more likely she was nervous seeing us in deep discussion and her woman's intuition understood what we were talking about.

I put my hand in my pocket and found several slips of paper with names and telephone numbers. I went to throw them away. "Wait, let me see who wants to tempt you" said Louise. I gave her the slips of paper and she read them. Ten were from women and one from a man. Louise laughed at some of them and made various remarks about their bodies, acting ability, parentage and general sexual desirability. Then I looked in my other pocket and found eight more.

"Wow Danny, nineteen propositions! I only got propositioned by ten men and two women" said Laure. "I better go take a look at myself in the mirror." Laure and Louise left together, chatting happily. When Louise came back W.C. Fields was with her. Fields was the star of *It's The Old Army Game* that Louise had just finished, and Fields was a big favorite of mine. He was a funny man but in person he was more reserved. Louise told me later that he had been rebuffed so many times by people he thought were friends that he was careful with everyone. Laure joined us and met Fields, who was in turn enchanted by her. Bill Fields walked away with Laure and Louise, an arm around each of them, telling them one of his stories as they searched for the liquor table. I chatted with Douglas Fairbanks who complimented me on playing the role of a hot new producer and no one caught on. He said that I should be a producer if I could get away with baloney like that. Douglas introduced me to Clara Bow, Myrna Loy and several others, and as a result I was never again starstruck when meeting a star. Later I found Clara's telephone number in my pocket.

Soon after that, people began moving toward the dance floor as the band started to play *The Charleston*. Laure and Louise were in front of the band doing the Charleston with a few extra moves that they must have just choreographed. Laure did a very energetic Charleston and together with Louise it was wild. Dancing together they did look like cousins.

I spotted someone who looked familiar and went up to her and introduced myself. She told me "You're that new producer in town. I'm Ann Little and I was an actress but if you're thinking about offering me a role, I have to tell you that I retired from acting last year and now I'm involved in other things. I came out today because Dorothy asked me to, and I want to help others recover from drug addiction."

"I'm very pleased to meet you Ann, and you probably hear this often but I enjoyed your movies with Wallace Reid, and I even met him near Chicago once when he had car trouble. That's why I'm here too, with my girlfriend Laure Brooks. We were both Wallace Reid fans."

"Oh yes, I remember Wally talking about the young fellow who fixed his lovely yellow Marmon. He remembered you, even thought of asking you to come out to California to take care of his automobiles. Too bad he never got around to do it, but he was beginning to be debilitated by his addiction. Maybe you remember Dawn?" I turned and there was Dawn, as lovely as the day I first saw her with Wallace Reid. Maybe even lovelier. She had a stunning presence and sexiness.

"Hello Dawn" I managed to speak somewhat clearly, remembering the evening we had spent together. Dawn was the only partner I had who Laure did not know about and I hoped that omission wasn't going to be my undoing.

"Welcome to Hollywood Dan. It's so good to see you again" Dawn said with a smile. Just then Dorothy Davenport was coming toward us and I began to feel light-headed. Did she and Dawn know each other? Dawn must have seen my concern. "Dan, relax. Dorothy Davenport and I have known each other for a long time. She knows I traveled with him, because I was his bodyguard, hired by the studio. His addiction was causing him problems and he would have trouble when he couldn't get his morphine quick enough, and some people tried to take advantage of him. My cover was that I was his girlfriend and everyone thought we were a couple. Maybe we were, occasionally. Wallace was a sexy man and things happened. I got your attention that day, and I recall our evening with great pleasure. I would like to do that again, wouldn't you?" and she gave me a look like I expected from Louise.

"Yes, of course" I said without thinking. "You were Wally's bodyguard? You don't look like a bodyguard. That wasn't meant to be critical; it's just not what I expected."

"People are taken by surprise because I'm not what they expect. It works for me every time." A security guard was walking by and Dawn called him over. "Try to hit me. Go ahead, try it" she said with a challenging look in her eyes.

"I don't hit women" the guard said.

"Don't worry – try to hit me" Dawn commanded. He tried a slap but Dawn caught his hand before it got anywhere near her. "I said try to hit me" Dawn repeated with emphasis. Ann Little was watching with curiosity so he raised his fist and swung. Faster than my eye could see, she flipped him over on his face. Dawn stood there with her foot on his back, completely calm.

"Can I learn how to do that?" Laure had seen the guard going ass over teakettle. I thought it would be a good idea for Laure to pick up some self-defense moves and encouraged her. Laure made arrangements to talk to Dawn later. It might be upsetting for Laure to find out that

Dawn and I had been lovers, but it was only one night and well before I had ever met Laure, but I decided to tell her about it myself.

A little while later Louise came in with a policeman who was looking for the owner of the red Duesenberg Phaeton, and I answered that I was. The cop told me that there were bullet holes in the rear bodywork and I told him they had been there since we witnessed a bank robbery in Kansas. Louise said "There's not much to do in Kansas except drink, screw, rob banks and shoot at cars, the more expensive the better. Where in Kansas did this happen?"

"A little town called Cherryvale, just south of..."

Louise broke out laughing and told us that's where she was born and raised.

www.ingramcontent.com/pod-product-compliance
Lightning Source LLC
Chambersburg PA
CBHW030023180626
46810CB00001B/182